About the Authors

BERNARD CORNWELL is the author of the acclaimed *New York Times* bestseller *Agincourt*; the bestselling Saxon Tales, which include *The Last Kingdom*, *The Pale Horseman*, *Lords of the North*, and *Sword Song*; as well as the Richard Sharpe novels, the Grail Quest series, the Nathaniel Starbuck Chronicles, the Warlord Chronicles, and many other novels. He lives with his wife on Cape Cod.

SUSANNAH KELLS is the pen name of Bernard's wife, Judy Cornwell.

Books by Bernard Cornwell

The Saxon Tales

THE LAST KINGDOM
THE PALE HORSEMAN
THE LORDS OF THE NORTH
SWORD SONG

The Sharpe Novels (in chronological order)

SHARPE'S TIGER
Richard Sharpe and the Siege of Seringapatam, 1799

SHARPE'S TRIUMPH
Richard Sharpe and the Battle of Assaye, September 1803

SHARPE'S FORTRESS
Richard Sharpe and the Siege of Gawilghur, December 1803

SHARPE'S TRAFALGAR
Richard Sharpe and the Battle of Trafalgar, 21 October 1805

SHARPE'S PREY
Richard Sharpe and the Expedition to Copenhagen, 1807

SHARPE'S RIFLES
Richard Sharpe and the French Invasion of Galicia, January 1809

SHARPE'S HAVOC
Richard Sharpe and the Campaign in Northern Portugal, Spring 1809

SHARPE'S EAGLE
Richard Sharpe and the Talavera Campaign, July 1809

SHARPE'S GOLD
Richard Sharpe and the Destruction of Almeida, August 1810

SHARPE'S ESCAPE
Richard Sharpe and the Bussaco Campaign, 1810

SHARPE'S FURY
Richard Sharpe and the Battle of Barrosa, March 1811

SHARPE'S BATTLE
Richard Sharpe and the Battle of Fuentes de Onoro, May 1811

SHARPE'S COMPANY
Richard Sharpe and the Siege of Badajoz, January to April 1812

SHARPE'S SWORD
Richard Sharpe and the Salamanca Campaign, June and July 1812

SHARPE'S ENEMY
Richard Sharpe and the Defense of Portugal, Christmas 1812

SHARPE'S HONOUR
Richard Sharpe and the Vitoria Campaign, February to June 1813

SHARPE'S REGIMENT
Richard Sharpe and the Invasion of France, June to November 1813

SHARPE'S SIEGE
Richard Sharpe and the Winter Campaign, 1814

SHARPE'S REVENGE
Richard Sharpe and the Peace of 1814

SHARPE'S WATERLOO
Richard Sharpe and the Waterloo Campaign, 15 June to 18 June 1815

SHARPE'S DEVIL
Richard Sharpe and the Emperor, 1820–1821

The Grail Quest Series

THE ARCHER'S TALE
VAGABOND
HERETIC

The Nathaniel Starbuck Chronicles

REBEL
COPPERHEAD
BATTLE FLAG
THE BLOODY GROUND

The Warlord Chronicles

THE WINTER KING
ENEMY OF GOD
EXCALIBUR

The Sailing Thrillers

STORMCHILD
SCOUNDREL
WILDTRACK
CRACKDOWN

Other Novels

STONEHENGE
GALLOWS THIEF
A CROWNING MERCY
THE FALLEN ANGELS
REDCOAT
AGINCOURT

BERNARD CORNWELL
AND SUSANNAH KELLS

THE FALLEN ANGELS

HARPER

NEW YORK • LONDON • TORONTO • SYDNEY

HARPER

This is a work of fiction. Names, characters, places, and incidents are products of the author's imagination or are used fictitiously and are not to be construed as real. Any resemblance to actual events, locales, organizations, or persons, living or dead, is entirely coincidental.

This book was originally published in 1984 by St. Martin's Press.

A paperback edition of this book was published in 2004 by HarperCollins Publishers.

FIRST HARPERTORCH EDITION PUBLISHED 2005.
FIRST HARPER PAPERBACK PUBLISHED 2009.

Library of Congress Cataloging-in-Publication Data has been applied for.

ISBN 978-0-06-172545-6

09 10 11 12 13 RRD 10 9 8 7 6 5 4 3 2 1

The Fallen Angels
is for
Sean and Kerry

". . . the age of chivalry is gone. That of sophisters, economists, and calculators, has succeeded: and the glory of Europe is extinguished for ever."

"Our antagonist is our helper."

Edmund Burke, 1729–1797
From *Reflections on the Revolution in France,*
published 1790

Prologue

Death's kingdom is the night. When the church bell strikes the small hours, when the owls hunt, when the land is black with night; death reigns.

They are the witching hours, when castle and cottage are closed against the dark, yet cannot stop the reaper who comes to grin his skull-grin and give the gravedigger employment.

At such an hour, on a night furious with storm, the Lady Campion Lazender woke into nightmare.

A scream woke her. She heard hooves on the gravel and a man shouting. His words were snatched to oblivion by the wind and rain that slashed dark at the castle's windows.

Edna, the maid whose scream had jarred Campion awake, pounded on the door. "My Lady! My Lady!"

"I'm awake!" Campion was already pulling a woolen gown over her nightclothes.

Edna opened the door. She held a candle and her face was as white as its wax. "He's bleeding, my Lady. He fell!" Her voice was half sobbing, half scared.

"Has the doctor been sent for?" Campion's voice was calm. She led the maid through the ante-chamber, out into the long corridor. "Has he?"

"I don't know, my Lady."

Servants, woken by the commotion, watched in the passages. Campion smiled at them, knowing they needed reassurance. The single candle, half shielded by Edna's hand, threw strange shadows on the high marble pillars and on the painted ceilings of the great rooms.

Campion ran barefooted up the marble staircase that led to the Upper Gallery. The longcase clock struck two.

The lights were brighter in this part of the Castle. Servants had lit candles and their flickering flames showed the open door of her father's rooms.

Campion stepped over a flax sheet, bright with blood, into her father's bedroom. Her father was on the floor. There was blood on the carpet, on the bed, and on the hands of the servants. Her father's terrible, sunken, dying face seemed paler than ever. His eyes were shut.

"What happened?"

Caleb, her father's manservant, answered. "Fell out of bed, my Lady."

On the table beside the bed was a spilt bottle of brandy. Doubtless, she thought, he had tried with his one good arm to reach for it to dull the pain that tormented him, and somehow his paralyzed body had fallen.

She knelt beside him, took his hand and stroked his cheek. His face was a grimace of pain. He moaned, but he seemed insensible to her presence. She dropped his hand and lifted the blanket that Caleb had put over the leg's stump.

The Earl of Lazen had been paralyzed these fifteen years, a strong man brought to pain and sickness and nightmares by a falling horse. Just one week ago the surgeons had taken off a leg because the gangrene had come in his foot.

"It opened up, my Lady," Caleb Wright said. She could see that the servant had twisted a silken bed cord about the thigh to staunch the blood flow.

"Lift him onto the bed," Campion said. She helped, and her father moaned as they put his wasted, light body onto the mattress. She put the blanket back over him. "The doctor's coming?"

"Yes, my Lady," Caleb said.

She stroked her father's face. "Father? Father?" But he could not hear her. She wondered how much blood he had lost. His breathing was slow, his chest hardly rising and falling, and she could scarcely feel the beat of his heart when she put her hand on his neck. She bent over and kissed him.

The wind rattled rain on the window by his bed. For fifteen years the Earl had looked on his estates through that window, and, through all those long seasons of his dying, his daughter had been his consolation and his joy.

She was called Lady Campion Lazender and, on this September night of 1792, she was twenty-four years old. She had been given beauty as few are given beauty, yet she seemed unaware of the gift. She was slim and tall, with pale gold hair that was the color of fine wheat two weeks before harvest. She had a face that was swift to smile, and her quick spirit flashed like sunlit gold in the huge halls and sickness-haunted rooms of Lazen Castle.

She could have been in London; she could have danced in palaces and taken tribute from every hopeful son, yet she would not leave Lazen. Her father was sick, her brother absent, and she had taken the reins of Lazen into her slim hands and it was she who was its ruler now. She was sensible, practical, and decisive. She could talk to plowmen or lawyers, millers or magistrates, and every man left her presence a little bit in love and ready to believe that Lazen was not cursed.

There was a belief that the castle was cursed.

The Earl was dying, drunk when he was awake, racked by pain when he awoke.

The Countess was dead, killed giving birth to a stillborn child.

The eldest son, who would have inherited Lazen, had been burned to death with his wife and child.

Lazen, the house of fortune, seemed cursed in all things but its daughter.

A servant piled coals on the fire. Campion still held her father's hand and she stroked his face as if she could drive her love through his insensibility. She prayed for the doctor to come quickly, that her father would not die, that he would live, at the very least, long enough to see Toby married.

Toby was her brother, the new heir, Viscount Werlatton. He was in Paris, a member of the British Embassy there, and now that the French had imprisoned their King and the revolution was turning bloodier by the day, he was coming home. He was bringing a bride with him, a dark-haired French girl of winsome and fragile beauty. There would be babies soon in Lazen and Campion was glad. Lazen needed babies, and she prayed that this pale, bleeding man would live to see them.

There was the sound of running footsteps, she turned, and William Carline, the Castle's ponderous steward, appeared breathless at the door. "My Lady?"

"What is it?" She knew it was bad news. She could tell by his face, paler than ever, and by the flicker of panic that ran like lightning among the servants.

"It's Doctor Fenner, my Lady. He's not home. They say he's gone to Millett's End." Carline's voice trailed away.

All the servants stared at her. She was twenty-four and on her slim shoulders rested this great house and all its possessions.

She lifted the blanket to look at the stump of her father's leg. She thought there was more blood on the linen, and she knew her father was going to die unless she acted swiftly. "Carline?"

"My Lady?"

"I want you to go to the stables, please, wake Burroughs, and ask for the horse needles and thread."

He blinked, then nodded. "Yes, my Lady."

"I want water, Caleb." She was trying to think of what else she would need. Candles, linen, and courage.

Her maid stared wide-eyed at her. "You're going to sew him up, my Lady?"

"And you're going to help me."

The storm had blown itself out by the time she had finished. She had untied the crude bandage, washed the stump, tied the broken artery, then, taking the flap of skin, stitched it into place. She had worked from instinct, doing what seemed to be necessary, frowning when the fragile skin tore under the thread's pull. Edna had held a candle close to her hands while Caleb and another servant held her father still.

Now, the room thick with the smell of lymph and blood, she untied the silken bed cord from her father's thigh. She watched in fear as the white skin flushed red with the released blood, the flush going ever closer to the newly closed wound, but, to her relief, the stitches held. A few drops seeped, but nothing more.

Her father would live, to know more pain and to count the slow hours of death's kingdom. Yet, Campion knew, he would also live to see his son come home with a bride to fill the castle with new life, fresh laughter, and the bright hope of glittering days that would obscure the memories of these dark nights.

Her father slept. Campion carried the hooked horse needles and gut out of the door, and the servants, who waited outside, looked to her for reassurance. She smiled at them. "All's well, and thank you all."

She walked slowly back to her rooms. She was Lady Campion Lazender, she was twenty-four, lovely as the dawn, and she had woken to a nightmare. Yet this night, in his own kingdom, she had cheated the reaper with his skull-grin, defeated him by her courage, but he would be back. He always came back. She warmed her hands by her fire, waited for the sunrise, and prayed for her brother to come home from Paris.

1

Fear, like the rumor of plague, can empty a city's streets.

Paris, on that hot September evening of 1792, seemed empty. The citizens stayed behind closed doors as though, after a week of slaughter, they were suddenly ashamed of the horrors they had fetched on their city. There was a silence in Paris, not an absolute quiet, but a strange, almost reverent, hush in which a raised voice seemed out of place.

Fear, on that evening, smelled like a charnel house.

Four horsemen rode through the streets. There was a menace in the sound of their hooves, a menace that made the hidden, listening citizens hold their breath until the sound passed. Death had become a commonplace that week, not decent death at sickness's end, but the death of the slaughterhouse. The hollow sound of the hooves was urgent, as if the horsemen had business with the horrors that had choked Paris' gutters with blood.

It was a hot evening. If it had not been for the stink in the city it would have been a beautiful evening. The roofs were outlined with startling clarity against a watercolor sky. Clouds banded the west where the sun, like a huge, blood-red globe, was suspended over the horizon.

The whole summer of 1792 had been hot. The soldiers who had gone north to fight the invading Austrians and

Prussians had marched through Paris with a grime of sweat and dust caked on their faces. Rumor said that those soldiers were now losing the war on France's northern frontier, and that too had made this city fearful.

The summer had been so hot that the leaves, withered and dry, had fallen early. On the day that the King was taken prisoner, he had walked from the Tuileries Palace to the National Assembly and his son, the *dauphin,* had kicked the piles of fallen leaves into the air as if it was a game. That had been the second week of August, only the second week, yet the leaves had fallen. Never, it was said, had there been a summer so hot, a heat that had not diminished as autumn came, that turned the corpses into the stench which fouled the exhausted city.

The four horsemen rode into a square where martins dipped over the darkening cobbles. They slowed their horses to a walk.

Facing the four men was a great building with an imposing archway. The gates were open. In the entrance of the building was a small crowd, oddly cheerful and noisy on this evening of silence and fear. The people in the small crowd were tired, yet the bottles from which they drank, and the memories of their great day, gave them a feverish energy and ebullience. Nearly all of them wore soft red hats that sat rakishly on their long hair.

The oldest of the four horsemen motioned with his hand for his companions to hold back while he rode on alone. The crowd, eager for more excitement, came to meet him.

The horseman looked over the group. "Who's in charge?"

One man stepped forward, a man with a great belly that sagged over the rope belt of his trousers. He looked up at the horseman and then, instead of answering, took a slow drink from his bottle. When he had finished all the wine, he belched. The crowd laughed. The fat man, pleased with his performance, spat, and looked truculently at the rider. "And who, citizen, are you?"

The horseman took a folded square of paper from a pouch on his belt and handed it wordlessly to the fat man who made a great pantomime with it. First he handed his empty bottle to a companion, then he brushed his moustache, then he planted his feet wide, and finally, with a flourish, he shook the square of paper open.

He read it slowly, his lips moving. He frowned, looked suspiciously at the horseman, then turned the paper over as though its blank reverse might hold an answer to his puzzlement. He turned it back.

He stared at the signature at the foot of the paper. He stared at the seal. "You're from the English Embassy?"

The horseman sighed. He spoke in patient French. "The British embassy."

"All of you?"

The horseman gestured at his companions. Closest to him was a young man with bright red hair. "That is Mr. Lazender, behind him is Mr. Drew, and my name is Pierce. Our names are all listed there." He did not bother to introduce the fourth horseman who hung back as if he did not wish to be associated with the three Englishmen. The fourth man was the only one in the group who was armed. At his left hip there hung a long, black-scabbarded sword.

The fat man frowned. The signature seemed genuine, and the seal seemed genuine, and the orders did not seem particularly troublesome. He scratched his cheek, pulled up his trousers, then handed the paper back to the man called Pierce. "Who are you looking for?"

"A woman."

"Name?"

"Lucille de Fauquemberghes. You've heard of her?"

The fat man shook his head. "Never heard of her." He looked at the fourth horseman, a young man dressed entirely in black who, unseen to the three Englishmen, gave the smallest nod to the fat man. The fat man seemed relieved by the signal. He waved carelessly toward the archway. "Go on, then!"

The three Englishmen dismounted and gave their reins to the man in black who tethered their horses to a grating beside the archway. His own horse, a superb black mare, he let stand free. He walked to the open prison gates. The gutter that came out of the building was darkly choked, smelly, and busy with flies. A dog, its ribs stark against its matted skin, licked at the black substance that clogged the drain.

The fat man watched the three Englishmen go into the prison. He waited till they had disappeared, then grinned at the man in black and offered his hand. "How are you, Gitan?"

"Thirsty."

Gitan leaned against the stones of the archway. Even in repose he was an impressive man with a lithe, strong, animal elegance. His face, dark tanned, was thin and handsome. His eyes were light blue, an odd color for a man with such dark skin and black hair. The contrast made his eyes seem bright and piercing. In any crowd Gitan would be remarkable, but among these sweaty, tired people he was like a thoroughbred among mules. He seemed to look on them with an amused tolerance, as though all that he saw he judged against the unfair measure of his own competence. He was a man whose approval was constantly sought by other men.

Jean Brissot, the fat bellied man, offered a wine bottle. Gitan did not take it at once; instead he fetched a scrap of paper from his pocket, some tobacco, and in Spanish style he twisted himself a small cigar. Another of the red-capped men hurried forward with a tinder-box and the black-dressed man leaned forward as though it was the most natural thing in the world for people to be solicitous of him. He blew smoke into the evening air then nodded at the horror inside the courtyard. "Been busy, Jean?" His voice was relaxed, his eyes amused.

"A hard day, Gitan. You should have been here."

Gitan said nothing. He wore a gold ring in his left ear. He reached for the wine bottle.

Jean Brissot watched him drink. "If you hadn't been with them I'd have said no."

Gitan shrugged. "The paper's genuine."

Brissot laughed. "I'm astonished the citizen Minister lets them poke around! Bloody English!"

The smoke from Gitan's tobacco drifted under the archway. Flies buzzed in the courtyard behind him. He picked a shred of leaf from his lip. "They say we don't want war with the English yet." He spoke lazily, as if he did not really care whether there was war or not. His name, Gitan, simply meant "Gypsy." If he had a real name no one used it. He was horse-master to the young red-headed man, described on the paper as "Mr. Lazender." Mr. Lazender, in truth, was Viscount Werlatton, heir to the Earldom of Lazen, but this was no week to advertise aristocratic birth in Paris.

Two girls came through the archway, laughing, their wooden sabots clattering on the cobbles. They saw the Gypsy and became coy, giggling and nudging each other. "Gitan!" one of them called.

He looked at them with his bright, amused eyes.

The black haired girl jerked her head. "You with the foreigners?"

The Gypsy smiled. "Which one do you fancy, Terese?"

They all laughed. Jean Brissot, sucking in his belly, looked enviously at the Gypsy. "Is there a girl in Paris you don't know, Gitan?"

"The Austrian whore."

That provoked more laughter. Marie Antoinette was imprisoned with her husband, the King.

Terese came close to the Gypsy. He smelt of leather and tobacco. She played with the laces of his black coat. "Are you at Laval's tonight?"

"No."

"Gitan!"

"I work! I sleep at the stables. If you ask my master he might let you in, but the straw gets everywhere." He blew smoke over her head, then cuddled her almost absent-mindedly. Brissot was jealous. The Gypsy, it was said, had a way with women as he did with horses. Now Gitan smiled down at the girl. "You're getting in the way of the bottle. Go on with you." He pushed her out into the square where the martins flickered between the dark houses.

Jean Brissot shook his head. "How do you do it?"

"Do what?"

"The women!" The plump man laughed. "If I had your luck, Gitan, just for one day!"

The Gypsy shrugged. "Women are like horses."

"You ride them, eh?"

The tall, handsome horse-master smiled. "You love them, you let them know who is master, and you always have a spare one."

"Gitan! Gitan!" The voice, peremptory and desperate, shouted from within the prison. "Gitan!"

The Gypsy tossed away his paper-wrapped cigar and shrugged. "Watch my horse, Jean."

Pierce, the oldest of the three Englishmen, stood by a flight of steps that led up from the courtyard. His face, always pale, seemed paper white in the fading light. "She's there. Upstairs." Pierce looked as if he had been sick.

The Gypsy nodded, climbed the steps and pushed past the men who loitered in the entrance. He climbed more stairs, noting how the still, hot air within the prison buildings seemed to have trapped the stench of blood and death so that it was thick in his nostrils and sour in his throat.

He saw Toby Lazender, Lord Werlatton, at the end of a long landing on the fourth floor. The young, red-headed man was leaning against the wall and he was lit by the last rays of the setting sun that filtered through a barred window and through the cell door. He did not turn as the Gypsy walked toward him, he just stared into the cell.

Gitan stopped by the door. He looked at Toby Lazender. He doubted whether, at this moment, the young Englishman was even aware that he was present. The young face was set harder than stone, the eyes empty of everything. He was utterly still. Beside him, a look of helplessness on his face, was Drew.

The Gypsy looked into the cell.

The sun dazzled him. Something stood on the window ledge.

He stepped slowly into the cell, treading gently as though in a flower bed.

"Gitan?" Toby's voice was low.

The Gypsy crouched and grunted.

The young Englishman's voice was filled with loathing. "Was there anything they didn't do to her?"

The Gypsy did not reply. There was no need to reply.

Lucille de Fauquemberghes had been twenty, lovely as the night, a creature of joy and love and beauty.

Now what was left of her was in this cell. She looked like cuts of meat, nothing more.

Blood was splashed a yard high on the stones. Flesh clung to bones. It was as if she had been torn apart by wild creatures.

Gitan stepped to one side, out of the sun's rays, and saw the object on the window sill. It was her severed head. Her hair, long and raven, fell below the sill.

"Christ!" The shout was like a wail, drawn out, wolf-howling, and the Gypsy turned, stepped over the horror and caught Toby Lazender about the waist. He pushed the young Englishman back against the landing wall, holding him there as Drew, an Embassy clerk, hovered helplessly. Drew, the Gypsy saw, had been sick.

"I'll kill them! I'll kill all those bastards! I'll kill them!"

Pierce, a Secretary at the Embassy, came running down the corridor. "Toby!"

Toby was sobbing the word "kill" over and over, and Pierce looked in horror as the Gypsy held the struggling young lord against the wall. It was in anticipation of this reaction, this anger, that Lord Gower, the ambassador, had ordered the men to ride without weapons.

The Gypsy spoke to Toby Lazender in French. "Go downstairs."

"No!" Toby howled the word. "No!"

"I'll bring her for burial. Go downstairs, my Lord."

"My Lord!" Pierce took the younger man by the arm. "Come on. Come on! Gitan will bring her." He looked despairingly at the tall gypsy. It had been the ambassador who suggested that Gitan accompany the search party; there was no man more competent, more accomplished than the Gypsy. Pierce saw the ease with which he pinioned Lord Werlatton. "You'll have to help us take him down."

The three of them took Toby Lazender down the stairs, down the steps into the yard where the bodies lay in muddled heaps, led him over the blood in the gutter, and even the grinning, blood-spattered men and women at the open gate looked nervous because of the anger and grief that was on the Englishman's face. Pierce talked to him all the time, talked in English, told him to make no trouble, to leave, to go back to the Embassy, and the horse-master untied their horses and watched them ride away.

The Gypsy let out a long breath. If Toby Lazender had lashed out just once then the crowd would have reacted, would have drawn their blood-stained swords and hacked the Englishmen to pieces. He waited until the three horsemen had disappeared in a dark alley and until the sharp sound of their hooves had faded into the gathering night.

He turned back to the yard of the prison. Torches were being lit and pushed into their iron brackets and the flames were lurid on the heaped bodies. There were men, women and children in the pile of corpses. Some of the children had been too young to have known what happened to them.

It was the same in half the prisons of Paris. The Commune, the new rulers of Paris, had howled that the aristos and the rich were sending messages to the Prussian and Austrian enemies and so the Minister of Justice had ordered them arrested and imprisoned. Then the rumor had gone around the little streets that the aristos planned to break out of the prisons and bring swords and knives to murder the Revolutionary government, and so the people had struck first. They had massacred the prisoners. Aristocrats, priests, servants; men, women, children, all dead in the prisons. Over a thousand had died in the week, hacked and raped and mutilated until the mob was tired of the killing.

Jean Brissot came and stood beside the Gypsy. "They found her then?"

Gitan nodded. "They found her."

"Which one?"

"Fourth floor. Cut up." Gitan's deep voice was laconic,

seemingly uncaring, but his words provoked the fat man to sudden enthusiasm.

"Long black hair? Pretty girl? Christ! We had joy with that one. Dear God!" He shook his head with remembered admiration. "They're different, you know."

"Different?" Gitan looked at the grossly fat man.

Brissot nodded. "White skins, Gitan, like bloody milk. They only brought her in this morning. I took one look and I couldn't believe our luck! God! A man could live a hundred years and not see a girl like that."

The Gypsy had rolled another cigar that he lit from a torch above his head. "Who brought her in?"

"Marchenoir."

"Ah!" The Gypsy nodded as though the answer was not unexpected.

Brissot looked nervously at the tall, calm Gypsy. "He knows you're here. I mean I sent word when you came with the Englishmen. You can't be too careful these days."

The Gypsy nodded. "True. You did the right thing." He smiled reassuringly at the fat man, then stared at the bodies; fat, thin, old, young, a mess of death. "So you had the girl, Jean?"

"Twice!" Brissot laughed. "You should have been here, Gitan. Skin like milk! Soft as bloody silk!"

The gypsy blew smoke over the lolling, black-streaked bodies in the yard. "I need to find a sack. I'm taking her away."

"Look in the storeroom." Brissot jerked his head toward a doorway. "Plenty of empty flour sacks." He watched the Gypsy pick his way among the corpses toward the store. "Gitan?"

"My friend?"

"Why did the Englishman want to find her?"

The Gypsy turned. He blew smoke into the torchlight,

and it drifted above a small child's corpse. He grinned. "He was going to marry her next week."

"Next week?"

The Gypsy nodded.

Brissot bellowed his laughter around the courtyard. "He should have hurried! We got her first! I hope the bastard knows what he's missing! Married next week, eh? Skin like cream! She was a bloody treat, my friend, I tell you. Still," his laughter died and he shrugged, "I suppose you've had lots of them." He sounded jealous.

"No," Gitan said, "I haven't."

"You haven't had an aristo?" Brissot was unbelieving. "Not this week?"

"Not ever." The Gypsy turned away to find a sack to serve as a shroud for a dead aristocrat.

The Gypsy worked slowly, the foul cell lit by a single candle as he scooped the remains from the stone floor and, with bloodied hands, pushed it into the sack.

When the work was half done he heard heavy footsteps on the landing. With them came the thick smell of cigar smoke. The Gypsy rubbed his hands on a corner of the sack, stood, and leaned against the wall.

A large, fierce-faced man appeared at the cell door. He was a man in his late forties whose shoulders were humped with muscle like an ox. He was huge-chested, massive-armed; everything about him spoke of strength and weight. His shirt had separated from his trousers, showing the straps of a corset that held in his belly. He looked at the mess on the floor and at the Gypsy's stained hands. "You'll forgive me if I don't shake hands with you." He laughed.

The man was called Bertrand Marchenoir. There had been a time when he was a priest, a fierce preacher made famous by the vitriol of his sermons, but the revolution had let him abandon the service of God for the service of the people. He was now a leader of the revolution; a man to fear or love, but never ignore.

Marchenoir bullied his followers; he preached, he shouted, he thumped tables into the night, he led, he harangued, he wept false tears to rouse the mob, his gestures were as expansive as his oratory. His voice, starting low and rising to a massive crescendo, had stirred the people from their slums out into the great streets of Paris. He had been at the Bastille, he had helped fetch the King from Versailles, and now his massive, terrifying force whipped the laggards in the National Assembly. "Forward! Forward!" was his cry, and this week in Paris, fearing that the revolution would go backward, Bertrand Marchenoir had led the slaughter in the prisons.

For those who wanted vengeance on their betters, Marchenoir was an idol. For those who wanted moderation, he was a scourge. No one was allowed to forget that he was peasant born; no gutter, he said, was lower than the one in which he had been spawned, and no palace, he shouted, was so high that it could not be pulled down. Forward, ever forward, and this week a thousand and more had died that Marchenoir's revolution could go forward.

This was the man who came to the cell, who looked almost disinterestedly at the mess on the floor, then back to the Gypsy. "So you're Gitan?"

"I am Gitan."

"You know me?"

"I know of you, citizen."

Marchenoir smiled and waved his cigar at the scraps of the body. "You're doing woman's work, Gitan."

"A man is lucky to have a job these days, citizen."

The heavy, jowled face stared at the Gypsy whose words had verged on criticism of the revolution. Then

Marchenoir twitched his unshaven cheeks into a smile, into a laugh, and he kicked at the sack. "Why are you doing it, Gitan?"

"The English lord wants to bury her."

"So let him do his own dirty work. Are you a slave?"

"I am a horse-master."

"And she's a corpse." Marchenoir stepped over the sack and peered at the face on the window ledge. "She took a long time dying."

"So Brissot said."

"Brissot has a fat mouth. One day I'll sit on it and fill it up." Marchenoir spoke without anger. "I let them have her first. They queued from her to the second floor!" He leaned against the wall, the candle throwing the shadows upward on his big, red face. "I should have charged two livres a go, eh?"

"Not a very revolutionary thought, citizen."

Marchenoir laughed. He was a leader of "the left," so called because they sat on the left side of the Assembly. They were revolutionaries who sought to abolish the crown, destroy the old privileges, and declare France a people's republic. The events of the last two months were bringing that dream to fruition. Now Marchenoir blew a plume of smoke over the cell. "I was thinking that we ought to have a people's brothel with girls like this. Every whore an aristo, yes? It would pay for the army." He looked at the girl's head. "Do you think she deserved to die, horse-master?"

"We all die," Gitan said. He was astonished at the brooding sense of power that was in this room. He had heard Marchenoir speak many times, he had seen the powerful arms beckoning at the crowd, listened to the voice arouse their anger and their hopes, yet still he was astonished at the sheer presence of the man.

Marchenoir chuckled at the non-committal answer.

"She had to die, Gitan, but why? That, my friend, is my secret." He stabbed with his cigar at the Gypsy. "Nothing can be done without blood, nothing! Even the church taught that! If we fear blood we fear life! Isn't that right, sweet child?" He had asked the question of the severed head. He chuckled, and pushed the stub of his cigar into the dead lips. He turned back to the Gypsy. "I wanted to talk with you."

"I'm here." Even with such a rising, powerful man as Marchenoir, the Gypsy seemed laconically independent, yet there was a hint of respect, of deference in his bearing. Marchenoir, after all, was in the new government.

Marchenoir sat against the far wall. He was a man of extraordinary slovenliness, his clothes filthy, torn, patched and held by loops of fraying string where the buttons had come free. Gitan, whose black clothes were spotless, saw the streaks of food and spittle on the politician's coat and reflected that such an appearance was a decided advantage for the ambitious in these days. It was certainly part of Marchenoir's appeal. The people saw him as rough, ready, lovable, and theirs. He spoke for them, and he killed for them.

Marchenoir had taken another cigar from his waistcoat pocket and he leaned forward to light it from the candle. "What else are you besides a horse-master?"

Gitan shrugged. "Just that."

Marchenoir stared at him. When his face was in repose it had a brooding aspect, as if his mind stirred above a pot of horrors. Slowly, he smiled. "I hear from Citizen Belleau that you are more." He ignored Gitan's shrug. "You are a spy, Gitan, a spy."

"If Citizen Belleau says so."

Marchenoir laughed. "Citizen Belleau does say so. You have, he says, given us much valuable information from the English Embassy."

Gitan said nothing. What Marchenoir said was true. For three years, while employed by Lord Werlatton, the Gypsy had passed news to whatever government ruled in Paris. Marchenoir took a scrap of tobacco leaf from his tongue. "Do you deny it?"

"No."

"So what happens to you, horse-master and spy, when the Embassy closes down?"

Gitan shrugged. The British Embassy was one of the last in Paris. After the slaughter of this week it would undoubtedly close. "There's always a job for a good horse-master."

"Like a whore or lawyer, eh?" Marchenoir's pouchy, bloodshot eyes watched the Gypsy. "Does your little English lord want you to stay with him?"

Gitan paused, then nodded. "Yes."

Marchenoir smiled. "Tell me, horse-master, do you know who your little lordling's father is?"

"He's an earl."

"An earl." Marchenoir said the word with distaste. His bitter hatred for the aristocracy was at the root of his fame. "But not just any earl, horse-master. Before his accident he was Britain's spy-master. Did you know that?"

"No."

"The British spymaster." Marchenoir said it as though he spoke of a terrible ogre to a small child. He laughed and spat another shred of leaf toward the blood. "Lord of the English spies! The Lazenders are so damned deep into spying that they've got eyes in their backsides. Your little lordling's a spy, isn't he?"

The Gypsy did not reply, though he knew the accusation was true. Lord Werlatton's job in the Paris Embassy was to entertain the politicians and bureaucrats of Paris. He would lavish champagne and luxury upon them, and leave the rest to their indiscretions.

Marchenoir pointed the cigar at Gitan. "So will you go to England with your lord, Gypsy?"

"I don't know."

Marchenoir stared at him, as if considering the truth of the answer. Slowly, he smiled. "I want you to go with him." The Gypsy said nothing. Marchenoir spoke softly. "I want you to go, Gitan, because soon we will be at war with England, and because the English will ask you to become a spy."

The Gypsy shrugged. "Why would they ask me?"

"God made the Gypsies fools?" Marchenoir's smile took the sting from the words. "They will have a French-speaking man whom they know has friends in Paris. Of course they'll recruit you! They will think you work for them, but really you will work for me." He said the last words slowly and forcefully.

"For you?"

"I need a messenger, horse-master, who can travel between here and London. A messenger who can travel in utter safety." Marchenoir's voice was low and urgent. "So let them recruit you. In England they will protect you, and in France we will protect you. What could be more perfect? Our enemy will be your friend."

The Gypsy did not speak or move. His odd, light blue eyes stared at the other man, his long black hair clung to shadow his thin face.

Marchenoir pointed to the candle with his cigar. His voice was still low. "It is not I who ask, Gitan, nor France. It is that."

The Gypsy looked at the flame. He knew the secret message that was being given to him. The candle gave light, and light was reason, and reason was the gospel of the *Illuminati*. "For reason?"

Marchenoir smiled. His voice was low. "For reason, which is above the law."

The Gypsy looked from the candle to the powerful man. For the first time the Gypsy smiled easily, his fear of Marchenoir gone. Now he knew why such an important man had sought him out. Even Gitan's voice seemed to change. He no longer was wary, he spoke now as if to an equal because he had discovered that this most dangerous, forceful man was, like himself, a member of the secret *Illuminati.* "I sometimes feared that the brethren slept."

"No, my friend. So? Will you be our messenger?"

Gitan still smiled. He gestured at the candle. "Of course."

Marchenoir grunted approval and struggled to his feet. "There will be rewards, Gitan." He waved his cigar at the body. "We're going to strip these bastards of everything, everything!" He stared at what was left on the floor. "She was going to marry your English lord, yes?"

"Yes."

"Your English lord." Marchenoir's voice was suddenly bitter. "His mother was a d'Auxigny. I grew up in Auxigny. We had to kneel in the mud if one of the family went past. Even if the coach was a half mile away we had to kneel. Even if we were thigh deep in muck we had to kneel. All between the river and the mountain belonged to Auxigny, and that included us." He laughed. "Do you know who the present owner of Auxigny is?"

Gitan smiled at the big man. "You, citizen!"

"Me!" Marchenoir pointed at his breast with his cigar. "Perhaps I'll turn it into a brothel of aristo bitches." He nudged the sack with his dirty boot. "That's one at least I won't have to kneel to again." He laughed as he walked to the cell door. "Good hunting, my friend. See me before you leave Paris!" He was in the corridor now, his voice booming behind him as he walked away. "Come and drink to our success, Gitan!" He laughed again, then sang a line of the new song that was sweeping through Paris. "The day of glory has arrived!" The smell of his cigar lingered in the stink of blood, urine and flesh. He shouted once more, his voice fading. "Forward! Forward!"

The Gypsy did not move for a long time after the politician had gone. He stared at the candle. Then, at last, he stepped to the window, took the damp cigar stub from the dead girl's lips, and threw it into the darkness.

He finished his work, tying the neck of the sack over the long, black hair of a girl who had been beautiful before this day, then he carried his soggy burden down to where carts were being loaded with the white, naked bodies of the enemies of the state.

His horse, untethered still, whinnied and came toward him. The Gypsy mounted, the sack heavy in his hand, and rode into a night that was filled with the smell of death, into a city exhausted by massacre. Yet he knew there would be more blood, far more; these deaths were just a beginning, enough to give the new men who had risen to power the taste of slaughter.

He thought of Marchenoir, of the candle's secret message, and smiled in pleasure. He was the Gypsy, the black dressed horseman who would ride through the horrors on the secret, silent path of the traitor, just as he now rode through a silent, dark, frightened city with his burden of death. He rode unafraid through a city of fear; he was the Gypsy.

2

Rain threatened Lazen. Since dawn the clouds had been low over the hills that edged the Lazen valley, and the wind that came from the west was cold as though it brought the chill of the long gray waves from beyond Cornwall.

The Lady Campion Lazender, dressed in a plain blue linen dress covered with a blue cloak, was riding, in a most unladylike manner, over a newly plowed field. She rode astride, careless that her ankles showed.

At the edge of the field she turned the horse back. The field was muddy, heavy with the rain that had fallen in the night. She kicked her heels to force the mare into a trot.

"She's a rare looking girl, Mr. Burroughs," said a tall, bald man who stood at the field's edge.

"That she is." Simon Burroughs was the castle's head coachman, a rank denoted by the six capes of his greatcoat and by the curled whip he carried in his gloved right hand.

"Mare goes well for her!" The bald man was hopeful that her Ladyship would buy the mare from him.

"Maybe." Burroughs would not commit himself.

Campion turned the horse again, and forced it into a canter. She leaned forward, trying to hear if the breath was whistling in the mare's pipes. "Come on, girl! Come on!" She slapped its neck.

The owner of the horse, Harry Trapp, was a farmer who had ridden this day from the Piddle Valley. He knew that Lazen Castle would always buy a decent horse.

Campion turned the horse again and this time she galloped the mare up the slope of the field, across the grain of the plow, and she kicked her heels back to see what speed the animal would show in this deep, wet ground. Mud flecked the skirts of her dress and cloak. She turned at the field's head and cantered toward the two men. Her cheeks were glowing, her face alive with pleasure.

She swung herself from the saddle, slapped at some of the mud on her cloak, and went to the horse's head. "She summered in a field, Mr. Trapp?"

"Yes, my Lady."

That, she thought, explained the horse's poor condition. She was newly shod, but the shoes had been put on over feet battered by a summer on dry land. "Has she had any oats?"

"No, my Lady. But she filled up nicely last winter."

Campion ran her hand down the horse's neck, down the forelegs to the chipped knee. The farmer shrugged. "That don't stop her, my Lady."

"Why are you selling?"

The farmer shrugged. "Ain't got no call for her, my Lady. Too good to pull a bloody cart."

"Don't you swear to her Ladyship," Simon Burroughs said.

"Sorry, my Lady," the farmer said.

Campion hid her smile. All the men in the Castle, Simon Burroughs included, swore freely in front of her, but were outraged if any outsider took the same liberty.

The mare was broad and firm at the root of her neck, and was hardly blowing because of the exercise. She would, Campion thought, make a good hunter, but would never breed the foal that Campion wanted which would be as fast as any in England. She opened the horse's mouth. "Six years old?"

"Yes, my Lady."

"Seven," said Simon Burroughs. "You tried to sell her last year to Sir John. You said she was six then."

"Seven," said Mr. Trapp.

"What do you call her?"

"Emma." He seemed ashamed of the name.

"It's a nice name." Campion was looking at the mare's eyes. There was a tiny fleck in the left eye, but not in the line of vision. "What are you asking?"

The farmer hesitated. He was not used to bargaining with girls, let alone the beautiful daughters of the aristocracy, and in truth what he was asking was inflated outrageously simply because he had come to Lazen which was famous for its fortune. He decided to brazen it out. "Squire at Puddletown offered me seventy pounds for her."

"You should have taken it," Campion said. "Feed her two pounds of oats a day for a week and I'm sure he'll offer it again." She smiled at the man and held him the reins. "Thank you for coming, Mr. Trapp."

"My Lady!" The farmer was blushing. "I thought she'd be happier here."

Campion gave him her most beautiful smile, pleased by the compliment. She knew what the horse was worth, and so did the farmer, but it would be unthinkable to buy the mare without going through the necessary bargaining. She pushed a muddy hand at her hair. "You can't expect me to pay top price for a horse that's been out at grass this long. It's going to take me a month just to put some muscle on her!"

"You rode her!" Mr. Trapp pointed out reasonably. "Wasn't pumping one bit when you brought her off the plow! She'll be fit for anything in a month!"

She ran a hand over the mare's chipped knee. "Did you splint this?"

But the farmer was not listening. He was staring instead at a vision that approached along the path which came from the Castle. The farmer's jaw dropped. No one would believe him in the taproom tonight.

A middle-aged man stepped precariously between the puddles. He wore breeches of dark blue silk, above tasselled boots of white leather that had been polished to glass brightness. His tail coat was of gray velvet, and his shirt and stock of white silk. He wore no hat or wig, instead his silver hair had been drawn back and tied with a black velvet bow. His fingers were lavishly beringed. In his right hand was a tall ebony cane, topped with gold and decorated with blue ribbons. On his thin, mischievous face there was powder and, on his left cheek, a black beauty patch. He smiled beatifically at the farmer. "May blessings rain upon your head, dear man."

The farmer shook his head. "Sir?"

"May the light of his countenance shine upon you, and give you peace." He spoke with a distinct French accent. "Is that a horse?"

Campion laughed. "Hello, uncle."

He grimaced. "Good God! Is that you, dear Campion? I thought it was a dairy maid. Mr. Burroughs." He gave the slightest bow. "I bid you good day."

"Sir," the head coachman said.

Campion patted the mare's neck. "We're buying a horse, uncle."

"I can't think why. You have so many, and all they do is clutter up the stables. You should buy a unicorn, dear Campion, a white unicorn with pearls upon its horn. I might learn to ride such a beast." He smiled wondrously at the farmer. "Can you see me in a unicorn's saddle, sir? I think reins of gold would suit me, don't you?" He put fingertips to his mouth. "You must forgive me, dear sir, for you have not the advantage of my name." He bowed to the farmer. "Achilles d'Auxigny, my most humble duty to you."

"Eh?" said the farmer.

"This is Harry Trapp, uncle, and you're not to embarrass him." Campion looked at the coachman. "I want her, Simon, but I won't pay more than we paid for Pimpernel."

Burroughs grinned. "Yes, my Lady."

"You'll forgive me, Mr. Trapp?" She smiled at him. "And thank you for bringing Emma here."

"You're welcome, my Lady." The farmer was blushing again because the Lady Campion was offering him her hand. He wiped his right hand on his smock and took hers. "Thank you, my Lady."

"And make sure you get something to eat before you ride home."

"I will." Harry Trapp smiled at her. He knew a real aristocrat when he met one, not some frippery floppery like the weird Frenchman.

Campion took her uncle's arm and led him back toward the castle. "You shouldn't be cruel to people." She spoke, as she always did in private with him, in her perfect French.

"I do enjoy teasing your yokels. They are so very teasable." He smiled at her. "You do look dreadful. Do you have to dress like a peasant? And can't you leave horses to grooms?"

"I like horses."

"It is time you were married," Uncle Achilles said irritably. "A good husband would keep you out of the stables."

She laughed at him. She liked her Uncle Achilles, her mother's younger brother. His elder brother had become the Duc d'Auxigny, and had inherited with the Dukedom the Marquisates of a score of French villages and become

Count of two score more, while Achilles, the younger brother, had inherited nothing except a minor title he refused to use, a noble name, and a clever head. Against his will he had been trained for the priesthood. His noble birth had ensured a swift rise to a rich bishopric, a rise that his scandalous, hedonistic behavior had not impeded in the least.

The revolution in France had let him slide, like Bertrand Marchenoir, out of the priesthood. He refused to take the Constitutional Oath, resigned his See, and when the burning of the great houses began, and when the stories of hacked, raped and slaughtered aristocrats spread through France, he had fled with his widowed mother to the Earl of Lazen's London house. The Duchess still lived on Lazen's charity, a charity she constantly criticized. Uncle Achilles, more independent, earned a living from the British government. He did not care to talk much about his work, but Campion knew from her father that Achilles d'Auxigny helped ferret out the secret agents who were smuggled into Britain as so-called refugees from the revolution.

They went through the kissing gate that led to the castle's gardens. Campion, holding her uncle's arm, smiled up at him. "I can't really imagine you as a bishop."

He pretended indignation. "I was a most loved bishop! I used to preach a very good sermon in which I would terrify a parish into making their confessions. I would then listen in the confessional and make a note of which ladies had committed adultery. Then, if they were very pretty, I would visit them and compound the offense, though with instant forgiveness, of course." He laughed at her expression.

Turning Achilles d'Auxigny into a priest had been his father's ambition. Achilles' father had been known in France as the Mad Duke. He had believed himself to be God and, for his own worship, he had built a shrine at his

Chateau of Auxigny in which, by careful mechanical contrivances, he would perform miracles. Undoubtedly the Mad Duke had hoped that his youngest son would preach the family gospel. Instead, as Achilles was fond of saying, his father had thought of himself as God and taught his children thereby that there was none. Now he looked at his niece. "I always told your father not to marry into our family. We're all quite mad."

"You're not."

He shrugged as if he did not care to argue the point. "I just made my farewells to your father. Everyone says you did a remarkably fine thing with his leg."

"I just sewed it up, uncle."

"Just sewed it up, indeed! I couldn't have done it. I would have fainted."

She laughed. She made him walk with her toward the ornamental lake. He complained that it would rain, that he had neither hat, umbrella, cloak or gloves, but consented to accompany her.

"I do hope Lucille can take to your English ways," he said dubiously. "Horses and walking. It's most uncivilized."

"She'll be too busy having babies," Campion said. Her brother would be coming with his bride within the week. "Lots of babies."

"How utterly dreadful. I do hate babies."

She laughed, refusing to believe him. Achilles d'Auxigny watched her as they walked. She was, he thought, the most beautiful creature he had ever seen. His sister had been beautiful, but in marrying the Fifth Earl of Lazen, his sister had created this extraordinary girl, hair as gold as pale wheat, eyes the color of the Virgin's dress, a face of strong lines, softened by the mouth and by an indefinable air of goodness that she carried quite unconsciously. She had, her uncle thought, the clearest skin he had ever seen, eyes that shone with happiness; she was a girl of delicate, wonderful beauty. He squeezed her arm. "When are you going to marry, Campion?"

She smiled at the question. "You don't give up, uncle, do you?"

"There are a hundred young men who would lay their souls at your feet! A thousand!"

"Nonsense." She looked away from him. "That coppice needs trimming. I told Wirrell last week."

"And don't change the subject," Achilles said. "You should marry someone, my dear Campion. It is time you were worshipped. That is what women are for! To be worshipped, to be stroked, to be adored."

"To be loved?"

"You talk of illusions."

"To be decorative, then?" she asked him teasingly.

"Of course," he replied seriously.

They had reached the strip of grass between the Castle's lake and the great, wrought-iron fence that fronted the Shaftesbury road. Achilles stopped and looked over the water. "Magnificent."

They were looking at the celebrated view of Lazen, the one that had been drawn and painted so often that Campion claimed the artists' easels had permanently marked the lawn at this spot.

From this lake bank Lazen Castle spread across their view in all its magnificence. The castle had taken two centuries to build, yet it was marvellously coherent. It was really three houses. To the right was the Old House with its Long Gallery and its great windows that reflected the day's gray light. The Old House was joined by a bridge of rooms to the Great House, and the bridge also formed the portico beneath which carriages drew up to deliver guests to the castle.

The Great House was the tallest building, topped by the huge banner of Lazen, and fronted by the fluted columns that reared so arrogantly from the great spread of gravel. It was there, in the Great House, that Campion's father had lain for fifteen years, ever since his best-loved hunter had fallen on him, rolled on him, and bequeathed him paralysis and pain.

To the left was the lowest part of the building, the Garden House that was joined to the Great House by a curving, pillared arcade. It had been built for Campion's mother, a gift from her husband, but now it was used as a guest wing. It was in the Garden House that Uncle Achilles had been staying on this visit that ended today.

Campion stared at Lazen Castle, seeing it reflected in the wide lake. It was home to more than two hundred people; grooms, maids, cooks, footmen, postilions, cellarmen, seamstresses, servants by the score, and all fed and paid by Lazen, their babies born in the town and raised in the Castle's shadow, their beer brewed in the Castle's brewhouse, their linen pounded in the Castle's fullery, their corn ground in the Castle's mill.

Her uncle stared at her. "Do you ever get tired of it?"

"Never!" She smiled wistfully, took his elbow again, and began walking. "Do you ever wish that nothing should change?" She looked up at him. "That everything would just stop?" She waved at the Castle. "Perhaps next summer? On a day of perfection? If we could just leave it like that forever?" She laughed at her own fancy.

He stopped walking, took her face in his long, thin hands on which, perversely, he still wore his bishop's ring, and kissed her solemnly on the forehead. "Dear Campion, may I say something offensive?"

"Uncle?"

"This is serious advice."

"Oh dear." She smiled.

"It is time you grew up." His face, thin and intelligent, was extraordinarily attractive. He was the cleverest man Campion knew, the most interesting, the most unexpected. The lines of age seemed delicately etched beneath the powder on his face. He smiled. "I've offended you."

"No."

"I should have offended you, then." He took her elbow and walked on with her. "Lazen is not yours, my dear. It will go to Toby and Lucille. You will lose Lazen just as I lost Auxigny. You have your own life to make and the sooner you make it, the better. You should not be here adding up columns of figures and worrying about the harvest and paying the wages; you should be in London. You should be dancing."

"That doesn't sound like growing up."

He walked in silence for a few paces. "Experience is growing up, Campion. What's your family motto?"

"Dare all."

"And you dare nothing! You stay here like a nun in a convent. Of course you're happy here. You live in the greatest house in western England, you live off the greatest fortune in the realm. You want for nothing, you only have to lift a finger and the servants trample each other to provide for you. I know!" He raised his gold topped cane to ward off her reply. "I know! You work hard. Yet you chose to do that, just as you could have chosen to do nothing. But you exercise your choice in safety. You are like a ship that must leave harbor, a beautiful ship, well built, splendidly rigged, and you dare not leave the quay." He stopped and smiled at her. "Yet one day, my child, there will be no more harbor, no more quay, no more safety."

She stared at him, sensing the seriousness in him, then smiled. "Lazen will go?"

"Of course not. It's eternal."

She smiled. "Toby will be here."

"Ah." He mocked her with faked comprehension. "So the nun will grow old in her brother's household? When you are really old your great-grandnephews and nieces will be brought to look at you; 'See the old lady! See how she dribbles!' "

She laughed. "It isn't true."

"Then marry."

She said nothing for a few paces. "Marriage will come, uncle."

He tutted irritably. "You make it sound like a disease!"

"I don't want it to be an escape."

"How clever you are, niece." He smiled at her as they climbed the gentle bank toward the driveway. "My beautiful, clever niece with a clockwork heart."

"Nonsense!"

"Then I expect to find you drowning in love's illusion when I return. I demand it! I expect you to be sighing and writing excessively awful poems about your love's eyes."

She laughed and they turned into the driveway, walking directly toward the great house. The huge stable block was visible now to the right of the castle, its entrance busy as the outriders' horses were prepared for her uncle's departure.

Hooves sounded on the gravel behind and Campion turned to see who approached.

At first she thought it was one of the grooms returning from exercising a saddle horse, but then she realized that not one of Lazen's grooms rode like this man.

This was a horseman. She had grown up in a house that prized horsemanship, that knew a thing or two about men and horses, but never had she seen a horseman like this. This was a horseman.

The horse, big, sleek and black, trotted superbly on the gravel, while the rider, long-legged and straight-backed, seemed arrogantly at home in his saddle.

The rider was dressed entirely in black. Black breeches, black boots and a black shirt. A black coat was rolled and tied to his saddle. He had long, black hair that moved with the horse's motion, and, as he came closer, Campion saw the glint of a gold earring in his left ear.

Her uncle, also staring in admiration, suddenly laughed. "It's a gypsy. He must have stolen the horse."

The gypsy's face was dark, thin, and savage as a hawk's. Campion stared at the face, struck by it, thinking suddenly that never, ever in her life had she seen so superb a man. He rode as though he trampled a conquered world beneath his mare's hooves.

He looked at them as he passed, his oddly light, bright, blue eyes passing incuriously over the man and girl. He did not stop, he did not acknowledge them, he seemed to observe them and then arrogantly dismiss them from his attention. Campion saw that the man's sinewy forearms were tattooed with the images of eagles. A sword hung from the saddle, incongruous for a man who was not a gentleman.

Uncle Achilles watched her face, then laughed gently. "Perhaps you don't have a clockwork heart."

She was embarrassed instantly. She blushed.

He took her arm again. "It's easier for a man. Just as my father did, we men can take our fancies of the peasant masses, indulge them, and pass on. It's so much harder for a woman."

"What are you talking about, uncle?"

"Oh, nothing!" He sketched an airy gesture with his ribboned cane. "Only he was rather a handsome brute and your face did rather look like that tedious little Joan of Arc when she heard her boring voices." He smiled at her. "Take him as a secret lover."

"Uncle!"

He laughed. "I do like to shock you. Perhaps I shall

find you a husband who looks like the gypsy, yes?" He laughed again.

To her relief a great drop of rain splashed on the drive and her uncle, forgetting the gypsy, groaned at the catastrophe. "My coat will be ruined!"

"Run!"

"It's so inelegant to run."

"Then be inelegant." She laughed, tugged his elbow, held up her skirts, and they ran in the gathering rain, past the old church, straight for the garden door of the Old House.

"Mon dieu, mon dieu, mon dieu!" Achilles d'Auxigny brushed at the sleeves of his gray velvet coat as they stopped within the hallway. The sleeves were hardly spotted with water, yet he sighed as though he had been drenched. "It was new last month!"

"It's not touched, uncle!"

"How little you girls know of clothes." He flicked his lace cuffs, then listened as the stable clock struck the hour. He sighed. "Eleven o'clock. I must go. Come and bid me farewell."

"You're coming back soon?"

"For Christmas." He smiled. "Or for your wedding, whichever is sooner."

She smiled, reached up and kissed his cheek. "I shall see you at Christmas."

He laughed, they walked toward the entrance where his coach waited, and Campion, amazed what one glance could do to her sensible soul, wondered who the tall man was who rode like a conqueror and looked like a king.

Uncle Achilles left. The servants were lined beneath the portico and grateful for the boxes he had left for them. Campion had a glimpse of his slim, ringed hand waving from behind the carriage window, then the horses slewed out into the rain and he was gone.

"My Lady?" William Carline, Lazen's steward, gave her his imperceptible bow. He was a man of enormous and fragile dignity.

"Carline?"

"A most strange man, a foreigner, wishes to talk with you. He is most insistent. He carries, he claims, a message from Lord Werlatton." Carline's sniff suggested that no foreigner could be trusted.

The gypsy. She felt her heart leap, and was instantly ashamed of herself, more so because she was sure that Carline would see her confusion, but on his broad, pale face there was no sign that anything was amiss. She nodded in acknowledgment, forcing herself to keep her voice casual. "Ask Mrs. Hutchinson to attend me in the gallery and send him there."

"Very good, my Lady." Carline gave another of his tiny bows and waved an imperious dismissal at the servants.

Campion felt a pang of excitement as she turned to go to the Long Gallery. She felt astonishment too. She had merely glimpsed a man, a gypsy, evidently a servant of her brother's, and one sight of his face had filled her with this odd thrill of anticipation. She felt, as she waited for Mrs. Hutchinson, her companion, a shame that she should be so moved by a man who was her inferior.

But nonsense or not, as a footman opened the door for the gypsy to come into her presence, she felt her heart beating in anticipation and excitement.

The Gypsy had come to Lazen.

Campion, as he entered the Long Gallery and walked down its panelled splendor, was struck again by the man's arrogant magnificence. He bowed to her. "My Lady." He held out a sealed letter and spoke in French. "I come from your brother."

She took the letter, wondering how a French servant, a gypsy, had learned to walk stately halls with such assurance.

The question did not linger in her thoughts. It was swept from them by Toby's letter, by the news that made her gasp as if struck by a sudden physical pain.

Lucille was dead.

Campion had met Lucille twice, long ago when travel to France had still been safe, and she remembered a girl of dark, almost whimsical beauty. She knew well her brother's adoration of Lucille, and in her heart she felt a dreadful sorrow for Toby, and a dreadful anger at what had happened.

She looked up at the Gypsy. Toby, in his letter, had named the man simply as Gitan. "You know how she died?"

"Yes, my Lady." Mrs. Hutchinson, knitting beside Campion, did not speak French, but she sensed from their voices that the news was bad.

Campion frowned. "How?"

The Gypsy's face was almost expressionless. "It was not a good death, my Lady."

"Who did it?"

He shrugged.

He seemed a strange emissary, this Gypsy, from a land of shadow and death, and perhaps because he had come from the horrors described in Toby's letter, because he had seen the massacres in Paris' prisons, he seemed to have an added attraction about him.

Campion pushed the thought away. She stood up, still holding the letter, and walked down the long carpet of the gallery.

Toby said that hundreds had died in Paris. The mobs had broken into the prisons and then slaughtered the inmates. Lucille, though, had not been in prison. She had been at her parents' house outside Paris and a squad of men had fetched her and taken her into the city and there killed her. Campion turned. "Why?"

"Do you mean why her, my Lady?" He shrugged. "I don't know."

Dear God, she thought, but Lazen is cursed! Mother, father, brother, and now Lucille. Her father would have to be told. Toby, not wanting his horse-master to face the drunken earl, had sensibly ordered Gitan to give the letter to the Lady Campion.

She walked slowly back down the gallery, listening to the comfortable click of Mrs. Hutchinson's needles. "What happened in Paris?"

He told her. He spared her the details, but even in outline the story was horrific. He told it well and Campion, sensing guiltily again her attraction to this man, resented that he had proved so intelligent. To be handsome was one thing, and to be struck by a good-looking servant was not so unusual, but to find then that the man was articulate and subtle only added to the attraction and made the rejection harder.

She sat again. Toby had sent this man to deliver the letter to Lazen, then to join him in London. Toby said he would come to Lazen, but not immediately. She looked up at the slim, tall man. "How is my brother?"

He did not seem to think it unusual that he, a servant, should be asked the question. He considered his answer for a second. "Dangerously angry, my Lady."

"Dangerously?"

"He wants to find who killed Mademoiselle de Fauquemberghes, and kill them in turn."

"Go back to France?" Her voice was filled with horror.

"It would seem to be the only way, my Lady," he said dryly.

She stared at him, and thought that his face, though extraordinarily strong, was also sympathetic. He had answered all her questions with a fitting respect, yet there was more to him than the blandness of a servant. He had somehow imbued his answers with his own character, with independence.

She realized that she had been looking into his blue eyes for some seconds and, to cover the silence, she looked down at the letter again. She made herself read it once more.

When she looked up she saw that he had turned to stare at the great Nymph portrait.

Of all the paintings in Lazen, this was her favorite.

It showed the first Countess, the first woman in this family to bear the name Campion, and it showed her in this very room, her hand lightly resting on the table where Campion had just placed Toby's letter. Sir Peter Lely, the painter, seemed to have caught the first Campion as she half turned toward the onlooker, delight and joy on her face, and family tradition claimed that the painting was indeed the very image of its subject. Legend said that the family had been forced to pay Lely a double fee, just so that he would not paint her as he painted everyone else, with pouting lips and languorous fleshiness, but as she truly was.

The first Campion was said to have been the most beautiful woman in Europe. Her hair was light gold, her eyes blue, and her calm face suffused by a kind of vivacious contentment. She was beautiful, not just with the lineaments of bone and lip and skin and hair, but with the beauty that comes from kindness and happiness within. The Gypsy turned from the painting and his blue eyes looked with amusement at Campion.

She was embarrassed.

She knew what he was thinking, she always knew what people thought when they saw the painting. They thought it was of her. Somehow, over the generations, the beauty of the first Countess had been passed to her great-great-great-granddaughter.

Yet there was more to the painting than its odd likeness to herself. There were stories in it, stories about the four golden jewels about the Countess's neck, and a story about its title, the Nymph portrait. The title puzzled some visitors, and most had to stay puzzled, for only a few, a very privileged few, were told to stand at the far side of the gallery and stare at the silken folds of the shockingly low cut dress worn by the first Countess of Lazen.

The dress was blue green, the color of water, and suddenly, by staring, and after it was pointed out, it was possible to see in the gorgeous drapery the shape of a naked girl swimming, but then a second later the onlooker would blink, frown, and swear there was nothing to be seen. Yet she was there, naked and beautiful, a nymph in her stream, and legend said that it was thus that the first Countess had been seen by her husband.

Campion, who knew the picture, could see the naked girl every time, but no visitor had ever spotted the nymph until she was pointed out. Campion had a sudden, outrageous urge to tell the Gypsy, an urge she suppressed with more embarrassment. The naked, swimming nymph bore the same uncanny resemblance to herself.

She suddenly felt angry with herself. At a time like this, when her brother was in mourning, she flirted with a forbidden attraction and she was guilty and ashamed and astonished that the thoughts, so unbidden, should be so strong. She looked at the man. "You are returning to London?"

"Yes, my Lady."

"You wish to stay a night in our stables?"

He hesitated, then shook his head. "My orders are to return quickly, my Lady."

She felt a wash of relief. She did not think that life would be easy if this tall, splendid, intriguing man was in Lazen Castle. "You can get food in the kitchens."

"Thank you, my Lady."

"And thank you for bringing this."

He bowed to her and, thus dismissed, walked from the gallery. She watched him go and, as the door closed on him, she felt as if her senses had been released from a sudden and unwelcome burden. She turned to Mrs. Hutchinson, her chaperone. "It's bad news, Mary."

"Oh no, dear. Oh dear, no."

Lucille was dead, there would be no babies in Lazen, and Campion cried.

Gitan left Lazen that afternoon, his fed and rested mare strong on the road eastward.

He smiled as he went into the wet woodlands that bordered the estate, the autumn leaves dripping monotonously with rainwater and the air rich with the smells of a damp forest.

He carried messages from Marchenoir to London, messages of secrecy, messages hidden within his sword scabbard.

He had come safely to England, brought by Lord Werlatton, but his true purposes were hidden, hidden as well as the naked swimming girl that he had seen in the great blue-green portrait in the gallery. He had almost laughed when he saw it, so lifelike did the image seem and so like the beautiful girl who was his master's sister.

He thought of fat Jean Brissot. He thought how the Parisians would like to have that girl in their hands. He patted his horse's neck and smiled. Bertrand Marchenoir would like her most of all; the rabble-roaring ex-priest who had led Paris into blood and more blood was famous for his dealings with the daughters of the fallen aristocracy, and there would be added pleasure for Marchenoir in the fact that this lovely creature was, on her mother's side, one of the hated d'Auxignys. Gitan laughed at the thought.

The wind blew the rain cold from the west as man and horse rode through the brown, wet woods of an English autumn. He stopped in a clearing on the hill's crest, turned in his saddle, and stared at the great house that was now beneath him. It was, he thought, a most beautiful house. It was also, though it did not yet know it, a house under siege. The Gypsy clicked his tongue and rode on.

"What is your name?"

The answer came from a man who stood alone in the center of a sunken, marble floor. The man was naked.

The room was brilliantly lit by a ring of candles, hundreds of flames reflected from polished marble, silver, and mirrors that threw the man's shadow in a complex coronet radiating from his bare feet. The room was circular and, high above the naked man's head, there was the gleam of gold mosaics that decorated the domed ceilings. It was a lavish room, fit for an Emperor or a great whore.

The questioner spoke again. He could not be seen and his voice came as a hoarse whisper that seemed to fill the room, coming from no direction and every direction. "What is your desire?"

"To join you."

"What gives light?"

"Reason."

"What gives darkness?"

"God."

"How do you apprehend this?"

"With reason."

"What is your name?"

The naked man answered again. His voice was strong

in the room, echoing from the marble and from the magnificent gold mosaics of the dome.

Another voice, also a whisper, echoed mysteriously about the great chamber. "What protects the weak?"

"The law."

"What is above the law?"

"Reason."

"What is your name?"

The man answered. He stood quite still. He was a tall man and well muscled. He did not seem uncomfortable with his nakedness.

A third voice whispered. "What is death?"

"Nothing."

Silence.

Real silence. No windows opened to the outside world in this extraordinary place. The doors by which the naked man had entered were of bronze, doors so heavy that it had taken all his strength to close them on the night.

It was October outside. In this room it could be any season, any hour, any year.

One of the whispers sounded. "Kill him."

Silence again.

The man expected this, yet he felt a crawling fear within him. He kept his face rigid. He was being judged.

"Why did you come here?"

"To serve you."

"Whom do we serve?"

"Reason."

"What bounds does reason have?"

"None."

"Kill him."

"Kill him."

The third voice did not sound.

Europe was rife with secret societies, most imitating the Masons, all offering a man the secret pride of belonging to a privileged group. Some, like the *Rosati,* were harmless, devoted to poetry and wine. Others, like the *Illuminati,* had more sinister purposes. Yet this gathering, in this strange marble hall that was like a mausoleum awaiting its dead, was a secret society within a secret society. These were the Fallen Angels of the *Illuminati.*

The *Illuminati* had come from Germany where the princes and dukes had persecuted the movement and driven it south to France where, in the ferment of revolution, the "Illuminated Ones" had found a home. It was said that more than half the leaders of the revolution belonged to the *Illuminati,* that the achievements of the revolution had been planned, not in political meetings, but in the secret halls of the society. It was rumored that the *Illuminati* were spreading like an unseen stain throughout the civilized world.

They had been given the light of reason. They were above the law. They were the future. They would take the world from the dark splendors of superstition into the brilliance of a planet governed by the intellect. The society of the Illuminated Ones existed to establish a new religion that worshipped reason, and to forge a universal republic. France had lit the way; France had proved that the old monarchies and the old gods could be destroyed.

The naked man had been *Illuminati* for five years. Now he had been offered a greater honor. He could join the Fallen Angels.

The Fallen Angels were not the only secret group within the *Illuminati.* Each group, like this one, had a task to fulfill. Just as cavalry rode ahead of an army to spy out the land and confuse the enemy with short, sharp raids, so did the secret groups of the *Illuminati* prepare the way for the coming age of reason. The Fallen Angels planned one such raid now and the naked man, standing on the echoing marble, was needed for a specific task. First, though, he must pass this trial.

The naked man, if he failed this test, would die. Simply by coming to this place he had learned too much about the Fallen Angels. If he passed the test then he would be given a new name, the name of a fallen angel; one of those bright creatures who had rebelled against God, who had fought the war in heaven, and who had fallen with Satan into the bottomless pit of defeat. The Fallen Angels took the names of those who had dared to fight God as symbols of their own rebellion against religion, superstition, and government.

A whisper sounded again. "What is your name?"

He told them.

"What do the Fallen have?"

"Reason."

"Do they obey the law?"

"They make the law."

"Do they obey the law?" The whisper had a suggestion of irritation.

"No."

Silence. The candle flames were still and bright. A few, their wicks untrimmed, shivered and raised thin streaks of smoke that darkened the ceiling of the circular alcove within which all the candles burned. The alcove, its rear wall mirrored, ran like a recessed shelf clear around the base of the dome.

The whispers seemed to sigh about the circular room. Then one voice rose above the others. "What is evil?"

"Weakness." The naked man had not been rehearsed in his answers, but his sponsor, one of the three men who questioned him, had talked of what he might expect. He might expect death.

"What is the punishment for weakness?"

"Death."

"What is your name?"

He told them. There was silence.

He felt the shiver of fear again, but he kept his head high and he stared at the veined sheen of the curved marble walls and tried to see from where the voices came.

The sigh came again, like a wind half heard far away. It died into silence.

The floor on which he stood was of green and blue marble. It was some forty feet in diameter and surrounded by white marble steps, four in all, that climbed to a mosaic pavement. The walls were decorated with columns, sculpted wreaths, and intricate bas-reliefs, any of which could hide the openings from which the voices must come. The chamber, though lavish and bright, seemed to be missing something, as though a throne or a great catafalque should stand within its barren splendor.

"What is your name?"

He told them.

"Kill him."

"Kill him."

The third voice, instead of confirming his doom, whispered that he should close his eyes.

The naked man obeyed. He could hear nothing, but there was a sudden shivering of colder air on his body as though a tomb had been opened.

Then he heard footsteps.

He heard naked feet on the marble floor. The feet approached him, walking slowly, and he had to fight the desire to open his eyes. He was shivering. He wanted to break away from the center of the floor and run from the slow, soft feet that came closer and closer to him. He imagined a blade reaching for him and he had to steel himself to stand still and keep his eyes closed.

Something touched his shrinking, crawling flesh and he almost jumped and shouted in alarm.

Fingers stroked his chest. Fingers that were soft and warm and gentle. The fingers traced down his ribs, over his belly, down to his loins. The relief was coursing through him. He had expected death.

"Open your eyes." The whisper echoed about the high chamber.

The naked man obeyed and, in front of him, smiling up at him, was a girl. She was pretty. She had a round, freckled face with red hair that had been tied back with a red ribbon. Her hair was full and springy because it had been washed. She smelled of soap because she had bathed before this ceremony. Like him she was naked. Her skin was pink, freckled, young and clean.

She smiled at him and her hands stroked him.

"Do you like her?" one of the whisperers asked.

"Yes." He felt embarrassed. Her hands were soft and shameless. They flickered and stroked, touched and kneaded his flesh.

The naked man guessed the girl was nineteen or twenty. She had big, firm breasts and the wide hips of a girl who would be strong in childbirth. She leaned forward and licked the sweat on his chest, then reached up to pull his head down to hers.

He kissed her. Her salty tongue was quick between his lips. She hooked a leg behind his legs and her strong thigh was warm on his skin.

"Take her," the whisper commanded.

She was pulling him down to the cold marble and he knelt, laid her down, and ran his right hand down her body.

The girl closed her eyes. The gentlemen who had hired her from the Dijon brothel had promised her a huge sum for this night's work. Half of it was already in her purse downstairs, the other half would be given to her after she had made this man happy. It was silly, of course, but what girl could refuse such a sum for such a small task?

She opened her legs, thinking what an uncomfortable bed cold marble made, and opened her eyes and smiled into the man's face. "Come, come."

The naked man ran his hands from her thighs to her breasts and she arched her back, moaned, and closed her eyes again. "You're so good! Come to me."

"Take her," the whisperer ordered.

He took her, and with a whore's skill she made him feel that he was a lover greater than any in history. Her head turned from side to side in false pleasure, she moaned softly, she reached for him to pull him down, she pushed up with her hips, and the man, propped on his hands that were either side of her shoulders, smiled down on her as she locked her ankles behind his thighs.

Each whisper so far had been in French. Now, suddenly, one of the hidden men spoke in English. "Kill her."

He froze, then knew that this was the test, that hesitation was failure and failure was death and he fell on her, his hands moving from the floor to her neck and he gripped her throat with his big hands, squeezed, and her eyes opened in terror as she still thrust at him, and then she twisted beneath him, tried to wrench her body free and she rolled on top of him, thrashing, kicking, clawing at him and he shook her head with his hands and forced her back to the floor again.

Her fingers pulled at his wrists, but her strength was nothing like his and he had her beneath him and he beat her head on the floor.

Still he squeezed. He could feel her pulse beneath his thumbs. Her legs beat on the floor. He knelt up, his knee slipping in liquid, and beat her head again. His teeth were gritted.

She took a long time to die. When he took his fingers from her throat, he thought they would never straighten again. He was panting.

Slowly he stood up. He stepped away from the body.

As he stood one part of the marble wall of the circular chamber suddenly moved. Two wooden doors, cunningly painted in the manner of poor church interiors to look like marble, opened before his astonished eyes to reveal a hidden room.

There was a table of black stone within the room. Candles stood on the table about which three figures sat. On either side of the table sat men in robes of black and gold, with great stiff cowls like monks' hoods over their heads. At the table's head, facing the naked man, sat a figure robed and hooded in silver. He was Lucifer, the day star, the prince of darkness, the leader of the Fallen Angels and, with due ceremony and courtesy, he welcomed the new member who henceforth, he said, could wear the black and gold habit of a Fallen Angel. The robe waited for him on a vacant chair. Then Lucifer gave the newcomer his name. From henceforth, he said, he would be known as Chemosh.

The Fallen Ones met in the shrine built by the Mad Duke who had thought he was God. The shrine was behind the splendid Chateau of Auxigny. The Mad Duke was long dead, gone to meet the God he had failed to be, and his eldest son, the present Duke, was imprisoned with his King in Paris.

One of the Fallen Angels did not sit at the black table, for he was a deaf mute. Lucifer had given him the name Dagon. He was a huge, shambling creature with the face of an idiot. The black and gold robe sat on his shoulders like a royal cloak draped on a dancing bear. His task was to care for the Chateau of Auxigny and its strange shrine, a task he did to the terror of the local children who spoke of strange things in the woods behind the castle.

When Chemosh had been admitted to the chamber, and

the doors had been closed again, Dagon took the body of the girl downstairs. He stroked it, and from his throat came strange noises. Later, when the Fallen Angels had gone, and when Dagon was again alone in the Chateau of Auxigny, he would take the body to the dark woods behind the shrine and he would leave it for the ravens and the night creatures and her body would be flensed and the bones scattered and the remnants covered by the falling pine needles. She was not the first girl to die in this place, for every new Fallen Angel was initiated with death, and Dagon, as he ran his huge hands down her still warm flesh, hoped she would not be the last.

Lucifer gestured with a silver-gloved hand at the wine. "Drink, Chemosh. You need some wine after that nonsense."

Chemosh smiled. "Nonsense?"

"Of course. Superstition! Yet we have to know if you believe what you say, that you believe reason is above the law, that you believe a reasonable man can do no evil. So we frighten you a little and give you a trifling test. Now you can forget it." He shrugged beneath the robes. His face was entirely hidden by the dipping cowl of his hood that made a black shadow from which his voice came so hoarse and low. It seemed to Chemosh to be an old voice, a voice that spoke from long and bitter knowledge. Once only, as the cowl was raised toward Chemosh, did the newcomer see the glitter of eyes that themselves seemed to be like two hard silver lights in the darkness.

Lucifer, his voice as dry as dead leaves in a cold wind, spoke of the purpose of the Fallen Angels.

He spoke of a war that would soon be declared between France and Britain. He spoke of the decision, by the *Illuminati,* to work for Britain's defeat.

His business, he said, was not with armies. France would fight, and France would win, and France would take republicanism and reason to Britain. But first the *Illuminati* would rot Britain from within.

He spoke of the British Corresponding Societies that supported the revolution. They would need money, help, and arms.

He spoke of the British journals and their writers, the scribblers who would take any bribe and spread any rumor.

He spoke of that "mad, fat King" who would be dethroned, of the scandals that would be spread in high places, of the foulness that would be smeared over Britain's leaders and aristocrats, until the people of Britain had no trust in their government and would welcome the cleansing flood of republicanism.

And all this, Lucifer said, would take money. "More money than you can dream of, Chemosh. The task of the Fallen Angels is to provide the *Illuminati* with that money."

The new silk robe was cold on Chemosh's thighs. He was still shaking from the effort of killing the girl. Her eyes, wide and bulging, still stared in his brain.

Lucifer drank water, then the silvery cowl turned to the newcomer again. Neither of the other two hooded men had spoken yet. Like Chemosh, they listened to their master's voice. "We are going to take a fortune in Britain, Chemosh, and your task is to help us." His voice was bitter and dry, soft and sibilant, yet even Lucifer could not hide the pleasure of his next words. "We are going to take the Lazen fortune."

Lazen! Chemosh knew of Lazen. Did anyone not know of the richest earldom in England? Lazen, with its sprawling great house and its London property and its estates in every shire, was rumored to have a greater income than that of most kingdoms. Lazen! He said nothing, but he wondered how, in Reason's name, these few men would take the fortune of Lazen.

Lucifer, his hands gloved in silver, told him how.

The Earl of Lazen was sick. He was dying. It was said he could not live another winter, that, indeed, he had almost died a few weeks before when the stump of his amputated leg began bleeding in the night. He would die, Lucifer said, and when he died the fortune of Lazen, with the title, would pass to his son, Viscount Werlatton. Lucifer turned to his left. "Moloch?"

The robed man opposite Chemosh pushed back his hood. He smiled at the newcomer.

Chemosh was suddenly frightened. He was staring at a face that had been lampooned by half the caricaturists of Europe. He was staring at a heavy, powerful, brooding, knowing face that was the very symbol of the French revolution. Moloch was Bertrand Marchenoir, the ex-priest who now preached his gospel of blood.

Marchenoir leaned forward, lit a cigar from one of the candles, then took up the tale. "Werlatton was in the British Embassy in Paris. He's an adventurer and up to his bloody neck in spying." Marchenoir blew smoke over the table. Chemosh saw how his black and gold robe was filthy with wine stains. The Frenchman gave a grim smile. "He was due to get married; you might remember the fuss the London papers made? We killed his bride and stopped him spawning more heirs. I now hear that he wishes to return to France, seek me out, and take his revenge." He laughed.

"We shall pray he does," Lucifer said.

"And when he does," Marchenoir went on, "and after his father's death, I shall kill him."

"After?" Chemosh asked.

The silver cowl of Lucifer looked at him. "We do not want the earl to change his will. The father will die, and the son will follow. The son is a fool. He should be rearing a family already, but he cannot resist adventure. So he will die, and the earldom will pass to a cousin. Belial?"

Chemosh knew who Belial was. He was another politician, a member of Britain's House of Commons who was famous for his impassioned speeches against the French and their revolution. Valentine Larke preached war against France in public, while in private he worked for Britain's defeat. Larke had sponsored Chemosh for the Fallen Angels and now he turned his hooded face toward his protégé. "The cousin is called Sir Julius Lazender. We have no problems with Sir Julius. Soon all that he will inherit will belong to us."

"How soon?" Lucifer asked.

"Two months? Maybe three."

The silver cowl nodded. "You see, Chemosh, by how slender a thread the fortune hangs? The earl, his son, and then it is ours. All of it. Except for one problem, a problem that you," and here a silver gloved finger stabbed at him, "will solve. Tell him, Belial."

Valentine Larke, MP, leaned back from the table. "There is a daughter. Her name is Campion." He said the unusual name slowly and scornfully. "She is, for a girl, remarkably well educated. At present she has all the responsibility for Lazen. Her father is ill, her brother absent, and she governs. She does it, I am told, well." He paused to sip wine. "Our problem, Chemosh, is simple. The earl knows how slender is the thread. He knows his son has no heir. He knows that Sir Julius might inherit and Sir Julius is a gambler. Lazen is in peril, and we believe that the girl is his answer. One. She might inherit, though I doubt it. Two, she might inherit part of the fortune, though I doubt that the earl will divide his inheritance. Three, and most likely, is that whoever inherits will find themselves still under her thumb. The estate, in short, will be entailed and she will have the governance of the entail." She shrugged. "We can't kill her now, because the earl will change his will, just as he would if the son died, so we must do something else."

"You must do something else." Lucifer spoke, and again his finger stabbed at Chemosh. "Your task, Chemosh, is to ensure that the Lady Campion Lazender is no threat to us. Specifically she is not to marry."

Chemosh understood that. If she married, then her husband would take her property and would have the governance of the entail or the estate. Her children, if her brother and cousin died, might inherit. "I stop her marrying?"

"You stop her marrying by any means short of death. Later she will die, but not until her father is buried."

Chemosh had his task now, he had earned it, and he was part of a conspiracy that would twist the history of the world into a new, clearer future. He felt privileged to be in this place where decisions were made which, like those which had led in secret council to the fall of France, would now lead to Britain's downfall. He was Chemosh, the name of the Fallen Angel that demanded human sacrifice, and he had escaped death by inflicting death. He understood now why they had made him kill for this initiation, for only a man without pity and who understood that Reason's servants are above man's petty laws was worthy to be a Fallen Angel. Chemosh's elation lasted as Lucifer gave his last instructions. He, Chemosh, was to take his orders from Valentine Larke, while Larke would communicate to France through Marchenoir's messenger. Yet to Chemosh these were mere details that were swamped by his exhilaration at this privilege.

Finally, Lucifer stood and the movement shifted the cowl for one second, and Chemosh saw again the glitter of eyes deep in the shadow. It seemed that even Lucifer's eyes were silver, then the hood settled back and the dry, rustling voice spoke again. "We are done. I shall go, the rest of you will follow in ten minutes. I wish you all a safe journey. I do not need to wish you success, for we are followers of Reason and therefore cannot fail."

Then, with a shimmer of his robes, he turned and went down the passage at the back of the chamber.

Marchenoir waited till their leader's footsteps had faded to silence, then stood, stretched his massive arms, and went to the painted, curved doors and pulled them apart. Chemosh saw that the body of the girl was gone. The marble floor glistened.

Marchenoir grinned. "Watch, Chemosh."

"Watch?"

The Frenchman jerked his head toward the empty, circular chamber.

There was silence. Chemosh gave a puzzled look to Valentine Larke who, now that Lucifer was gone, pushed his hood back from hair that, despite his fifty years, was still glossy black. It was rippled like the hard sand on a creek bed. Beneath the hair was a broad, flat, intelligent face, an impressive face even, a face of such judiciousness that any free-holder would think this man worthy of a vote with or without the election bribe. His eyes stopped his face from being handsome. They were of a blandness so unnatural as to be frightening; dark eyes in flattened sockets. They were the eyes of a quiet, watching man, but they were also eyes of horrid implacability. Valentine Larke did not forget or forgive his enemies. Now, though, he smiled and gestured toward the main room of the shrine. "Watch!"

Chemosh turned to the brilliantly lit chamber where he had killed the girl.

He saw nothing strange, but then, deep in the building, he heard the rattle of a chain, a creaking sound like the windlass of a well, and to his astonishment he saw that the brightness of the gleaming shrine was dimming. A shadow seemed to flow down the walls like blood, like an artificial twilight, a shadow that flicked over the statuary, became darker and then, with an awesome finality, extinguished the last flicker of candlelight with the huge room. In just seconds the brilliance of the shining room had been dimmed to darkness.

Only the candles on the black stone table stayed lit. The shadow had swallowed the marble chamber.

Marchenoir laughed at the newcomer's expression. "The Mad Duke's little palace of tricks!" He gestured toward the dark dome. "Just an iron shutter that drops in front of the candles. Dagon turned the handle downstairs. It was built so the mad bugger could shout 'let there be light' and a dozen peasants would haul on the chain!" He laughed and shook his head. "Our job was to worship the crazy bastard. There used to be a tunnel under here so he could suddenly appear in our astonished midst. They bricked that up when the bugger died. But I suppose we were impressed by it all." He tossed his cigar onto the darkened marble floor, then turned his hard, brooding face to the newcomer. "I envy you, Chemosh."

"Envy me?"

"I hear that the Lady Campion is a pearl of great price. She is said to be beautiful." He walked to the black table and lit another cigar. The Gypsy, who was the messenger between Marchenoir and Larke, had told the French politician that the Lady Campion was more beautiful than a dream. Marchenoir blew smoke into the huge, dark chamber. "Very beautiful indeed."

"A pity," Larke said dryly.

"Pity?" Marchenoir asked.

"Because the easiest way to stop her marrying," the Englishman said quietly, "is to make her unmarriageable. If you scar her face, Chemosh, and scar her body, and scar her mind, who will want her?" He sipped wine. "Have her raped. Hire a poxed man to rape her and scar her and drive her wits a little mad." He smiled. "You see how easy your task will be?"

Marchenoir laughed. "Send her to me."

"You'd like that, wouldn't you?" Larke smiled. "A virgin aristocrat at your mercy."

Marchenoir laughed. "I am the killer of aristocrats." He said it simply, boastfully, then walked to the edge of the dark chamber and stared up at the dome where the iron shutter had dropped over the candles. "They're different. They have white skins, soft skins, skins like silk. They squeal." He laughed again, and the sound echoed back in the Mad Duke's chamber. "I would like her. God, how I would like her." He turned, and his broad, powerful face stared at the newcomer. "If it is possible, Chemosh, if in all this wide God-ridden world you find it possible, then bring her to me." He paused, then the voice that had roused Paris against its King, and France against its civilization, roared in the marble emptiness. "Scarred or poxed, whole or savaged, Chemosh," he paused and he shouted his next four words slowly and distinctly, so that the echo of one faded before the next was uttered. "Bring her to me!"

The early winter weeks were hard for Lady Campion Lazender, harder than she dared admit to herself, and made so by the constant visits of the Gypsy to Lazen Castle.

It was not that she saw much of the man called Gitan, yet she found that when her brother was in residence she would deliberately find a reason to visit the dairy or brewhouse, to see how the new wall of the kitchen garden was progressing, or to count the stock in the game larder; any excuse, indeed, for going close to the stable entrance. She made herself stop the subterfuge.

Yet still she would glimpse him. Sometimes he would be a black, upright figure schooling a horse in the meadows to the east of the drive, and once she saw him leaning at the kitchen door drinking a glass of ale that had been fetched for him by one of the maids. The maid, a pudgy little girl with a hare lip, stared up devotedly at the tall, dark man, and Campion was astonished by the streak of jealousy that stabbed at her, wrenched at her, and she felt the humiliation of this attraction and the wretchedness of suppressing it.

Yet suppress it she did. She threw herself into her work of which, the harvest having failed for two years running, there was plenty. The Castle, with all its estate and pensioners, had to be fed. The tenancies had to be managed. What harvest there was had to be eked out from the rick-yard and storerooms.

There was Christmas to prepare for, her father to care for, and estate decisions to be made. Campion chose which timber should be cut for winter fuel, which coppiced, and how many animals should be kept alive through what promised to be a hard, hungry, cold season.

She had no need to work. The Castle had a steward, as it did the estate, and there were lawyers ever eager to charge fees for their services. Yet she hated idleness. She had begun to interest herself in the Castle's management when, at eighteen years old, she made the chance discovery that the housekeeper was buying more sheets each autumn than existed in the whole Castle. That housekeeper was long gone, the accounts straightened, and even in the hardest winter Campion had cut the estate's expenditure by a third. No one went hungry, nothing was skimped, yet the family was not robbed. She liked the work, she was good at it, yet this winter its best advantage was that it kept her from what she knew were humiliating, unfitting thoughts of the Gypsy.

She even wondered whether it was her reluctance for the Gypsy to leave the Castle that made her so adamant in her opposition to Toby's plans.

He was returning to France.

He had told her and she had exploded in sudden and unnatural anger, telling him his duty was to stay at Lazen, to look after Lazen, to marry and have children, and her words had whirled about his stubborn red head with as much force as snowflakes.

He was not thinking of Lazen. He was thinking of scraps of ragged flesh tossed about a cell.

She shook her head in bitterness. "Suppose you die?"

"Then Julius gets what he's always wanted." He

laughed at the thought of their cousin, Sir Julius Lazender, inheriting the earldom.

She was too angry to speak.

He tried to explain. He tried to tell her that there were men in France who prepared to fight against the revolution, men faithful to the church and to the King, and men who looked to Britain for help. He was not, he said, going alone, but going with the blessing of Lord Paunceley.

"Then Lord Paunceley's a fool!" she said.

Toby laughed. "They call him the cleverest man in the kingdom."

"Then that makes all Englishmen fools!"

He shrugged. Lord Paunceley, a mysterious man of immense power, ran Britain's secret service. He had been a lifelong friend of their father, though the friendship was now conducted entirely by correspondence.

Toby smiled. "I'm taking the rebels muskets, powder, and money. I shall be safe!"

"You'll be dead."

"Then I'll be with Lucille."

And that had been the final straw for her, a reply of such stupidity and such an evasion of his responsibility, that they had parted on terms of strained affection. She did not want him to go, she could not stop him going, yet, in the end, there was a certain relief that the tall, black-dressed Gitan was leaving with him.

She said farewell to Toby on a cold morning in November. She hugged her brother tight. They had always been close, always affectionate, and it seemed to Campion that only these last weeks had brought some barrier between them. "Be safe, Toby."

"I shall be safe."

She looked up at the mounted Gypsy, black cloaked, his blue eyes so unreadable. And on this last glimpse, as on her first, she felt the force of the man's looks and personality strike into her soul with undiminished impact. She nodded coldly, wishing him a safe journey, keeping her voice as tight and controlled as ever when she was in his presence.

He smiled and answered in his strongly accented English. "Thank you, my Lady."

Then she hugged Toby again, her eyes closed and her arms about him. He gently pulled away and climbed into the travelling coach. He went to his revenge, to his chosen work, and Campion watched the tall, black figure that rode beside the coach until the gatehouse hid him from view. They were gone, and there was the sense of a burden lifted.

Yet sometimes, in the long evenings, when her father was lost in the solace of his liquor and the Castle was slowly closing itself for the night, she would find herself before a large, pagan portrait of Narcissus that hung in the castle's Great Chamber and see, in that old painting, the same arrogant, competent, strong face that she missed. The Narcissus in the painting was naked, and she was ashamed that she should be drawn by the strong, sleek body. She was ashamed and she was astonished that she, who was so controlled, so sensible, so practical, should find her emotion so uncontrollably arrested by a common groom. He was the Gypsy, and he had ridden into her dreams to make them sad.

Her father saw it. He looked at her from his bed one bright, cold morning at November's end. "What's troubling you?"

"Nothing." She smiled. She was dressed to go out, cloaked and furred and wrapped against the winter's cold.

"You look like a dog that's lost its nose. Are you in love?"

"No, father!" She laughed.

"Happens to people, you know." He grimaced as pain lanced through him. "One day they're perfectly sensible, the next they're mooning about like sick calves. It's nothing that marriage won't cure."

"I'm not in love, father."

"Well, you should be. It's time you were married."

"You sound like Uncle Achilles."

He looked her up and down fondly. "There ought to be someone who'd marry you. You're not entirely ugly. There's Lord Camblett, of course. He's blind, so he might have you."

She laughed. "There's that curate in Dorchester who thought I was the new milliner in town."

"He wet himself when he found out," her father laughed. "Poor booby. Why didn't you tell him?"

"He was being very sweet. He showed me over the church." The curate, nervous and hopeful, had escorted her from the church to find a carriage and four waiting outside, postilions and grooms bowing to the girl he had thought a milliner. He would not be consoled for his mistake. Campion smiled. "If I'd have told him he'd only have been more nervous. It's quite nice sometimes to be treated like everybody else."

"I could always throw you out of the castle," her father said hopefully. She laughed, and he held her hand. "You're not sad?"

"No, father." How could she tell him about the Gypsy? He would think she was mad. "Except I wish Toby wasn't in France."

He shrugged. "Wouldn't be much of a man if he didn't want adventure, would he?"

"No, father. I suppose not."

Hooves and wheels sounded on the gravel and her father laboriously turned his head to look at the horses that stopped beneath his window. "They're looking good."

"Marvellous." She said it warmly.

The bays were her joy. A matched pair that were harnessed to a carriage she had chosen for herself, a carriage that her father considered flighty, dangerous, and welcome evidence that his beautiful daughter was not entirely a sensible, practical and dutiful girl.

She had bought herself a phaeton.

Not just any phaeton, but one of the highest, swiftest phaetons in the country. The bays were as spirited as the carriage itself, and the earl, whenever he saw the equipage drawn up on the forecourt, felt a pang of fear for his daughter.

The phaeton, her father thought, could hardly weigh more than she did! The earl had ordered ballast placed above each axle, but still the fragile assembly of steel, leather, and wood frightened him.

He looked at her from his pillow. "Simon tells me you took the ballast off the axles."

"A bit."

"A bit!" He laughed. "I don't know why you don't just glue bloody feathers on it and try to fly."

"Perhaps I will." She kissed him. "I'll see you at lunch time."

"Drive slowly."

"I always do."

"Liar." He smiled at her.

This morning she was driving to Millett's End. The village was a remote place, lost in the southern heaths, but it was a journey she took each fortnight as part of her duty. Most of the villagers were tenants or pensioners of Lazen, the vicar was appointed by the Castle, it was as much a part of Lazen as the larger, closer, richer town on the Castle's doorstep. Campion went there for duty, yet she admitted to herself the pleasure of letting the bays run free on the high, straight, heathland road.

Not that today she could go fast. The frost had rutted the roads dangerously hard, though once up on the heath she knew she could steer onto the grass and let the bays stretch their legs.

Simon Burroughs shouted from the stable-block doors. "You want company?"

"No!" She smiled at him. Sometimes a groom would accompany her on a saddle-horse, but Campion knew the grooms were instructed to keep her pace slow. Today, on this crisp, cold, hard day she wanted to be alone.

The wheels blurred as the bays trotted down the long, curved driveway, over the small bridge that crossed the stream which fed the ornamental lake. It was here, she thought, that she had first seen the Gypsy, and then she pushed that thought away as she rattled between the gate-houses and onto the cobbled street that led to Lazen's market place.

She raised a gloved hand to those who greeted her, called a welcome to Mrs. Swan who was brushing out her cottage, and pretended not to notice the lurch as two children jumped onto the back axle stand. Two only was the rule, and only as far as the mill bridge, but it was no fun unless she pretended not to notice.

She let the horses go faster as she crossed in front of the covered market. She had seen Simon Stepper, the bookseller whose business was almost entirely owed to the Castle, wrapping a scarf about his neck in his shop doorway. He was a clever man, but once he began talking he would never stop. She looked the other way, laughing as a man who stacked logs beside the glebe cottages gestured for her to go faster, and then Simon Stepper was left behind and the phaeton, its shadow leaping from cottage to cottage, slowed to approach the mill bridge. She heard a gasp and laughter as the children fell clear.

The water was high, spilling gleaming from the mill

pond. The smoke from the mill kitchen chimney was whipped away by a stiff breeze and Campion caught a whiff of roasting meat and then she was driving past the town's clink, the small single cell jail with its door open onto mysterious shadow, and she was through the town. She slowed as the cobbles ended and the road climbed between black, frost rimed hedges toward Two Gallows Hill.

She went slowly here, remembering how in spring these hedgerows were thick with flowers and fragrance. Spring, she thought, seemed so far away. The road climbed more steeply. Joshua Cartwright, who farmed on this edge of the town, would bring his horses to help wagons climb this incline, yet the bays pulled the phaeton without apparent effort. She looked right at the single, empty, leaning gibbet on Two Gallows Hill, then the road twisted through pasture land, heaved up one more steep slope, and levelled itself onto the heathland above. The gibbet was left behind, the sky was immense now over the flat landscape, a landscape bare of features except for the road, a few, windbent trees, and the curious, humped ridges of the old earthwork fort to her left.

It was a cold day, the sky was cloudless and the sunlight slanted low and bright onto the bushes. She took the bays off the road onto the wide, flat verge, and let them go into a trot. Their breath whipped back past their gleaming flanks. Her spirits rose with the speed.

She let them go faster. The ground here was quite level, quite safe, free of hidden stones that could tip a fast-moving phaeton and smash it to tinder. She shook the reins again and it seemed to her that she rode a chariot in the sky. The bushes blurred as she went past them, she felt the joy of it, the excitement of it, the reins quivering against the tension of her forearms, and she let the horses go faster still.

The wind put tears into her eyes and lifted the cord of the whip. She thought the speed might even pluck off the fur bonnet that was pulled so low over her ears and about her face, but still she shouted at the horses, laughed, and felt the pure exhilaration of the speed.

The Reverend Horne Mounter, dining in the earl's rooms last week, had explained the scientific fact that there was an absolute celerity beyond which a human body could not travel.

The earl, sitting up in bed, and grumbling about an itching in his mended stump, had opined that such a scientific fact was garbled mumblelarkey.

The Reverend Mounter had laughed politely and complimented the earl on his spitchcock'd eel.

"Always liked eel," the earl said. His thin face had been flushed. The room had a sour smell in it, a smell of sickness. At least, though, he was sober. Campion had cut more of her father's food, then smiled at the rector.

"An absolute celerity, Reverend Mounter?"

"Indeed so, my Lady." The Reverend Horne Mounter swallowed his mouthful of eel and helped it with some of the castle's best claret. "At speeds, they say, in excess of one equivalent to thirty miles in an hour, it is certain that the blood of the body would be driven by the excessive motion to the rear of the body. Unless, of course, one was travelling backward, in which case it would be driven to the front of the body!" He demonstrated this fact with copious movement of his plump, white hands. "Starved of the blood the front, or back, half of the body would die! It's quite certain!"

"It's quite fiddlededee!" the earl had said.

Now, her wheels spinning and bouncing on the frost-hard turf, Campion shook the reins again and let the horses go into a gallop. She wondered how fast they travelled and whether the tingling on her skin was the blood being driven backward by the celerity of the carriage. She laughed aloud at the thought, and as she laughed, so she saw the shape rise from the gorse to her right.

She stood no chance.

The man ran at the bays, shouted, and hurled a thick bough of dead gorse at their feet. They swerved, Campion leaned on the reins, felt them sawing at her wrists, but the horses had panicked to their left and dragged the light carriage onto the uneven road.

The wheels of the phaeton bounced, slammed down, and caught on the thick, frost-hardened rut at the road's center. Campion shouted at the horses, pulled the right reins, and then the front left wheel splintered in shards of varnished, gleaming wood and the carriage crashed down, dug in its spinning axle hub, and Campion was thrown clear, by a miracle the reins uncurling from her hands, and she screamed because the phaeton seemed to be falling on top of her, but it lurched back, was crashing past, and she fell onto the grass of the road's center, the breath driven from her body, and she heard the horses slowing as the tangled, broken mess of the phaeton dragged them to a stop.

The man laughed.

Campion's right hand was on one of the splintered spokes of the wheel, fractured in the crash so that the varnished wood, picked out with yellow paint, was now sheered into a wicked point of fresh timber.

There was pain all over her. She was dazed, but she swung the feeble weapon at the shape above her, kicked, but then her makeshift spear was held and a foot was clamped heavily on her ankle.

The man's breath rasped loudly in his throat.

For a second he did not move.

Her vision cleared. She could not see him at first, so bright was the sky about his head, but she could smell him. He pulled the broken spoke effortlessly from her hand and tossed it far into the gorse.

He chuckled hoarsely as he knelt beside her. She struck at him with her right hand, but he caught her wrist and forced it to the ground, then seized her left wrist. She saw his face and screamed.

He was unshaven. There was an open sore by his right eye. He looked like any vagabond, any tramp, except that his skin was oddly pallid as though he had been in a sunless prison. His face was scarred by old boils. His hair was lank, littered with straw ends, and his mouth, as he leered at her, was filthy with blackened stumps of teeth. His nose was flat and crooked, as though it had been broken repeatedly. He felt hugely strong to her. She had a glimpse of a great barrel of a belly, dirty where his rags gaped to show a red boil, and she lashed out with her right boot, sobbing, but he put his knee between her thighs, pinning her by the skirts, and his spittle dribbled onto her face as he leered above her.

"You be nice to me, you be nice! I'll make it easy on you if you be nice to me, girly!" He laughed as she tried to kick at him. "Don't do no good fightin', girly. I be one of the fancy, I was." As if to demonstrate his point he let go of her left wrist, and his fist, that had been bruised, skinned and broken by the bare-knuckle fighting so loved by the gentry, slammed into her belly.

The breath was pushed again from her, she lay helpless, pounded by the blow, and she felt the vomit rise with the panic.

She could not move. The blow had hurt her. He let go of her other wrist that hurt from his cold grip, and pushed her woolen cloak away from her body. He laughed. "Pretty." He moved his knee, grunted, and hauled her skirts up. "Oh, pretty! Pretty!"

She screamed as he touched her thighs, lashed at him

with both hands, but he just laughed and caught her fists, and held both her slim wrists in the huge grip of his left hand. She felt as if her wrists would snap as she tried hopelessly to pull away from him.

She was powerless. She tried to kick at him as he fumbled with frost-chilled fingers at the string which held up his ragged trousers, but he just laughed at her feeble efforts. "You be good, girly!"

She twisted, jerked, and could do nothing. Her thrashing dislodged the collar of her cloak and the man saw the gleam of the gold chain she wore at her neck. He had untied his trousers and now he reached for the chain.

He tugged the chain free, his fingers scrabbling at her throat, and she twisted away, the sickness thick in her gorge, and then he let go of her wrists, gripped the cream linen dress she wore beneath her blue, fur-lined cloak, and jerked her with savage force as he tore the dress down to her waist.

He hit her hands out of the way, hooked his fingers on her petticoat, and she screamed again as he tore at it. The force of his tearing hands lifted her body from the grass and, as the petticoat ripped open, she fell back, screaming and sobbing.

He was kneeling over her, straddling her body, and she could feel his spittle dripping on her cold, naked breasts. His nose was running, dribbling to his mouth. He was laughing, the laughter choking in his slavering throat, and he forced her hands aside to look at her body and he laughed. "Pretty girly, pretty, pretty girly." He held her arms on the ground.

"No!" She screamed. "No! No!"

He leaned back, the better to see her, and she could smell his breath like ordure and hear the air rasping in his throat. He let go of her arms and she clasped them over her breasts and then she felt his hands tugging at her waistband and she struck at him and he slapped her stingingly on the face. "You be good, girly! You be good!"

She tried to kick him, but his weight was on her thighs, and he laughed as he took from somewhere in his rags a small, rusted knife and began to saw at the dress's belt. His trousers had fallen to his thighs. He grunted as he ripped at the cloth, beat her hands aside again, and cursed as she twisted desperately and the tangle of cotton and linen snatched the small blade from his hand. He thumped his fist onto her bare belly to make her quiet. His orders were to disfigure her, to scar her, to pox her, to scab her, to make her a thing that no man could ever desire. He fumbled for the knife, impatient to cut her clothes off, then, losing patience as she twisted so desperately beneath him, he raised himself up and simply pulled her skirts above her waist and forced her legs apart. "You be good now, girly! You be good!"

She screamed in despair. The scream sobbed helplessly as she twisted and then, from nowhere it seemed, came rescue. Into her lonely place of horror came help.

It came with a shout, with the thunder of hooves, with a cry of alarm from the man who pawed at her and who suddenly scrambled away, gibbering and shouting, and Campion clutched her torn clothes to herself, rolled over, and it seemed as if the air was filled with the noise of hooves, the shadow of a great horse that pounded within inches of her head and she had a glimpse of a mounted man who held a streak of light in his hand.

"No!" her attacker shouted. His shout was one of pure, sudden terror. He stumbled, one hand holding his trousers, the other warding off the sudden brightness of the long sword. Campion's eyes were closed. Over the thunder of hooves, over her attacker's cry for mercy, she heard the hiss of steel in air. Then silence.

Except it was not silence. She could hear the hooves on

the grass. She could hear the creak of a saddle, the chink of a curb chain.

She pushed herself to her hands and knees. She vomited.

"Madam?" The voice was crisp, educated, and solicitous. "Dear Lady?" The man had dismounted, had come close to her.

She shook her head. Her breath came in huge, stomach-heaving gasps. She was on all fours and she could see the scraps of her cream colored dress hanging down by her breasts. A small, rusty knife was on the ground beneath her. She sobbed.

She screamed as something touched her, but the man's voice was gentle. "Quiet now! Quiet! Gentle, dear lady!" A great cloak was dropped about her shoulders, a cloak that enveloped her. It smelled of horses. The man's voice was soothing, as if he spoke to an unbridled colt. "Quiet now. Gentle now!"

Slowly she knelt up, clutching her own and her rescuer's cloak about her torn clothing. Her fur bonnet had fallen on one side of her face and she shuddered as she felt his hands put it back into place, but his touch was gentle and she was glad of it.

"Dear lady?"

She looked up.

Her rescuer was in uniform. The sight was somehow astonishing. Here, on this lonely heath, was a cavalryman in his finery, a blue jacketed and breeched uniform, bright with red facings and gold lace and looped with frogging and sword slings. An embroidered sabertache swung at his side. Small gold chains hung from his epaulettes. His voice was anxious. "Are you hurt, dear lady?"

"Only in my pride." It came out as a squeaking sob. She tried to say it louder, then saw the man who had attacked her.

He lay dead. He could not be alive. His dark rags and his lank hair were red with blood. His trousers were about his thighs. His neck had been half cut through by a great sword, steel bright, blood stained, that her rescuer had plunged into the turf. The man had died in an instant.

Campion's breath came in huge gasps. A gobbet of blood, thick as honey, trickled down the sun-reflecting brightness of the big sword. Vomit retched in her throat and she forced it back.

The cavalryman turned to look at his victim. "I shouldn't have killed him."

She frowned. "Sir?"

"He should have hung." Her rescuer's voice was suddenly full of outrage. "God damn him. He should have hung!"

Oddly it seemed funny to her. She gave a choking laugh. She knew she sounded hysterical, but she could not help laughing and crying and sobbing at the same time.

The cavalry officer crouched beside her. "Gentle now! Gentle!"

She shook her head. She swallowed. She took a great gulp of air. "I'm all right, sir." It came out as a sob again and she forced calmness into her shaking voice. "I thank you, sir." The words made her cry.

The cavalryman took from his sleeve a handkerchief, offered it to her, then realized that both her hands were gripping the cloaks to cover her nakedness. He seemed embarrassed by her tears and stood up. He went to the sword, plucked it from the turf, and cleaned the bright blade with the folded handkerchief. He had to scrub at the blood and, when he was done, he tossed the handkerchief away.

He turned back. She had stopped crying. She knelt on the grass and stared at him. He smiled reassuringly. "My presence, dear lady, was most fortunate."

"Indeed, sir." She managed to say the words clearly. Everything seemed unreal, yet slowly the universe was putting itself back together. She could see the chalk scars on the earth ramparts of the old fort, the shadows of the gorse, the black blob of a missel-thrush nest in a bare, stunted elm.

He smiled at her. "I'm travelling to Shaftesbury. Someone said this was a short cut." He pushed the sword back into the scabbard, the steel ringing on the metal throat. "My servant's following tomorrow." He seemed to be filling the silence with inconsequential words. She nodded.

"You were alone?" he asked.

"Yes, sir." She swallowed. The world seemed to want to spin about her. She closed her eyes. In her mind's memory she heard the thick chop of the blade in flesh.

The cavalryman went to look at her phaeton and she opened her eyes and turned to see him unbuckling the harness and leading the miraculously unhurt bays from the wreckage. She was still on her knees. She was shaking. She wiped spittle from her mouth onto the collar of his cloak.

The cavalryman's hat had fallen off in his charge. The sun glinted on his golden hair and moustache. He had a round face, red from the cold, and she guessed his age close to thirty. He worked efficiently, tying the bays by their reins to the broken splinter-bar of the phaeton.

He slapped his hands together when he was done, then took big, white leather gauntlets from his belt and pulled them on. She saw that the right gauntlet was speckled with bright blood. He smiled. "That's the horses looked after, now for you, madam."

She felt the need to apologize. "I'm sorry."

"Dear lady! You're sorry! God! It's I that should apologize. A moment sooner and I might have stopped the whole damned thing." He stooped beside the dead body and picked up the gold chain with its diamond drops. "Yours? Hardly his, I suppose?"

He said it so lightly that she laughed. It was a slightly hysterical laugh.

He stood up, still holding the jewel, and bowed. "My name is Lewis Culloden, Lord Culloden. Major in the Blues when the fancy takes me, which is not often."

She looked up at him. "Lady Campion Lazender, my Lord." That too struck her as funny, to be introducing herself from the grass. She wished she could stop the hysterical swinging between tears and laughter. She wished she had brought dogs with her, that the groom had come, that the horrid man with his dripping nose had not pawed at her. She cried.

Lord Culloden let her cry. He waited till the sobs had faded. He cleared his throat and sounded astonished. "You're Lady Campion Lazender?"

"Yes, my Lord." She was ashamed of herself for crying. She was ashamed of it all. She obscurely felt that it was her fault, and that annoyed her because she knew it was not true.

"From Lazen Castle, my Lady?"

She nodded. "Indeed, my Lord."

"My dear lady! Good Lord!" He seemed quite flummoxed suddenly, as if St. George, having rescued the maiden, discovered that he was too shy to talk with her. He blushed. He looked at the crumpled figure on the turf. "He must have been mad!" he blurted out.

She tried to stand, stumbling because she needed to keep her hands within the cloaks, and Lord Culloden came forward to take her elbow as though she was made of porcelain. She smiled her thanks. "Do you have any water, my Lord?"

"Water?" He said it as if she had asked for the moon. "Ah! Water! No. I have rum, my Lady?"

"Can I beg you for a sip?"

He walked to his horse and Campion felt another shudder of revulsion as she saw the bent neck and still body of her attacker.

"My Lady?" Lord Culloden nervously offered her a flask. She could not take her hands from within the cloaks; he seemed to understand and held the flask to her mouth.

She almost choked. She used the first mouthful to swill the sickness from her tongue, spat, and then she drank some of the crude spirit, and she saw her rescuer's smiling, anxious face and she felt a great rush of warmth and gratitude.

He led her to the phaeton so she could lean against the wrecked, tipped carriage. He smiled. "How do we get you home? Can you ride?"

She nodded.

"And what were you doing alone on the blasted heath?" He was patting her bays' necks. "I thought fair maidens stayed away from such places. Too many dragons!"

"Apparently," she said. "It has always been safe."

"That's what King Harold said about Hastings." He grinned. The sun was bright on the gold wires and lace of his uniform. "Now, my Lady, you will ride my horse and I'll take yours." One of the bays was shivering, the whites of its eyes showing. Lord Culloden ran his gauntletted hand down the horse's back. "You're recovered enough, my Lady?"

She nodded. "Indeed, my Lord, thanks to you."

"Thank the rum, Lady Campion." He smiled. "Is it far to Lazen?"

"No, my Lord." He was, she thought, despite his gaudy uniform, a plain, honest looking man. She could imagine him in a saddle for a day's hunting, a squire with a voice that could carry for two wet fields against the wind. He was obviously awed by this meeting with the daughter of one of England's great families. His eyes, slightly hooded, added a dash of humorous languor to his face, hinting that he might possess a wry wit. He was not, at first sight, a man of startling handsomeness, yet at this moment he was, to Campion, more handsome than St. George and all the angels. She made herself stand upright. "If we could go to Lazen, my Lord, I would be most obliged."

"To Lazen we shall go. I would dream of going nowhere else." He was leading his own horse toward her. She was shaking still. She could see the dark ruin that had been her attacker's throat and she closed her eyes on the sight.

"Lady Campion?" Lord Culloden's voice was gentle.

"My Lord?" She opened her eyes, forcing herself to be calm.

He was blushing, making his blond moustache seem even lighter against his red skin. "If you clutch the cloaks so tight then I fear I will have to lift you onto the saddle, can you bear that?" He smiled.

She nodded.

He lifted her easily to set her sidesaddle on his horse, then used the wrecked phaeton as a mounting block to settle himself on one of the bays. He gathered its long driving rein into his hands, took the reins of the other, and smiled at her. "To Lazen, my Lady. The dragon's corpse we will leave behind!"

She was suddenly freezing, shivering despite the two cloaks, but the relief of it all was overwhelming. She even felt lightheaded now, laughing as Lord Culloden talked to her and they descended the steep hill toward the town. He was still nervous of her. He looked at her often for reassurance that some small witticism was well received, and he touched his moustache in an habitual gesture whenever she smiled at him. He became shyer as the excitement of the rescue faded, embarrassed almost to be in her presence. She remembered some story of his family, of his father gambling away much of the property. She guessed that Lord Culloden was not accustomed to glories such as Lazen.

They rode through the town and earned inquisitive looks from the people who watched them pass and then, as they came to the gatehouses, Lord Culloden reined in. He shook his head in amazement. Before him, like a hill of stone and glass, was the grandeur of Lazen. Seen thus for the first time it was easy to imagine why some people called Lazen "The Little Kingdom."

"It's magnificent! Magnificent! I'd heard so, of course but . . ." His voice trailed away.

She smiled. He could have said nothing better calculated to please her, such was her love of this place. "My father will want to thank you, my Lord."

He blushed modestly. "I could not impose, my Lady."

She dismissed his modesty, urged him onward, and together they rode into Lazen.

5

It was the first time in three years that the fifth Earl of Lazen had left the castle.

First he was carried downstairs by three footmen, then carefully placed on the cushioned seat of Lazen's most comfortable travelling coach. He hated leaving his rooms. He hated outsiders to see his weakness.

He was sober this day. His face was pale and drawn, the face, Campion thought, of an old man. She was not going with him, but as she watched the blankets being tucked about his thin body she thought how the raw, winter light made him look a score of years older than fifty. His manservant, Caleb Wright, climbed into the coach and the door was shut.

The earl nodded to Wright, who rapped on the coach roof, and then the earl grimaced as the coach jolted forward. Even small movements gave him pain, yet he had insisted on going out this day.

There was not, after all, far to go.

The coach went down the driveway, through the huge gates with their stone carved escutcheons that showed the bloodied lance of Lazen on either post, past the gatehouses that curved forward in elegant wings, and then slewed right on the cobbles of the market place to take the Shaftesbury road.

Lord Culloden rode beside the coach. His face looked grim and wintry, suitable for this occasion.

Simon Burroughs, Lazen's chief coachman, had brought extra horses and, when they reached the field at the bottom of Two Gallows Hill, they were harnessed to the six already pulling the coach so that the great vehicle could be hauled to the summit of the hill.

Waiting at the hilltop, as the coach heaved and jolted upward, was a common cart. It stood close to the pitch-painted gallows that leaned eastward toward the town.

A small group of men stood about the cart. They were cold. The Castle lay like a great stone monument in the valley beneath them. The smoke from its scores of chimneys drifted flatly over the winter-hard land.

The coach, creaking and swaying, reached the gentler slope at the hill's top. The men standing about the cart pulled off their hats as the door was swung open. They could see the white face of the sick earl staring from his seat. He raised a hand in acknowledgment of their muttered greetings.

The door had been opened so he could see what was about to happen.

Lord Culloden dismounted. "You're ready, my Lord?"

"I am." There was a grim pleasure in the earl's voice.

The turf about the gallows was worn thin. To the south Lord Culloden could see the heathland where he had rescued Campion. The sky above was gray and white. He nodded to the waiting, cold men about the cart. "Do your duty!"

The body of the man who had attacked the Lady Campion Lazender had been fetched from the heath. It had been stripped naked, then bound in a net of chains. The links jingled cheerfully as the men hauled the body off the cart, as if thumped on the ground, as they dragged it by the feet to the gallows.

The earl watched.

The ladder had been forgotten, but one of the small boys who had come to watch shinned the upright and sat astride the crossbeam. A rope was thrown to him that he threaded through the rusted iron ring that was bolted to the beam. The lad stayed there.

They tied the rope to the chains at the nape of the dead man's neck, then hauled him up so that he hung like a misshapen sack. He would rot now, the chains holding his decomposing flesh as the birds tore at him. By winter's end he would be nothing but bones in rusted chain.

The Earl watched with grim satisfaction. It was a pity he could not have hanged the bastard alive, but he would hang him dead and in a place where, each dawn, the body could be seen from the Lazen valley; a warning to others who dared attack his family.

The small boy, while the men supported the weight of the dead man, tied the rope at the ring iron. The men let the body hang. It turned slowly, the head slumped down on the chains about the half cut neck. Lord Culloden stood back, touched his blond moustache, and looked at the Earl through the open carriage door. "May God damn his soul, my Lord."

"God can have his soul," the Earl said, "but I'll have his bones. I'll grind them for the pigs." He grimaced in pain. "Give the men their cash, my Lord, and add a half guinea for that lad! Then home!"

Campion, watching from the Long Gallery, saw the dark speck hanging on the skyline. Beside her, Mrs. Hutchinson, her companion and chaperone, frowned. "Hanging's too good for him, dear."

Campion smiled at the old woman. "Where he's gone, Mary, he's suffering far worse."

"I hope so, dear, I hope so. You know me, I'm not vengeful, but I'd have torn his heart out with my own hands! I would, too!"

Campion laughed. "You can't kill a moth!"

Mrs. Hutchinson tried to look fierce and failed hopelessly. "Well at least Lord Culloden is staying on! I thank the good Lord for him, dear, truly I do."

Campion looked at the old lady and smiled. "So do I."

"And you'll pardon me for saying it, dear, but it is nice to have a gentleman about the house again! It's been too long! Entirely too long."

"It has, Mary, it has." Campion smiled, and there came, inevitably and annoyingly, a sudden image of a black-haired man laughing with the small maid at the kitchen door, and she angrily thrust the image away. "I'm glad he's staying." She made herself say it warmly, and she told herself, as she had told herself a dozen times since the awful attack on the heath road, that her meeting with Lewis Culloden was a miraculous providence of heaven.

Lewis Culloden's dramatic entry into her life had made her look up a half forgotten passage in Mr. Burke's book "Reflections on the French Revolution," a passage which said that "the age of chivalry is gone. That of sophisters, economists and calculators has succeeded." Mr. Burke, she thought, was wrong. The age of chivalry had come with a bright sword and the hammer of hooves on the lonely road to the south. A maiden had been rescued, a villain hanged, and a lord had come to a castle. Chivalry, she tried to persuade herself, yet lived.

"If they kill their King," Valentine Larke said, "we should turn Paris into a slaughterhouse. To do nothing is to condone the crime. We will have to fight!"

His companion laughed. "With what? We've reduced the army again!" The Prime Minister believed that Britain would not need an army now that the French nation, as Burke had prophesied, promised to destroy themselves in blood and fire.

Larke said nothing. He was staring into the Westminster night, waiting for a cab or chair to come to the steps of Parliament. Sedan chairs, now that London was growing at such a rate to make their journeys impossibly laborious, were increasingly rare. Larke's broad face looked grim in the light of the great lanterns. Sleet was falling on the cobbles.

His companion shivered within his greatcoat. "You'll get your war, Larke, but the Prime Minister wishes you wouldn't call for it quite so fiercely."

Larke laughed. "I owe Pitt no favors."

"But he can do you some." His companion smiled. "You're coming to White's?"

"No."

"Working again, my dear Larke?"

"Working." At that moment the lanterns of a cab appeared and a linkboy ran forward with his flaming torch. Larke crammed his hat on his crinkly, black hair and nodded to his companion. "Mine, I think."

Valentine Larke ran for the cab, climbed in, and shouted his destination to the driver. He could hear the sleet pattering on the tarpaulin that covered the driver's knees.

Inside the vehicle he smiled. Again, in the candlelit chamber of the Commons, he had given a ringing call for war. He knew Britain was not ready for war, he knew that Pitt would do all he could to avoid war, so this was the perfect time to rattle the saber and demand slaughter. Valentine Larke, Belial of the Fallen Ones, was establishing impeccable credentials as a man who hated the French and their damned revolution. He laughed aloud.

"You said something, sir?" the driver called out.

"Damn your eyes! Just drive!"

The cab rattled behind its slow horse through the cold London night. Larke, sitting well back in the leather seat, saw the whores sheltering in the doorways, the drunks who would die in this cold, and the children sent out to beg while their mothers whored at home. Larke thought how much he loved this city. He knew it as a rat knows a dark, shadowed and fetid yard.

The cab stopped in one of the new streets of London's west end. The houses were big, white-stuccoed, with elegant iron railings supporting torches. He handed two coins to the driver and waited for the cab to go into the slanting, cold sleet.

He did not climb any of the elaborately porticoed steps. Instead he walked into a dark alley, unlit and stinking of urine. He lifted the skirt of his huge cloak as he walked, crossed a mews that was thick with the stench of horse manure, and then, stepping over a moaning drunk who reeked of gin, he entered another alley. He had a pistol in the pocket of his dark coat beneath the great cloak, but he walked without fear. This was his city. He moved through it with the skill of a hunter in a forest.

Music sounded ahead.

He could have ordered the cab driver to drop him at the glittering, impressive facade of the building that he approached, yet deviousness had become second nature to Valentine Larke. He approached the rear of the building, not because he came in secret, but because he always preferred the hidden approach. He was Belial.

The alley opened, under an archway, into a small brick-enclosed yard that was piled with scraps thrown from a busy kitchen. It was a foul place of rats and cats, a place where the sun would not enter except on a summer's midday.

Three men were there. All were richly dressed. They wore no greatcoats or cloaks. Their coats were unbuttoned, showing frilled shirts and high silk stocks. The door at the top of the steps leading into the great house was open, letting a wash of yellow candlelight into the yard.

The three men, if they saw Larke, ignored him.

One of the three, a pugnacious, ugly man, was laughing as he tried to unbutton the flap of his breeches. The man belched, then finally succeeded in pulling the flap open. He held onto the wall. "Hitch her skirts up, Robin!"

An old woman, a drunkard, had come scavenging in the kitchen yard. She had either collapsed in gin-sodden unconsciousness, or else had been knocked down by the three young men who laughed at her helplessness.

"Company!" A tall young man whom Larke recognized as the Honorable Robin Ickfield drew the word out as if he was a drill sergeant. "Company! Fire!"

All three pissed on her, laughing loudly as she tried to drag herself out of the way.

Valentine Larke moved silently behind them and climbed the steps into the house. The young lordlings were at play and that was never a good time to disturb them. There were few things in life more dangerous than the idle, bored young men of London society.

Larke went into the house, through an antechamber, and then into the great, well-lit hallway into which the front-door of the house opened. A footman, hugely muscled beneath his elaborate uniform, started as Larke silently appeared from the back of the house, but then recognized him and relaxed. "Mr. Larke, sir."

While Larke was giving the man his cloak, hat and cane, a door to the left of the hall opened and a huge woman, middle aged and grotesque, came into sight. She was dressed in lurid purple silk, her piled hair surmounted by a feather dyed the same color. At her huge breasts hung a pendant of gold. She stopped when she saw Larke, sniffed, then nodded coldly. The feather quivered above her head. "Mr. Larke, I see."

He bowed to her. "Your servant, Ma'am."

"You'll want food, I suppose," she said ungraciously.

"Indeed, Ma'am."

"And no doubt you'll settle the bill, Mr. Larke?" Her small eyes glared at him from the shapeless, pudgy face that seemed like a lump of dough piled haphazardly at the top of her massive cleavage. She seemed to have no neck at all. She jerked her monstrous head, making the pearls shake where they hung in her piled hair. "I am not a charity, Mr. Larke."

He smiled. "Indeed you are not, Mrs. Pail."

She sniffed and swept on, attended by two small footmen who fussed behind her like pageboys.

Her name was Abigail Pail, and these were her Rooms. Mrs. Pail's Rooms were famous in London, not just for the food, which was superb, or for the gaming, which was fast, but most of all for the girls, who were superb and fast. The ugliest woman in London ran the best whorehouse. It was here that the rich and the titled came to play, where their fortunes were lost, where their every need was attended to at a price that was extortionate.

The three men who had relieved themselves in the kitchen yard came noisily back into the hall. The pugnacious one, whose wigless black hair was cut short as a curry-brush, had vomit stains on his red silk coat. He saw Valentine Larke and laughed. "Christ! They let you come here?"

Larke smiled and bowed. Sir Julius Lazender, he thought, had one merit; consistency. He was offensive all of the time.

Sir Julius brushed rain off his coat. "Abigail lets you paw her girls, Larke?"

The Honorable Robin Ickfield snickered in a high voice. "I thought politicians preferred boys."

"You should bloody know, Robin," Sir Julius laughed.

He belched drunkenly. "Christ! I could tup a bloody horse tonight." He pulled himself up the stairway, then turned with a malicious grin on his face. "You've come for the Countess, Larke?" He said it accusingly.

"The Countess, Sir Julius?" Larke's voice was unctuous.

"Don't tell me you didn't know!" Sir Julius's breeches' flap was only half buttoned. "The old faggot's got a French Countess here, Larke, but then I don't suppose you can afford her, eh?"

"She's expensive, Sir Julius?"

Sir Julius laughed. "Five years ago the sniffy bitch wouldn't look at you! Now her Ladyship will rub her tits on your ass for a shilling." He leered at Larke. "But only if you're a gentleman." He turned away, pleased with his insult, followed by his companions.

Valentine Larke watched the three climb the stairs, his hard eyes showing no offense. Valentine Larke had not been born into the gentry, but if Sir Julius Lazender was a measure of gentility then Larke was glad he was no gentleman. Sir Julius, nephew to the Earl of Lazen, was a belligerent, drunken, pugnacious, rude wastrel. Larke smiled. Sir Julius would live to regret every sneer and every insult.

He turned toward the gaming room. The footman, who knew that Larke was neither a lord nor conspicuously rich, only opened one of the two leaves of the door.

He walked slowly through the lavishly appointed room, acknowledging the silent greetings of three of the players, and then climbed the far stairs that led to the dining room.

It was almost empty at this time of night. The waiters stood solemnly at the sides of the room watching the few patrons who remained. The food at Abigail's was famous. Within an hour, Larke knew, the tables would be crowded with men from Parliament who saw no disgrace in eating their chops beneath Abigail's bedrooms. One of the waiters hurried forward to usher Larke to a table, but Larke dismissed him. He walked the length of the room and through a door that would, by a short passage, bring him back to the main stairway which led to Abigail's girls.

Another door, marked "Private," led from the short passage.

Larke paused, looked left and right, saw that no one was watching, and took from his waistcoat pocket a key. He fitted it into the keyhole, grunted as it turned reluctantly, and then, with a last look left and right, went into the room. He locked the door behind him.

He sat. On a table beside him was a tray with glasses. He poured himself some wine. A great book, bound in morocco leather, was beside the tray and, pulling the candelabra nearer to his chair, he opened the book on his lap.

"Recorded. That Lady Delavele will drop Twins by Easter Day, between Mr. Tyndall and Ld. Parrish. 200L."

"Recorded. That Ld. Saltash will Consume Bishop Wright's Tomcat, prepared in Mrs. Pail's Kitchens, Entire. Between Ld. Saltash and Bishop Wright. 150L." Beside it was written, "Ld. Saltash the winner."

"Recorded. That Mr. Calltire's Bucentaurus will beat Sir Simon Stepney's Ringneck, the owners up, between Tyburn and St. Paul's. The race to Commence at Midnight, Christmas Eve. Between the Owners. 2000L."

"Recorded. That Ld. Saltash will Consume Bishop Wright's Marmalade Cat, Without Benefit of Onion Sauce, entire, prepared without Any Sauces or Gravies, in Mrs. Pail's Kitchens. Between Ld. Saltash and Bishop Wright. 300L."

Valentine Larke smiled. The commission on wagers recorded in Mrs. Pail's book was twenty percent. A key sounded in the lock of the door.

He looked up, his bland, flat eyes wary in the candlelight.

Mrs. Pail herself stood in the doorway, her white, podgy face grim.

Larke stood. "Dear Mrs. Pail."

"Mr. Larke." She shut and locked the door, then turned and gave him a clumsy curtsey.

He smiled. "I find you well?"

"Indeed, sir. Yourself?"

"Never better, Mrs. Pail." He put the book on the table. "Things seem to be flourishing?"

"Flourishing they are, flourish they had better." She said it grimly, then smiled and bobbed her head as Larke poured her a glass of wine.

He raised his glass to her. "What's this I hear about a French Countess in the house?"

"Dear me!" Mrs. Pail gave a coy laugh. "A spinet maker's daughter from Birmingham! Father was a rich man, raised her to speak French, but he's bankrupt now." Mrs. Pail shook her white, shapeless face. "Not the most beautiful of my girls, but I took her as a favor. She does well. She jabbers in French while they work. You'd like to see her?"

Larke smiled. "No. But a splendid idea to call her a Countess. I do congratulate you."

Mrs. Pail blushed with pleasure. "You're too kind, sir, entirely too kind."

"Please sit, Mrs. Pail."

Valentine Larke was the sole owner of Mrs. Pail's Rooms, though only she, he, and a select few others knew it. He owned a dozen other such establishments in London, places where the gentry went to lose their money at cockfighting, cards, women, or prizefighting. He was insistent that, in public, she treated him as one of her less valued customers, such was his passion, his need for secrecy. He waited till she was seated, then sat himself. "I'm sorry to intrude on your evening with business, Mrs. Pail."

The doughy, powdered face screwed itself into a sympathetic smile. "It's always a pleasure, Mr. Larke."

He smiled. "I won't detain you long. I merely wish to know how much Sir Julius Lazender is in your debt."

She thought for two seconds. "Not counting tonight, Mr. Larke, nine thousand four hundred and twenty-two guineas."

He raised his eyebrows. It was a huge sum, yet he did not look displeased. "You still lend him money?"

"Of course, sir. You told me to."

Larke nodded and sipped his wine.

Abigail Pail watched him without speaking. She did not know why her employer had instructed her to let Sir Julius Lazender run up such a vast debt. Sir Julius did it without difficulty. To Abigail Pail's knowing mind Sir Julius Lazender was a brute, a brute with an appetite that drew him back night after night. He lost at the tables, he became drunk, and he went upstairs to the lavish, soft rooms and never was asked to pay a penny. Even his gambling debts were settled by the house. Sir Julius Lazender, on Valentine Larke's specific instructions, had been given the freedom of London's most exclusive and expensive whorehouse.

Larke knew that freedom should not end yet. His timing in this matter of Sir Julius had to be exquisitely right. He put his glass down, steepled his fingers, and smiled at the woman. "You will see Mr. d'Arblay and instruct him, upon my authority, to prepare a summons for ten thousand guineas. But it is not to be served, you understand?"

"Of course, sir."

"Nor is Sir Julius to know that the summons exists. He may continue to come here and you will continue to welcome him. If you need money then my bankers will, of course, oblige."

"You're very kind, Mr. Larke." The white, blubber face sniffed in disapproval.

Valentine Larke saw it and smiled. "Something troubles you, dear Mrs. Pail?"

"Not my position to be troubled, sir." She said in a tone that contradicted her words. "But he's going to be the ruin of us!"

"I assure you he is not." Larke smiled.

She chose to ignore his assurance. "Only this week, Mr. Larke! He bit a girl! Horribly, Mr. Larke! I can't work a scarred girl!"

"You put it on his bill?"

"Of course."

"And the girl?"

Mrs. Pail frowned. "I can't put a girl on the streets just before Christmas, Mr. Larke! It's not Christian!"

"Indeed not." He stood, to show that the interview was over. "Indeed you may keep her in the house, Mrs. Pail, so long as you wish." He knew the loyalty that Abigail had to her girls. She educated those that could not read and always ensured that those who were not communicants in the Church of England learned their catechism and were confirmed by a bishop who was one of the house's steadier patrons. By day the bishop conducted the girls toward heaven, and at night they returned the favor.

Larke bowed over her fat, ring-bright fingers. "I will stay a few moments."

"Of course, Mr. Larke." She smiled archly. "You'd like company?"

He shook his head. "Thank you, but no."

When she had gone, and when the door was locked, he took from his waistcoat pocket a message that had come to him at the House of Commons. He opened it, read it for the third time, then tossed it onto the grate that was piled with glowing coals. He watched the letter curl, burn, and break into wavering scraps of black ash.

Chemosh had not done what he had said he would do.

Larke stared into the fire.

Chemosh had promised that the girl would never marry because no man would marry her. She would be poxed and scarred, yet she was neither. She lived still with her beauty and her virginity. Chemosh had not done what he had promised he would do.

He put his head back, the corrugated black ridges of his hair crushed on Mrs. Pail's chairback, and he wondered when the Gypsy would next come. The Gypsy was the messenger who connected Larke and Marchenoir, carrying the coded letters that none but those two politicians could read. Larke hoped the Gypsy would come soon for he needed to pass on to Lucifer, by way of Marchenoir, the news of Chemosh. Lucifer would have to decide what was to be done. The timing of this thing was like the workings of a chronometer; gleaming, valuable, and exact. Chemosh was threatening to fail.

They dared not fail. Valentine Larke, staring into the fire, thought that they could not fail. Lord Werlatton was hunted by Moloch, Sir Julius by Belial, and the Lady Campion by Chemosh, and the joy of it was that not one of the victims knew of the hunters. He sipped his brandy and thought of Chemosh. The man had not done what he had promised, but he had not yet necessarily failed. Nor, Larke reflected grimly, would he fail. They were the Fallen Ones, and they did not fail.

Nor would he fail with Sir Julius. He smiled and took another sip of the wine. Sir Julius was baited and hooked, and Larke could reel him in whenever he wished. It could wait, he decided, till after Christmas, and then Belial would strike and the Fallen Ones would tighten the invisible ring that would choke the life from Lazen Castle. He smiled. He drank to the victory that would follow Christmas, to the victory that would lead the Fallen Ones to the Day of Lucifer and the fall of Lazen.

Uncle Achilles ran the blue ribbons through his fingers. "You're going to wear these?" His tone suggested that perhaps she should burn them instead.

"I won't wear anything if you stay here."

"My dear Campion, I am far too old to be excited by a woman getting dressed, let alone undressed. Besides, you forget that I'm still a priest. They never unfrocked me."

"And I'm not unfrocking while you're here. Go away." She smiled at him and kissed him on both cheeks. "I'm glad you came."

He smiled. "And glad that my mother didn't?"

"She would have been welcome."

He laughed. "I like your Lord Culloden."

"He's not mine."

Mrs. Hutchinson was laying out a dress of white crepe with Brussels lace at the neck and cuffs. Uncle Achilles looked at it where it lay on her bed and smiled. "A wedding dress?"

"Go away."

"But I do like him, truly!" Uncle Achilles took a pinch of snuff, crossed to her dressing table, and sat down. He opened a pot of rouge, dabbed a finger in it, and rubbed it experimentally on the back of his hand. "Not my color."

She crossed her arms. "I'm going to be late, uncle."

It was only four o'clock in the afternoon, yet already Campion had ordered candles lit in her bedroom. It was gloomy outside, the sky gray and darkening over the Lazen valley. Uncle Achilles twisted on his chair and stared down at the townspeople who walked in excited groups toward the Castle's entrance. "You English make a great fuss about Christmas."

"We don't make any fuss at all. We simply have a good time. Those of us, that is, who are allowed to dress."

He grinned at her. He was clothed, Campion thought, lasciviously; there was no other word. He had a suit of gold cloth, a new wig with silk tails, gold-buckled shoes of satin, stockings of white silk, and the faintest touch of cosmetics on his face. He saw her looking him up and down. His voice was teasingly anxious. "You think I'm presentable?"

"You look wonderful. Just like a bishop."

He laughed. He dipped her powder puff into the china bowl and brushed it against his hand. He held the hand out to the window and frowned critically. His nails were varnished. "In London they think I'm very elegant. But then I'm French which always impresses the English. They feel inferior to us for one very good reason."

"Because they are?" She smiled. She thought how bored Achilles must be; an elegant, clever Frenchman only half employed in a strange country. He smiled at her.

"Exactly, dear niece. You are so sensible for a mere woman." He crossed his legs, taking care not to crease his silk stockings. "The English have a sneaking suspicion that we know something about life and elegance and beauty that they do not know, and it is every Frenchman's duty to continue the illusion. It is even, dear niece, the duty of someone like yourself who has the blessing of being half French." He smiled seraphically. "Has he asked you to marry yet?"

"I haven't known him five weeks yet!"

"How proper you are, dear niece." He smiled and turned to the dressing table again. He dipped his finger into the cochineal ointment she would use on her lips and painted a heart on her mirror. He ignored her protests. He pierced the heart with an arrow. Above its fletches he wrote "CL," by its point he wrote "LC." He inspected his work. "There's a certain symmetry to the two of you."

Mrs. Hutchinson, who had not understood a word of the French they had been speaking, understood the drawing. She laughed.

Campion, who was dressed only in a full length bed robe of colored Peking silk, sat on the chaise longue. She smiled at her uncle. "You think the symmetry is important?"

"I think it's wonderful!" He was fastidiously wiping his finger on one of her towels. "After all, lovers always seek fate's happy signs. One says 'I was born on a Monday' and the other says 'and I also!,' and from that mere, unimportant coincidence they deduce that heaven has had a hand in their conjunction." He shrugged. "I think CL and LC come into that happy, heavenly category, don't you?"

"You want me to marry him?"

He smiled wickedly. He liked teasing her, not the least because she never took offense, however shocked she might be by his words. "Do you wish to marry him, dear Campion?"

"What I wish, uncle, is to get dressed."

He stood, bowed, and smiled again. "I retire defeated from the field. You will dance with me?"

"Of course."

"If Lord Culloden will let you. Do you think he's the jealous kind? Men with moustaches often are."

"Go away."

He did, crossing in the doorway with Edna, Campion's maid, who had fetched a bowl of warm water and hot towels.

It was Christmas Eve, the traditional day of celebration, the day when the town came to the Castle and the Castle provided bowls of frumenty and plates of pies and vats of punch and music from the gallery and fires in the great hearths and hogsheads of ale and puddings that had seeped their smell from one end of the huge building to the other and, as midnight drew near, great platters of roasted geese would bring cheers from the throng in the Great Hall.

A throng which expected the Lady Campion to marry. The word seemed to haunt the castle. The rumor was like a whisper in every room, in every corridor, in every smiling face that greeted her. Lord Culloden had been in Lazen just a few weeks, yet all the Castle, all the estate, expected there would be a marriage.

Lord Culloden had said nothing. He was correct, polite, and charming, yet the mere fact of his presence fed the rumor that, before the leaves fell again, the Lady Campion would be wed.

She dressed with more care than usual.

Mrs. Hutchinson cooed over her, patting the dress where it did not need adjusting, twitching hair that was like pale, shining gold. "You look a picture!"

"I feel exhausted, Mary." Campion, as usual, had organized the day's celebration.

Mrs. Hutchinson smiled. "You look lovely, dear, quite lovely." What she meant, Campion knew, was that she looked lovely for him.

For whom, though?

For the Gypsy was also here.

She had seen him and the sight of him after so long was like an arrow thrust into the heart. She had thought she had forgotten him, she thought that the memory of that slim, dark, oddly blue-eyed face was just that, a memory. She had persuaded herself that her thoughts about the Gypsy were not about a real man, but about an idealized man, about a dream, and then she had seen his smiling, strong, competent face, and it seemed as if her heart stopped for that moment, there had been a surge of inexplicable, magic joy, and then she had turned abruptly away.

He had brought a letter from Toby. Toby was still in France, working for his mysterious master, Lord Paunceley. The letter asked his forgiveness that he could not be in Lazen this Christmas. Instead the Gypsy was in Lazen and on this night of Christmas Eve, just as at the old Roman feast of Saturnalia from which Christmas had sprung, the servants in Lazen would join the festivities with those they served. Tonight the Gypsy was her equal.

The blue ribbons were threaded into her sleeve so that, when she danced, they would hang and swirl.

About her neck were sapphires.

In her hair were pearls.

She stared at herself in the mirror. CL and LC.

Lord Culloden had come into her life in a blaze of heroism, in a manner of a Galahad or a Lancelot. He was tall, he was eager to please, and he was happy to make her happy.

She could not think of a single thing that she disliked about Lord Culloden, unless it was a slightly supercilious air toward his inferiors. She guessed the superciliousness came from his family's lack of money, a fear that with a little more bad luck he would become like those he despised. On the other hand, as he became more comfortable with Lazen's great wealth and privilege, he was displaying a dry and sometimes elegant wit. She smeared the red arrow with her finger and she thought that CL did not dislike LC. She might even like him very much, but there was the uncomfortable fact that when she saw him about the Castle she felt nothing. Or, at least, she did not feel the delicious, secret thrill that the Gypsy gave her.

She wished the Gypsy had not come. She stood. She stared for a moment at the gray, lowering clouds beyond her window. The hills across the valley looked cold, their crests twisting like agony to the winter sky. At the top of Two Gallows Hill, like a black sack, hung the man who had attacked her.

She shuddered, closed the curtains, and turned. Tonight there would be music and dancing, the sound of laughter in the Great Hall and flamelight on its panelling. Yet none of that, she knew, gave her the tremulous, lovely, guilty anticipation that sparkled in her eyes as she left the room. She had dressed with care, she had made herself beautiful, and, though she could not even admit it to herself, she had not done it for Lord Culloden. She walked toward the music.

There was applause as she walked down the stairs, applause that grew louder as more people at the edges of the room turned to watch her. The compliment made her smile shyly.

"I hope you know how lucky you are, my Lord," Achilles d'Auxigny said to Lord Culloden.

Lord Culloden smiled. His eyes were fixed on Campion. "Give her wings and she would be an angel."

Achilles raised his plucked eyebrows. "The church fathers maintained that angels did not procreate, or how would you English say? They don't roger?"

A look of utter shock passed over Lord Culloden's face, as if what a man might say in the regimental Mess of the Blues was one thing, but quite another to hear it said of a girl like Campion. He smiled frostily at Achilles, then walked forward with his arm held out. "My dear lady?" He bowed.

"My Lord."

And the sight of the two together, the one in white crepe and blue ribbons, sparkling with precious stones, and the other in gleaming uniform, served only to make the applause louder. The sound reached the Earl of Lazen, whose room Campion had just left, and he smiled proudly at the Reverend Horne Mounter. "Pretty filly, Mounter, eh?"

"Undoubtedly, my Lord. I suppose she'll be married soon?"

"That's up to her, Mounter, up to her." The Earl's tone made it quite plain that he was not going to discuss his daughter's marriage plans with the rector. "I'll oblige you for another glass."

The Reverend Horne Mounter, who doubted whether the Earl should be drinking frumenty at all, reluctantly poured the glass and put it at the bedside. He took a volume of sermons from his tail pocket. "Can I read to you, my Lord?"

The Earl seemed to shudder. "Save your voice for the morning, Mounter." He drank the frumenty in one draft, sighed, then smiled as the liquid warmed his belly. "Put the jug by me, then go and enjoy yourself, Mounter. Parsons should enjoy themselves at Christmas! Your lady wife has come?"

"Indeed, my Lord." The rector smiled eagerly. "I'm sure she would be most happy to greet your Lordship."

"Not up to parsons' wives tonight, Mounter. Give her my best respects." He clumsily poured another glass. "Go on with you, man!"

Few at the Castle would be drunk so quickly as the lord of Lazen, but few had such good reason. All had good means. The frumenty was a speciality of Lazen, brewed for days in the great vats at the brewhouse. Despite the bad harvest the Castle had kept sacks of wheat aside that had been husked, then boiled in milk. When the mash was thick it was mixed with sugar, allowed to cool from the boiling point, and then liberally laced with rum. The recipe claimed that enough rum should be added to make a man drunk with the fumes, at which point the amount of rum should be doubled. The frumenty was cooled. At the last moment, before serving, it was heated again, mixed with egg yolks, and brought to the hall before it could boil. It was drunk only on Christmas Eve, it was too strong for any other day. The Reverend Horne Mounter, who allowed himself some sips of the Castle sherry on this night, secretly believed that the frumenty was a fermentation of the devil, but to say so was to risk the Earl's displeasure.

In the Great Hall Lord Culloden watched in amazement as the liquid was served. He had taken a cup himself and drunk it slowly, but the tenants and townspeople were drinking it like water. He smiled at Campion. "How long do they stand up?"

"Long enough. They deserve it." She smiled up at him. "You're not bored?"

"Good Lord, no! Why should I be bored?"

"It's hardly London, my Lord."

He looked at the noisy, shouting, drinking throng. "I always enjoy birthdays." He laughed.

The local gentry had come, and Campion saw how they kept themselves at one end of the hall while the common folk kept to the other. She walked through both ends, greeting old friends and neighbors, introducing the tall, golden haired cavalry Major at her side. Already, she thought, we behave as though we were married. She looked constantly for a tall, black haired figure, but the Gypsy could not be seen.

The dances were hardly the dances of London. They were country dances that all the guests knew, dances as old as Lazen itself. The Whirligig was followed by Hit and Miss and then Lady Lie Near Me. The church orchestra played fast and merrily and the dancers slowly mixed the two ends of the hall together. Once in a while, in a gesture toward the gentry, Simon Stepper, the bookseller and flautist of the church orchestra, would order his players to provide a minuet.

There was applause again when Campion and Lord Culloden danced to one such tune. The floor seemed to clear for them.

He danced well, better than she would have expected. He smiled at her. "Your father spoke to me today."

"He did, my Lord?" The room turned about her in a blur of happy faces, candles, and firelight on old panelling. Lord Culloden made the formal, slow gestures with elegance. The month's easy living in Lazen, she saw, had thickened his neckline so that the flesh bulged slightly at his tight, gold-encrusted collar. He smiled. "He wanted my advice."

Campion smiled at Sir George Perrott who, bless him, had led Mrs. Hutchinson onto the floor. For that, she thought, she would give Sir George a kiss under the mistletoe. She could not see the Gypsy. "About what, my Lord?"

"Your cousin."

"Oh Lord!" Campion said rudely. She smiled at the miller who, with pretensions to gentility, had insisted on dancing this minuet with his wife and had bumped heavily into Campion's back. "About Julius? What about him?"

Lord Culloden frowned as the tempo of the orchestra underwent a frumenty-induced change. He adjusted his steps. "It seems he has written asking for money." He had to speak loudly to be heard over the riot of conversation and laughter from the lower end of the hall. "He's in bad debt!"

"Again?"

"That was your father's word."

Uncle Achilles, with grave courtesy, was leading Lady

Courthrop's nine year old daughter about the floor. The townspeople, she could see, were laughing at the odd looking Frenchman. She planned another kiss under the mistletoe.

Lord Culloden turned at the upper end of the hall, his feet pointing elegantly in the small steps and glides. "It seems that he's spent his allowance for the next ten years. Can you believe that? Ten years! I mean a fellow has to live, but hardly ten years at a time." He smiled. Campion supposed that all tonight's guests were waiting to see if she kissed Lord Culloden under the mistletoe. She thought she would not like to kiss a man who wore a moustache.

"I'm hardly surprised," Campion said.

She did not want to talk about Julius. She disliked Julius intensely. He was the son of her father's younger brother, her uncle who had died in the war against the American colonists. That uncle, she knew, had had the reputation of a rake, and Julius, with a foulness all his own, seemed determined to outdo his father. When Campion had been sixteen, and Julius twenty-two, he had attacked her in the stables, and though it had not been as horrid as the attack on the heath road, she had never forgotten it. He had pawed at her, pushed her into the straw, and it was only the intervention of Simon Burroughs, the castle's chief coachman, that had ended what Julius had whined was "cousinly fun." Burroughs had broken Julius's nose, a wound that had to be blamed on a fall from a horse. The Earl, at Campion's insistence, was not told of the incident.

Lord Culloden bowed to her as the music raggedly ended, then politely applauded the musicians. He offered her his arm. "Your father believes that no more money should be sent."

"I trust you agreed with him, my Lord."

"It's hardly my place to agree or disagree, is it?" He looked at her with a smile. "I would not want you to think me presumptuous."

"If my father asked you, my Lord, then I would not think you presumptuous."

Campion climbed with him to the dais where the top table was set with wine and punch. She took a glass of claret and sipped it. She might look after Lazen, but there were some things that her father kept from her. The allowances to his English relatives was one of those things, and Campion had never been consulted, nor sought to influence him. She looked at Lord Culloden. "You must say whatever you think best, my Lord."

He was marking her card, she thought, demonstrating that he was already a part of the family. She wondered whether he had already approached her father to ask for permission to seek her hand in marriage. She wondered what she would say when that moment came, if it did come, and the thought made her search the great, happy room for a sight of the Gypsy. The dance now was the Old Man in a Bed of Bones, violently native in its crude exuberance, and, seeing no sign of Gitan, she wondered if he had stayed away in wariness of such an overwhelming English occasion. She smiled as she saw Uncle Achilles, who had no such inhibitions. He capered wildly with two girls from the town.

A crash sounded from the far end of the room and Campion knew that someone had fallen down drunk. They would not be the last. The orchestra, without missing a beat, moved into the Friar and the Nun, provoking laughter, and she looked up at the hooded eyes of Lord Culloden. "You know this dance?"

"Indeed, no, my Lady. My education was sadly lacking." He smiled. "Are you going to teach me?"

She grinned happily. "No, my Lord, you're going to watch me. Sir George?"

Sir George Perrott had danced these tunes before Campion's mother had been born. An ironic, happy cheer went up as the two stepped down to the floor, for the privileged of Lazen were expected to join in these revels. Lord Culloden, smiling and watching from the dais, thought he had never seen her face so happy and so vivacious. He laughed as they mimed the old story that, each year, shocked the Reverend Horne Mounter and his stout, proper wife.

Culloden joined in the applause. Simon Stepper waved his flute, shouted, and the orchestra went rumbustiously into a new tune. The hall cheered, Sir George laughed, and Campion linked her hand with the old man's for Cuckolds All in a Row.

The music filled the hall, the clapping from the crowds at the room's edges seemed to shake the floor, to shiver the air with this day's happiness. This was the Little Kingdom at its best; united and glorious. Campion's face was lit with the joy of it. She let go of Sir George's hand and, laughing and smiling, she was swung from man to man, from servant to miller, miller to brewer, brewer to squire, squire to farmer, and farmer to Gypsy.

His face caught her utterly by surprise. The touch of his hand seemed to freeze her, made her pause on the next step and run to catch up. Her missed beat provoked a cheer from the hall.

She turned at the end, looked for him, but he seemed to have gone as quickly as he had come. It was as if the touch of his hand and the single glance from his blue eyes had been a dream. The music was speeding again, she went forward, her hands holding her dress up so that her ankles showed, and then she was whirled violently about by Sir George, she went backward beside the innkeeper's wife, and the music ended. A huge cheer went up. The musicians, hopefully, went into Up Tails All, but Campion, thinking that dignity must have a limit, smiled and shook her head.

She walked back with Sir George who, with the license of old age and old friendship, put an arm about her waist. "They're getting very drunk, my dear."

"You sound like Mrs. Mounter, Sir George."

He laughed. "God forbid. Where is the lady?"

"Probably looking for dust in the Garden Room," Campion laughed. The rector's wife terrorized the parish with her visitations, and even Lazen Castle had been reprimanded for slovenly housekeeping. Campion steered Sir George to the left, and checked him beneath the mistletoe.

He looked at her. "My dear?"

She kissed him on both cheeks. "A happy Christmas, Sir George."

He laughed. "It will be now, if the excitement doesn't finish me off. Come, my dear, I must give you back to your handsome young officer."

Even Sir George, she thought, considered that Lord Culloden was her man. His Lordship smiled as she climbed the steps, clapping her gently by touching the tips of his fingers on the opposite palm. "Some food?"

Her eyes were shining, her whole face suffused by happiness. Even without the diamonds and pearls she glowed this night. She smiled at Culloden and let him lead her to the Old House's Garden Room where chafing dishes waited for the guests of quality.

The servants who had drawn the short straws of the lottery and thus had to work this evening welcomed them to the Garden Room, held their chairs, then brought plates of food and a cooler of champagne. Lord Culloden had led her to a private table, set in a window alcove that was curtained against the raw night outside. The music was distant now. He smiled at her. "It's a magnificent Christmas."

"You really think so?"

"All Christmasses should be like it."

She laughed, pleased with the compliment. Christmas at Lazen was special to her. "It was better when my mother was alive. She used to dance them all off their feet, all of them!" She smiled. "I was little. I used to watch from the stairs. Toby and I liked to watch the drunks."

"No one minds them getting drunk?"

She laughed. "It's Christmas! Some of them have to be taken home in farm carts. Church tomorrow will be groaning with regret." She sipped her champagne. "You're sure you're enjoying it, my Lord? Our country ways are not too crude?"

"Aren't country pleasures the best?"

It was deftly said. Country pleasures were pleasures of the flesh, the tumbling of bodies in hay, yet he had merely picked up on her words, teased her, and she could do no more than smile.

"Speaking of which," Lord Culloden went on, "are you riding on Tuesday?"

She nodded, her mouth full of pie.

"Your father," he said carefully, "would like me to stay through the season."

She suspected that he wanted her approval for the idea. She gave him a bland answer instead. "The Blues keep you that busy, my Lord?"

He smiled. "I'll have to go to the regiment for a week or two, just so they don't forget me. I'd like to stay, though. You must have the fastest hounds in England!"

"They should be." Her father, whose accident had been on the hunting field, still had a passion for the sport. He had appointed a huntsman to breed lighter hounds, for even if the Earl could no longer follow the pack he was determined that his guests should be thoroughly rattled by the chase. He was regarded as a dangerous innovator by those who preferred the fatter, staider, more traditional hounds, but it was obvious Lord Culloden liked the quicker sport.

He began talking to her about the Lazen hounds, saying how much sharper the hounds appeared when they were hunted with a few bitch couples among them. She nodded, smiled, made the right responses, but her thoughts, with the dreadful inevitability that she feared, insisted on remembering the sudden, warm touch of the Gypsy and the startling look of those odd blue eyes. She had been astonished by the shiver that had tingled throughout her body as his fingers so lightly gripped hers and passed on. Her uncle had said, before she dressed, that lovers look for small coincidences as signs of heaven's favor, and she found herself dreaming that the shock of the Gypsy's touch was just such a sign. Dear Lord, she thought, but this was madness!

Lord Culloden had spoken to her, and she had let the words go straight past her. She looked at him and smiled. "I'm sorry, my Lord?"

"You were miles away," he said with a smile.

"I was wondering if Carline had remembered the puddings. One year they boiled dry."

He smiled again. He was looking into her face that was so quick to smile and laugh. "Did you not hear what I said?"

She looked contrite. "Truly not, my Lord."

He looked down at her ringed hand, then his hooded eyes came up again. He had, she thought, an oddly attractive and crooked smile beneath the moustache. "I hope I offer you no offense, my Lady."

She smiled. "Offense?"

"I want to stay, but not just to hunt the fox. I would have you know that, my Lady."

She sensed the eagerness with which he sought her reassurance, and though his words were undoubtedly too eager, even verging toward insolence, she knew, too, that his actions on the heath road had given him the right to ask for reassurance.

She smiled. "If my father has asked you, my Lord, then no further invitation is needed."

He ignored her evasion. "From you, my Lady, I would ask such an invitation."

She guessed from his words that he had not yet asked her father for her hand, though her reply to this question would undoubtedly influence whether or not he did. The music still played. She heard laughter and shouts from the hall. She found herself wishing, suddenly and profoundly, that this conversation was not taking place.

"My Lady?"

To say yes, she thought, was to set in motion the pavane that led to marriage. He would ask her father, he would ask her, and what then? Marriage, pregnancy a year from now?

And why not? Love was only something that fell from the stars to gild the world for fools. Marriage, she had decided, was a compromise, it could be nothing else. And if CL and LC was a happy coincidence pointing to fate's hand, then how much more was the coincidence of their meeting on the Millett's End road?

"My Lady?"

She stared unseeing at the champagne bottle and, as unbidden and unwelcome as ever, the image of the Gypsy swam before her eyes and she felt an anger at that unworthy attraction. I am not worthy, she thought, not worthy.

She had known this man just a few weeks, yet the suddenness of their introduction, the horror of the man pawing at her on the heath road had led so swiftly to this question. Marriage, she thought, should be a blaze of glory, not something insidious and relentless, creeping up on her with all the appeal of a winter fog.

She smiled at that. Marriage, her father had once said, is like buying a horse. Look at the teeth, the legs, and don't expect a unicorn. She smiled because she knew that somewhere in her life she had been infected with the disease of romance, the expectation of a unicorn. It was unfair on this man, this good man, and she looked at him with her eager, bright, welcoming eyes, and smiled. "Of course, my Lord."

What else, she thought despairingly, could she say?

He took her hand, his eyes still on hers, and raised it close to his mouth. "I am your servant, my Lady." He kissed her fingers. The moustache pricked at her ungloved knuckles.

By such small words, she thought, and tiny, polite deceptions are the courses of our lives fashioned.

A scream interrupted them, a scream that pierced from the hall. Lord Culloden stood, his hand moving to his sword hilt.

Campion smiled. "Someone's drunk, my Lord. Fighting over one of the girls, I expect." She wiped her fingers on the napkin and stood beside him. "Perhaps if I appear it will calm things down." Lord Culloden still frowned, and she put her arm into his as they walked toward the Great Hall. "It happens every year."

There were shouts now, the crash of breaking plates, and Lord Culloden pushed through the people who crowded the dais to stare at the bedlam on the floor.

It was a fight, but such a fight as Campion had not seen

for many a year. A dozen of the town lads were hammering at each other, while as many of the men were trying to pull them apart. Women screamed while the Reverend Horne Mounter was trying, without success, to shout silence and calm into the melee. Simon Stepper and his musicians, oblivious to it all, were playing the dance Dissembling Love.

Lord Culloden's parade ground voice made the musicians pause, but no more. "Stop it! Stop it I say!"

A boy reeled out of the fight with blood coming from his nose. He staggered, fell, then forced himself upright and charged back into the mill of fists and boots.

Campion was laughing.

Two of the town girls were screaming encouragement and she guessed that they had started the fight. The drink was helping it along. Most of the townspeople grinned as they watched. There was nothing for the fighters to damage except themselves, and Christmas at the Castle was hardly Christmas without one good fight to talk about in the coming nights. Why else was all the valuable furniture and china moved from the hall?

Simon Burroughs, the coachman, bobbed his head at Campion. "You want me and the boys to knock their pates together, my Lady?"

"What started it?"

"Cartwright's boy. Thought someone was taking his girl."

"Were they?"

Burroughs shrugged. "Like as not, my Lady. I reckon he came here wanting trouble. You want me to tear his head off?" He asked it eagerly.

Campion smiled and shook her head. Lazen's huge head coachman seemed too final a solution for a boy wounded by Cupid's arrow. "I think they're calming down, Simon."

"Falling down, I think," Lord Culloden said. Two bodies were flat on the floor, blood on their faces.

It did seem as if the fight was ending in drunken exhaustion. The older men, who had tried to break it up, began to pull away, brushing their hands and laughing at the bloodied boys who staggered and reeled and swung their fists hopelessly in thin air. Campion smiled. "I think it's time for a minuet."

Then George Cartwright, the son of the man who farmed the slopes of Two Gallows Hill, drew a knife that was hidden within his coat and slashed at the man closest to him. Mercifully, he missed. He was screaming now, all control gone, the spittle showing at his mouth as he spread his anger about the room.

"Christ!" Simon Burroughs ran forward, shouting in a huge voice, but another man, closer, jumped at the boy. George Cartwright, his eyes mad with jealous passion, turned and sliced at his attacker. The boy was a hugely muscled seventeen year old who spent his days on heavy farm work. The man shouted and staggered back with blood showing on a cut hand.

The youth was screaming his challenge like a banshee and the knife, a twelve inch flensing blade, made a glittering space about him which none dared invade. Simon Burroughs, frowning, slowed to a prudent walk.

Campion looked at Culloden. "My Lord?" She did not want an unarmed man to approach the boy. "I think your sword is needed."

Lord Culloden did not move. He seemed appalled by the sudden violence.

"My Lord!"

The boy saw Burroughs coming, turned, and suddenly ran toward the two girls who had encouraged the fight. He was blind with anger, maddened with jealousy, tormented by those who had mocked his muscled simplicity.

"My Lord!" Campion pushed Lord Culloden toward the floor.

There were screams from the women. The knife slashed at a man who tried to trip the boy, the blade whirled in a savage arc that cleared people from his path, and the two girls shrieked in terror as he ran at them. Simon Burroughs could not reach him, the knife went up, Campion flinched.

And the knife stopped.

A hand held the boy's wrist.

The boy shouted at the man who held him, pulled away with all the strength of his plow-hardened body, but the Gypsy did not move an inch. He seemed, to Campion, to have come from nowhere, to have stepped from the shadows in silence, and now he stood, quite still, gripping the wrist of the boy's knife hand.

His hand tightened. The Gypsy, though taller, looked almost frail beside the great barrel chest and thick arms of the youth, yet, with chilling confidence, he waved Simon Burroughs back.

It was the boy who suddenly looked alarmed. The pain in his wrist seared at him, increased, and he swung his left fist at the Gypsy who simply swayed out of the way and squeezed harder.

The knife dropped.

The Gypsy let go of the boy's wrist, slapped him lightly on the face with his left hand, and, as the boy turned to face that challenge, hit him in the belly with his right hand.

The boy folded with a grunt, was caught by the black-dressed man who lifted him onto a shoulder and walked over the floor as though his burden weighed nothing.

Someone cheered. "Well done, froggie!" The cheer was taken up, spread, turned to clapping, and Campion laughed aloud.

"My Lady?"

She looked left and saw the boy's father. "Mr. Cartwright?"

The poor man was terrified. His hands were clasped and shaking, his head bobbing. "I apologize, my Lady. I'll hit the daylights out of that young bugger, so help me God!"

Someone opened the door for the Gypsy, he paused, then tossed the Cartwright boy out into the gravel. Campion smiled. "Mr. Cartwright, you will stay and enjoy yourself." She turned to the table, nodded to a servant, and held out her hand. The servant, not quite sure what she wanted, gave her the first thing that came to hand, a glass of wine. She presented it to Cartwright as a public symbol that Lazen held no grudge for him. The liquid shook as he took it. "Thank you, your Ladyship."

She raised her voice. The room was silent. "Your son, on the other hand, Mr. Cartwright, you will send to me on Wednesday. Tell him he will have to apologize, and tell him it will not be a pleasant conversation."

The farmer nodded. "Yes, my Lady." It was rumored that the Lady Campion Lazender had a rare temper when she wished to show it. He looked at the wine that trembled in his hand. He wondered if he was supposed to drink it.

Campion smiled. "Now, if you will excuse me, Mr. Cartwright, I have to thank our Frenchman."

She stepped down from the dais and walked across the floor in silence.

The whole room watched her.

She looked superb. The light of a thousand candles touched the pale, pale gold of her twisted, piled hair, flashed from the pearls, the gold, the sapphires, from her large, blue eyes, from the high cheekbones and the full lips. She looked fit to rule an empire, while inside, seeing his face, she felt like a kitten.

Why the Gypsy did this to her, she did not know, yet seeing those oddly bright eyes, so pale in the dark face, and the savage, handsome features, made her heart jump and the blood tingle in her veins.

She stopped. She smiled. She spoke in French. "We owe you our thanks, Gitan?" She deliberately made his name a question.

He shrugged. He smiled, making his face so suddenly brilliant. He ignored the interrogatory that she had inflected on his name. "A small thing, my Lady, not worth a remark." He bowed to her gracefully and then, straightening, his vivid eyes caught hers again.

"Two seconds later and there would have been a badly wounded girl." She smiled. "I think we owe you something." At least, she thought, by playing the great lady, she hid the turmoil he put within her.

Gitan smiled again. "Then may I have the temerity to name my reward?"

For a moment she thought he was going to ask to dance with her and she feared that all this room would see her excitement and guess her shameful secret. She bent her head graciously. "Please."

Somehow, without offense, he managed to make his smile personal, as if they were conspirators. "I merely ask your Ladyship's permission to visit the long room to see the portrait again."

She blushed, she knew she blushed. For a desperate, terrible second the thought slipped across her mind that he had seen the naked nymph hidden in the Lely portrait, but she knew that was impossible. Then, with certainty, she knew he was complimenting her, giving her a message that was as forbidden for him to give as she to receive. Yet how could such a simple request, such a modest request, be denied? She nodded. "Of course. I'll tell Carline. Tomorrow?"

"Tonight, my Lady." He spoke humbly. "I leave in the morning."

"Christmas Day?"

"Alas, yes."

"Then tonight." She turned away, sure that the whole room, even if they did not understand the foreign tongue, would still have seen her confusion. Yet no one looked at her oddly, no shocked mouths whispered behind hands, no murmur of rumor sounded in the hall. She waved to Simon Stepper for his musicians to begin playing. Slowly the noise of conversation, of laughter and of dancing began again.

"An odd looking fellow!" Lord Culloden said.

"He's French," she said, as if it explained everything.

"Oh!" he said, as if it did. "I thought a sword would be over-egging the pudding, my Lady."

She was tempted to say that he could have stopped the boy's madness without drawing his sword, as the Gypsy had done, but she smiled instead. "I'm sure you're right, my Lord."

He touched the tips of his blond moustache. "I think this is meant to be a minuet. Shall we?"

She danced with the man whom she had encouraged to approach her father for her hand in marriage and she knew, as she felt his hand on her arm, that the Gypsy's request had been more than a compliment. It had been an invitation.

She told herself she would ignore it. She danced. She dazzled the room, she turned, she whirled, she danced. It was Christmas.

* * *

The Castle's guests who were staying for the season had mostly retired by two o'clock. A few, like Sir George, were staying the course with those townspeople and servants who still danced to the single violinist who had survived the frumenty. Campion herself, kissed on the fingers by Lord Culloden, went to her bedroom a few minutes past the hour.

Her maid was excited. "It's such a good ball, my Lady."

Campion smiled. "Go back to it, Edna. I'll undress myself."

"I wouldn't hear of it, my Lady! And that Frenchie?" Edna giggled. "They're ever so handsome, aren't they?"

Jealousy stabbed at Campion. She was shocked by it, ashamed by it. She took Edna by the shoulders, turned her, and pushed her toward the door. "Go back. Enjoy yourself. Maybe you'll find your Frenchman!"

She waited till the girl had gone, till the corridor was quiet, and then she locked the bedroom door. She crossed to the far side and unlocked the door that led to the gallery.

Her heart pounded as though she faced death.

She should not do this. This was wrong. This was more wrong than anything she could imagine, yet nothing would stop her. It seemed she did this thing with a volition that was not her own.

The door swung open.

She walked into the Long Gallery. She was doing the single most exciting and dangerous thing of her life. She went to the gallery because she thought that in the Gypsy's polite request had been more than a desire to see the Lely portrait. There had been a statement that he would be there and she could meet him. Now, by some impulse of seething delight, and against all common sense, she went into the gallery.

A single candle burned at the western end, its flame unwavering in the still air, its light showing nothing.

Nothing but the furniture, the glass of the windows, the great painting on the wall. He was not there.

She felt a surge of relief. It had been three hours since she had told Carline to let the Gypsy up here, ordering a candelabra to be given him. He had come here and he had gone, leaving a single candle to light his way out. He had gone.

She stood in the light that came from her bedroom and she stared at the single candle in the Long Gallery. It was cold here, the fires dead since the afternoon. She felt the relief that he had gone. She felt the sadness that he had gone. She was astonished at the mingling of her feelings. The shame that on this night a lord had virtually asked for her hand, she had accepted, and then she had hoped for a clandestine meeting with a servant. Mixed with that was a terrible disappointment that the Gypsy was not waiting in the light of the single flame that burned so still at the gallery's western end. She turned back to her room.

She walked slowly into her bedroom. She closed the door, leaving only the single candle in the Long Gallery. There was the sound of her key turning in the lock, then silence.

A man who breaks horses must know patience. He must know when to bridle a colt, and when to do nothing. The Gypsy, in the darkness of the gallery's eastern end, watched her and thought she was the most lovely woman he had seen, more desirable than loneliness could dream of, more beautiful than danger itself. For a second he was tempted to call out, to walk toward her, but he stayed silent. There was a time and there was a season, but the time and season for the Lady Campion were not now.

Gitan had waited at the dark end of the gallery for a message. He would have waited all night. The message had been given. She had come. She would come again.

On silent feet he went downstairs. He walked through the frost bright night to the stables, to the room he used when he was in Lazen. He slept on the floor, covered with a cloak and blanket, and beside him, pale in the night, was a naked sword. By Christmas Day's cold dawn he was gone.

It was a miserable Christmas in Paris, a cold and hungry Christmas, its only solace the good news from the war against the Prussians and Austrians. The armies of France had repelled the northern invaders and were poised to take the war to the enemy lands. Indeed, to all lands, for the French government had decreed that they would help any and all countries to throw off the chains of superstition and monarchy. The grim jest in Paris was that France merely wished to send its hunger and poverty abroad.

The new year brought cold rains. The people of Paris hunched into the foul weather and dreamed of a time when shops were filled with warm, fragrant bread. Yet on one January day there was joy in the city, a great celebration that let the citizens forget their cold and hunger.

It was a Sunday. It rained.

It was a bitter, sleety rain that slanted in needle slashes through the thick smoke that lay in a tattered layer above the rooftops of Paris. Everything seemed grimy. Everything seemed touched by the greasy, dirty slime of winter. The Seine was like the River Styx. The bodies of dogs and dead cats floated in the gray, pocked water to the far off sea.

The great days of the summer seemed long ago, the days when the people had stormed the Tuileries and ransacked the great rooms and hunted the King's guard to squalid deaths in the sun drenched courtyards. Today the palace was still empty, its windows still being repaired, its plaster ceilings still chipped by the bullets of summer.

The winter crowd that trudged past the palace gave it scarcely a glance. They had a greater attraction waiting to the west, waiting in the wide square that had been triumphantly renamed the Place de la Revolution.

Toby Lazender, Lord Werlatton, went with them.

If his sister had seen him she would not have known whether to laugh or to cry. He had not shaved for a week. He wore, on his unruly, uncut red curls, a redder cap, the cap of Liberty. He wore ragged trousers, as much a sign of revolutionary fervor as the red cap itself. A man in breeches was suspected of elitist sympathies.

On his feet he wore wooden sabots, too big for him and stuffed with straw. He had a torn coat, tight belted with string, covered with a crude cloak of dirty sacking. In the Palais Royale he had caught sight of his reflection in a cutler's window and he had laughed at the astonishment his appearance would have caused in Lazen.

He sometimes thought of his sister's pleading words. Campion had said, with truth that he was ready to admit but not to follow, that his duty now, as Lazen's heir, was to ensure the succession. He should, he knew, be in England. He should be choosing one of the innumerable girls who would want nothing more than to be the next Countess of Lazen.

He had never wanted to be the heir. The death of his elder brother had thrust the responsibility unwillingly on Toby's shoulders at a time when he was already enmeshed in Lord Paunceley's secret world. He was reluctant to leave that world and the death of Lucille had determined him not to leave it.

If Lucille had lived, he thought, he would have taken

her to Lazen and been satisfied. No one knew how she had touched his life, how her very presence had given him happiness, how her death had left him with a bleak and awful anger.

Lord Paunceley, that most clever and least principled of men, had seen the anger and been glad to use it for his own ends.

Lord Paunceley had sent Toby to the Vendée, an area of French countryside to the south of Brittany, and there Toby's job was to determine what hope its people had of successfully rebelling against the new French Republic. The Vendeans wanted their King on the throne, they wanted their church restored, and they wanted nothing to do with Republicanism and its shibboleths of equality and liberty. Yet on this January Sunday in 1793, this historic, wet Sunday, Toby had left the Vendée to be in Paris.

He had stayed the night with twenty others in a room of a small lodging house in the Rue des Mauvais Garçons. He gave his name there as Pierre Cheval, astonishing the landlord by writing it himself in clumsy, block letters in the book. Peasants from the country were not supposed to be able to read or write. He had eaten a meal that cost him six sous, then gone out into the cold, sleety streets of Paris. He had gone to a drinking club called Laval's. At first, being a stranger with a country accent, he had not been welcomed, but when he said that his friend Gitan had sent him he was taken into the drunken company of the main table.

Now, as he approached the Place de la Revolution, he saw the girl he had met the night before. Terese. She was a black haired, bright eyed girl who, at Gitan's name, had pushed next to Toby and questioned him about the Gypsy's whereabouts.

Her voice, as she saw Toby in the street, was eager. "Did you find him?"

"Not yet." He had lied to her. He had told her he was in Paris to meet the Gypsy.

She fell into step beside him. "He is coming?"

"He promised." Toby grinned at her. "Won't I do?"

She pouted, but took his arm nevertheless. "He is coming?" she insisted.

He nodded. "He said he'd meet me here. If not today, tomorrow. Either me or Jean Brissot."

Toby had gone to Laval's to find the fat Brissot who had boasted that Lucille de Fauquemberghes' skin was like milk. The man had not been in the tavern. Terese, sure that he would be in the Place de la Revolution, had promised to meet Toby and point Brissot out to him.

Now, as they walked westward in the great crowd, she looked up at the tall, red-headed man. "Why do you want to meet Jean?"

"I told you. Business."

"What business?"

Toby shrugged. "Gitan's business."

The answer satisfied her. The Gypsy, it seemed, could do no wrong. The mere mention of his name made her smile. She stopped to let a legless beggar swing past on muscular arms. "I hate Brissot. He's a pig with hands."

"Hands?"

"Hands everywhere. It's Terese this and Terese that and his hands are up you and down you and around you, squeezing and mauling. He's a pig!"

A pig, Toby thought, who had raped his Lucille. He smiled at the girl beside him. "You just find him for me."

"And you keep his bloody hands off me."

She seemed happy enough to be with Toby. She enjoyed playing the city girl who showed the country boy the sights of Paris, none of which was more impressive than the great machine erected in the center of the Place de la Revolution.

If there was one symbol of equality in the new France, then surely this machine was that symbol.

In the old days only the nobly born could expect the quick execution of a swift axe. The peasants were not so fortunate. They might be burned, hanged, disemboweled, or killed in some other slow, imaginative way that would amuse the crowd. Yet today was the age of equality and now all condemned men and women died in the same privileged way. They lost their heads and they lost them swiftly.

The machine was not a French invention. It had been used in Britain, Germany and Italy, yet French genius had refined it. Dr. Joseph Guillotin, a member of the National Convention, had recommended the adoption of the machine and, under the supervision of the Academy of Surgeons, he had refined its operation by testing it on live sheep and dead lunatics. Now it stood, massive and high, a product of equality and science.

Terese and Toby, arm in arm, shuffled toward the great machine. The angled blade, beaded with water, was held at the top of the two uprights by a taut rope. The crosspiece above the blade had been whitened by the pigeons that huddled against the rain.

Terese licked her lips and stared at the machine. "You've seen it before?"

He shook his head.

She laughed. "Sneezing into the basket."

That was what the people of Paris called the death that this machine gave. The sound of the falling blade was like a sneeze, and the motion of the head, twitching up as the blade struck then going violently down as it bit, was like the jerk of a man sneezing. Toby laughed. "Sneezing?"

"Atishoo."

The crowd pushed them away from the machine. The rain fell steadily. From Toby's left came the sound of boots on the cobbles and he could see the bright slashes of bayonets over the crowd's heads.

Terese stared about her. "I don't see Gitan."

"Patience." Toby was astonished at the loyalty the Gypsy engendered in girls. This one had not seen Gitan since the previous autumn, yet the mere mention of his name had made her face flushed. To take her mind off the Gypsy, he bought them both some *petits pains* from one of the many hawkers. The bread tasted of sawdust. "Do you see Brissot?"

The soldiers cleared a path through the crowd and held it open with their steel-tipped muskets. Cavalry, ragged men with curved swords, clattered down the cleared path and arrayed themselves beside the machine. The platform was tall enough for the crowd to see over the horses. They waited.

Terese was worrying. "He'll never find us!"

"He said to meet him at the bridge if he couldn't get through the crowd," Toby frowned. "But he might not come till tomorrow!"

Not that anyone could now hope to get through the huge throng that filled every inch of the great square. Even the hawkers had given up trying. The crowd, packed and expectant, waited. Voices made a great buzzing hum, broken by laughter or a child's crying. The rain fell. The pigeons on the tall machine strutted up and down as if bemused by the noise and the great crowd that stretched in every direction.

Then, oddly, there was silence.

As if by agreement the crowd stopped talking. Heads turned to the north side of the square.

"Brissot," Terese whispered and nudged him. "There!"

"Where?"

"There! The man with the bottle!"

Toby saw a lank haired, pudgy man tipping a black

bottle to his lips, and then the movement of a tattered umbrella half hid the man.

Over the heads of the crowd he could see the roofs of carriages, the leading one a dark green that glistened from the rain. The crush of the crowd created warmth. Terese had an arm about his waist.

Toby stood on tiptoe and moved his head till he saw the plump, grinning Brissot again. The sight of him, the thought that that pig had raped his Lucille, stirred a sudden, terrifying anger within him. He put a hand inside his ragged, string tied coat, and felt the handle of the knife that was strapped to his body.

Drums sounded from the procession that approached the machine, drums whose skins were made soggy by the weather, but which were thumped energetically by the drummers who had been told to keep the sound going until all was over.

The coaches stopped. Now, from his place in the crowd, Toby could see nothing of what happened. He could not see a pale, fleshy man descend from the green carriage and be stripped of his brown coat and hat. He did not see the shears slice off the collar of the white shirt and then cut the long hair from the nape of the man's plump, white neck.

He did not see the priest, dressed, as the law demanded, in lay clothes, mutter his prayers against the crowd's silent enmity.

He did see the man climb the wood stairway to the platform where three men waited for him. The priest, the rain soaking his book, followed.

The fleshy, pale man's arms were tied behind his back, lashed from wrist to elbow so that his shoulders were unnaturally forced back.

As the plump man came in sight of the crowd so there was a kind of sigh that went through it. Terese, her tongue between her lips, stood on tiptoe, one hand on Toby's shoulder. Her eyes were bright. For a moment at least she had forgotten the Gypsy.

The man walked to the platform's edge. Toby saw his fat, white neck, his double chin, and his fleshy, drooping lips. The man began to speak and, miraculously, the drummers stopped. Toby frowned as he tried to catch the words.

"I pray God that the blood you are about to shed will never be asked of France . . ." and then the wind seemed to snatch the next words of the fleshy man away. Someone shouted by the machine, shouted angrily, and the drummers guiltily began to beat their soggy skins again, the noise rising to drown the man's words.

"Fat bastard," Terese said.

The three men who had waited on the wooden platform, the executioner and his two assistants, moved toward the man. One assistant took his left upper arm, the other the right, and they guided him forward to the plank.

Clumsily the man lay down. The two assistants lugged him forward as if he was a sack of barley, pulled him until his head was under the uprights. Then the executioner dropped the wooden brace that trapped the man's neck beneath the blade.

The assistants stood back.

The priest knelt. He made the sign of the cross.

The drummers, their wrists weary, kept their sticks moving. The crowd seemed to hold its breath.

The executioner stepped to the taut rope. He unlooped it, jerking drops of water from the twisted hemp, then let it go.

The blade scraped in the grooves. It fell. The rope, snatched by the weighted steel, snaked and danced and looped upward.

The man screamed.

The scream went on. The blade had fallen, yet all of Dr. Guillotin's experiments with sheep and lunatics had not allowed for a neck this thickly fleshy.

The scream came pathetic and shrill over the drums' failing sound. Not one of the great crowd spoke or cheered as the scream rose and fell, sobbed and faded. The executioner, startled into action by the awful scream, hauled on the rope so that the great blade rose jerkily to the top of the shafts again.

The scream faded. The blood on the wide blade, diluted by rain, ran pale down the slanting edge. The executioner gave one more tug, stepped back, and the rope snaked up again.

The blade caught speed, hissing, rattling down, and the plump man sneezed into the basket with a snatch of the head and a thump as the blade bit through his neck and sprayed a fan of bright blood on the kneeling, praying priest.

Silence.

Toby thought the crowd drew its breath.

And then the cheer came, a cheer that startled the pigeons up into the gray, wet air, a cheer that sounded like the thundering of a great sea within the elegant facades of the huge square, a cheer that told France that its King was dead, that tyranny had met the blade, that the Republic had cut its last ties with the past.

Louis XVI was dead. Pigeons circled the square. A soldier jumped onto the scaffold and held the dead man's head by the hair. He rubbed it against his trousers to provoke the mocking laughter of the crowd.

The priest, his clothes spattered by the King's blood, hurried into the anonymity of the crowd which was reluctant to go back to the cold, hungry hardships of winter.

Slowly, still excited, the great crowd dispersed.

Toby struggled to stay near Jean Brissot, fighting against the tide of bodies. Terese, gripping his cloak of sacking, wanted to find the Gypsy and Toby suggested she wait at the bridge to the south of the square. "He said that's where he'd meet me."

"What if he's not there?"

"Meet me at Laval's tonight!"

He watched her go, then pushed through the crowd toward the plump man who had gone beneath the wooden scaffold to dip his finger in the blood of a King.

Toby stayed with Jean Brissot. He followed him through the day, through the alleys, followed him until the fat, loud man went into a dark courtyard to relieve himself of the wine that had celebrated a monarch's death.

Compared to Louis XVI, Jean Brissot was fortunate. He had little time to contemplate his death. He had listened with horror as the red-headed man talked of a long dead girl, a horror that turned to panic as he tried to run and shout for help. But Toby tripped him, turned him, stood astride him, and gutted him from groin to chest. He did it for Lucille de Fauquemberghes, for whom death had been far, far worse, and when it was done the small courtyard seemed awash with the fat man's blood.

Toby dropped his blood-soaked cloak of sackcloth over the body. A cat licked at the blood which was pecked by falling sleet. Dusk made the courtyard dark. Toby could hear a violin playing in the tavern from which Brissot had swaggered to his death.

Lord Werlatton went back to the Rue des Mauvais Garçons, to the small, filthy lodging house where the name Pierre Cheval was written in the book.

He did not go into the building.

He watched instead from a street corner and saw what he expected to see. Only the Gypsy had known that Pierre

Cheval was the Lord Werlatton, and only the Gypsy knew that Lord Werlatton planned to stay in that lodging house on that street.

And that was why the soldiers were searching the house, driving the people out with musket butts, smashing open cupboards and ripping up floorboards.

Toby, the knife hidden again, turned back into the alleys of Paris where he would hide till the roadblocks at the city gates were lifted. Lazen, though it did not yet know its enemy, was fighting back.

"It's war," the Earl said. "Damned war! The fool's caught up in a war!"

Campion looked at *The Times,* published four days before in London. France, in the wake of murdering their King, had declared war on Britain. War. The word seemed so unreal to her, so stupid. There was war between her mother's and her father's countries. Britain was at war.

The Earl grimaced as pain caught him. "Scrimgeour brought the newspaper." He gestured at the fat man who smiled at Campion as he stood up from behind the table where he had established himself. The Earl growled, "You do remember Scrimgeour, my dear?"

"Of course." She acknowledged the fat man's bow. "You're well, Mr. Scrimgeour?"

"Of course he's well," the Earl snapped. "He's a damned lawyer. Evicted any widows or children lately, Scrimgeour?"

"One loses count, my Lord." Scrimgeour, who was Lazen's London lawyer, was oblivious to the Earl's attacks. He smiled constantly. Campion always thought that he would have made an excellent Renaissance Cardinal with his fat, smooth face, his unctuous smile, his ingratiating manners, and sly wit.

The Earl pulled *The Times* toward him with his good

hand. "Your brother, my dear, is in a war. He's a fool." He smiled at her. "I hear you had a good run yesterday?"

"Picked up a scent in Candle Woods and then all the way to Sorrell's Ford."

"And lost him there?"

"Went to ground."

The Earl laughed. "You lost the same old dog last year! He'll live longer than all of us! How did Pimpernel go?"

She shrugged. "He was whistling by Abbotshill."

"I knew it! I knew we shouldn't have bought that horse! That damned French Gypsy of your brother's said it was no good, but you can't tell Correy. He won't listen! Boring you, am I, Scrimgeour?"

"Indeed not, my Lord."

"I try, I try. D'you hunt, Scrimgeour?"

"Only malefactors, my Lord." The lawyer's shoulders heaved with silent laughter.

"Christ!" the Earl groaned. He looked back at his daughter. Much of his swearing and grumpiness was for her benefit; she pretended to be shocked, but he knew she liked it. After her mother's death it was inevitable that Campion would grow up in a male dominated household, inevitable that she would be teased. She was also loved by this ill, clever, frustrated man who now smiled at her. "You're out on Friday?"

She nodded. "We're drawing Sconce Hill."

"What are you riding?"

"Hellbite."

He laughed. "He'll have you on your ass. You'll end up like me, good for nothing, lawyer's bait. Sorry, Scrimgeour, forgot you were here."

The lawyer laughed. "Your lordship is ever thoughtful." He looked at Campion. "Such wit!"

She dared not look at her father. She would have burst into laughter if she had caught his eye.

"Now!" her father barked. "We are gathered here for a solemn occasion. What happens when I die." She looked at him with sudden shock and he scowled at her. "Don't you cry, Missy. I can't stand weeping women! Your mother never wept, God bless her. Nothing worse than a weeping woman, ain't that right, Scrimgeour?"

"They are a bane, my Lord." Scrimgeour was delicately hooking the wire earpieces of half-moon spectacles beneath his scrolled wig.

"So." Her father gave her a swift smile. "You sit and say nothing, my dear, and listen to us men talk. Tell her what's in the will, Scrimgeour."

Campion looked from the lawyer to her father, and back to the lawyer again. She had known, of course, that Cartmel Scrimgeour had come to Lazen, but she presumed that it was no more than one of his normal visits. She had been summoned to her father's room and had expected only to talk about the domestic accounts. Now this? Her father's will? She wanted to protest, but the fat lawyer, his thumbs and fingers splayed above the papers as if he was casting a spell, spoke first.

"You understand, my Lady, that despite this egregiously woeful topic, we all, of course, wish your father a long and most happy life."

"Christ!" The Earl groaned. "Get on with it."

Scrimgeour lifted a curling sheet of paper. "In the unhappy event, dear lady, of your dear father's death . . ."

"Father!"

The Earl looked innocently at her. "Seen a spider?"

"What are we talking about?"

He smiled at the shock in her voice. "I am doing, dear child, what the priests tell us to do. I am preparing for my death."

"But . . ."

"Be quiet, Campion. Carry on, Scrimgeour, she's usually more sensible than this."

The lawyer smiled ingratiatingly. "In the unhappy event, dear lady, of your dear father's death, the estate, and the title, of course, descends to your brother, Lord Werlatton."

"She knows who her brother is, Scrimgeour!"

"Your Lordship is quite right to tell me!" He gave the Earl a happy, grateful smile. "Shall I add the details of Lady Campion's own settlement?"

"No. Let her wait till I'm cold." The Earl smiled at her. "Periton House and a decent income. You won't be cold. Will you please stop looking as if you've seen a spider?"

She reached for his hand and held it in both her own. She supposed she should say something to him, but this cold-blooded and sudden immersion into the details of his will had left her too shocked to open her mouth.

Her father seemed to understand for he raised her right hand to his mouth and kissed it. Then he nodded to his lawyer. "Go on, Scrimgeour, don't mind this touching display of fatherly affection."

"It warms my heart, your Lordship." Mr. Scrimgeour, as if to prove his point, dabbed at one protuberant eye with a plump finger. He smiled at Campion. "Unfortunately, dear Lady Campion, your father has felt it necessary to make precautions against a more unhappy outcome."

"What he means," her father said, "is that if my damn fool son catches his death of a French bullet, then your cousin inherits the Earldom. Making Julius an Earl is like making an ape into an Archbishop, or a lawyer into a gentleman. Carry on, Scrimgeour, don't mind my interruptions."

"They are always most illuminating, my Lord."

Campion had scarcely thought of the eventuality, yet

suddenly it seemed horribly real. There was war. Toby was, at his own insistence, in France, and only Toby barred the Earldom from Sir Julius. She remembered her cousin pawing at her in the straw, she remembered his foul language, and she shuddered to think of him as master of Lazen.

Cartmel Scrimgeour ran a finger beneath his stock. "In that event, Lady Campion, your father has decided that the property will be entailed upon Sir Julius's issue or, if he has none, upon your own children."

"Let's hope he has none," the Earl growled. "Let's hope it's rotted off by the pox." He squeezed her hand and she squeezed back.

Scrimgeour went on as though the Earl had not spoken. "That would mean that Sir Julius, as Earl, would have no power over the estate. He may live at Lazen, he will receive an income sufficient to his needs, and a very generous one too, but you, Lady Campion, will have the administration of the estate until the death of Sir Julius, or, should he predecease his issue, until the majority of his heir or, should he have none, your own." He smiled.

She was astonished. In effect the whole estate would be given to her if her brother died to hold in trust for the following generation.

She stared at the lawyer. Her father laughed at her. "Don't pretend you're surprised."

"Father!"

"Christ! You think I'd let Julius have this? God! He'd gamble the whole damned thing away in a year! Wrote to me a month ago wanting more money. I told him enough was enough and now he's praying for my death and Toby's death. I just wish I could see the little bastard's face when he finds out we've entailed the damned place. Do go on, Scrimgeour."

The lawyer waggled his eyebrows, a sure sign that he

was approaching a difficult topic. "There is always the sad possibility, Lady Campion, that you will predecease your cousin in the sad event of your brother not succeeding to the Earldom."

"He means," the Earl said, "that all my children will be dead. A united family once more. Go on."

"In which case, Lady Campion, the new will provides that your husband will continue your responsibilities, in which discharge he will be aided by Achilles d'Auxigny and by your humble servant."

"He means himself."

Scrimgeour bowed to her in his chair. "Your dear uncle and myself are named, in any case, to be your fellow trustees."

She smiled, trying to cover her astonishment. "I'm glad, Mr. Scrimgeour."

"Oh God! Don't be nice to him. He's a lawyer. He'll have the skin off your back if you're nice to him."

"Such wit," murmured Mr. Scrimgeour.

Her father drew his hand back and pushed himself up on the pillows. "Your uncle may be French, but he's got more sense than anyone else in the family. As for Scrimgeour, well, he tells me he's honest. He's a lawyer, but he says he's honest. Such wit."

Cartmel Scrimgeour let the jibes roll off his ample, sleek flesh. He smiled at Campion. "Let us fervently hope, Lady Campion, that our advice will not be required, and that your brother will live to a hale, hearty age to be much pleased with his own children."

"Amen," Campion said fervently.

"But if not," her father said, "then you look after Lazen. And I mean you! You'll make the decisions. You'll get advice from Achilles and Scrimgeour, but the power is yours! I know you're a girl, but you've got good sense. You should have been born a boy."

"You'd have liked that, father?"

"Girls aren't much use. All headaches and hair pins."

She put her tongue out at him. He laughed and reached for her hand. He held it and looked at her blue eyes. He smiled. "You may be a mere girl, Campion, but you're the best of my litter." He ignored her protest. "Your elder brother was a bore. And Toby?" He shrugged. "Toby doesn't want the aggravation of it all. He wants to be a hero. I think he fancies a grave in Westminster Abbey."

"Nonsense, father."

"It's not nonsense. And what it means, mere girl, is that Lazen hangs on a very thin thread. I'm using you to strengthen the thread."

She smiled. "A mere girl?"

"Which makes it important," her father said, "that you choose your husband wisely. However, there is no connection whatsoever between that statement and the next matter I wish to raise. Read it, Scrimgeour."

The lawyer dropped one piece of paper and selected another. He licked his lips, peered archly over his spectacles at her, then read from the sheet of paper. "Lewis James McConnell Culloden, fourteenth . . ."

"Forget his titles," her father growled. He looked at Campion. "I asked Scrimgeour to find out who he was."

She knew she was blushing. She said nothing.

Scrimgeour smiled at her. "Went to Eton College, of course, but didn't we all?" He laughed lightly. "Then Kings, naturally, but did not stay up for his baccalaureate. The family lost their Irish lands, I fear his father was a gambler. Enough was saved from the wreckage for his Lordship, on succeeding his father, to buy himself a commission in the Blues. A most excellent regiment, of course. House in London, very fair, and property in Lancashire, Cheshire and the remnants of a small estate in County Offaly. All the latter mortgaged. No scandals, my

Lord. He's a communicant member of the Church of England, of course, and he has only spoken twice in the House of Lords; once on the subject of turnips, and the other time he advocated the adoption of the Austrian pattern of cavalry sword. His reputation, my Lord, is as a steady, quiet, solid man, plenty of bottom, whose family has fallen on hard times. He has never married." Scrimgeour smiled and put the paper down.

"What he means," the Earl said, "is that Lewis ain't got the pox." Campion blushed, and the Earl smiled. "Upon which good news, Scrimgeour, I'd be obliged if you left us."

Cartmel Scrimgeour stood. He bowed. "My Lord. Lady Campion." He walked with immense dignity from the room.

"Well?" her father said.

She stood. She walked to the window, rubbed a patch of glass clear of condensation, and stared at the light scattering of snow that had fallen in the night. The hedgerows seemed very black against the unusual whiteness. She hoped it would be warmer for Friday's meet.

"Well?"

"Well what, father?" She turned.

He stared at her. Her beauty was a constant solace to him, more beautiful even than his wife whose portrait, on an easel, had stood these fifteen years at the foot of his bed. "You're not going to weep on me, are you?"

"Why should I?"

"Because my bowels, child, that I cannot control anyway, have started to pass blood. Fenner, who knows nothing, says it means nothing. He's lying. Doctors always lie. They're worse than bloody lawyers. I have pain like the very devil and I'm dying."

She wanted to cry. She wanted to throw herself onto his bed, into his arms, and cry.

She stood still. She looked at him and felt the tears prick at her eyes.

"Don't weep on me, girl. Weep after I'm dead, but give me a smile while I live."

"Father."

He laughed at her, held out his good arm, and she went to him, let him hold her, and she cried anyway. His hand stroked her neck. "Get me a brandy, girl."

"You shouldn't drink, father."

"It's for you, fool."

She laughed. He always had been able to make her laugh. She dried her eyes on his pillow, smearing it with cosmetics, and the look of her face made him laugh. "Get us both a brandy, girl. Get drunk with your father, not many girls do that."

She gave him a small brandy, provoking a snort of disdain, and gave herself an even smaller one. "Well, father?"

"Do you want to marry him, eh? Scrimgeour says he ain't poxed, says he's got bottom!"

She had guessed that the question would be asked when he had dismissed the lawyer so brusquely. She said nothing.

Her father drained his glass. "You've been looking miserable as a hound without a nose these last two months. Don't you like him?"

"I like him, father." Yet how could she tell her father of her shame? The memory of going to the Long Gallery on Christmas morning, of going in hope that a servant would be waiting there. Each time she remembered it she winced at the thought, at the agonizing embarrassment of the thought. "I do like him."

"If you're not going to drink that, give it to me."

She sipped and made a face. "Here."

He laughed, took the glass and drained it. "He wants to marry you. Stood there like a new-born foal, all twisted legs and shyness, asking for the privilege of your hand. God damn it, girl, it is a privilege. You're the prettiest filly in the country."

"Father!"

He stuck his tongue out at her. "So I told him to wait for a month. By that time Scrimgeour would have found out his bloodstock and you could give me your answer. So?"

She shrugged. "I don't know, father."

He watched her as she walked back to the window. He sighed. "You want certainty?"

She nodded. "I suppose so." On the steamy part of the window, out of his sight, she had drawn a heart. She pierced the heart with an arrow. At the feathered end she traced her initials, CL. With a slow finger, with trepidation, she put a C beside the point of the arrow, and then crooked a line to make it into a G. She rubbed it out, full of shame, despising herself, unable to explain it to herself, wishing she had the sense and practicality that everyone else claimed to see in her.

Her father patted the bed beside him. "Come and sit."

He looked at the portrait of his wife, and then at Campion. "Would you say your mother and I were happily married?"

She nodded. She had only seen them together when she was very small, but she remembered their laughter.

He smiled. "I didn't know if I was doing the right thing. I know Madeleine wasn't sure. Certainty isn't part of it."

"It isn't?"

"No." He shook his head. "But we were happy. You grow into it. It's a responsibility. God, I'm being serious. It must be death creeping up on me."

She smiled because he wanted her to smile. She took his hand, seeing how thin it was, how his wedding ring hung loose on his finger. She raised the hand to her lips and kissed it. "I love you, father."

"Christ! You want me to cry?"

"No."

He smiled. "Can you love Lewis?"

"Should I?"

He shrugged. "I don't know, child. I know one thing. I'm going to die, and not all the liars in England can stop that happening, and when I do die, my child, the wolves are going to come to Lazen. And if Toby's dead then you'll have to stop Julius stripping the flesh off Lazen's bones."

"Toby should come home."

"I know. But bloody Paunceley wants him, bloody Paunceley would. And you can't blame Toby, my child, because a young man should go out and dare the world. So let him be." He squeezed her hand. "But if Toby dies, then every bastard in the kingdom will try to take Lazen. You need a man beside you, a good man, a strong one."

"Because I'm just a girl? All headaches and hair pins?"

He laughed. "All tits and troubles, eh?"

"Father!"

He laughed again, the laughter turning into pain. "And if you die, my dear child, and women do die in childbirth like your mother did, then I need to know that a man, good and strong, is holding this Castle against the crucifying bastards."

"You want me to marry Lewis, father?"

"Is there anyone else?" he teased her.

She thrust the thought away, the ridiculous, stupid, demeaning, flighty thought, and shook her head. "Of course not."

Her father smiled. He looked so old, so tired, and so pained. "I think he's a good man. I think he will look after you. So what do I tell him?"

She half smiled. "You like him?"

He nodded. "He's good with hounds."

She laughed. She supposed her father was right, that certainty was a luxury, no more to be looked for in a betrothal than the fool's gold of romantic ecstasy. Yet could there not be some small magic? A dash, no more? Since Lord Culloden had rescued her there had been only the slow, growing, undramatic certainty of their marriage.

"Well?" the Earl asked. He seemed anxious.

She squeezed his hand and smiled. "Tell him yes, father, tell him yes."

He smiled back. "Thank you. I'll get Scrimgeour to talk to him. Lewis ought to know the will." He gripped her hand. She could sense the relief in him. He pulled her toward him and kissed her cheek. "You always were my sensible one."

She wished he had not said it, for what lady of sense would hold the memory of a horse-master in her heart? But what was said could not be unsaid, and she could only wait for the proposal and for the future which, this day of lawyers and snow, had begun to look so hard and cold and close.

8

"Louis was a fool." The voice was grating, harsh and unforgiving. "A damned bloody French fool."

"Yes, my Lord."

"A fat fool! They should have boiled him down for rushlight. He was no God-damned use for anything else!" The man who spoke was an old man of awesome ugliness. He had a small, round head that was perched on an unnaturally long neck. His skin was wrinkled and dark. There was something reptilian about him. He wore a dirty, old-fashioned wig over his baldness. His mouth seemed no more than a lipless slit.

He sat behind a huge desk, a desk covered with papers and brilliantly lit by ranks of candles. In the center of the desk, just before his angry, sardonic gaze, was a large book of engraved pictures. It was a rare and inventive volume of pornography that his Lordship was savoring. Lord Paunceley, government servant, was a collector of such things.

He turned a page that crackled as he handled it. He stared at a picture depicting Leda and the Swan. "If you were to disguise yourself, Owen, for the purposes of rape, would you adopt the guise of a swan?"

"No, my Lord."

"Do you rape women, Owen, or for that matter boys?"

"No, my Lord."

"You, being Welsh, would doubtless choose something less flamboyant than a swan. Would you be a peewit?"

"No, my Lord."

"A priapic peewit?" His Lordship laughed to himself. "Better a priapic peewit than to be King of France. It took two drops of the blade, eh?"

"Indeed so, my Lord."

Lord Paunceley relished the information. "He screamed?"

"So they say, my Lord."

"I wager he screamed! I wager he soaked his royal breeches too." Lord Paunceley smiled at the thought. "I would heartily like to see their execution machine work, Owen."

"I'm sure it could be arranged, my Lord."

"On fat George, you think?" Lord Paunceley chuckled evilly. "Damned Hanoverians! Why we have foreigners for Kings I do not know, and why we choose fat foreigners I cannot think, and why, of all the blubbery mad idiots in the world, we choose farmer George the God-damned bloody Third I have no idea. Doubtless you will report me now, Owen, and have the pleasure of watching my humble neck stretched in the noose?"

Geraint Owen smiled. He was Lord Paunceley's secretary, Lord Paunceley's memory, Lord Paunceley's admirer, and, to a certain point only, Lord Paunceley's confidant. His Lordship, from his lavish Whitehall office, fought a secret war against Britain's enemies about the globe. He did it, Owen thought, brilliantly, despite an avowed hatred of his King.

Lord Paunceley leaned back in his chair. He wore a massive fur-lined cloak over his old, thin body, a cloak so big that, with his long neck and ugly questing head, it made him look uncannily like an ancient, malicious turtle. A fire roared in the hearth. Curtains and closed windows tried to shut out Whitehall's winter drafts. "So tell me what that young fool Werlatton was doing in Paris. I didn't send him to Paris. He's a fool. I should have sent him to Wales, that would have been punishment."

Geraint Owen refused to take the bait. He was as thin as his master, with a shock of black, unruly hair that fell over his forehead. He gestured with Toby Lazender's letter. "He went on private business, my Lord."

"Private business!" Lord Paunceley spat the words out. "His only private business is to unhook his breeches and give Lazen an heir. If he's capable of it."

Geraint Owen forbore to remark that Lord Werlatton might well have done just that if only Lord Paunceley had not leapt at the chance to employ him. Men whose French was as fluent as their native English were rare in this service, rare and valuable. "He went to Paris, my Lord, to kill one of the men who killed his bride."

Lord Paunceley stared at Owen. On his Lordship's face, wrinkled like old leather, there appeared an expression of mock astonishment. "God in His insane heaven! He went to kill a man who killed his bride?"

Owen nodded. The Welshman had a manner of modest diffidence that he had learned as a charity scholar, yet the diffidence, as Paunceley knew, hid a sharp mind. Owen was the only man who could test Lord Paunceley at chess. His Welsh voice was soft and gentle. "He says, too, my Lord, that the French attempted to apprehend him."

"You can't blame them," Paunceley said reasonably. "Anyone with hair that red is asking for trouble."

"They had no cause, my Lord. We were not at war at the time, and they could not have known of this man Brissot's death. It is his belief, my Lord," and here Owen shrugged as though he did not fully believe what he had read in Toby's letter, "that the French have a particular and peculiar interest in his household."

Lord Paunceley began to laugh; a croaking, hoarse, terrible sound that grew like the cackling of a strange bird. "He thinks what?"

"He says, my Lord, that the death of his bride was particular. She was selected, not at random, but with precision. He cites his own experience in Paris. He claims that the names of his bride's killers were given to him to lure him into captivity." Owen gestured with the letter. "It's all here."

"His brain's addled. He must have Welsh blood."

"Most of the great families do, my Lord," Owen observed mildly and with satisfaction. He was rewarded with a thin smile.

"Go on."

Owen put the letter on his Lordship's desk. "You did yourself warn us that the French, if war came, would be looking for a source of money within this country. Could they be trying to take Lazen's money?"

"Bah!" Lord Paunceley stared at the Welshman. "You shouldn't listen to me, I'm an old fool."

Geraint Owen pushed the hair off his face. It was sweltering hot in this room. The fire would still be burning, he knew, in August. "Lord Werlatton begs you to consider his proposals, my Lord."

Lord Paunceley picked up Toby's despatch as though it was smeared with the Black Death. "Begs me! Proposals! No doubt, Mr. Owen, he wants his fat Britannic Majesty's resources diverted to his own private end, if he has one?"

Geraint Owen always knew when he was being dismissed. At that moment he was, for the first and only time, called "mister." "It would not hurt to read his letter, my Lord," he said as he stood up.

Lord Paunceley held Toby's despatch over his waste-paper basket. "Hurt? It will pain me extremely!" He let the letter drop among the other litter. "Tell him to get on with what I sent him to do. Tell him to forget his fancies! Tell him, with my profoundest respects, that he is a cretinous ape." He smiled. "Good night to you, Owen."

Owen paused, as if he wanted to argue with his master, but he knew it would achieve nothing. He nodded. "My Lord."

Paunceley waited until the door was closed, until he heard the creak of the floorboards that told him Owen was some feet down the corridor, and only then did he lean to his right and pluck Toby Lazender's letter back from the basket.

He laid it on Leda and the Swan. He read it through once. Then, with apparent effort, he stood and shuffled to the fire. He threw both sheets of the letter onto the coals and watched till the last scrap had been consumed.

He went back to his desk, moved the precious book and took a clean sheet of paper. He unstoppered his ink, selected a quill, and wrote a letter that would not, quite definitely not, be entrusted to His Britannic Majesty's messengers. The letter concerned itself with the fortunes of Lazen. As his Lordship's quill scratched quickly down the single page his face seemed set in an expression of pure malice. He sanded the letter, folded it, sealed it, then, as the bells of St. Margaret's sounded the witching hour, his Lordship sounded the bell that would summon his coach.

It was convenient, he thought as he carried his rare book with the letter hidden its priapic pages, that the Gypsy was in London. The Gypsy would carry this letter, for the Gypsy was a servant of Lord Paunceley, and this letter concerned the matter upon which the Gypsy was engaged. His Lordship, as he climbed into his coach, peered up into the smoky darkness of London's sky as though he could smell in that sooty blackness the tendrils of evil and intrigue that went from here to Paris and to every capital of Europe. Evil, intrigue, plots, and stratagems; those were the business of Lord Paunceley, that ancient, most savage, most clever and secret man.

March brought a thaw to the valley. It brought brisk winds that tossed the bare trees and drove gray clouds low over Lazen.

It also brought to the valley a Festival of Loyal Britons that declared, not to anyone's surprise, that Republicanism would never sully this corner of Dorset, and that if the Damned French marched up the Dorchester Road then they could expect many a stout blow from Lazen men. The Festival, in truth, was not so much an affirmation of patriotism as an excuse to force the Earl to provide two oxen that were roasted whole, a dozen hogsheads of beer with which to toast the monarch, and wine for the men of substance to drink in the Lazen Arms' Assembly Room that overlooked the humbler festivities in the main street. A good time was had by all, undisturbed by Republicanism or French invaders. George Cartwright, whose jealousy had blazed at Christmas Eve, married the heavily pregnant cause of that jealousy. Spring was coming. Marriage was much in Lazen's mind.

Yet March did not bring a proposal of marriage to the Lady Campion Lazender.

April's first day brought sunshine to light the primroses in Lazen's hedgerows. The second day brought a letter from Toby.

The Earl of Lazen showed the letter to Campion. He watched her as she unfolded it. "What is it? You look as if you've seen a spider."

"Nothing." She laughed. Instinctively her heart had

quickened at the thought that the Gypsy must have brought the letter, yet she dared not betray her interest by asking. She tilted Toby's letter to the window.

He was well. He was fighting. The Vendée was in full rebellion, Frenchmen fighting Frenchmen. He had, he wrote, adopted a nickname to frighten his enemies. Campion laughed.

"What?" her father said. Caleb Wright had just brought him luncheon on a tray. Campion knew he would eat little of it.

"Calling himself *Le Revenant!*" A revenant, in English as in French, meant a creature come back from the dead to haunt the living. She laughed again. "He should call himself carrot head."

Her father smiled. "Young men are full of fancies, my dear. I know another young man who suffers the same way."

"Who?"

"Look out the window."

She did. She dropped the letter. She put her hands to her mouth. Her father thought it was a gesture of delight. "Go down."

"Father!"

"Go on! Caleb and I will watch."

She went downstairs, out to the forecourt, then to the lakeside where a line of amused servants stood waiting for her. Lord Culloden bowed as she approached. In his hands was a white rope.

At the far end of the rope, graceful and gleaming, floated a pleasure barge.

Campion knew that the barge existed. The second Earl was supposed to have built it, and Campion remembered seeing the old boat, its paint long flaked, upside down on hurdles in one of the dim, dusty Castle buildings. Over the years it had been stacked with timber, had been home to mice, sparrows, and cats, gathering dust and cobwebs like so many other half-forgotten splendors in the Castle's storerooms.

Now Lewis Culloden had rescued it. He had more than rescued it. It looked new. It gleamed with white and gold paint.

The barge was thirty feet long with benches for six oarsmen at the bow. Above them, rearing proudly upward, was a gilded, carved prow that bore the arms of the Lazenders in fierce colors.

The stern half of the barge, where the gunwales flared outward, held a small pavilion, curtained beneath an elegant, white-painted, wooden roof. The curtains were drawn back, showing cushions heaped about a table spread with food. Behind the pavilion was a small platform where a helmsman could stand.

Lord Culloden smiled. "If we were doing it properly we would have a second barge, with musicians."

"Doing what properly?"

"Our voyage of discovery." He bowed and offered his hand to let her step on board.

"Voyage!" She laughed. It was a forced laugh. She knew why this thing of beauty had been rescued and repainted. She guessed that all the servants knew too, and that their smiles and laughter were not just for the boat, but for the question they knew would be asked within its curtained pavilion.

She took his hand, stepped precariously on board, and the servants clapped her as if she had done a great thing.

Lord Culloden followed. He shoved at the spongy bank with his foot. "Into the cabin, my Lady!"

The servants were laughing. The barge rocked alarmingly as Lord Culloden took up a long pole and thrust it into the lake bed. The barge moved from the bank.

Campion peered from beneath the carved canopy. "Aren't we to have oarsmen?"

"Your servants are all landlubbers!" Lord Culloden said. "You're going to pole us? We're going in circles!"

It was true. The barge, rather than cutting a straight, elegant course into the lake's center, lumbered in an erratic circle as Lord Culloden thrust the unwieldy pole into the water. He drew it out, weeds and mud dripping from its tip, and swung it inboard. "We shall drift, my Lady."

Drifting into marriage, she thought. She had wondered, as winter turned to spring and the bright leaves showed budlike on the trees, why Lord Culloden had not asked for her hand. Her father's permission had been given, and then nothing had happened! Now that the moment had come she felt oddly unprepared, though she had thought of little else in her private moments.

She leaned back on the cushions. She wondered, for the thousandth time, what she would feel when the question was asked. She decided it was all rather embarrassing. Perhaps, she thought, these things would be better done by letter. She laughed at the thought and Lord Culloden smiled to see her happy.

The sun was reflected in ripples of light on the white-painted pavilion ceiling above the lavish food. There was a cold pheasant with sauce, a frilled ham, two raised pies, tarts, a custard, and three bottles of white wine that lay in ice. Lewis took a corkscrew and opened the first bottle, carefully pouring the liquid into the crystal goblets.

Campion threw bread for a duck that swam past. The servants, as the barge drifted away, turned back to the Castle.

He handed her some wine. "Your health, dear lady."

"And yours, my Lord." She supposed that, once the question was put and answered, he would kiss her. It all seemed rather indelicate. One of her friends who had married the year before had told Campion not to worry. Being kissed was just like being nuzzled by a horse.

Luncheon was delicious, unsullied by any proposal of marriage. He fed her plate with the best morsels, and kept her glass full. The barge, turning with the small breeze, finally lodged gently on the mud by the reeds at the western bank, swung broadside to the lake and stopped. Lewis undid silken cords that let three of the curtains fall, thus making a pavilion with an open side that looked out onto Lazen.

Campion, sitting with her knees drawn up, stared at the Castle. "It's beautiful."

"More so than any house I know." He grunted as he pulled the second cork.

The house looked wonderful, its elegant facade showing against the bright emerald leaves of early spring and the gentle hills where the lambs were growing. She smiled. "Perhaps the barge should be left here. We could come and sit and watch Lazen through the seasons."

"I think it intends to stay anyway."

"What!"

He laughed, cleared some cushions and rugs, and lifted the boards. The water was dark in the bilge beneath them.

"We're sinking!"

He smiled at her. "I think it would be more accurate to say we have already sunk. George Hamblegird said we should soak the thing to let the wood expand, but if we'd have waited for that we'd be waiting till summer."

"How do we get off?"

"I shall summon a boat." There was a small dinghy that was kept by the old church on the Castle forecourt, used to clean the lake's banks and cull the lilies that threatened to spread over the entire surface. Lord Culloden put the boards back. "We'll sink no further."

She leaned back on the cushions, still staring at the Castle, and listened as he told her of the secrecy that had surrounded the rebuilding of the barge. Three of the estate's carpenters had worked on it, under Hamblegird's instructions, always fearful that she might discover the gorgeous craft in their long workshop. Lord Culloden admitted that he had half expected the boat to sink the moment it was launched.

"Didn't you caulk the seams?" she asked.

"Are you trying to teach us sea-faring men how to make ships? Of course we did. Still sunk, though," he laughed.

She turned to look at him. His downward slanting, hooded eyes looked amused. His moustache was flecked by the custard. She decided she did not like his moustache. The water slapped on the boat's side. She laughed at the thought of sinking.

He held out the bottle. "More wine?"

She wondered if he was using the wine to raise the courage to propose to her. She suddenly thought the whole thing was funny and then she thought how mortified he would be if he knew, and that thought also seemed funny to her, and to cover her untimely hilarity she held out her glass for more wine. "We should do this every day."

"Sink?" He smiled and leaned back on the cushions. He looked at her, his face suddenly serious.

Dear Lord, she thought, here it comes.

He frowned. "I must go to London in two weeks."

"You must?" She thought she had sounded rather relieved, so she repeated the words in a more anxious tone.

"I have some small business with the regiment." He shrugged as if it was unimportant, and poured her more wine. "You had a letter from Toby?"

She began to think that perhaps he was not going to propose after all. "Yes."

"How is he?"

"He's tediously bloodthirsty. He claims to have killed eight French soldiers. I'm not sure if I approve."

"That's because you're half French."

"True." She closed her eyes. It was warm. The three closed curtains had stopped the wind coming into the pavilion. She decided that if he was going to ask he would have asked her already. Then came the thought that perhaps he wanted her to sleep so that he could wake her with a kiss. She wondered if the Sleeping Beauty's Prince had a moustache. She decided the wine had made her sleepy. She wondered if people always got drunk to propose marriage. Perhaps that was the best alternative to an engagement by letter.

Lord Culloden said nothing. He stared at the fitful sunlight on the gray water and saw the clouds thickening to the north, and then he looked down at Campion and saw the extraordinary delicacy of the girl, the clearness of her skin, the beauty of her face. Her eyes were closed. He thought of their meeting, and he knew that if it had not been for his slicing sword on the winter road, he would not be here now. He smiled at the memory.

"What's funny?"

He looked down to see her very blue eyes staring at him. "I thought you were sleeping."

"I'm not. Why are you smiling?"

"It's forbidden?"

"When you're in a sinking ship, yes."

"Sunken?"

She laughed. She closed her eyes again. The water made a pleasant, gentle slapping sound against the gleaming paintwork of the barge. Occasionally the craft would lift sluggishly as the wind tugged at the pavilion and bellied the curtains. Campion felt the barge move as he shifted his weight on the cushions, coming closer to her.

"Will you marry me?"

The question came so suddenly, in just the same, bantering tone of voice that he had been using about the old sinking barge, that Campion was startled. It was as if the cold, lapping lake water had suddenly risen into the pavilion.

She opened her eyes.

He smiled down at her, a quizzical look on his face.

She had been waiting for the question since January. Now, suddenly, with the question finally asked, she seemed struck dumb.

His fingers brushed her forehead, stroking her gently. "You don't have to answer me now. I've thought long about it, my dear, long and hard, and it is only fair that you should do the same." The words sounded stilted. She supposed such words always did.

She sat up, driving his hand away, and turned to face him. "Lewis?"

"Campion?"

She was not sure what she wanted to ask. She had thought, when she had thought about this expected moment, to say "yes" on the answering beat of the question, yet now, quite suddenly, she found her practical, sensible mind wanting to probe, to explore, and she shook her head uncertainly. "Marry?"

He smiled. "People do it, you know."

She smiled back. She wished there was not custard on his moustache.

She thought of her father and his wishes. She should marry. She looked at Culloden's pink face, a hint of fleshiness about the eyes, and she supposed that her father was right. This man, this solid, dependable man would hold Lazen against an uncertain future.

He took her hesitation for doubt. He sat up straighter and drew his knees up as hers were drawn up, making the barge rock slightly on its muddy bed. "I don't want to spoil your life, I wish only to make you happy." He touched both ends of his moustache. "I'll leave the regiment, of course, that's why I'm going to London, to sell the commission. Lazen is your life, it has to be, and even when Toby is back we'll live close by." He shrugged. He seemed as uncertain again as the first days after they met. She thought of the bones on Two Gallows Hill. She thought of her father decrying certainty. She thought of LC and CL traced scarlet on a mirror.

He smiled. "I know how you feel about London. I wouldn't ask you to live there, and . . ."

"Lewis!"

He stopped, surprised.

She smiled, shaking her head. She had listened to him and felt a sudden pity for him. He had done all that he could to make this day special, to bring her to a magic place, to make it a day to be treasured in her memory, and then he had seen that she wanted practical, sensible proposals instead of a moment that should be wreathed in gold as splendid as that which circled the Lazen crest on the boat's prow. She took a deep breath. Her decision, of course, had been made weeks before when Cartmel Scrimgeour had visited the castle and drawn up the marriage agreement. This conversation in the barge was merely a polite formality and she must play her part as nobly as Lewis. The words seemed to need a great effort, but she managed to give her answer a smiling certainty. "Of course, Lewis, of course!"

He stared at her.

She smiled. "Yes!"

"You mean?"

"I mean yes! Yes!" He gaped at her in amazement, and she laughed. "Did you expect me to say no?"

"I thought . . ."

"Thought what?"

"That I am not worthy of you."

"Lewis!" She reached for his hands. How could she

tell him that it was she who was not worthy, that it was she who had harbored thoughts of such shame that she could scarce admit them to herself? This very morning, when her father had given her Toby's letter, had not her first thought been of the Gypsy? "Lewis," she had to think of what she ought to say in this circumstance. "I shall be most fortunate in you!"

He took her hands and looked bashfully into her eyes. "I have thought much about it."

"I know."

"I will do all for our happiness. You do know that?"

"Of course!" She wondered why it all seemed so unreal.

He drew her toward him, clumsy on the cushions, and he put his arms about her and kissed her on the mouth.

She closed her eyes.

She had never been kissed like this. She had often wondered what it was like and wondered why there was not one single touch of mystery about it. She pushed her lips against his, wondering if the magic came later. His moustache was definitely uncomfortable. It pricked and it tickled. Being nuzzled by a horse was definitely nicer.

"My dear Campion." He leaned back from her, reached over her shoulder and pulled the cords of the last curtains, shaking the green cloth down so that it seemed they were in a closed, luminous tent that lay on water. "My dear, dear Campion."

He pulled her gently, turning her, stretching her on the cushions and his hands were gentle on her face, on her neck, and he kissed her eyes, her cheeks, her mouth, and she knew he was being gentle and she wondered why she had this terrible, dreadful need to laugh. His kisses pushed her lips onto her teeth. It was uncomfortable, and then she felt his hand slide down to her body. "No, my Lord."

He smiled. He stroked her breasts, the silk dress smooth to his touch. "No?"

She put her own arms about him and pulled him down so that his face was beside hers.

His hand, denied her breasts, slid to her thighs and she found herself wanting to laugh again. It was so silly! All this fuss over marriage and having children? His hand moved upward and she pushed him away. She smiled. "No."

Somewhere in the back of her mind a tall, black haired, blue eyed man laughed at her. She blotted the vision away, angry at herself. She sat up, her hands rearranging her hair. "When I marry, my Lord, I will come to you," she hesitated, "as you would want your bride to be." God! She thought, but this is embarrassing! "Besides." She smiled.

"Besides what?"

"The servants! They'll be thinking the Lord knows what!" She pulled one curtain back and tied its cord.

He untied it. "Let them think."

"No! They shall know we are to be married." She was tying the cord again. "And they shall know that we are to be married properly."

He smiled. "Forgive me."

"For what?"

He shrugged. "Impatience?"

That embarrassed her, but she knew the proper response. "That's very good in a husband to be, yes?"

"I don't know, I've never been one."

It was done then, she thought. It had been, she decided, about as bad as she had expected it to be. No worse, but no better either. It had felt odd to be kissed by him, odder still to feel his hand pressing on her body. It was all odd, all rather embarrassing, and all tempting her to unseemly laughter. She wondered whether any of the custard from his moustache was on her mouth, but thought it would be rude to be seen wiping it with a napkin. She looked at him. "I'm very happy, Lewis." She said it as a test, to see if it was true. She was not sure that it was, but perhaps happiness, like the magic of love, was something that came with time.

"As you shall ever be."

She stared over the water, wondering if her father watched them from the window by his bed. She did not know what to say. The wind ruffled the lake and died. Coots swam red and black by the reeds. She remembered a question that was important on these occasions and smiled at him. "When?"

He smiled back. "I'm impatient. Soon?"

She blushed. "There must be preparations."

"Preparations?"

"The tenants have to be fed. Musicians." She shrugged. "The usual things. A betrothal party to make it proper." She laughed. "We can have the betrothal party when you come back from London. You can take the invitations with you."

"Dear, practical Campion."

She wondered if she would ever enjoy being kissed, but at least he had been gentle. She had rather feared that making love would be like a prize-fight.

The boat unexpectedly lurched, sliding on the shelving mud, and Campion gave a cry of alarm. "Lewis!"

He laughed. "We're shipwrecked."

"My God, we are!" The barge was canting and moving, sliding into deeper water and she could hear the gurgle of the lake coming between the sprung planks. "We'll have to swim!"

"I'll carry you."

"You can't!"

He could. Every movement seemed to lurch the pretty barge farther into the depths, but he made her crawl out from the pavilion and then he carried her carefully forward, over the newly painted thwarts, until he could put her feet on the forward seat. The barge seemed to be still again, but half its width was under water. He jumped over the gunwale.

He shouted with surprise as he sank into the mud, the water bitterly cold and up to his thighs. "Come on!"

"You'll drop me!"

"Never! I'm rescuing you again!"

She laughed, put a hand on the great, surging prow, a foot on the gunwale, and then half sat, half dropped into his arms. She was laughing, he was laughing, and then he turned, sucking his boot out of the clinging mud and forcing it into the roots of the tall reeds.

"You're dropping me!"

"I'm not!"

"Careful!"

He pulled his other boot free. "Stop laughing! You're shaking me!"

"It's fear, not laughter."

He forced his way up the bank, through the reeds, stumbling at the very last to fall to his knees, making Campion laugh and shout in alarm, and then he stretched himself out to drop her, almost gently, on the very edge of the park's grass where it met the swampy bank.

Behind him, half hidden by the reeds, the gorgeous barge tilted in the water.

She laughed at him. The front of his clothes was soaked by thick mud. "It's very romantic, my Lord."

He smiled down at her. They were hidden from the house by the tall reeds. He bent his head, kissed her, and before she knew what was happening, his left hand ran strongly down her body from her breasts to her knees, and the shock of it made her gasp and his tongue was between her teeth and then, as swiftly as he had stooped down to her, he lifted his head. His hooded eyes were dark above her. "You will make me very happy, my love."

She nodded. She found it hard to say the expected words. "And you me, my Lord."

It suddenly did not seem funny anymore. The kiss had been too savage, too quick, too suggestive of that bigger hurdle which lay beyond marriage. She sat up, shivered, and suddenly went utterly still, her eyes huge and fixed on the castle.

"What is it?" Culloden frowned. Campion had gone white. She sat, one hand at her breast, staring across the corner of the lake as if a ghost walked the castle's forecourt. Culloden could only see a groom exercising a horse. The man was tall, dressed in black, with long black hair. The groom, Culloden noted with a cavalryman's eye, rode superbly. He looked back to his bride to be. "What is it?"

"Nothing."

Culloden squeezed her hand. "We should tell your father."

"Yes, my Lord." She knew the Gypsy had seen her. He must have brought Toby's letter, she thought. She could see his face, a hundred yards away, turned toward them, then the horse pranced, he put his heels back, and rode toward the stables.

She stood slowly. He was there, and suddenly she knew there would be no happiness for her so long as the tall horseman hovered at the edge of her life. Lord Culloden still frowned at her. "You're well, my dear?"

"Yes, my Lord." She sounded subdued. "I'm well."

They walked about the lake, engaged.

It rained that night. It started slowly, a mere mist that beaded the windows. By nine o'clock the wind was lashing water at Lazen, a seething storm that crashed on the forecourt's gravel and rattled the doors of the castle.

Campion and Lord Culloden dined with the Earl. She made herself happy. She told herself that the art of marriage was to fashion contentment from the flawed cloth. She laughed at her father's familiar stories, smiled at Lord Culloden, and tried to forget that single glimpse across the lake's corner of the mysterious horseman.

"The lake will be flooded," the Earl said. He was drinking brandy with Lord Culloden.

Campion stood. She went to the window and stared into the turbulent darkness. A shaft of lightning made her jump. It splintered, blue-white, down to Two Gallows Hill and outlined the horror hanging at the gibbet.

"Can you see the lake?" her father asked.

But she was not looking. She was staring at the corner of the Long Gallery. She knew that the gallery was unused this night, that its fires were dead, its candles cold, yet a single flame showed in the western window.

"Campion?"

"No." She let the curtain drop, turned, and smiled at her father. "It's too dark."

"Dirty bloody night." Her father took another glass from Lewis Culloden. "A night for dirty, bloody business, eh? Broomsticks and cauldrons." He raised the glass. "Your happiness, my children."

Campion smiled. She was nervous again, frightened and excited. A hundred hundred times since Christmas she had told herself she was glad that the Gypsy had not been in the gallery that night, told herself she was fortunate to escape, yet now, beckoned by the candle, she forgot the relief. "You'll forgive me if I retire, father?"

"So you should, dear. Leave us men together." He smiled. There were patches of color on his sunken cheeks, put there by the liquor. She kissed him.

"I'll ring for your girl?" Culloden asked.

"No. She'll be waiting for me." She gave her betrothed her hand. He kissed it, his moustache prickly.

Thunder hammered at the castle, rolling over the sky like hogsheads trundled in an attic. Crossing the bridge between the New and Old Houses Campion saw the lightning flicker to ground, showing in its sudden glare the seeping, spreading lake water.

She passed the door to her rooms. She blushed. She knew she blushed. She should have gone to her rooms and let Edna help her to bed, instead she went to the upper lobby and turned to the Long Gallery's main door.

Perhaps Edna had lit the candle. Perhaps a footman had come to fetch something and left the solitary flame burning. The door handle was cold. She pushed it down and went into the room.

And through her, as sudden and bright as the lightning on the lake, went relief. The Gypsy was there.

He stood before the Nymph portrait. He turned to look at her and, as if her entrance meant nothing to him, he turned back to the portrait. He had drawn his hair back and tied it with a ribbon.

She stood watching the Gypsy, her hand on the door handle. She knew she should say something, demand an explanation for his presence, but she seemed dumb.

He turned to her again. The candle flame was reflected in his oddly light eyes. "Should I be here, my Lady?"

"No." They spoke in French.

"Then I hope my presence doesn't offend you." He spoke comfortably, as if to an equal. She did not reply. He stepped back from the portrait and gestured at the western door of the gallery. "Isn't that room haunted?"

"So they say." Still she did not move.

He smiled. "Your brother says a man was murdered there."

"I've heard it, yes."

"But you don't believe in ghosts?"

"Do you?" She said it defiantly. She knew she should send him away, she knew she must play the great lady, but she wanted to talk with him, she wanted to see the candlelight on his thin, superb face, she wanted to hear his voice in her ears.

He smiled again. "Yes." He gestured about the room. "I think that everybody who was happy here and everyone who was sad here left part of themselves, don't you? Would the room be the same if it had been built yesterday?" She said nothing. He half bowed. "I hear I must congratulate you, my Lady, on your own happiness."

"Thank you." She wondered how it was possible to have a conversation like this. She let go of the door handle and walked a few paces toward him. "I think you should go." It seemed an extraordinarily hard thing to say.

He stared at her. His smile seemed to suggest that he knew what she had wanted to say. "Yes."

Neither moved for a few seconds. If he stepped toward her, Campion thought, then she would step toward him. If he lifted a hand she would lift hers. If he opened his arms she would go to him, and she waited, expecting it, wanting it, and almost moved toward him when his hand did move.

He picked up the candle. "My Lady?" His voice was soft as velvet, dark as the night. He sounded so strong to her. She said nothing. She was trembling like a colt feeling the bridle for the first time.

He turned toward her, smiling, and he saw that her lips were parted, her eyes bright, and he thought that at this moment she was even more beautiful than the splendid, smiling woman in the Nymph portrait. He stepped one pace, his own heart beating with the fragility of the moment, when the door opened.

The Gypsy smothered the candle flame with his hand instantly.

Edna stood in the light that opened from Campion's bedroom into the Gallery. The light of a dozen candles flooded from behind her. "My Lady?"

"Edna?"

The maid was sleepy. "I thought I heard voices."

"I came to find a book."

"In the dark?" Edna laughed. "I'll fetch a candle. Raining something terrible, isn't it?" She turned back to the room. Campion, like a conspirator, looked to gesture the Gypsy into hiding, but the gallery was empty. Like a cat, like a shadow in a shadow, silent as a dark thing in darkness, he had gone. In less time than a heart fills and empties, he had gone. She felt a sadness, as if he had spoiled a game, and then Edna came back with a flickering candle and asked what book Campion sought.

"Red leather cover. I'll manage."

But the maid had frowned. "I know I shut that door!" She walked to the gallery's end where the last door, the door to the haunted room, let in a draft. "It must be the ghost, my Lady."

"Yes."

"I know I shut it before!" She pulled it hard closed. "There. You've got your book, my Lady?"

Campion had picked a book at random from one of the tables. "Yes."

Edna smiled nervously. "You look as if you saw the ghost!"

Campion smiled. "To bed, Edna." Campion went to her room with thoughts of what had happened this day and what had not happened. She went in sadness. She wondered what kind of man it was who called himself a horse-master, yet moved like a ghost in great halls. In one second more, she knew, she would have forgotten her place, would have forgotten the marriage that was now arranged, and would have been in his arms.

She dressed for bed, and even in her room she could hear the wind savaging the great house. It came from the northwest, a wind from the ocean beyond Wales, and it was made turbulent by the hills and heavy by the storm water.

It hammered at the castle windows, blew boughs down in its woods and lifted thatch from the cottages.

It took the barge, the pretty pleasure craft, and lifted it in one last voyage from the mud to topple and float and slowly sink. The cushions floated free. Three empty bottles bobbed unseen on the dark lake. Uneaten food, the crystal, the silver forks and knives, the white linen, all slid from the table and then, unnoticed in the storm's anger, the barge sank.

In the morning, on a lake littered with twigs and timber broken from the park's trees, only one corner of the shining pavilion roof was above the gray water. Campion saw it then, saw the light reflected bright from the white paint, but she spoke to no one of the barge's fate, preferring it to be unsaid, just as the word love had been unsaid the day before. The die was cast, her promise given, a man to be forgotten, and a life to be lived. She would be married.

9

On the day before Lord Culloden left for London the bones that had hung on Two Gallows Hill were brought to the castle. They were pounded in a stone trough and, true to the Earl's word, the sieved powder was mixed with the feed of the Home Farm pigs. The Earl declared that he wonderfully looked forward to the bacon. Campion, busy answering letters of congratulation, tried to ignore the jubilation that attended the final destruction of her attacker.

The next day, the day on which Lord Culloden would leave, brought her the pleasure of a new phaeton that she had ordered from London. It was even more dashing, more dangerous than the old vehicle. Simon Burroughs looked suspiciously at the gleaming, fragile carriage that had been brought on a great wagon and unloaded down wooden planks to the forecourt. "Looks like a crow's nest on wheels, your Ladyship."

She laughed. "It looks fast, Simon!"

"Oh fast! It looks fast," he said dubiously. "But you bit one stone in that, my Lady, and it'll just be tinder for next winter's fires."

She insisted that the bays, their coats clipped and gleaming, should be harnessed to the carriage. Burroughs, as the horses were backed into place, was relieved to see Lord Culloden strolling toward them. His Lordship touched his moustache ends with his gloved fingertips and walked around the new carriage. "Marvellous! Marvellous!"

"You'll take her Ladyship out, my Lord?" Burroughs said hopefully.

"Of course! Why not?" He smiled at her. "Rattle down to Periton, my love?"

Campion, who had ordered the carriage herself, had wanted to be the first to drive it, but she succumbed with good grace. The sad truth was that Burroughs, like every other man in Lazen, did not believe that a girl could drive as well as a man.

Lord Culloden gave her his hand and she climbed to the buttoned leather seat and felt the vehicle sway as her betrothed climbed up beside her. He gathered the reins, pushed the whip into its socket, and shouted at Burroughs to let go of the offside leader's head.

They went slowly over the town's cobbles, the hooves sounding crisp, and then they gained the dry, earth surface of the Shaftesbury road and Lord Culloden let the bays go into a quick trot. The wind tried to lift her skirts and she had to tread on their hems. She laughed with the speed of it, the marvel of the light carriage's motion.

To her right the Castle was spread in the spring sunshine, the vast banner of Lazen lifted over the Great House. She saw, on the sun-sparkled surface of the lake, the small white patch of the sunken barge's roof, and then the road dropped into a grove of beeches and hid Lazen from her. The manes of the bays were bouncing with the speed, the bright new leaves of beech seemed to whip past in a blur of light and shadow. She laughed.

"You're happy?" He smiled at her.

"I'm happy, my Lord." They both had to shout over the noise of hooves and wheels, and then he handed her the reins and she let the horses run where the road bordered the Lazen stream.

Two miles from the Castle she slowed the horses and turned them over a stone bridge that led to stone gateposts. The gatehouse, no bigger than a toll cottage, was empty. She trotted the horses up a drive that curved between thick laurel until the gravel opened out before a large, white painted house. It had been rebuilt in the fashionably classic mode, its lines severe, its windows regular.

She let the horses slow and stop.

Lord Culloden smiled. "Shall we go in?"

She shook her head. The plaster inside was still damp and smelling, indeed, would not be dry, the builders said, for three more months; longer if the spring was wet. Then, when all the alterations were complete, and the plaster dry enough to take the paint and gilt, this would be their marriage home, Periton House. Stacked on the forecourt, amidst a litter of timbers and ladders, were bales of horsehair and barrels of lime, the ingredients for the plaster that still had to be put into the big reception room.

Lord Culloden frowned. "There's no one working!"

"It's the Spring Fair at Shaftesbury," she explained. "Father said they could go."

He grunted in apparent disapproval.

Behind the house the hill climbed steeply, thick with beeches, while before it a great lawn sloped to the Lazen stream. In the trees that edged the lawn she could see the haze of bluebells that would thicken in the next few days.

Lord Culloden was leaving this day. He travelled to London in one of Lazen's coaches, going to his regiment to sell his commission and wind up his affairs, and when he returned they would be married. First there was to be a great party, a celebration before the event, for which musicians were coming from London and fireworks from

Bristol. The wedding, two weeks later, would be a quieter affair, as the fashion was; merely the Bishop, a few score guests, and a meal in the Great Hall that evening. The Earl, whose disease was wasting him and drawing ever deeper lines on his ravaged face, had sent to Lord Paunceley demanding, even ordering, the return of Toby for the celebrations.

Campion looked at the windows above the pillared carriage porch of Periton House, windows that looked dark against the limewash, and she thought that there, behind the dark glass, was her new bedroom. That was where the mystery of marriage, the mystery that seemed so commonplace and uninviting, waited for her.

Culloden's gloved hand rested on her forearm. "We shall be happy here, my dear."

"Yes, my Lord." She said it dutifully. She knew that he wanted to kiss her. She smiled and picked up the reins. "Home, my Lord?" She meant Lazen, and she turned the horses skillfully on the gravel turning circle of the house.

She said her private farewell to Lord Culloden in the Long Gallery. Mrs. Hutchinson expressed her fear that, instead of selling his commission, his Lordship would discover the regiment riding to war and, as a true-born Englishman, go with them. Lord Culloden smiled at her. "If that happens, dear lady, I will bring a thousand banners to lay at your feet."

Mrs. Hutchinson laughed and lifted the sewing that lay on her lap. "Not too torn by your sword, I trust!"

"And for you, my dear," he lifted Campion's hand and kissed it, "I will bring the crown of France, that France does not want, and make you a queen."

She laughed. She saw how the flesh of his neck bulged at his collar. In ten years, she thought, he would be as fat as butter. He smiled at her. "May I ask a favor of you, my Lady?"

"Of course, my Lord."

He turned to one of the many tables in the Long Gallery and picked up a small, framed portrait of Campion. "That I may take this as a foretaste of joys to come?"

The painting had been done three years before. It showed Campion in a dress of cream silk. In her hands, held at her breast, was a bunch of pink-red campion flowers, and her face was an expression of shyness and delight.

Mrs. Hutchinson smiled. "That's my favorite of her!"

Lord Culloden looked at the portrait in its gilt frame. "It is most beautiful, my Lady, but does not do you justice. But I would still ask it as a favor of you."

She laughed. "Then take it, my Lord, with all my heart." And as she said it there came a memory of another man, taller and darker, who had stood in this room and stared at the Nymph portrait and, as she watched, the small portrait picked up by Lord Culloden, she wished, with all her heart, that it was another man who took her likeness for his remembrance.

He left in the spring sunshine. Campion, when the coach had disappeared between the gatehouses, went to her father's room. She had made it her duty to clean him these days, to share with Caleb Wright the blood and the mess, and to give her father the love that alone made his pain and dying bearable. At least, she thought, her father would see her married before he died, and for that, if for nothing else, she was glad.

Lord Egmont Paunceley was a contented man as he sat alone in his parked coach. He was well wrapped in a fur cloak that he had bought when, as a young man, he was attached to the British Embassy in Moscow. On his right side was a basket of comestibles; jellied duck, pies, a plum cake, and four bottles of good Burgundy. Lord Paunceley was on a day's outing.

On his lap was a book, a fine edition of the *Histoire de dom B,* a piece of illustrated French pornography that was deservedly famous among collectors. It was, he reflected, so much finer than the badly illustrated, crude, uncivilized works that now came from Paris. The new fashion, he thought sadly, was to write about perverted peasants, while his Lordship's taste ran more to the humiliation of high-born virgins.

It was a mild spring day, the crowd large, the hawkers of pies and lemonade loud. Lord Paunceley's coach was within the private enclosure. He closed his book, placed it carefully in a pocket, then drew back the curtain of the right hand window. He nodded with pleasure at what he saw.

The public stands were full. That was good. Moreover the crowd was in a good mood, which was interesting. Nothing could tell the temper of the country better than this crowd. Lord Paunceley raised a glass of wine to his ugly face. What was most astonishing, he decided, was the number of people present! Did they not have work?

He saw Geraint Owen coming across the grass and he rapped on the window. He scowled as the Welshman climbed into the coach. "You're letting in a draft, man!"

"Good morning, my Lord! A fine one, yes?"

"Passable. You brought the dispatches?"

"No, my Lord, I threw them into the Thames." Owen placed them on the table that folded down in front of Lord Paunceley.

His Lordship stared distastefully at them. "Well?"

Owen smiled. "You have the papers from last week's meetings of the Committee for Public Safety, my Lord. Nothing of note except a letter to the American President requesting that he keeps his treaty obligations and declares war on us."

"Ha!" Lord Paunceley stared out of the window. "Is that all?" For a man who had just been given papers purloined from the highest committee of the French government, he sounded distinctly churlish.

"A private letter for you, my Lord, from the Earl of Lazen."

A wrinkled, dry, claw-like hand was abruptly thrust from beneath the great cloak of wolf fur. "Give it to me."

Owen wondered whether he would be offered wine. He was not so fond as his master was of these expeditions, and a little wine would help him bear the festivities. As Lord Paunceley scrabbled the letter open and tilted it toward the light, Owen leaned forward to look out of the right hand window.

Beyond the glass was a small, scrubby area of mud where a few blades of grass tried to survive. The patch of ground was almost entirely surrounded by tiers of seats, high enough to obscure the new buildings that had spread out from London to encompass what had once been the dairy land of Tyburn.

In the center of this arena was "Albion's Fatal Tree." Once, Geraint Owen supposed, there truly had been a tree on this spot, but if so it had long since disappeared. It had been replaced by a great timber construction, three posts placed in the ground and joined, at their tops, by three long beams that formed a triangle supported twelve feet in the air.

A ladder was against the beam closest to the private enclosure. A man straddled the great timber, looping a rope that ended in a noose.

Lord Paunceley put down the Earl of Lazen's letter, then spooned some jellied duck into his mouth. "Our fellow goes first, I trust?"

"Indeed, my Lord," Geraint Owen nodded.

Their fellow was a Frenchman. He had claimed to be

secretary to the executed Duc de Sallons, but Achilles d'Auxigny had asked him what color were the silk hangings of the Duke's bed and the so-called secretary had said blue. Achilles had sighed. "They were pink, dear boy, always pink. Rather pretty, as I remember." A search of the émigré's luggage had revealed a paltry code book and instructions for the man to find out what ships were being constructed in Britain's naval dockyards. He would be hanged this fine morning.

Lord Paunceley waved his spoon at the rope. "It won't be quick, I hope!" he said anxiously.

"No, no!" Geraint Owen reassured him. They never hanged spies quickly. It spoiled the crowd's enjoyment.

Lord Paunceley peered at Owen. His Lordship's reptilian, questing face was screwed in displeasure. "Do you drink wine in Wales, Owen? Or only water? Ale, perhaps? Or do you have some particular Welsh beverage? Crow's blood? The bile of toads? The juice of virgins squeezed at midnight into coconut shells?"

"A glass of wine would be most pleasant, my Lord."

"It's very good wine," his Lordship said dubiously.

"I'll do my best to survive it, my Lord."

His Lordship poured him a generous glass. "I do so enjoy these occasions. When you are my age, Owen, you will find that an execution is a most marvellous tonic. To be old and to see the young die! That is a measure of success, is it not? There. Sip it. I paid four shillings a bottle, and God only knows how high this war will drive that price. Where's Lord Werlatton?"

The sudden question merely confirmed Owen's suspicion that the Earl's letter had been about his son. "In the Vendée, my Lord."

"Not murdering people in Paris?"

Owen smiled. "He's in the Vendée, my Lord."

"How soon can we send word to him?"

Owen shrugged. "Within a week."

A great cheer spread through the tiers of seats and Lord Paunceley peered anxiously through the window. "Ah ha! Our work, you see, is not in vain!"

The Frenchman, dressed in boots, breeches and shirt, was a fine looking man. He stood in a cart, his head held high and the wind stirring his dark brown hair. Lord Paunceley chuckled. "A loss to the ladies, eh?"

"Indeed, my Lord." Owen was thinking that his Lordship would have done better to let the wine sit in his cellar for another two or three years. He decided it was best to say nothing.

The cart that held the prisoner passed close to Lord Paunceley's carriage. His Lordship laughed. "A brave young fool, Owen."

"Indeed, my Lord."

"And all so laughably pointless! They only had to read the Naval Gazette! Still, we must not be ungrateful for the entertainment they will give us." Paunceley rubbed at a speck of dirt on the window. "The Earl of Lazen, Owen, wishes us to summon his son home. He is to come for his sister's nuptials. Her virginity is to be sacrificed to some lumpen ape of the aristocracy and I am supposed to bring Werlatton back so he can watch the proceedings! Oh, splendid!" This last was because the Frenchman, who had reached the gallows in his cart, was trying to make a speech about liberty. One of the jailers brought the speech to a swift end by the simple expedient of punching the man in the belly. The blow doubled him over and conveniently allowed the noose to be slipped over his dark head and tightened.

Lord Paunceley was leaning forward, tongue between his teeth, watching. "Gently now! Gently!"

The carthorse was urged slowly forward, and the Frenchman forced to walk backward by the tension of the rope about his neck. The crowd were silent. They grinned. There was small sympathy for the death of a Frenchie, except for a few women who thought it a terrible waste of a good looking man.

"Gently! We don't want to lose him!" his Lordship said anxiously.

The prisoner's feet came to the end of the cart, they were seized by the executioners who had jumped to the ground, and, as the cart went away, they took the man's weight and lowered him slowly so that the rope tightened, his head tilted to one side, and then they let him hang.

"Good!" Lord Paunceley smiled. The man would choke to death slowly, very slowly, his legs dancing for the entertainment of the crowd. "Very finely done, Owen, very finely done!"

Geraint Owen looked, frowned, and looked away. French spies had to die, of course, but he would have preferred them to die a soldier's death, standing before a firing quad. Yet he allowed that this slow, agonizing death might be a deterrent to others.

The Frenchman jerked, his legs moving as though he were trying to swim upward in the air and take the choking, blinding pain from his neck. Lord Paunceley smiled as the crowd cheered. "That will teach him to count His gross Majesty's ships!"

"Indeed, my Lord."

"It seems, Owen," Lord Paunceley had his head turned away from the Welshman, "that the Earl is dying. He would like his son to be at his deathbed. Touching, yes?"

"Indeed, my Lord."

"Ah! He's watered!" Liquid dripped from the Frenchman's dangling boots to the pleasure of Lord Paunceley and the crowd. "I like Lazen, he's a good man. You know he once held my office?"

"I did know, my Lord."

"He wasn't as good as I, of course. Oh but this is magnificent!"

The Frenchman was twisting on the turning rope. His right leg was in spasm. Lord Paunceley watched avidly. He came frequently to the gallows for this entertainment. "The French are so inhumane, Owen."

"They are, my Lord?"

"Machines for killing people! What next? They call it 'sneezing in the basket'!"

"I had heard, my Lord."

"Ridiculous! This is the natural way, Owen, God's way! It gives the man time to dwell on his transgressions, to repent, to prepare his soul." Lord Paunceley's fur-swathed shoulders shook with laughter. "So how do I get Lord Werlatton back to England in a hurry? Tell me precisely so that I may reassure Lazen."

The prisoner choked, loud enough for Lord Paunceley to hear. The man was twisting and jerking and the crowd was roaring its approval.

Geraint Owen had leaned back on the seat so as not to see the death agonies. He closed his eyes. He blotted out the baying of the crowd and thought instead of the small ships that plied the channel and decided the Navy was wrong for this task. To use the Royal Navy meant making a request of their Lordships of the Admiralty and answering God alone knew how many ridiculous questions. Instead, the Welshman decided, he would use one of the many smuggling ships that ignored the war to keep the gentry supplied with brandy and good wine. "I can have the *Lily of Rye* there within two weeks, my Lord."

"The what of what?"

"The *Lily of Rye,* my Lord."

"Sounds like a harvest whore. And have it where?"

"There's a village called Saint Gilles. It has a small quay. We've used it before."

"Then use it again, pray. What day should Werlatton be there?"

Owen thought again. In his remarkable head he kept, along with the myriad details of the secret war, a tide table of the Channel. "He has to be there on the nights of the fifteenth and the sixteenth, my Lord. The usual signals."

"Whatever they may be. How you do enjoy your work, Owen. Very well. I will write to Lazen and tell him that His corpulent Majesty's resources will be laid at the altar of his daughter's virginity, and you will inform Lord Werlatton to come and witness the loss of his sister's purity. Do you think she is a virgin, Owen?"

"My Lord, I have not the first idea."

His Lordship chuckled. "One does doubt it. So few girls are these days. It goes out of fashion, Owen, like a full-bottomed wig. Soon it will be a mere word in the lexicon and the young will need to have it explained. Oh, how sad!" This last was not for the extinction of virginity, but rather because the prisoner's twitching was slow and fading. "He's going! You remember the one who lasted four hours?"

"The Gascon?"

"The very same." Paunceley watched the hanging man and frowned. "He's gone! It was hardly worth the journey, Owen." The prisoner's knees were slowly drawing up. "From being His Majesty's prisoner, he has become His Majesty's corpse. Do you think vulgar George would like it if I presented the body to him? With an apple in its mouth?"

"I would never presume upon the tastes of my betters, my Lord."

Paunceley laughed. "Fat George isn't your better, Owen. He's not fit to lick your impediments. So, Saint Gilles? The fifteenth or sixteenth?"

"Indeed, my Lord." Owen had never known his Lordship be so interested in the minutiae of an expedition.

"The Harvest Whore?"

"The *Lily of Rye,* my Lord."

"Then so be it. Arrange it. Expedite it!" The tortoise-like face turned to Owen. "I suppose Lord Werlatton has not whined to you anymore about his family being persecuted?"

Owen smiled. "No, my Lord."

"No tales of hooded men besieging his sister?"

"No, my Lord."

Paunceley laughed. "I knew there was nothing in it! Nothing at all! What nonsense young men do utter!" He turned back to the window and watched as the body-men scrambled to cut down the corpse. They could fetch fifteen guineas from an anatomist for such a fine specimen. Paunceley smiled. "I intend to stay for more pendant pleasures, Owen. I believe we have a brace of women this morning! You wish to stay?"

"Your Lordship is very kind . . ."

"You were ever an accurate man."

"But I will decline, my Lord."

"So be it, Mr. Owen, I bid you good morning. Pray do not ventilate the carriage as you go!" Lord Paunceley shivered ostentatiously as the Welshman left, and then, before the next victims arrived, and before even returning to the book in his pocket, he wrote down the details of the ship and the rendezvous that would fetch Lord Werlatton home. He was getting old, he thought to himself, and the memory was not what it was, not what it was at all. Then, the details noted, he tucked his pencil and notebook away and settled back for more immediate and entertaining pleasures.

On a May night, a night warm and glorious with spring, Campion sat at her table in the Long Gallery. The windows were open. The curtains bellied slowly like a line of strange white ghosts.

Most of the gallery was in darkness. A few candles burned on her table where she sat beneath the Nymph portrait. The candle flames shivered in the soft breeze.

Before her, on the table, were four jewels.

"I love him, I love him not, I love him, I love him not." She said the words aloud, sadly and slowly, placing the jewels one by one from her left to her right side. Each jewel had a long, golden chain that trailed on the table.

These were the jewels of Lazen.

They were seals for marking hot wax. Each golden, jewel-banded cylinder was tipped by a mirror-image of steel. One mirrored the axe that had taken St. Matthew's head, the next St. Mark's winged lion, the third bore a winged ox for St. Luke, while the last showed a serpent wound about the poisoned chalice of St. John.

She looked up at the Lely Nymph portrait. The first Countess, the first Campion, wore these jewels about her neck. It was said that these jewels, these seals of the Evangelists, had once controlled all of Lazen's fortune, all its future.

Each of the gold cylinders unscrewed. Within each seal was a second symbol, fashioned in silver, though the significance of these hidden symbols had long been forgotten. In St. Matthew was a crucifix, in St. Mark a naked woman, in St. Luke a tiny pig, and in St. John was nothing. There had been something once, but someone in the past had taken the symbol out.

She unscrewed the seal of St. John and felt with her finger the rough edges of the small claws that had held whatever had once been inside. Something missing.

She felt an extraordinary sadness.

At least, she thought, the Gypsy was far away. She tried to persuade herself that her unworthy madness was over, that his face was a fading memory, and her shame a secret that receded into a forgotten past. Yet she knew she had not forgotten him. The prospect of marriage was made worse by the thought, the hope, that the Gypsy would come to Lazen with Toby. On a day when she should be most happy, she would be forced to see that haunting face and feel the awful, shameful, secret longing.

She slowly joined the two halves of the seal of St. John. Once this house had been under siege, and all of it for these jewels. Now they were kept in a locked box in a locked room and she doubted whether they were looked at from one year's end to the next.

The age of chivalry, she thought, is gone. That of sophisters, economists, and calculators has replaced it.

Soon she would be married.

She touched the seals one by one. "I love him, I love him not, I love him," she paused with the seal of St. John in her hand, then slowly put it with the others. "I love him not."

The servants smiled differently at her, as though the prospect of marriage had changed her. It was childhood's end, she supposed, her initiation as a woman was close, and she wondered why she felt nothing when Lewis Culloden touched her. She wondered if there would be magic in his kisses if he shaved off his moustache.

Marriage, she told herself for the hundredth hundredth time, is a compromise. It is a decision about money, about lands, about inheritance. It is an arrangement.

Love, she told herself for the hundredth hundredth time, is a fiction for kitchen girls. Love was not a sudden glory of light that dazzled and changed the world, it was something that grew. It was a responsibility.

She looked again at the splendid, smiling woman who was buried in Lazen's old church, yet seemed to live on in the great portrait. The family said that she had fought for this house, that she had gone through the valley of darkness and hatred and war so that Lazen could exist. Did it all come down to marrying Lewis Culloden? Was all romance, and all glory, and all magic just a child's tale, as insubstantial as the naked nymph who swam in the water-silk? Was love really this insidious, slow, calculating progress toward marriage?

Yet she was being unfair, and she knew it. Sometimes, in the dark nights of winter, she remembered the leering, filthy face that dribbled on her nakedness, the way the man had fumbled with his knife at her waist, and then she remembered too the savage joy of the hoofbeats, the sweep of the great sword that sounded so triumphant, the shout of fear, the crunch of the blade going home, then why, she thought, was love not invested with the same glory? Did Iseult feel disappointment when Tristan kissed her?

It seemed almost unfair that it should have been Lord Culloden who had rescued her, and she knew that to be an unworthy thought. Yet there were times when she imagined that it had been a man with black hair and an arrogant face who had ridden to her rescue. She imagined the Gypsy's hands comforting her. She would try to fight that waking dream, but in her longest, loneliest nights it had been a curiously comforting dream to have.

There were times when, instead of shame at the memory of the two nights when she had come into this gallery to seek the Gypsy, she felt only regret. To be touched once, she thought, just once and feel the glory. If the glory existed.

She suddenly felt a terrible, terrible fear, as though that empty darkness above Two Gallows Hill was her future. The thing in its chains no longer hung there, but it seemed to her that the dry corpse, mere bones held by sinews like bowstrings, still danced and mocked at her.

She was to be married, and where there should be life and joy and expectation was only a sullen dread.

And then, sensibly, she decided that her thoughts were no more and no less than the thoughts of any other young woman on the threshold of marriage. She was not special. She had no right to expect more from love than anyone else. In all things, she told herself once more, she had been blessed above others. In this one thing, marriage, she would be ordinary.

She smiled. She was a calculator too.

She put the seals in their box.

One by one she closed the windows, saving the servants the task, and shut the darkness out with the mirrored reflection of candlelight.

There was no certainty. There could be no certainty. The only thing to do was to live. Soon she would be married, she had promised it, and with that promise she had abandoned the hopeless dreams of love and had accepted the realities of life.

She closed the lid on the golden seals.

She was a calculator.

Then so be it. She picked up the box and went to bed.

10

The walls of the room were undressed stone. Water dripped to make puddles on the stone floor. Despite the spring weather it was cold in this great, echoing hall of stone that was lit by high-bracketed torches. There were no windows.

It was night.

The echoes rose, fell, then rose again. Grunts, the slap of feet on the stone floor, the sound of flesh hitting flesh.

There was a deep shadowed gallery at one end of the hall, a place for people to watch the proceedings on the flagstoned floor below, though on this night the gallery was empty. It should not have been empty. Valentine Larke, one of the men in the hall, kept looking to the gallery to see if Chemosh had yet arrived. Larke frowned. If Chemosh did not come this night, then Chemosh would have failed the Fallen Ones and Chemosh would die.

Valentine Larke, Belial of the Fallen Ones, owned these premises. London knew them as Harry Tipp's Rooms and it was here that the gentry came to meet the Fancy, the prizefighters, to box with Harry Tipp himself, to fence in the long hall, and to exchange stories in the steam baths that Harry Tipp kept filled with lithe-bodied foreign manservants who understood the needs of tired gentlemen.

Yet the greatest appeal of Harry Tipp's Rooms, greater even than the curtained alcoves of the steam room, was the presence of the criminals who came to meet the gentry in the liniment stinking halls.

The gentry and the criminals were, in Larke's view, made for each other. Each had a distaste for work, a passion for gambling, and no aversion to tipping the odds their way. The hungry, cruel men who came from the rookery of Saint Gilles could find employment of a sort at Harry Tipp's; mostly commissions from gentlemen who wanted an enemy maimed, killed, or merely terrified. Harry Tipp's was where a young man came to prove the part of his manhood that Abigail Pail's establishment could not satisfy. It was a masculine institution, loud with shouts and brave with boasts, and, with the exception of Abigail's profits, it was Valentine Larke's most lucrative business.

Yet tonight the curtained alcoves of the steam baths were empty, the plunge pool's surface was still, the punching bags rested, and no shoes squeaked on the French chalk of the fencing hall. No cooks served pie and eels in the echoing dining room, and the wine cellar was locked. Harry Tipp's Rooms were closed by order of Mr. Larke. Closed but not empty.

In the echoing, stone hall Valentine Larke motioned with his hand for the big man to cease his work. He walked past him and stared at the naked man who was sprawled on the floor. The man was bruised and bleeding. One eye was almost closed, his lips were swollen, yet still the naked man seemed to spit hatred and defiance at Valentine Larke.

"Bugger's got nerves," Abel Girdlestone said grudgingly.

Abel Girdlestone, more than six feet tall, was one of Harry Tipp's prizefighters. His face was mashed from the times he had stood toe to toe with opponents and hammered with bare fists for more than a hundred rounds. Girdlestone had once gone a hundred and eight rounds with the Jew, Mendoza, before that famous fighter had pounded him insensible to the turf. That defeat was among Abel Girdlestone's proudest memories. His fists, hardened by spirit and the leather punching bag, were like hammers of scarred flesh and bone. He was stripped to the waist, his great chest gleaming with perspiration.

"Bugger's got nerves," he said again. "If you'd just let me hit him proper, sir." He added eagerly.

Larke shook his head. "He has to live."

"We have all night." The man who had spoken, his voice like something from the pit, was even bigger than Girdlestone, a man of such vast size that to look at him was to be astonished. Harry Tipp was a Negro, rumored to be an escaped slave, and seemingly made of ancient, blackened oak. Tipp had stood a hundred and nineteen rounds against Mendoza until, in awed admiration, the Prince of Wales had declared the fight to be drawn and then ordered the cheering spectators to pull the two bloodied heroes back to town in an open chaise.

To be a confidant of Harry Tipp was now the height of fashionable ambition in London. He called no man "My Lord," even the Prince of Wales only received an occasional and grudging "sir." To be praised by the huge, unsmiling Negro was an achievement more prized than the Garter itself. He stood over the naked man, looked at him with an expert eye, then turned to Larke. "Use the girl."

Larke considered the black man's suggestion. Behind him, at a small table, the two lawyers said nothing. They were awed by the two huge men, terrified of the violence they had seen, and hoping only that this night's work would soon be done. Larke nodded slowly. "The girl mustn't know I'm involved."

Tipp jerked his massive head at the balcony. "Watch from there."

Sir Julius Lazender moaned. His tongue, exploring his swollen, bleeding lips, found a tooth missing. His body seemed to pulse with the pain of the great fists, yet, like a mastiff that would not see that the bear had him beaten, he tried now to get to his feet and strike at Valentine Larke who had arranged for this pain and humiliation.

Harry Tipp casually slapped Sir Julius down. Girdlestone laughed. "You snicker him, Harry."

"The girl will be quicker. Help me with him."

There were iron rings high on the stone wall, rings left from the time when the hall had been a warehouse, and the two huge men lifted the naked, bleeding Sir Julius and, ignoring his kicks and shouts, tied his wrists so that he hung with his back to the stone. There was blood in his cropped, black hair, blood on his ribs and thighs, yet still the belligerent, twisted face snarled and cursed them.

Valentine Larke left them. He climbed the winding gallery stairs. He ducked under the low door at the top and there stopped. He felt a sudden, welcome relief. At the balustrade, silhouetted against the flamelight of the fighting hall, was the tall figure of Chemosh. The man had evidently just arrived, was even now shrugging his caped greatcoat from his shoulders, Larke, who had feared treachery, suddenly knew that the plans of the Fallen Ones were still intact.

Chemosh stared down at the naked, beaten, bleeding man. He turned as he heard Larke's footsteps. "He doesn't give in easy."

"He's stupid. He has a brain of bone. You're late."

"For which I apologize." Chemosh sounded unworried by the curt, ungracious words. He dropped his hat and cane on the floor. He was superbly dressed, his silk stock tied to perfection, his blue jacket brilliant with embroidery. Beside him Valentine Larke, in dull, dark cloth, seemed drab. Drabness had become a way of life to the politician, a man who preferred to stand in the shadows and let others dazzle the fools in the crowd.

Valentine Larke's father had been the tenth Earl of Melstead. His mother had been the wife of Lord Melstead's coachman. Valentine Larke was the eldest son of an Earl, and all for nothing because he was a bastard.

He had hated his coachman stepfather who had fawned on Lord Melstead, bringing up his Lordship's bastard and thanking his Lordship for that honor and for every new favor. And favors there were many. Lord Melstead educated the boy, encouraged him, and secured him employment as a clerk in the Admiralty. Valentine Larke spent his long days copying state documents and working his silent, obedient way up the hierarchy of the civil service.

And his nights he spent as a hunter.

The tenth Earl of Melstead died and was succeeded by his son, and Valentine Larke hated his young half-brother who had set about dissipating the fortune which, according to Valentine Larke, should have been his birthright.

At night, the ink still on his fingers, Valentine Larke followed the eleventh Earl until he knew the places where the Earl whored and gambled and drank and vomited and whored again.

There was war then. A French army, helping Washington's rebels, was driving Britain out of the thirteen American colonies, and somehow the French government always knew when new British Battalions sailed and where they sailed to, and how many ships escorted them, and what the fleet orders were.

Valentine Larke had a sober, serious, painstaking reputation as an Admiralty clerk, while his air of discretion and willingness to work long hours brought him advancement. He worked on papers of the highest secrecy and each paper, carefully copied, was paid for by the French. At night that money was used for other purposes.

He gambled and discovered that his intelligence, his love of science and mathematics, made him a formidable player of whist. He never won too much, and took care to lose when it was politic to lose.

He was tolerated by the quality. They did not know who he was, except that he spoke well enough, dressed with modest elegance, and paid his debts. If he needed to cling to their coat-tails then they were happy to let him. He was the butt of their jests, the object of their insults and a willing runner of errands. They thought it was pathetic to see the gratitude he showed whenever he was noticed.

The eleventh Earl of Melstead, ten years Larke's junior, did not even recognize his half-brother. They had rarely seen each other in childhood, and Larke did not remind him of their relationship. He did not even give his first name when they met.

"Larke! Old coachman called Larke!" Melstead guffawed. "Up early, what!"

Larke ruined him that night. No one knew, of course. They saw Larke win a modest thousand pounds and took no notice when Melstead pushed his note of hand across the table with a bored air. "Settle you soon, Larke."

"Of course, my Lord. Thank you, my Lord."

The eleventh Earl had turned his fat, stupid face to the rest of the company. "Anyone fancy Mother Tillie's tonight?"

They left Larke and went noisily into the night and Melstead tupped his last whore. He came out of Mother Tillie's in the small hours and found two men waiting. They were huge men, one black, the other white, and they had been hired for this night's work.

"Larke! Damned inconvenient. They were positively rough!"

Valentine Larke had not said a word. As if laying cards on the table he put down the Earl of Melstead's notes of hand. He had bought them, bought half the Earl's debts, and on his broad, intelligent face there was no sign of mercy.

"The bailiffs will be at all your houses today."

"Larke!"

"You call me 'sir'!"

He had, too. Larke smiled at the memory. The fat fool had begged on bended knees, had wept when Larke had threatened him with debtor's prison, but had fallen into abject, terrified silence when Larke played his last card with exquisite care.

"You want the world to know that your coachman's son is now your master?"

The Earl of Melstead had signed the papers prepared by Larke's lawyers and then, on that same morning, blown his brains out. Two huge men who wanted to make their names in the Fancy ensured that he did so, and thus did Valentine Larke secure his first great property, mortgaged to be sure, but redeemable. He had left the Admiralty, regretted by all, claiming that a maiden aunt had left him a modest windfall.

Wherever the quality went to enjoy themselves, there Larke was. He was mocked still, no one knew he was the money behind the whorehouses and behind the gambling clubs and cockpits. He was Valentine Larke, rumored once to have been a clerk and now, by a lucky will, a man of independent means. He was still good for an occasional loan, for a bottle of champagne, even to run out into the rain to call a coach, yet no one ever thought to connect Valentine Larke with the men who disappeared, who ran from their country, who committed suicide, who sold their last acre and last jeweled pin.

He became a member of Parliament, buying a Midlands constituency that he never visited, but which regularly returned him to Parliament in return for his gold. He bought it, not to be respectable, but because the *Illuminati* had ordered it. They hoped for a revolution in Britain, a revolution like the one they had sparked in France, and Larke spied out the land for them. He was a politician, a man of business, yet above all he was a hunter.

He hunted the privileged. He enticed the gaudy beasts into his garden of earthly pleasures, and there he picked his prey. Only one of his victims had escaped, and that was Chemosh. Instead of running or fighting, Chemosh had recognized Larke's strength and had proposed that they join forces. Chemosh went where Larke could not go. He scouted victims for Belial. They had hunted together for seven profitable years.

Now Chemosh smiled as he stared down into the wet, stone hall. A girl had been admitted through a side door. "Who on earth is she?"

"A whore." Larke stood in the shadows. "One of Abigail's."

"She's very fetching."

"She was."

The girl crossed the stone floor and the sound of her rustling dress carried easily to the balcony. She had lustrous, heavy hair, dark brown, that was looped beneath her ears and pinned with pearl clips. Her face was sensual, wide mouthed and big-eyed.

Sir Julius Lazender watched her approach. His breath rasped in his throat.

The girl stopped six feet from him. Harry Tipp stood on one side of her, Abel Girdlestone on the other.

She stared with loathing at the naked man, then, slowly and deliberately, she untied the laces of her bodice. She did not speak. Sir Julius licked his swollen, bloodied lips.

She pulled her dress down to show scarred breasts. She let Sir Julius stare at her. "You did this."

He shook his head in pathetic, hopeless denial.

She pulled the dress up and tied the laces. She turned to Harry Tipp and held out a hand. The Negro took pincers from his breeches pocket and placed them in the girl's palm. "There's a razor too." Harry Tipp held the girl back for a second. "And don't touch his right hand."

She nodded. "I don't want his right hand. I want the teeth he bit me with." Harry Tipp let go of her shoulder and, for the first time since she had entered the room, she smiled.

"No!" The shout was a wail, a moan, a scream that rose as the two big men came to hold Sir Julius's legs and the girl walked slowly forward.

On the dark balcony Valentine Larke smiled. "Harry was quite right. She'll break the bastard." He turned to Chemosh. "I think we need somewhere quieter."

The noise faded as Larke led Chemosh to Harry Tipp's private quarters. One scream seemed to linger in the deserted buildings, but then was cut off as Larke closed the sitting room door. The noise was replaced by the sound of a spinet, an odd sound for such a masculine establishment. Larke gestured Chemosh toward a chair. "You're getting fat."

"So?" Chemosh smiled. "Aren't husbands supposed to get fat and comfortable?"

"I have never," Larke said, "been married." He grunted as he pulled the cork of a bottle of Sillerys. "Harry Tipp is not pleased with you. He's distressed about Scurdon."

"I'm sorry." Chemosh did not sound sorry. He sounded surprised that the matter of Jemmy Scurdon had even been raised.

"Tipp's a very loyal man. He looks after his people. He wanted my assurance that Scurdon had to die."

"Of course he had to!" Chemosh said.

Jemmy Scurdon, poxed, drunken and long past his fighting prime, had been hired to attack Lady Campion on the Millett's End road. Chemosh had travelled to Lazen to scout the attack, but his first glimpse of the girl, six days before Scurdon arrived, had put the idea of marriage into his head. What better way to effect an introduction than to save her from rape? It was so simple that any fool could have thought of it. And what better way to ensure that she did not marry the wrong man than for one of the Fallen Ones to be her husband? Thus, at the last moment, he had changed his plans and, instead of depending on Scurdon's ravages, he had decided to sacrifice the London man.

Larke raised his glass. "My congratulations on your betrothal, my Lord."

"You're very kind, Larke."

"You've done well." Larke was grudging.

Lord Culloden laughed. "I've been the bashful suitor, Larke. I've had to put up with the God-damned country! Have you ever spent Christmas in the country?"

"No."

"It's positively barbaric! Hunting's decent, but as for the rest!" Lord Culloden shook his head. "Do you know I even go to church for her!"

Larke did not smile. "I hear she's uncommonly beautiful."

Culloden sat, reached down to his coat on the floor, pulled it till he could get his hand into one of the capacious pockets, and brought out a paper-wrapped package. "See for yourself."

It was the gilt-framed portrait that showed Campion in her cream silk dress with the flowers at her breast. Larke sat opposite Lord Culloden and stared at the small painting. "A good likeness?"

"Excellent. If anything she's prettier."

"A figure to match?"

Culloden laughed. "Scurdon showed me enough of it." He sipped his champagne, remembering how he had stared from the bushes as Campion's clothes had been torn from her. He could see the thighs now and remember his excitement that had been so intense that he had almost been too late in fetching his horse that had been hidden in a hollow. "She's quite beautiful, Larke, quite utterly beautiful. Better than anything you keep at Abigail's."

Larke still stared at the portrait. "She's half a d'Auxigny, of course. Marchenoir said her mother was beautiful." Larke smiled and hefted the portrait. "Perhaps we should send this to Citizen Marchenoir, eh? Whet his juices a little."

Culloden said nothing. In the next room Mrs. Tipp played her spinet, the notes tinkling and bright.

Larke's voice was low. "Are you in love with her?"

Culloden laughed. "In love? I fancy her, any man would, but by God you couldn't live with her! She's so . . ." he paused and waved his hand, "dutiful? I had almost forgotten what goodness was like, Larke, how utterly boring it can be. And I do not really think I can live with that unending passion for horses and books. Yet she does have such obvious compensations, don't you think?"

Larke stared at the portrait. "She does. Indeed she does. You could fetch a hundred guineas a night from her." He laughed. "I think I shall send it to Citizen Marchenoir. He likes pretty aristocrats."

"Likes them?"

"Likes killing them." Larke smiled and gestured with the portrait. "You don't mind?"

"My dear fellow!" Lord Culloden said expansively.

Larke put the portrait carefully on the table, stood, and

his rippled, oiled hair shone in the candlelight as he crossed the sitting room that was lavishly decorated with red velvet and with framed prints of Harry Tipp's famous fights. There was a large portrait of Mrs. Tipp smiling in young, coy prettiness toward the artist. She was indeed young, she was pretty, but hardly coy. She ruled the huge fighter with the same ease with which she ruled the finances of his business.

Larke drew back a curtain and stared down into the street. "Lucifer is worried." Culloden said nothing. He was expecting this conversation. Larke let the curtain drop. "He is worried because the will was changed."

"Hardly to our disadvantage," Culloden said mildly.

"Not to yours, my Lord."

For a few seconds neither man spoke. The spinet stopped next door, paused, then Mrs. Tipp made another attempt at a difficult trill of ascending chords. The ormolu clock on Harry Tipp's mantel whirred, then struck midnight.

Larke returned to his chair. "How is the Earl?"

Lord Culloden shrugged. "Half dead."

"Good."

"I just have to marry the girl before he goes, I can't wait through a period of bloody mourning."

"No, you can't." Larke's voice was soft, his face unreadable. "And then, Lewis?"

Lord Culloden smiled. "When her brother dies, she inherits."

"Which will leave you as heir to Lazen. And when she dies, Lewis, it will leave you as owner of Lazen, and you do know that she has to die, don't you?"

Lord Culloden said nothing. He twisted the champagne glass in his fingers, wondering where the bubbles came from that appeared magically and streamed endlessly from the bottom of the glass. He watched for a dozen heartbeats, then turned his oddly hooded eyes to Larke. "Sir Julius gets five thousand a year. His heir will inherit Lazen, not me."

"And if he has no heir?"

"Then I inherit," Culloden admitted. He put his glass down and smiled. "Does that worry you, Larke?"

"Oh no!" Larke's voice was sarcastic. "We've only worked for two years to give you the biggest damned fortune in England. I've only spent forty thousand to get nothing! Of course it doesn't worry me, Lewis, whatever made you think it worried me?" He stared malevolently at Chemosh. "Does it worry you?"

Culloden said nothing.

Larke looked at the portrait. "It must be a pleasant prospect, Lewis. Bed her, take her money, and let Lazen protect you? Had you been thinking that? Had you been thinking that as lord of Lazen you would be beyond the reach of the Fallen Ones?"

Culloden, who had considered just that, smiled. "Of course not."

Larke closed his eyes and leaned his head back. "It must be most tempting, Lewis, most tempting, but don't think of it, don't even think of thinking it." He opened his eyes and stared at the moustached man. "You do not know Lucifer, but I will tell you one thing, Lewis, and that is that he is clever." He let the word hang like a threat. "Clever! He knows your temptation. Do you think he has not planned against it?" He reached into his pocket and brought out a sheaf of papers. "It was your idea, Lewis, to marry the girl rather than make her unmarriageable, but did you think Lucifer would not take some precautions against the danger of your changing loyalty?" He threw the papers on the table next to Lord Culloden. "You will sign these, my Lord. You will sign and you will seal them. If you do not . . ." He did not finish his statement.

He did not have to. Culloden had seen what Abel Girdlestone and Harry Tipp had done to Sir Julius. He had been summoned from Lazen and he had thought hard about refusing the summons, but Lord Culloden, better than most men, knew Valentine Larke's hidden reach. If he had refused, then he would have had to guard his back every moment until his marriage, and the likelihood would be that no marriage would take place because the groom would be dead. Lord Culloden, who had enjoyed tantalizing Larke these few minutes, knew that enough was enough. He reached for the papers.

The first was a confession that he had hired James Scurdon to attack the Lady Campion Lazender and that he had then murdered Scurdon as a means of ingratiating himself with the Lady Campion.

The second paper only became effective at his marriage. It agreed that whatever property he thereby acquired, and whatever property he inherited at the death of his wife, was transferred to . . . there was only a blank space. In consideration of this forfeiture the agreement promised Lord Culloden an income of twenty thousand guineas a year for life.

Culloden tapped the blank space. "Lucifer?"

"Of course. I've signed a similar paper, Lewis."

Lord Culloden smiled. He was signing away a fortune, yet he knew it was a fortune he could never have held. The Fallen Angels would see to that. In its place he was receiving a prince's income. It was, he knew, a fair agreement. It was what he had hoped for when he came to London in answer to Larke's summons. He scrawled his name on the papers, dripped wax, and stamped his signet ring down to make two bright seals. He lifted the paper that was a confession of murder. "What will you do with this?"

"Trust me, Lewis. It will be safe. When we have won

it will be returned to you. Until then?" Larke smiled and reached for both sheets of paper. He put them into a pocket, then poured more champagne in a gesture of conciliation. "You say the Earl will die soon?"

Culloden laughed. "It's astonishing he's alive. The Castle believes he clings on to see his dear daughter married. After that?" He clicked his fingers. "Goodbye."

"And Lord Werlatton, you'll be delighted to know, is trapped. He will not be at your wedding." Larke did not expand that good news. "So we can be sure that father and son will be dead within a few weeks. One by sickness, one by war." He smiled at the thought. "Deaths, Lewis, which no one can lay at our door. And after that, we must find a similarly elegant solution for your wife."

Culloden stretched out his shining boots. "A riding accident. She's utterly besotted with horses. Told me the other day she wants to breed the fastest damned horse in Britain. Why can't she take a fall? Break her pretty neck? It's simple enough, Larke, no one will be astonished. But do give me time to roger her first. It's not often I get a hundred guinea whore for free." He laughed.

Larke gave a dutiful smile. "I see one difficulty."

"What, for God's sake? She takes a fall! What could be simpler?"

Larke sipped his champagne. "Her father dies, her brother dies, then she dies. I think some people would smell something foul, don't you?"

"Then wait!" Culloden brushed the difficulty away. "Give her a year or two."

"I doubt that Lucifer will want to wait that long." Larke spoke mildly, but there was a subtle threat in his voice. "Think about it, Lewis. Maybe you're right, maybe she can tumble off her horse, but there must be no foul stench." He said the last three words slowly. "I don't want lawyers buzzing around that honeypot."

There was silence. Lord Culloden was not sure how to prevent such a scandal, but it was a problem that could be delayed. First he would marry her, then deflower her, and only after that would he consider the manner of her death. He sipped his champagne. "And what happens to Sir Julius?"

Larke smiled. He put his champagne glass beside the portrait "Shall we see?"

Lord Culloden followed Larke through the long fencing hall, past the racks of foils and épées, the sound of Mrs. Tipp's spinet fading behind them. They went over the upper landing, past the billiard hall, and onto the gallery of the fight room.

The girl had gone.

Sir Julius no longer hung from the iron rings. He was sitting at the lawyer's table, a blanket about his naked shoulders. His right hand, undamaged in the evening, held a quill. Lord Culloden could see spots of blood that marked a trail from the rings to the table.

Larke leaned over the balustrade. "Mr. d'Arblay?"

One of the lawyers held up a hand. Sir Julius scratched with the quill, then leaned back. His mouth was a pit of blood.

Mr. d'Arblay took the papers, then turned with a smile to the balcony. "They're signed, Mr. Larke."

"I am most obliged to you, d'Arblay."

"The obligations are entirely mine, sir."

Culloden knew what Sir Julius had signed. He had signed what most of Larke's victims signed, a paper that gave away their future inheritances. Sir Julius had been led into debt, and then the trap had been sprung. Now Larke would reap the harvest.

Larke smiled. "Mr. Girdlestone?"

The huge prizefighter turned his face to the gallery. "Sir?"

"Sir Julius is now in your charge. Treat him kindly! He may have liquor, comfort, and a whore! Remember he is to be Earl of Lazen, so treat him with respect!"

"Sir!" Abel Girdlestone seemed to come to attention.

"And be ready to move him to Lazen on my orders, Mr. Girdlestone."

"Sir!"

"Mr. Tipp?"

The Negro looked up, but said nothing.

Larke smiled. "I shall need eight or nine other men. You can provide them?"

"Of course?"

"And yourself?"

Harry Tipp frowned. "No, Mr. Larke, you know that, Mr. Larke. My Betty!"

"Of course." Larke laughed. He straightened and turned to Culloden. "You see the dangers of marriage, my dear Lewis? Look at him! Even the Prince of Wales fears him, yet that slip of a girl has him under her tiny thumb. She won't let him leave London for fear of highwaymen!" Larke laughed at the Negro, then clapped Lord Culloden on the shoulder. "Be grateful to me, Lewis, that you will not be burdened long with a wife."

Culloden smiled. He knew that Larke's unnatural jollity came from the knowledge of victory. This night's events, the papers that had been signed, had brought the triumph of the Fallen Ones very close. The Earl was dying, Lord Werlatton was trapped, Sir Julius baked in the lawyer's pie, and Lady Campion was marrying Chemosh. Lazen was doomed. The day of Lucifer was close.

11

"It's horrid!" Lady Campion grimaced at the portrait.

"It's mother!" Uncle Achilles protested. "She has discovered, she tells me, that desiccated plums assist her digestive system. She says she will live to be a hundred and ten."

Campion laughed. The yellow drawing room of Lazen was slowly filling with wedding gifts. The Duchess d'Auxigny's had just arrived, a portrait of herself. She simpered out of the painting, all her lines removed by the artist, and her hair piled impossibly with a profusion of stones, feathers, and pearl ropes. Campion shook her head. "I can't think that Lewis will want it."

"Lewis is an Englishman. He'll probably think it's wonderful art." Her uncle flicked a speck of dust from his velvet sleeve. "Mother would like to come with her plums for your wedding. Do you think you can bear it?"

"I can bear it."

"Poor mother." Achilles said it lightly. "She's pretending to be in mourning for Philippe. She isn't, of course, but you'll have to endure the sobs and gulps. She plays the bereaved mother rather as I imagine a hippopotamus would. Do hippopotomae exist? I can't think so, they seem such an unlikely aberration by the Almighty, but then, I suppose one could say that of mother."

Achilles d'Auxigny, once Bishop of Bellechasse, was

now the Duc d'Auxigny, Marquis of a score of obscure villages and Count of two score more. He thought it laughable. His elder brother, by insisting that the revolution would blow itself out like a freak storm, had found himself and his sons in a Paris tumbril that carried them to Dr. Guillotin's machine. Achilles thought his elder brother a fool to have stayed, and now that the slew of titles had descended upon his middle-aged, elegant shoulders, he shrugged them off. "If people think I'm a Duke, dear niece, they'll only wish to borrow money. I'm as poor as a church mouse."

"Then you shouldn't have bought this. It's lovely." Her uncle had brought his own present to Lazen, a one hundred and thirty-eight piece set of Meissen porcelain, the glaze as hard and delicate as anything from China. She kissed his cheek. "It's much too generous."

"Nonsense. As I expect to retire to your house some day I thought the least I could do was make sure you serve my meals on decent plate."

She laughed. "Not French porcelain?"

"Meissen is better." Her uncle sighed. "However I will expect a Sevres chamberpot in my bedroom."

"It will be yours."

At one end of the great table was a basket filled with scarlet and white sword knots of twisted silk. In the French fashion they would be presented to all the men who attended the wedding. Beside them, in a second basket, were fans of ivory and Nottingham lace for the women. The rest of the table was heaped with porcelain, silver, gold, paintings and jewels. Cartmel Scrimgeour had sent from Lincoln's Inn a golden basket heaped with gold and silver fruits. Campion showed it with delight to her uncle. "Isn't it generous?"

"Considering the fees he takes from Lazen it's a mere bauble!"

"Uncle!"

He laughed. "Of course it's generous. Scrimgeour is one of those rare things, an honest and generous lawyer. What on earth is that?"

"That" was a japanned work-basket sent by Aunt Lucretia on behalf of herself and her son Sir Julius. Achilles lifted the lid and frowned at the array of colored threads. "She thinks you're a seamstress?"

"At least she remembered."

"My dear girl, she never forgets! Once you and Toby are safely out of the way she'll be the mistress of Lazen, and God help it then. She'll put green curtains everywhere and paintings of small, plump children. Quite ghastly. Toby and yourself have a duty to survive in the interests of art. I do like this." He lifted a crystal decanter, mounted in silver, from among the matching goblets.

"That's from Sir George Perrott. He apologized for the paucity of the gift."

"I like Sir George," Achilles said. "He's not complicated." He ran a finger down a marble statue of Ceres, crowned with harvest wreaths. "Who gave you this?"

"The Earl and Countess of Fleet. They're distant relatives."

"I'm sure they were glad to be rid of it. My God!" This last was occasioned by a vast, gloomy painting that showed St. George and the dragon. A half naked maiden, chained to a rock, strained forward for the benefit of the spectator, revealing huge white breasts, a snack denied to the dragon by St. George's bloodied lance.

Campion laughed. "Lord Paunceley."

"My God! You are honored. He probably found it in some forgotten room of his house. She's not nearly nude enough for him and he'd much prefer it if the dragon was nibbling at her. What are you going to do with it? Hang it in the stables?"

"And frighten the horses?"

"True." Uncle Achilles laughed. "Does he still write to your father?"

"Every month. Do you ever see him?"

Achilles shrugged. "I'm admitted to the presence every few weeks to offer my humble opinion on some poor émigré." He smiled. "I suppose you'll have to thank Lord Paunceley for that monstrosity, but then he is a monster."

"Truly?"

"A monster! A most ugly monster. But very clever." Uncle Achilles lifted a Wedgwood cup, part of a great set of jasperware. "You're getting a rather good painting from the town."

"I'm not supposed to know that."

"Well you do now." He put the cup down with a grimace that suggested English china was not worth a Frenchman's perusal. "They're painting Lazen for you. The man's rather good. I gave him a few suggestions about technique." Uncle Achilles smiled at her. "You're happy, then?"

"Resigned to it, uncle."

"That's the spirit. Like a lamb to the slaughter, dear. What are you going to wear?"

"White silk, Brussels lace, orange pinners and the Lazen jewels."

He pretended to think about it, then nodded. "It will do. I shall find something to match, something that won't put you entirely in the shade."

She smiled. Uncle Achilles would give her away. Her father had promised to be in the old church for the ceremony, but he was sicker than ever and sometimes Campion thought that it was pure strength of will that kept him alive just to see her married.

Uncle Achilles stood back and stared at the profusion of gifts. "At least marriage looks profitable."

"Doesn't it?"

"And Toby will be here?"

She smiled. "That's the best news."

"The best?" He raised his eyebrows. "My dear niece, I thought the best news was that you will be united in matrimony with a fine, upstanding Lord?"

She smiled, took his arm, and walked with him through to the oval drawing room, and then to the great chamber. "People keep telling me that I mustn't look for magic."

"They do? How insufferable of them!"

"Well, you told me!"

"I did? I must have been in an avuncular mood that day." He stopped, smiled and looked into her eyes. "If you had the choice now, my dear Campion, to marry or not to marry, what would you say?"

She looked back at him. She paused, she shrugged, she smiled shyly. "I think I'd say 'no.' "

"Truly?" His fine, intelligent face was serious. "Truly? You want me to stop it?"

"Oh, uncle!" She took his arm again and went with him down the great, curving stairs which led to the ballroom. "Am I very silly in wanting some magic?"

"Are you looking for it?"

She smiled. "I suppose so."

"Then you won't find it. I do remember telling you that." They walked out of the ballroom, through the wide folding doors and beneath the Gibbons carvings to the front hall. The great doors that were usually left shut had been folded back and measurements were being taken for carpets that would be laid on the pedimented front steps. It was from here that the guests would watch the fireworks launched from the lake's far bank.

They stopped on the top step. Uncle Achilles drew his cane along the square base of one of the pillars. "Do you remember my father?"

"The Mad Duke?"

"He always wanted magic, and that's why he built that stupid shrine." Achilles's voice, talking about his father, was tight with displeasure. "All the candles to go out at once! The doors opening to show him in his chamber, the secret tunnel, the hidden chambers for the musicians. The secret funnels for turning water into wine!" He shook his head. "I learned one thing from him, my dear, that there is no magic. I used to think that place so special! Standing in the darkness, knowing I was alone and the drawbridge was pulled up, and then there was my father!" Achilles flicked his fingers open from his thumb. "Pouf! I was astounded! He had worked a miracle! He was God! Then I discovered it was all done by simple, simple machines, and a tunnel under the moat! So simple as to be laughable!"

She smiled sadly. "So there is no magic?"

He walked with her down the steps. "Oh, there's magic. The spread of stars? A daffodil? Even your face." He smiled at her, then shrugged. "If you don't marry him, there'll be scandal. You'll make him unhappy, even your father unhappy. The lawyers will be like pigs in a sloppy trough. None of that matters. It's totally unimportant. If you can look at me and promise me that you know this is wrong, that this will condemn you to unhappiness, to a life of dislike and envy and hatefulness then, I promise you, I will stop it."

She stared at him. She felt the temptation. She said nothing.

"Think! Better now than on the day. It's so embarrassing when everyone is in church."

She smiled. "I suppose it's just nervousness. Are all brides nervous?"

"All brides are nervous and all brides are beautiful. I suppose you're terrified of the nasty business that follows marriage, yes?" She shrugged, but said nothing. Her uncle laughed. "I can't blame you. It always seemed to me to be a business suitable only for peasants. It's cheap, they find it pleasurable, and the necessary equipment is widely available. I never did quite see it as an aristocratic pursuit. It lacks an element of civilization. It also produces children, but you probably want children, yes?"

"Yes."

"You poor thing." He smiled. "Do you think Lewis is a bad man?"

She shook her head. "No."

He touched her cheek with his finger and looked lovingly at her. "Are you in love with someone else?"

"No, uncle!" She laughed and turned away from him.

Achilles's voice was soft behind her. He stirred the gravel with his cane. "You think I know nothing of life, child?"

"More than anyone I know."

Her uncle's voice was still soft. He spoke almost casually, as if he talked of the weather or what they might eat for luncheon. "He's French, so of course he's good looking. He's more than that. He's splendid! I grant you that, splendid as a great horse can be splendid, or an eagle can be splendid. It's just nature, child, blooming a great blossom on a crude bush."

She turned to him. She was truly aghast, astonished that he knew. She shook her head, unable to say anything. He laughed and held up the hand which bore his bishop's ring.

"No one knows! You've been so discreet, my dear niece, but you forget that I was with you when you first saw him." He took her elbow and walked a few paces toward the lake. "And I watched you on the night of Christmas Eve. He was brave where Lewis held back. You think I didn't notice? That I didn't watch you with him? You desire that tall, mysterious Gypsy, don't you?"

She could not admit to it. She said nothing. She felt tears of shame pricking at her eyes.

"You want him," Achilles said, "and that is entirely natural. But you can't have him."

"I know." She said it so softly that she wondered if he even heard.

He dropped his cane and put his hands on her shoulders. "You are a lady, dear niece. You come from a great family. You have the blood of kings in you. If this world has a future, then it needs that blood. You do not mingle it with dross."

"I know."

He smiled. "Don't be ashamed. No one knows except me, and that's because I watch like a hawk. I wasn't even sure till just now and I couldn't resist finding out." He said it mischievously, making her laugh. He patted her shoulders. "You must marry good blood, child. You can have him as a lover, but he must not father bastards on you."

"Uncle!"

He laughed. "Is he the problem?"

"I don't know." She smiled sheepishly.

"Has anything happened?"

"Of course not!"

"Forgive me for asking, my dear." He stooped and picked up his gold topped cane. "So, do you want me to stop this marriage?"

She turned away from him and stared at the sunlight which glinted on the roof of the sunken barge. She thought of the Gypsy, of the lone, still candle in the gallery, of the sudden touch of his warm hand in the dance. She felt an odd relief that Achilles knew, that he had understood, that he had told her that the shameful feelings were natural.

"Well?"

She looked back to him. She thought of the scandal if

the marriage did not take place. She thought of her father. "No, uncle. I don't want you to stop it." She spoke decisively, and she saw relief show on his thin face. He leaned forward and kissed her cheek.

"Well done, O most favorite niece of mine."

She smiled. "You didn't want to stop it, did you?"

"No. I just wanted to see if you wanted me to stop it." He laughed at her, pleased with himself. "Do you think we can go inside now? The sun is so bad for my complexion."

She took his arm and went back into the Castle that was being prepared for the ceremony and celebration of her marriage.

The *Lily of Rye,* a fine schooner, was a smuggling ship. No exciseman could touch her, she was too fast and too well sailed. Yet Captain Nathaniel Skeat's disdain of the Excise cutters and the Royal Navy did not stem from his ship's speed, but rather from the piece of paper in his cabin that bore the seal of His Britannic Majesty and guaranteed that the *Lily of Rye* was hired to the British government for services unspecified.

Those services, in addition to providing the brandy and wine that would find its way to Lord Paunceley's table, consisted of taking British agents to deserted parts of the French coast. Sometimes the same men would appear a month or so later to be picked up, but too often Captain Skeat never saw his passengers again.

The French navy or privateers could be troublesome, but the French did not have a single ship that could outsail the *Lily,* and on his frequent rendezvous with French smugglers Captain Skeat was told which enemy ships were ready for sea and where they would patrol. Then English gold would pay for French brandy and the *Lily,* her sails looming in the darkness, would bend for home.

Captain Skeat expected no troubles on his present task. He was riding off the northern Biscay coast, waiting for midnight, and he had Geraint Owen's assurance that the shore here was in the hands of the rebels. He still took no chances. The ship carried no lights except for the shielded lantern over the compass. His sails, like many a smuggler's sails, were dark as night. The hull was painted black.

A longboat was in falls at the ship's stern, its crew ready to row ashore. Captain Skeat had no intention of risking the tall, lovely *Lily* even in a safe harbor on the French coast. A ship like the *Lily* could make any man rich, even a rebel of the Vendée.

"D'ye see anything?"

"Nothing."

"Wait."

The wind sighed in the rigging, waves slapped at the hull, the timbers creaked. The *Lily* waited. If, Skeat reflected, Lord Werlatton did not come within the next two hours, then the *Lily* would have to return the following night. He stared at the dark hint of land, smelled the resin of the pines on this coast, and waited.

Ashore, in the deep darkness beneath a stand of pines that grew on a sandhill behind Saint Gilles, Toby Lazender also waited.

He lay on his belly. The trunk of a pine was sticky to his right. He had not moved in an hour, not even when an owl stooped close to him, claws reaching, to snatch a wriggling lizard to its airy death.

Toby stared at Saint Gilles. He saw the houses as dark blobs against the lighter strip of sand, beyond which the waves fretted ragged white. He could smell the salt.

Once, he was not sure, he thought he saw the dark shape of a ship to sea, and he had thought of the signal he would have to give from the small, stone jetty that served as Saint Gilles' harbor. Beneath his right hand, the oil of its lock pungent in his nostrils, was a musket. On his back, in a knapsack, was a lantern and a tinder box, both wrapped in cloth so that, when he moved, they made no noise.

There was a price on his head, a price sufficient to keep a French family alive for two years. He was *Le Revenant,* the leader of one of the rebel bands that harried the French government troops in the small, tight fields and woods of the Vendée. A score of his men were a half mile behind him, waiting for a signal that would tell them to come forward and collect the barrels of fine, English powder that the *Lily*'s longboat would bring to France.

Nothing moved in Saint Gilles, nothing except the endless rill of surf.

He could not smell fire, and he suspected the villagers had gone. The fishermen of Saint Gilles, even on a warm night, rarely let their fires go out; fires that simmered the inevitable great pots of fish soup and kept the pitch warm for the boats and the nets. The village seemed deserted.

He waited another twenty minutes, still nothing moved and then, silent as a ghost, a revenant, he moved down the sandhill into a gully which led to the beach.

The surf was louder here.

He stopped at the dunes behind the beach and watched again.

A great wooden frame reared up on the foreshore and something moved there. He stared at it, seeing at last that it was hung with nets which stirred in the small wind. He moved again, going closer to Saint Gilles, closer to the small jetty from which he should embark for England and Campion's marriage.

He found the first sentry ten minutes later. It was a boy, scarce sixteen, who had fallen fast asleep in a bowl of the dunes. Toby saw him because of the shimmer of light on the lad's bayonet. The position of the sentry told him where the French troops would have their cordon and he crouched, unmoving in black shadow, and at last saw a second man take off a hat and scratch his head.

They were silent. He knew they expected him. Not one had lit a pipe, which proved that their discipline was good. They had waited in silence and if he had not half expected them, and if he had not moved with such silent caution, their skillful positions might well have been sufficient to surprise him.

He went back the way he had come.

He stopped where a hedgerow came to the dunes and there, hidden by the earth bank on which the thick hedge grew, he discarded the useless knapsack with its lantern that would make no signal now to the dark sea. He pulled back the flint of the musket, put it to his shoulder, and aimed it in the general direction of the village. At this range the ball had no hope of accuracy.

He fired.

The flash of powder in the pan momentarily dazzled his open right eye, while the burning grains stung his cheek. His shot whistled over the dunes and smacked into the hanging nets, startling the French sentries and provoking them into a panicked, ragged volley.

Toby climbed the hill toward the pines, knowing his men would bring his horse forward. He stopped once to see if the French would send patrols out, hoping they would so that his band could cut one off and chop it down, but the troops stayed in the village. He could hear them shouting, he could see the lanterns unmasked and hear the officers yelling for order, and then he turned away to his waiting men and his saddled horse. He had been betrayed.

In the village the Colonel, who had come with his men to Saint Gilles after dusk in a convoy of fishing boats, swore foully. "Who fired?"

Everyone had fired, yet the sentries swore that they had been fired on first, that, indeed, a whole army of rebels had blazed at them from the sand dunes and the Colonel, who had been an army butcher before the revolution had opened up the ladder of promotion, kicked some of the younger men, swore once more, and went back to the fishing hovels from which, as his men landed, the inhabitants had precipitately fled. God damn and God damn and God damn! He wondered if the *Le Revenant* would try again tomorrow.

If, he thought, there were to be any tomorrows left for him. His orders had come from Paris, signed by Citizen Marchenoir himself, orders that were astonishingly specific. They named the dates, they named the place, and they named the time when *Le Revenant* would come to this rendezvous.

The Colonel had failed. He had been pointed toward an enemy of France and, as his orders said, all he had to do was wait for the Englishman to walk into his arms. The ambush had failed. It was unlikely that the Englishman would come on the morrow.

Such failure, the Colonel knew, led to that last sneeze into the bloodstained basket. He shouted for one of his officers who could read and write, shouted for a lantern, demanded wine. The officer, a subtle Captain called Tours, sat quietly opposite the Colonel. "Sir?"

"You will concoct a story, Tours."

"A story?"

"Why *Le Revenant* did not come. We are told he's ill. We're told . . ." the Colonel's invention ran out. "Write something, you fool." The Colonel poured himself wine. He decided he hated Paris and its secret men and its power and its ability to make him shiver with fear on this warm coast. God damn *Le Revenant,* God damn Paris, God damn everything. He drank.

And at sea, where the *Lily* jerked against the waves, the crew saw the sparks of the musket flames and heard, a few seconds later, the rattle of shots come over the water.

Captain Skeat clapped his hands. "Wear her round!"

The jibs were tightened and the beautiful ship creaked as the wind pushed her, as the bows swung to the open sea, and then the staysail caught the breeze, the *Lily* dipped, and suddenly all the great spread of canvas was driving the lean, black ship away from the enemy shore toward the safety of the empty ocean.

Toby was betrayed and still in France. He rode eastward, far from the sound of the sea, and in his thoughts were Lucille and revenge. He rode, the revenant, toward the dawn.

12

Lord Culloden was no longer a Major in the Blues. He claimed he had sold the privilege for close to four thousand pounds, yet he still wore the gorgeous uniform. Seeing him at the stairhead, waiting for her, Campion even wondered if his uniform was new. He had lost none of his new weight, yet his neck no longer bulged at the embroidered stock, and the tunic was not stretched at its buttons. He bowed as she approached. "Ready, my dear?"

"As I'll ever be." She smiled.

The Earl had wanted to see them before the ball began, to look at them in their finery, to imagine how they would look when they descended the great staircase. He had smiled at them, wished them well, but his humor had been driven away by the pain. "Go, children. Enjoy the evening." He had waved them to the door. Campion had held back and kissed him. "Thank you for all this."

He tried to smile. He reached out to touch her hand. "I suppose your brother hasn't come?"

"No, father."

He sighed. He could scarce move his head. His red rimmed eyes rolled away from her as he coughed. Dr. Fenner was mixing laudanum and brandy. The Earl waited eagerly for the drink. "Go, my love. Go."

The Castle was filled with guests. A host of relatives

had come for Lord Culloden, and with them had arrived a dozen young cavalry officers, loud mouthed and braying, who had churned up the south terrace lawn with a horse race the day before. Aunt Lucretia had come, sniffing into odd corners of the Castle as though planning what she would do if her son, Sir Julius, inherited them. The dowager Duchess d'Auxigny, Achilles' mother, had descended in billows of black silk and white powder, wishing to know why the flag on the Castle staff was not at half mast for her elder son. She brought an expensive mercury thermometer to test the heat of the water in her washing bowl, declaring that water too chill would prematurely age her already wrinkled face. The Duchess, with her drove of maids and servants, was given the Garden House, making the rest of the Castle even more crowded.

And on this night, the celebration before the wedding, there were the local gentry, officers from Dorchester, the mayor of Lazen, and the rector, the Reverend Horne Mounter, who fussed at the castle entrance in anticipation of the Bishop's arrival.

Campion, as she waited at the top of the stairs, was dressed in colored Pekings, the silk brilliant, the colors seeming to shimmer as she moved. She wore silk gloves that reached to her elbows. Her hair, piled high and held by a comb of gold, was crowned by ostrich feathers. About her neck were the four jewels of Lazen, the chains now of differing lengths so that the seals seemed to make a bar of jewelled gold at her breasts. She had decided, for a reason that seemed whimsical but good to her, that the seals should be seen. They had been locked up too long, these symbols of Lazen's pride. She put her arm into Lord Culloden's and thought how much her father wanted her to enjoy this night. For his sake, she decided, she would.

Culloden smiled down at her. "Forward? The full charge?"

"Shouldn't we wait for the music?"

"I rather think it waits for us."

"Oh!" She laughed. "I'd have stood here all night!"

Lord Culloden's spurs and sword-sling jingled as he stepped forward. The two of them went from the shadows of the upper hallway into the chandelier-lit brilliance of the ballroom.

Septimus Gheeraerts de Serckmaester, who was in truth called Ernest Gudgeon, but who had found his musical services more in demand when he assumed a continental name, rapped with his hand on the lid of the pianoforte. The orchestra had rehearsed for two days and now, resplendent in wigs and livery, the musicians bent to their instruments and played a triumphant processional that had been commissioned for this occasion.

Applause rippled through the ballroom, it swelled, and Campion, dazzling on the stairway, smiled shyly.

Lord Culloden wondered if this would be the last time that the great house would ever see such a ball. Within months this place would be stripped, its treasures sold, and the money used to bring down an even greater edifice, Britain itself. Yet Lord Culloden had no great desire to see Britain humbled, or Reason, whatever that was, triumph. His membership of the *Illuminati,* like his membership of the Fallen Ones, was merely an extension of his partnership with Valentine Larke.

It was not, it could never be, an equal partnership. Larke was inestimably more powerful because Larke was inestimably more rich. And now, on top of all his riches, Larke possessed the confession of murder which would ensure that Lord Culloden would surrender all this magnificence when the day of Lucifer came.

So there was some regret in Lord Culloden on this

evening of music, applause, and display; on this evening when he walked with such loveliness beside him. He had embarked on this marriage for the Fallen Ones, the expenses of the courtship had been paid by Larke, yet Culloden regretted what he must give up. In marrying Lady Campion Lazender he gained riches and honor beyond his most extravagant desires. He could see that fact written on some of the faces above the applauding hands. The faces smiled, but he sensed the bitterness within, the jealousy, because an unknown lord had taken the most eligible heiress in the country. Lord Culloden sometimes thought that he deserved this marriage. It was he who had play-acted so skillfully, dissembled so politely, who had watched his tongue and guarded his behavior and steered her gently toward their engagement. Yet Lazen could not be his, he knew it, its bride must be sacrificed, and he consoled himself that, on Larke's coat-tails, he would rise above the lordship of Lazen's "Little Kingdom" to the pinnacle of Reason's empire.

His white-powdered head high, his face stiff with pride, he led her with a delicately poised hand into the center of the floor and waited for Septimus Gheeraerts de Serckmaester to slide the music into the first minuet.

They did the tiny steps, the glides, the hand movements and the salutations with exquisite grace. The applause continued. Slowly other dancers came to the floor, but always leaving space for the handsome couple in the center. Only after this dance would the ball become general.

They danced the quadrille, the pavane, the polonaise, while softly the dusk descended outside, making the brilliance of the ballroom more startling yet, a brilliance that was reflected from jewels and gold, from crystal and silver. This was Lazen at its most splendid, the men in velvet, silk and satin, their white gloves making intricate, pleasing patterns as they gestured together in the courtesies of the dance. The women were dazzling in sapphires, diamonds, emeralds and rubies. It was a splendor better seen than smelled. At the edges of the room, where the over-dressed, warm people crowded together, where satin, silk and gossip rustled close, there was a distasteful odor of bodies and stale powder that no perfume could quite overcome.

Campion danced with Sir George, with the Earl of Fleet, with a Captain of the Blues who seemed to blush throughout his minuet, and with Uncle Achilles. Achilles, who danced with wonderful grace, shrugged at her as they passed in the minuet. "So no Toby?"

"No."

"A pity."

"I know."

He bowed to her, she curtseyed. He stepped toward her, away, and he smiled over his shoulder. "I see the Bishop has arrived. I suppose you'll have to kiss his ring."

"We don't kiss rings in the Church of England, uncle."

"How very boring of you. I used to put a speck of mustard on mine when a particularly tedious person came to see me."

She laughed, and the watching guests thought how beautiful and happy she looked, the very image of a bride in her loveliness and innocence. To see her was to smile. There was jealousy too, from those women who hated a rival and from the men who could not hope to possess her, yet those who knew her wished only that the happiness they saw would be hers forever. She was lovely. The Bishop, as she approached him, applauded her loveliness. "Dear Lady Campion! You look clipped and brushed!"

She laughed. She liked the Bishop. He inquired about the prospects of the harvest, remarked that there was a damned fine pike in the river at the foot of his garden, apologized for his wife's absence, "She's got the vapors again," and invited Lady Campion to a day's coursing. "How are the partridges, my dear lady?"

"Promising, Wirrell tells me."

"Good shooting, eh? Perhaps you'll let me go over the ground come October?"

"My pleasure, my Lord."

"Splendid!" The Bishop turned to his chaplain. "You'd better keep me a week free of bloody confirmations, Jenkins. My God!" He raised his hands in mock amazement. "This must be the lucky man! You've snaffled the likeliest filly in the county, my Lord."

Campion introduced Lord Culloden who clicked his heels and nodded formally. "My Lord."

The Bishop smiled. "You'll let me thump around the floor with your lovely bride, my Lord?"

Culloden touched his moustache. "Of course."

The thump had to be delayed. As a minuet ended to applause, the folding doors of the ballroom were pushed fully back and Carline's voice announced that the fireworks would be ignited at the pleasure and convenience of the assembled company.

The Bishop took Campion's arm. "If I stand by you, my dear, I'll get a good view." He raised an affable hand to Sir George Perrott, bellowed a greeting to Lady Courthrop, and turned back to the beautiful girl on his arm. "How did your hounds run this year?"

"Fast."

"That's what I heard." He sounded gloomy. "I never got down once. I was riding with a fat pack in Somerset. Couldn't catch a pregnant duck. Why I can't find a diocese with a decent hunt close to the palace I don't know. There's that idiot McDonnell in Leicestershire, all prayers and psalms. A waste of a good See." He shook his head gloomily then turned to his right. "Ah! Mounter! I suppose I'd better relinquish the bride for the dubious pleasure of your company. Your lady wife is here, I see. Wonderful, wonderful! Jenkins? There must be some brandy in this bloody place. Look, man!"

Lord Culloden took her arm, the crowd parted for them, applauded them, and she smiled left and right as Lewis led her to the portico and the waiting night sky. Footmen pulled back their chairs. The Duchess d'Auxigny, Campion saw, had already claimed the highest row of seats. She was calling loudly for wraps and furs, complaining about the cold English night. Campion smiled at her, then sat by Lord Culloden.

Despite the complaints of the French Duchess, the night was dry and warm. The stars showed above Two Gallows Hill and there was enough moonlight to reveal the mysterious preparations on the far side of the lake. Behind Campion, within the castle, the music played on.

Lord Culloden led the applause as the first stars of fire exploded in the darkness.

Campion had been nervous about his return to Lazen, yet oddly she had found herself calmer than she expected. She wondered whether she had at last accepted the inevitability of marriage, had recognized that it was a commonplace and not something of wonderful strangeness. She had even begun to look forward to Periton House, to entertaining there, and she had felt that sudden, inexplicable yearning for motherhood. She was, she supposed, accepting marriage with decent grace, though she did not see why the graciousness had to extend to every small detail of her new life. She smiled at Lord Culloden. "Would you ever think of shaving off your moustache?"

He turned astonished from the fireworks. "Shaving it off?"

"Yes." She mimed a pair of scissors with her fingers in front of his mouth. "Like that."

He frowned. "What's wrong with it?"

"Would you like it if I had a moustache?"

"Not excessively."

"It's like being kissed by a horse brush. That's pretty."

Culloden turned to look at the flaming comets that were reflected in shaking streaks on the water. "I rather like my moustache."

"You must preserve it, my Lord, if it's very precious to you."

There seemed to be a struggle on his face. He touched both ends of the offending hair, then shrugged. "Of course, if you really want it off, dear Campion, I shall get Mellors to shave it tomorrow morning."

"If you make that sacrifice," she said, "I shall have to marry you, my Lord."

He laughed. Mrs. Mounter, the Rector's wife, who stood protectively beside the Bishop, saw their happiness and pointed it out to her companions. "Made in heaven, I say! Made for each other!" She sniffed.

The Bishop swirled his brandy. "She's a good filly! Best damn seat on a horse I ever saw! Good Lord! Look at that! Isn't it splendid!"

The crowd applauded the pretty fires that laced the sky and fell like stars into the water. Great clouds of smoke, shot through with colors of the fireworks, drifted over the lake. In one great burst of white flame Campion saw the gleaming roof of the sunken pleasure barge. Servants moved among the great crowd with salvers of wine and plates of food. The townspeople were thick on the driveway, their applause echoing that from the Great House steps.

"Magnificent!" Culloden applauded. The crest of Two Gallows Hill was suddenly spitting fire that arced red into the air like a great crown, a crown that grew and grew until the whole sky seemed to be suffused with the color. The hanging gallows were touched scarlet.

Then the men from Bristol lit their masterpiece and the cheers echoed from the Castle. On the huge, wrought iron fence that stood so grandly between its ten foot high stone pillars along the Shaftesbury road they had hung an arrangement of fire that glowed white, showered sparks, and spelled the names Lazender and Culloden. The names were wreathed in hearts and surmounted, as was fitting, by the escutcheon of the Earl himself. The crowd seemed to sigh as the fires died and as the last sparks fell red from the iron frame. The shield was the last piece to fade, the lance blazing in a final burst as a challenge to the darkness.

Campion hoped her father had seen the fireworks. She looked impetuously at Lord Culloden. "I'm going to see father."

He frowned. "You think he'll be awake?" She knew he meant sober.

"I'll go and see."

"You have some free dances?"

She looked at the card that was held by a tasselled cord to her wrist. "Major Farthingdale. Give him my apologies and say I'll save a dance for him later."

Culloden bowed over her hand. "Remember we have a polonaise."

"I'll remember."

She walked through the hall, smiling at friends, then up the western staircase to avoid the crowds on the main flight. Two strange servants ran past her with wraps for their mistresses who wished to take the air. She wondered whether beds had been found for all the servants; more had come that she had anticipated, and then she decided she could not worry about such things on this night of music, fire and dance.

A couple were embracing in the shadow of the great Roman statue on the main landing. She smiled when she saw that they had extinguished the candles nearest them. She smiled at the women who waited by the Chinese screens erected in front of the chamberpots, and then she turned into the corridor that led to her father's rooms. The music reached up here, fault and beautiful, like a reminder of past times in the great house.

She walked beneath the pictures of horses. Her heelless satin slippers were silent on the thick carpet. Candles in smoked glass chimneys stood on the small tables every few feet.

Her father's manservant smiled and stood as she came into the ante-chamber. "He's asleep, my Lady."

"I won't wake him, Caleb. I'll just look."

The Earl slept peacefully. His face, for the first time in weeks, looked calm. His breathing was gentle. The candles either side of her mother's portrait burned steadily. Campion leaned down and touched her lips gently on his gray hair.

She would not wake him. Good sleep was a rarity for her father, and sleep as gentle as this, sleep that had taken the lines of pain from his face, was almost unknown now. She smiled at him, then walked to the farther window and stared down at the forecourt.

People strolled in the light of the great lanterns which lit the facade of the castle. On the far side of the lake, their torch flames rippling on the reflecting water, the firework men cleaning up their apparatus. On Two Gallows Hill the fires started among the thorns by the fireworks were beaten out by farm laborers hired for this night.

There was laughter beneath her and she saw three couples dance into her view. They were being applauded by the strollers on the forecourt. There was happiness down there, a great party in a great castle, and all for her marriage. She looked at her father. Was his sleep due to contentment? Was her marriage the solace of his pain-filled days? She smiled. She felt a welting surge of love for him, of pity for his pain, of gratitude.

She still smiled as she looked back at the forecourt. The dancers circled the fountain now. Someone had put a candelabra on the stone wall that held the fountain's pool, and in its tight she could see two lovers kiss. The girl, Campion thought, leaned so willingly forward, stayed so lingeringly.

To be touched once, she thought, by that magic. Just as the fire rippled and swayed and shivered on the lake, so she wanted to know what that girl knew.

She looked left toward the town. A horseman trotted on the grass by the lake and she half frowned, thinking that one of Lord Culloden's cavalry friends had saddled a horse for some night-time mischief, and then the rider stopped.

She knew who it was. Even in shadow the man and horse looked like one being. Only one man rode like that. He had come.

She had wanted him to come. She had wanted him to see her in her splendor. She had wanted to see his face. Nothing Achilles had said could change that. The guilt, the shame, the excitement, all mingled and seethed in her. She stared at the shadow within the shadow and she put a hand to her breast as though she wanted to quell her heartbeats.

The shadow did not move.

She turned.

She saw herself in the mirror across the room and it was as if she stared at a stranger. That girl in silk and feathers and gold was a girl arrayed to marry a lord. She wanted to weep suddenly, and that offended her, and she straightened her head, refused to turn back to the window, and walked slowly toward the door.

Caleb stood as she approached. He shut the door of the Earl's bedroom softly. "You look as if you've seen a ghost, my Lady!"

She smiled. "No, Caleb. I think it's just the excitement."

"You should be excited this night, my Lady. Now you go on down. They'll be missing you! And you do look lovely, my Lady, if you'll forgive an old man."

"It's only clothes, Caleb!" She plucked at the colored Pekings.

"Ah! Get on with you! I remember you in swaddling, my Lady, and you were a picture then!"

She laughed. She went from her father's room, back to the ball and its glory, back to the excitement which a shadowed horseman had brought so suddenly to this night.

She sipped champagne, she danced. The Bishop insisted on a minuet, raising his feet as though he was a carthorse and clumping them down in a travesty of the dance's minute, precise, calculated movements. He boomed at her how he had spent the morning helping his groom to blister the hocks of his hunters. Campion smiled, made polite answers, and searched the crowds who lined the room's edges. She knew the Gypsy would not come into this splendor, but she looked.

She danced with a gloomy French count, one of the exiles who kept bitter court at her grandmother's house, who frowned at the other dancers and spoke hardly a word to her until he bowed elegantly at the music's end. "You are to be married, my Lady?"

"Indeed, my Lord."

"If you are bored, madame," and he twitched the lace cuff of his threadbare sleeve, "I am always at your service. I am, of course, discreet."

She stared in astonishment as he walked away. Her uncle laughed at her as he took her to the pillared drawing room for champagne beneath the great Vecchio ceiling. "He propositioned you?"

"I think he did, uncle."

"That's how he makes his living."

"But he's so gloomy! And ugly!"

Achilles laughed again. "I am told by my lady friends, dear niece, that he is exquisitely skilled." He raised his eyebrows at her and presented her with champagne.

She leaned with him at the doors which opened onto the Water Garden. The gravel paths which led to the small stone bridges above the shallow, carp filled canals were busy with couples who walked, stood, talked, and kissed. Ropes had been strung from the castle to tall poles at the western edge of the garden from which hung paper Chinese lanterns.

"Exquisitely skilled." Her uncle's words intrigued her. She felt nothing when Lord Culloden kissed her, nothing except distaste at his moustache. She wondered what the skill would be that Achilles described, but dared not ask. She felt oddly childish. Perhaps marriage, and the duty of marriage, would initiate her into this world she did not understand, this world that she could glimpse only by half understood gesture and elegant innuendo. There was a secret, and she did not share it, and she felt that these people, even her uncle, laughed at her innocence. Then she remembered the single Christmas touch of the Gypsy and thought there was a clue in that memory to what her uncle spoke of.

She looked for the Gypsy in the Water Garden and she could not see him. She told herself that Caleb had been right. She had seen only a ghost in the shadows at the edge of her happiness. She had seen a horseman, no more, and she had decided that the horseman must be he. She had been wrong.

Achilles smiled at her. "You look forlorn, dear Campion."

She laughed. "I have to sit with your mother."

"Then let me not keep you from the awesome presence."

She dutifully found her grandmother who held stately court on a small dais at one side of the ballroom. The dowager Duchess d'Auxigny felt the colored Peking dress with an ancient finger and thumb, sniffed, and supposed that it had been "cobbled in London"?

"Indeed, *Grandmère.*"

Her grandmother was resplendent in black silk, mourning her son who had been guillotined in Paris. The Duchess had hated her son in life, but now his death had made her a small celebrity among the émigré community. She felt qualified now to pass absolute judgment on the revolution in France, a judgment that none was allowed to question. Her liveried servant, a black band about his yellow-sleeved arm, stood a precise two feet to her left and held a bowl of prunes. The Duchess ate them slowly, leaning over to spit the stones into a silver dish held by Madame la Retiffe, her paid companion. She pointed a finger at Achilles who danced with the Marchioness of Benfleet's small daughter. "Achilles grows more stupid every day."

Madame la Retiffe, holding her silver dish, hissed an echo. "Stupid!"

Campion could not understand how anybody could think Uncle Achilles was stupid. "I think it's nice of him. He always dances with the ladies who feel left out."

Her grandmother ignored the compliment. "It is ridiculous to think of him as Duc d'Auxigny! Like an ermine wrap on a monkey!"

"Monkey!" hissed la Retiffe.

"I think he looks very distinguished," Campion protested.

"Distinguished! Distinguished! His father was distinguished, child, not that grinning monkey. I should have drowned him at birth!" Achilles's father had been the Mad Duke, the man who thought he was God, the man who made simple, child-like miracles to happen with clumsy, expensive machines. The Duchess spat another prune stone out of her mouth, ejecting it in a small spray of yellowed spittle. "Distinguished! Now that is what I call a distinguished man!" She smiled, caking the thick powder in her wrinkled face. "He must be a Frenchman!"

It was not a ghost, not a desire seen in the shadows.

The Gypsy had come.

The Duchess had spotted him across the room and now she simpered at the tall, handsome man who stood carelessly at the edge of the dance floor.

The Duchess was not the only woman to notice him. He was not dressed as a servant this night, but as a gentleman. His clothes were black, except for a lilac colored shirt and silk stock. His suit was elegantly cut, his hair drawn back, and his left ear was bare of the gold ring.

He was tall, slim, and he wore a full length sword instead of the small dress-swords of the other men. The women watched him over their fans. He was the handsomest man in the room and his air of arrogant self-sufficiency intrigued them.

"Who is he?" the Duchess asked.

Campion was tempted to tell her that the distinguished man she so much admired was a servant. She shrugged instead. "I don't know."

"Madame!" The Duchess turned to her sour, pale, thin companion. "I wish to meet him. Go."

Madame la Retiffe put down her dish of damp stones, stepped from the low platform, and walked obediently across the floor.

The Gypsy, as the woman approached, looked past her at Campion. It seemed, at that moment, as if there were just the two of them in the crowded room, as if those odd, pale blue eyes were reading her very soul. He gave her a flicker of a smile and a hint of a bow.

"He's seen me!" the Duchess said.

William Carline, Lazen's steward, who moved magnificently among the guests to check that the servants were doing their duties, saw and recognized the Gypsy. He frowned. He looked at Campion, edged an offended head toward the man he knew to be a servant, and raised an eyebrow that asked whether Campion wished the man to be ejected from among his betters. She gave a tiny shake of her head. Carline, his sense of propriety wounded, stalked toward the hallway.

Uncle Achilles, pausing in the dance, saw the tiny shake of Campion's head. He sighed. He smiled at the ten year old child he gallantly danced with. "Do you know what happens when you put a black cat in the dovecote?"

"No, sir."

"Blood and feathers and lots of trouble!" He laughed. "I do like nonsense, my dear, I do so like nonsense!"

Madame la Retiffe led her prize across the floor. The heads of the women turned. Some of the servants looked astonished.

The Gypsy stopped in front of the Duchess. He gave her a bow that would have pleased Louis XIV. The old woman simpered and tapped Madame le Retiffe's chair with her folded black fan. "You may sit beside me, monsieur." She looked at Madame le Retiffe. "Introduce me, then!"

It seemed Madame le Retiffe had not discovered the name of the intriguing, tall man who had caused such a stir by his presence.

The Duchess looked at him. "Well, who are you?"

He looked at Campion, and the meeting of their eyes seemed to hold the breath in her body. He smiled, changing his face utterly. "The Lady Campion knows who I am."

The old face glowered at Campion. "You said you didn't know!"

"I don't know his name, *Grandmère.*" That was not quite true. She knew him as Gitan, but that seemed more of a nickname than a name. She smiled, enjoying the moment. "I just know that he's my brother's groom, *Grandmère.*"

She could not resist saying it, not to humiliate the Gypsy, but to see the horror on her grandmother's face when it dawned on her that she had invited a servant to sit beside her. Campion stood, ignoring the gaping, shocked mouth of her grandmother, and stepped down from the small dais. She made her face cold, her manner stiff, and she reflected that this man deserved humiliation for coming among his betters. "What are you doing here?"

"I come from your brother." His voice was lazy and confident.

"You have a message?" She addressed him in a voice of aristocratic command, yet his face, so full of life and promise, stirred something deep inside.

He smiled. "No." He had turned his body subtly and forced Campion to take a further step away from her grandmother so that, to the room as a whole, it seemed that the tall, black haired stranger was deep in private talk with the golden haired bride. "I have brought you his wedding gift."

It was insufferable, yet he managed to imply that his coming with the gift was the most important part of this evening. He smiled again, and she felt her defenses breaking down. His arrogance, his charm, and the confidence on his slim, dark face, astounded her. She straightened her back. "The steward will receive it."

"I doubt it if he can!" He sounded amused. "I thought I might give it to you at the temple in the park."

"My dear?" The voice, cold and lazy, came from behind her. She turned. Lewis Culloden, seeing her with the handsome stranger, had come to find out who he was. He frowned at the Gypsy with dislike, as though sensing that the man was a rival. "I don't think I have the honor, sir?"

Lord Culloden had forgotten seeing this man at Christmas, and in truth there was no reason to connect the servant who had disarmed the boy in the Hall with the gentleman who now stood at Campion's side.

She had discomforted her grandmother by revealing that the man, despite his clothes, was a servant. Yet now, with Lord Culloden beside her, she found she could not repeat the assertion. She did not want to see the Gypsy humiliated by Lord Culloden, who, she was sure, would indignantly demand that the man return to the servant's hall. That decision was hers, not his. She heard herself tell the lie and she was astonished at herself and she felt the delicious amusement of it even as she spoke. "This is the Prince de Gitan, my Lord."

Culloden looked startled. Princes were as common in French aristocracy as earls among the British, but Lord Culloden did not like to be outranked by the tall stranger. He bowed coldly.

The Gypsy had smiled as she invented the rank. He spoke to Culloden in French, complimenting him on his bride, and the discovery that the Prince de Gitan spoke no English seemed to irritate his Lordship even more. He put a proprietorial hand on Campion's arm. "I think I am named for the next polonaise, my dear."

"Of course." She smiled at him, then turned back to the Gypsy and spoke in French. "The temple?" She thought, as she said the two words, that she had entered a conspiracy of shame, a conspiracy she could not resist.

The Gypsy bowed. "The temple, my Lady."

Culloden pulled at her arm. "My dear?"

She let herself be led to the dance. In a few moments, she knew, she would leave this ball. She would leave a celebration arranged for her marriage and go into the darkness to meet the man who had given her dreams, had haunted those dreams, and who had come again to Lazen to tempt her with the unthinkable. She would go to the temple.

13

The polonaise finished. She curtseyed. She smiled weakly at Lord Culloden. "I'm feeling distinctly faint, my Lord."

"Faint?" He frowned.

"The champagne, perhaps?" She touched her forehead. Faintness was so common an excuse, so expected of a woman, that he would think nothing of it. Yet, for all its ordinariness, it was an excuse she had never, ever used in her life. Now, as he put a hand on her shoulder, she felt a horrid premonition that the excuse would run like a threnody of unhappiness through her marriage. "I'm going to lie down for a few moments. I'll come back."

He bowed. "You will be missed, my dear."

She climbed the stairs, crossed the windowed bridge, and went to her rooms like a guilty person. She could feel her heart beating. It seemed like a crime, like a delicious, secret crime.

Her maid was not in the rooms. Campion locked all the doors. She lit new candles from the guttering stubs of the old, took the ostrich plumes from her hair, sat at the mirror and put new powder on her face. She put shadow-cream on her eyelids. She took the dance card from her wrist, looked wryly at the names of the men whom she was disappointing, then dropped it on her dressing table. She smiled a conspiratorial smile at her own reflection.

From the wardrobe she took a long, hooded cloak of midnight blue. She listened to make certain no one was in the corridor, then, her every sense heightened by excitement, she turned the key and slipped into the tangle of Tudor rooms at the back of the Old House.

She went down servants' stairs, past the silver vaults, through the old laundry, and out into the kitchen garden. She pulled the cloak's hood over her hair of pale, pale gold.

The night air was fresh and warm. She could smell the herbs. The music came to her across the dark lawns that lay to the north of Lazen Castle. The gate of the garden creaked as she opened it.

She walked on the grass, her satin slippers thin enough to impress every small bump on the soles of her feet. The orchard blossoms made a haze of whiteness to her right.

She skirted the mound that had once held the keep when Lazen was a real castle. At its foot, where she hugged the dark hillock, were the castle's beehives.

She stopped at the edge of the mound and saw the lights brilliant in the castle's northern windows. Couples walked in the gardens, couples whose laughter came soft over the grass.

She walked on. There was an exhilarating, nervous pleasure in this secrecy, this assignation on such a night as this. She wanted to laugh aloud, she wanted to kick off her slippers and run barefoot on the grass. How many brides left their betrothal ball to meet another man? The thought made her laugh.

To her right was Sconce Hill, a tangle of bushes and darkness, and ahead were the ruins of the old gatehouse. Once Lazen Castle had faced north. Now, when it was no longer a place of war, but one of the great mansions of England, it had turned its face to the warmer south.

She could see the bright couples walking beneath the paper lanterns in the Water Garden. She could not go that way. Like the guilty person she felt herself to be, she must stay in the darkness. She went to her right, crossing the northern approach road, and going into the long, tangling grass beyond.

Laughter bubbled inside her. Practical, sensible Campion was doing what no one would believe she could do. She could scarcely believe it herself.

She had to pull the colored Peking above her knees to climb the barred fence that divided the grassland from the park. She climbed carefully, not wanting to tear her satin stockings, and then, unsnagged, she jumped safely to the far side.

She went more slowly now. The park was rough pastureland, its dips and bumps scarcely lit by the moon or the brilliant light that came from the castle. She lifted the skirts of her dress and cloak above the long grass and searched ahead for a sight of the small temple on its low rise.

She heard muffled laughter to her left. She stopped, crouched and listened. She could hear voices, a man's and a woman's, and then she heard a long moan, a laugh, and she knew suddenly that a couple had gone to the shadowed secrecy at the bottom of the ha-ha. The ha-ha was a ditch that separated the formal gardens from the park, a ditch with one sheer face that no deer could climb, thus keeping the view from the castle unimpeded by a fence and the gardens unravaged by deer. And Campion, listening to the sound, felt as though she was a part of the happiness of illicit love that was spreading about Lazen this night. A pang of excitement and apprehension shot through her as she rose and walked on. She was being foolish, she knew it, and it was delightful, delirious foolishness.

She justified the foolishness by telling herself that she came only to receive Toby's present. She tried to persuade herself that she did nothing that would offend Uncle Achilles' concern for her dignity. She would take the present, whatever it was, thank him graciously, and walk away.

She saw the moon whiteness of the footpath, turned onto it, and there, faintly pale against the beeches behind, was the elegant temple. Her grandfather had built it, a small pillared fancy that stood on a stepped pedestal and was crowned by a white, domed roof. She had sometimes climbed the steps and chased about the floor with Toby when she was a child. Her father had spoken of pulling it down, yet it still stood, deserted and odd, the retreat where the fourth Earl of Lazen had written his huge, unpublished attack on the Copernican system.

She walked to the bottom of the steps. The Solomonic pillars twisted to the white dome. A wall, low enough to sit on, edged the temple's floor. She looked up. She wondered if she should call his name. She wondered if she should turn back to the castle.

She could hear the music of the dance, so faint now as to be like the music of the fairies that her mother would tell her to listen for in the night-time woods behind the castle.

"Hello?" Her voice seemed small and shy.

Silence, but for the trees moving in the wind.

She felt sudden fear. She was alone in the darkness to meet a man she did not know, a servant. She told herself that she should go back to the castle, that she should abandon this foolishness.

"Hello?"

Two bats skittered through the temple's pillars, twisting and darting into the darkness.

She turned. A shadow moved in the park, a swift, dark

shadow against the blackness of Two Gallows Hill. She heard the hooves on the turf, the jingle of curb chains, and she knew he had come and she felt something close to panic in her, a panic edged with excitement. She stood unmoving as the shadow resolved into a black horse, a black-cloaked rider on its back.

The Gypsy stopped five yards from her. The black cloak was draped on his horse's rump. He leaned on the pommel of his saddle. The moonlight made his light eyes bright in his dark face. "My Lady."

She said nothing.

He turned his head and gave a short whistle. She heard a snort, heard more hooves, and then, trotting obediently to his command, came a horse of wondrous beauty.

She guessed, in the moonlight, that it was chestnut. It was not a big horse, but it had long fronts, deep shoulders, straight hind legs, and, as it trotted, it showed a long, full action that promised speed and stamina. The Gypsy smiled at the horse, reached out, and let it nuzzle his hand. "She's called Hirondelle." He spoke in French. The name translated as the Swallow.

Campion walked to the mare and stroked her muzzle.

The Gypsy smiled. "Your brother's gift. He ordered me to buy the best horse I could find. I found her in Kent. She's a beauty."

Campion smiled. She ran her hand down the strong neck. "She's lovely." The mare trembled under her touch. "Why a French name on an English horse?"

"I named her."

"It's a good name."

"Five years old, well enough nagged. You can hunt her next year."

Campion stopped, one hand on the horse's back. She looked over Hirondelle at the black-cloaked man. "What did you say?"

"Well enough nagged."

It was a common phrase, meaning that the horse had been well schooled. It was not the phrase that surprised her, but the fact that the Gypsy had spoken in English. There had been no trace of a French accent. She stared at him. "You're English." She said it accusingly.

The Gypsy laughed. He swung from his black horse and, carrying a saddlebag, climbed the temple steps. His voice was cheerful. *"Mandi Angitrako Rom, rawnie."* He sat on the wall to the right of the entrance, one leg bent in front of him, his back leaning on a pillar.

She knew this was the moment when she should thank him for bringing the gift, order him to stable Hirondelle, and then she should walk back to the castle. She knew, too, that he had deliberately intrigued her so she would stay. She looked at him from beneath the cowl of her hood. "What did you say?"

"Mandi Angitrako Rom, rawnie." He smiled. "It means 'I am an English Rom, my Lady.' "

"Rom?"

"You call it Gypsy. My tribe is the Rom, and their language is the Romani, and I come from that part of the tribe that lives in England. My mother, though, was French Rom." He had taken a bottle of wine from his bag and two glasses. The glasses were familiar to her, both had come from the castle. He poured the wine and placed one glass at the end of the wall as an invitation to her. He leaned back, raised his glass, and smiled. "My congratulations on your forthcoming marriage." He managed to inflect the formal words with inoffensive irony.

She knew she should not stay, but why else had she come? Hesitantly she walked toward the temple. She climbed the steps. The floor of the temple was incised with the signs of the zodiac about a great half globe that protruded from the floor's center. At the top of the half globe was Britain, and at the very top, where the globe was flattened as an impractical table, was the word Lazen. Campion ignored the wine. She walked left about the globe to be on the far side from him. Her feet stirred the dead, dry leaves that had collected on the floor. She frowned at him, as if to show that her presence here was not incompatible with her dignity. She tried to think of something to say that would be natural, that would explain her staying at the temple. "Hirondelle came from Kent?"

The Gypsy nodded. His teeth were white in the darkness. "From Hawkhurst. Put a martingale on her for a few weeks. That'll teach her not to star-gaze."

Campion smiled. She could talk about horses forever. "So she's not perfect?"

"She will be. She's fast."

She felt a trembling inside her. When he smiled, and his face was transformed with a kind of mischievous joy, she felt her heart beat faster. In repose there was a savagery to his face that was exciting, but the smile promised other things. She hid her feelings. "We were sorry my brother could not be here."

He laughed. It occurred to her that he was laughing at the formality of her words. He sipped his wine. "Toby wanted to come, but the French were waiting for him. He's safe, but he had to go back inland."

He had used her brother's Christian name as if it was normal.

She frowned. "Yet you came."

He smiled. "But I move about France, my Lady, with the permission of the French, and about England with the permission of the English."

The words tantalized her. She supposed they were meant to. "So what does that make you?"

"A Rom."

She smiled. She sat on the wall, the movement tentative as though expressing that she ought not to be here. She stared at him across the hump of the half world. "How does a horse-master get permission of warring governments to move where he pleases?"

He turned and stared at the castle which seemed to float on a great surge of light. "Because, my Lady, I am not a horse-master."

"What are you then?" She could feel herself trembling beneath her cloak.

He took a twist of tobacco from a pocket, a slip of white paper, and wrapped the one in the other. He opened his tinder box, struck a spark, and blew the charred linen into a small flame. He bent his head to the flame and she thought, as she stared at the strong, fire-lit features, that she had never seen so magnificent a man. Smoke whirled into the darkness as he closed the box. "For ten years, my Lady, I lived as a Rom. Then my parents died, killed in a ditch by a farmer. You remember the laws?"

She nodded. The Gypsy Laws, repealed only ten years before, had made it a crime even to talk with a gypsy, while the death of gypsies had worried no one, certainly not any Justice of the Peace.

The Gypsy blew more smoke. "The farmer said they'd stolen his child. It was nonsense, of course, but that didn't stop him shooting both of them. He searched the wagon and there was no child, except me. He tried to kill me."

He told the story in such a commonplace way that it astonished her. She frowned. "He tried to kill you?"

"With a knife. I wasn't worth powder and shot." He grinned. "I killed him instead. Slit his belly open with my own knife." He looked at her as if waiting for a reaction. She said nothing. He smiled. "So I went to work in stables. I was good with horses. Suddenly people wanted me."

"Wanted you?"

"To make their horses go faster. And other people wanted to stop me. I became better with a knife, learned to use guns and a sword. I was paid fortunes by the quality to win races," he shrugged, "and I got bored with it, so I set off for Italy."

"Why Italy?"

"Why not?" He smiled. "I liked the sound of it. I was eighteen, my Lady, and at eighteen you think the world is all yours and that the roads have no ending."

"How did you live?" She had become fascinated. When the Lazenders travelled it was with thirty or more servants, their own cooks to take over inn kitchens, and their own lice-free beds to put into the best rooms.

He smiled. "A good horseman can always make a living, a good thief makes a better one, and we have a saying that the best bread is begged bread. I lived."

She laughed. It felt utterly natural to be talking with him. She had come here in a mixture of excitement and shame, not knowing what to expect, knowing only that there existed a great gulf between them that should have kept them decently apart. Instead, though the excitement was still there, she felt this odd, happy comfort in his company. "Where did you go in Italy?"

"Venice, Padua, Florence, Rome, Naples." He shrugged. "It was in Naples that I met the Marquess of Skavadale. You've heard of him?"

"He came here once." She smiled. "When I was very small."

The tip of the Gypsy's tobacco glowed a hard, bright red. "I liked Skavadale. He was digging up Roman relics. You've probably got some?"

She nodded. There had been an insatiable passion among the great houses for the relics of ancient Rome, a passion that had been blown to white-heat by Edward Gibbon's *The Decline and Fall of the Roman Empire.*

Lazen had not been immune. Wagons had brought old, expensive, battered statues that still stood in unlikely corners and in the more remote bedrooms. The Gypsy sipped his wine, then leaned his head on the pillar. "Someone was stealing from Skavadale and I stopped it. He was grateful. He taught me to read. He made me his chief helper, his guardian, his whipper-in." He smiled. "He also discovered that I wasn't baptized so he found some Anglican clergyman who was touring the ruins and had me christened in the remains of a Roman bath-house."

"With what name?" She asked it quickly.

He turned to look at her. He shrugged. "Christopher Skavadale."

"I like it."

He shrugged. "It's not my real name. You don't take a new name at twenty."

"Why not? You expect women to do it all the time."

He laughed. "That's true." He raised his glass to her. "Lady Campion Culloden?"

She said nothing. She was wondering what the names Lazender and Skavadale would look like wreathed in white fire on a nighttime fence. She thrust the thought away. "What happened then?"

"He sent me to London five years ago. He made me take a gift." He held out his tinder box. "It was a Roman lamp, just this size, one of the oil lamps with a spout for the flame, and a lid that covered half the bowl. On the lid was a bas-relief. It showed a man and a woman. They were doing what I think a couple of your guests are doing in the ha-ha."

She laughed. "You heard them too?"

"Half the county must have heard them. There was a crowd watching them when I came past."

She liked the way he had said it. Her uncle, dear

though he was to her, could not have mentioned the couple without being sly, or without insinuating that there was something horrid and fascinating about their lovemaking. Lord Culloden would not have mentioned them at all, or, if forced to, he would have pretended disapproval for her benefit. Christopher Skavadale had talked of them as though it was the most natural thing in the world.

He flicked the small cigar into the darkness and poured himself more wine. "I had to take the lamp to a Lord Paunceley. It seems to me now that Skavadale was doing me a favor." He shrugged. "He couldn't take me back to his own house; there were too many bitter women and under-worked sons there, so he gave me his name as a gift and sent me to Paunceley instead."

Lord Paunceley the spy-master, the subtle man in the center of his sticky webs that had entangled her brother. "Which is how you met Lord Werlatton?" she asked.

He smiled at her use of her brother's title. "Toby pretended that I was a French Rom that he'd hired as a groom. It was obvious that the French would recruit me to spy on the British, and they did. They never knew I'd been recruited already." He looked at her. "I don't suppose I'm meant to tell you any of this."

"Then why are you?"

He shrugged. "You asked what I am, so now you know. I'm an agent of the British government, a spy." He looked at her as though waiting for an adverse reaction.

"Why did you tell me?"

He smiled. He stared into the wine glass, swirling the liquid about. "I can't impress you with a uniform fit for the fairy queen," she knew he meant Lord Culloden's cavalry uniform, "and I'm not bowed into great rooms because I'm rich, so," he looked at her and smiled ruefully, "I lay what little I have before you."

"I'm impressed. Prince of the Gypsies?"

He laughed. "Thank you for that."

She laughed too. She was suddenly nervous. So much had been said in their seemingly innocuous words of the last seconds. She changed the subject deliberately, steering it away from the sudden intimacy of their shared laughter. "How's Toby?"

"He's well. Strong as an ox and needing to cut his hair. He's happy. He'd like to be here, but . . ." He shrugged. "He's hunting the man who killed his Lucille."

"He knows who killed her?"

Skavadale was making another of his Spanish cigars. He paused and looked at her. "Bertrand Marchenoir."

It was like a shock of cold water. Marchenoir! The man whose name had become a byword for blood and savagery, the man who could shock Europe, the man who fed the machine of death in Paris. Uncle Achilles, when he had first heard that the ex-priest had risen to infamy, had exploded in rare wrath. "He comes from Auxigny. His mother was the town whore! We educated him! We took him from the dungheap and made him a priest, and now look at him!" She stared at the Gypsy. "Why?"

He shrugged. "Probably because she was engaged to Toby. Marchenoir hates the Auxigny family. He'd like to kill all of them, including you." He pointed at her with his unlit cigar.

"He doesn't even know I exist!"

Skavadale smiled. "He knows. There's nothing he doesn't know about the family, or its English connections. There is a rumor," he sounded uncertain suddenly, as if he might offend her, "a rumor that he was one of the Mad Duke's bastards."

He did not offend her. The Mad Duke of Auxigny, her grandfather, had spawned too many bastards for the family to take offense at their memory. "He'd be my uncle." She said it wonderingly. "Do you know him?"

Skavadale nodded. He had struck a light and bent his head to the flame. He lit his cigar and the flame was snuffed out. "I know him." He gave her his quick smile. "I assure you there's no family resemblance. He calls me *mon ami.* He puts his arm around my neck and tells me I should marry for France and breed a family of republican cavalrymen."

She laughed nervously. His mention of marriage touched a raw nerve this night. "Are you?"

He smiled. "Getting married? Yes, I'm twenty-eight, it's past time, but I won't marry for France." He looked out at the moon silvered parkland. "I want to breed the fastest damned horse in the world."

She had said the same thing herself once. She felt suddenly jealous because this man, this Gypsy, would have the life she wanted. She felt jealous of whoever would share his life and the jealousy drove out her thoughts of Bertrand Marchenoir. She made her voice light, determined not to show the jealousy. "What's breeding a fast horse got to do with marriage?"

"I can't do that and cook for myself at the same time."

She laughed as she was meant to. She looked at the floor by her feet and kept the tone of her voice casual. "Who are you marrying?"

"When I meet her I'll know." He paused. The wind stirred the dead leaves at her feet. When he spoke again his voice sounded to Campion as dark as the night itself. "She will be fairer than the dawn, and in her eyes stars. At her feet grow lilies, and in her hands, love."

He took her breath away. The words seemed to shake her. He had been talking so calmly, in such an ordinary way, and then the sudden poetry. She looked up at this disturbing, handsome man. "Who wrote that?"

"I did. You don't go to market without knowing what you want."

She laughed, but it was a nervous laugh. He had turned the subject to love, and it would be so easy to turn it away, but somehow she did not want to draw back at this moment. She spoke slowly. "I'm told love is an illusion."

"Who by?"

"My uncle," she shrugged. "Even my father says there's no certainty." She heard herself saying the words and she wondered at it, yet still it felt so natural to talk with him. She could speak to so few people about love. Her uncle mocked her gently, her father cared only to see her secure, her friends were as ignorant as she was herself. Somehow this man, with his gentle, confident voice, neither mocked, nor spoiled, nor thought the subject odd.

"There's no certainty." He finished the glass of wine and poured another. "But who wants certainty? If every dawn and sunset were the same, why would we look at them?"

"My uncle says," she said, "that you won't find love if you're looking for it."

"That's because we don't know what to look for."

"Do you?" Her heart was beating so strongly that she could feel it shifting the gold seals at her breast.

He answered in French, with a sentence that she had read long before and had half forgotten. " 'The heart has reasons that reason does not know.' "

"Pascal?"

He nodded, then smiled. "You're surprised that a nothing of mongrel gypsy can read Pascal?"

"No!" Yet she had been thinking exactly that.

He laughed at her protest, then swung his leg off the wall. He picked up the glass of wine he had poured for her and walked about the swelling globe. He held the glass to her. "Do you think love is real, my Lady?"

"I suppose so." She was embarrassed now.

"Do you know what it is?"

She said nothing. She took the glass from him.

He spoke gently. His words, for all their meaning, were edged with humor. "But suppose love came to you from nowhere, out of a sudden dark night, would you know it?"

She looked up at him. His eyes were bright in the small moonlight. He had a half-smile that made his savage face gentle. She knew suddenly why it felt so natural to be here, it was because he had made it so. She could feel his strength, his assurance, his ease. She thought of the hours in which she had tried to persuade herself that Lord Culloden was a strong man, but now, sitting on the low wall, she knew that Christopher Skavadale was setting a standard against which any man might fail. This man was strong enough to know when to be gentle. His strength was almost frightening.

He smiled, as if he knew she would not answer his question. He touched her glass with his own. "Here's to the fastest horse in the world, my Lady. May it run like the north wind."

Her hand was shaking. She raised her glass. "May it be faster."

She sipped the wine. He stepped away from her. He stood by the next pillar and watched her.

She knew what was happening. They talked of love and it seemed as if they skirted some dark, forbidden place where, if she but dared walk boldly in, she would find the magic that she sought. She did not dare. She trembled on the edge of that place, advancing, fearing, retreating. In that mysterious place the soul was naked. She knew the answer to his question. She knew what love was when it came from nowhere on this sudden, dark night, but she could not answer him. She stared at the globe. In the moonlight she traced the words chiselled at its base. "Terra Incognita."

"We Rom have a thing called *dukkeripen.*"

His sudden words startled her. She looked up, grateful that he had broken the silence. "What is it?"

"Telling the future." He smiled at her. "Most of the time it's nonsense, just like the belief that we control fire, but it's useful nonsense. We just tell people what they want to hear, and it's odd how often, once someone tells you that something will happen, you make it happen. You just needed to be told once. Shall I *dukker* you?"

"Tell my fortune?"

"Shall I?"

She shrugged, as though it did not matter whether he did or not. "If you'd like to."

"You have to give me a hand."

"You're going to read my palm?" She sounded disappointed.

"No. Hold your hand out, just hold it out. You'll have to take the glove off and close your eyes."

She peeled down her right glove and put it beside her glass on the wall. She closed her eyes. It felt like a child's game. She smiled nervously.

She held her hand out. She knew he was going to touch her. She wanted him to touch her. The fortune-telling was her excuse, no more, a means to persuade herself that she did not flirt with that dark, forbidden place.

She heard his glass clink as he placed it on the wall. His scabbard scraped on stone and his boots rustled the dead leaves. She waited.

His hands, dry and warm, closed on her hand.

She shuddered. She shuddered in every part of her. With one touch he had answered all the questions. When Lord Culloden touched her there was nothing, yet Skavadale's touch spoke of mystery and wonder and she had to stop a mad impulse to close her fingers on his and draw him toward her.

He stroked her hand. He was gentle. She felt his fingers flicker about her wrist, trace down her palm, stroke magic into her own fingers. She wanted him to kiss her. She wanted to shout a triumph at the whole, dark world because she had been right. The world had told her that love held no mystery, that she must settle for the commonplace, and now this.

His hands seemed to move fast over hers, touching, tingling, and then suddenly pressing. She wanted that touch never to leave her. She let her thumb caress his hand and, as it did, so his touch went away.

"You can open your eyes."

She opened them. She was almost astonished that the world had not changed. He walked around to the far parapet and she looked down at her hand and wished that he still held it.

She looked at this tall, cloaked figure. "Well?"

He was staring at the Castle.

"Mr. Skavadale?"

He turned back to her. "I can't tell the whole future. I don't have the skill."

"What can you tell?"

There was silence. The music came soft over the park. A bat swerved close to the temple's entrance and disappeared.

He stared at her with his light eyes. "You are going to move in shadows, in death, in horror, but you will not be hurt."

She shivered. She was in Dorset, in a park, and this man talked of shadows, death and horror. "You're making it up." She drank her wine and put the glass down. "You're trying to frighten me." She said it defiantly.

He shook his head. "Nothing will be what it appears to be, but you will be safe. Remember that. You will be safe."

She smiled. "That's not a fortune, Mr. Skavadale. That's just pessimism."

He shrugged. "You wanted me to raise the spirits of the dead? Make the earth tremble?"

"It would have been more impressive."

He laughed. "I told you the truth, you must do what you want with it. I wish I could tell you more, but I don't have my mother's skill at *dukkering*."

"Did she tell your fortune?"

He nodded.

"So what did she tell you?"

"That I would find what the Rom are searching for."

She smiled. "And what are the Rom searching for?"

He walked back to her and leaned against the globe, smothering the marble with his black cloak. He had a pleasant smell of leather, horses, and tobacco. "My people have a story."

She looked into his humorous, light eyes. She wondered how many girls dreamed of this man. "Tell me your story."

He smiled. "When the gods put man onto the earth, they gave him a choice. He could do two things. The first was that he could work and make the earth rich. To help him, the gods gave him lordship over every beast; the ox to plow for him, the dog to hunt for him, the cow to feed him, the sheep to clothe him, the horse to carry him. All that, the gods said, man could have." His soft, deep voice paused.

"And the second choice?"

"The second choice was to be poor, to raise no crops, to herd no cattle, to build no monuments. Instead, the gods said, man could pursue happiness. And what, man asked, is that? And the gods said that they had made one creature after man, the last creature they made, and though that creature could be beaten, whipped, twisted, gutted, skinned, and killed, it could never be mastered. Yet if man could find the creature and make the creature come willingly to him, then man would find happiness. So man asked 'What is the creature?' The gods said that the creature was fairer than the dawn and man would know when he had found it. So all the tribes, one by one, chose riches; all the tribes except the Rom. We stole a horse to make our search quicker, and we have roamed the earth ever since and hunted the last and brightest of creation. We have hunted for the creature who is fairer than the dawn."

She laughed. The sound was nervous. She felt as if there was no world outside this small, white building.

He leaned forward. Very slowly, very gently, he raised his hands. She saw them coming and did not move. He pushed the hood of her cloak back so that her pale gold hair shone in the moonlight. "Fairer than the dawn, my Lady, and in her eyes, stars."

She looked into his eyes. "There are no lilies at my feet, Mr. Skavadale."

"You never looked."

The sadness was immense. The music came faint across the park. It told her that another man had her hand, her promise, her body to be his in marriage. She pulled the hood back over her head and took a deep breath. "This is foolish."

"Is it?"

He had taken her to the place she feared, to where truth, however wrapped in the finery of fable and flattery, demanded her response. She could not give him what he wanted. She could not look at him. "I am to marry, Mr. Skavadale. I should not be here."

"Then go, my Lady."

She looked up at him sharply, but said nothing.

He stood. "This need not be said, my Lady, but no one will know we have met."

She began to reply, but fell silent. Tomorrow, she thought, she would have feared just that.

His voice was no longer soft and gentle. "I'll put Hirondelle in the stable for you. Don't let the grooms tighten the throat latch too much, they do that here."

"Yes." She stood. She shook her cloak straight. She was embarrassed. "Yes, they do."

He walked to the top of the steps. "I apologize if I have offended you, my Lady."

She walked to the other side of the entrance. The sky was black, star-spattered, huge. She did not know what to say. She knew he did not want her to leave, to walk back to the music and the candles. Nor did she want to leave.

She did not look at him. "Do your people have a story about what happens when man finds his creature?"

"I've not heard it." He said it casually, his eyes staring up into the stars.

She looked at the Castle. Her place was there, among the dancers who led her toward the well-ordered marriage with Lord Lewis Culloden who would give her children and stand beside her when the children married and lie beside her in the tomb. She felt the immense sadness of it, as if an infinite desolation awaited her.

She looked at him and caught his gaze as he turned his eyes on her. She felt as if she was at the turning point of the earth, in a tiny place, that one move would spin her into chaos.

She could not speak.

Slowly, with infinite gentleness, he raised his right hand and she watched it come close to her face and she told herself that she must move, but then the fingers touched her cheek in a gesture so soft, so comforting, that she shuddered again as he stroked her skin down to her jawbone and then slid his hand, warm and gentle, to the back of her neck.

She stared up at him, her eyes huge.

He kissed her.

She closed her eyes and was astonished.

She kissed him and she felt as if the shudder had started deep inside, had shaken her, warmed her, and she felt, to her astonishment, the same in him. She slid her lips from his, laid her cheek on his shoulder and clung to him with an arm behind his back. She was crying.

Neither spoke. There was nothing to say.

His hand stroked her back. Slowly she stopped the sobs. She kept her eyes shut.

It was impossible. She was to be married. She had come here, she thought, like a young girl who thought that this guilty assignation would be like a naughty game. Instead she had found a power deeper than her comprehension.

He gently tilted her head back, kissed the tears from both her cheeks, and smiled at her. "I promise to come back, my Lady."

She said nothing. She would be married.

He stepped away from her. "And remember. No harm will come to you." He stooped, picked up his saddlebag, and walked down the steps. "I leave you the wine, I'll take Hirondelle to the stable."

She watched him. Her throat was full. She did not know what to say. The memory of that one kiss was like a burning on her, as if a star had fallen to earth.

She watched him mount his horse. He looked at her from the saddle. "I will come back. *Ja develesa, shukar.*"

She watched him ride into the night. She wondered what his last words had meant. She felt an immense solitude as if she was the only creature on the surface of the whole, dark planet.

She did not want to go back to the Castle, that would be worse than loneliness.

She sat on the parapet and poured herself wine. She raised the glass in a toast to herself, a toast to foolishness.

She drank alone in the temple, beneath the stars, and knew that nothing, after that kiss, would ever be the same again. She wept. She was to be married and she would never know happiness. The Gypsy had seen to that. She should not have come, not because of the shame, but because it would be better to live without this memory forever mocking her compromise with love. She leaned her head on a pillar and stared at the tear-blurred stars.

She knew she should go back to the castle. Slowly, as if she was immensely weary, she stood. She looked for her long silk glove and found it had gone. Skavadale must have taken it when her eyes were closed, and that made her smile. He had said he would come back and the missing glove somehow persuaded her it was true.

She walked slowly down the temple steps, her cloak trailing on the white stones. She was alone, but he had promised to come back. He had promised.

14

The fastest horse in the world, she thought, could be bred out of Hirondelle.

The Swallow ran like the wind.

She rode the horse next morning, taking it first beneath her father's window, and then trotting through the town, up past Two Gallows Hill to the Millett's End road. The blossom of yellow broom made the heath bright.

She rode side-saddle. Lord Culloden and his cavalry friends escorted her and she took Hirondelle to the top of the rings, to the earthen bank that had been built in the far off past when men painted themselves blue and fought with bronze and stone. She watched the young men ride among the bushes below, their healthy shouts loud.

It seemed to her that the Gypsy had come in a dream and gone in a dream, leaving only this horse behind. Lord Culloden, whose moustache had not been shaved off, was curious. "Where did you get her?"

"It's Toby's wedding gift."

Lord Culloden seemed rather put out. A wedding gift should be to a couple, not just one person, and Hirondelle was not a horse large enough for his Lordship. He frowned at his friends who played an intricate game on the heath, slashing with their swords at the bushes of broom. "You didn't come back to the ball last night."

"I'm sorry, my Lord, I was feeling unwell."

"Too much champagne?"

"It must have been that." She was appalled because, suddenly, she found it hard even to talk with Lord Culloden. That was not his fault. She had allowed herself to be tempted to the temple in the park, she had flirted with danger, and now she had to struggle against her feelings. Nothing that had happened last night changed her betrothal, nothing had been said that could change it. A part of her yearned to smash her ordered life, to declare the marriage would not take place, but for what? A gypsy adventurer? To be sure he was not a servant, but still he was not a man who would be thought worthy of her. She felt a flash of anger. Even if he was just a servant, Christopher Skavadale was a man worthy of whatever he achieved.

Lord Culloden nodded toward the track that led over the heath. "Bad memories, my Lady?"

She made the proper reply. "Memories of your timely courage, my Lord."

He smiled. He touched first one end, then the other, of his moustache. She wondered if he had forgotten his promise to shave it off. His face, on this morning after the champagne of the long night, looked fleshily heavy as if hinting at what he would look like in middle age.

She turned Hirondelle. His Lordship looked surprised. "You're going?"

"I promised father I'd read to him."

"Splendid! Splendid!" He smiled.

She let the horse gallop to the hill's brink, a gallop that made her feel free and happy. She curbed Hirondelle where the road fell down between the heavy, flower-bright hedges. The valley of Lazen, the Little Kingdom, spread before her. She looked at the far horizons, hazed by the sun, and wondered where in this wide world the

Gypsy had gone. He would come back, he had promised, and that thought gave her a happiness that rose like the song of the larks tumbling over the heath. He would come back.

It happened in the night, an attack so sudden and so painful that the castle was aroused by the sudden fear flickering like flame in the passages.

Dr. Fenner was sleeping in the Earl's rooms. When Campion, a robe wrapped about her night-gown, met the doctor his hands were bright with blood. Caleb Wright, his face grim, hurried past her with an armful of stained, slinking sheets.

The doctor plunged his arms into a bowl of water. "Wait, my Lady."

"Wait?"

"He's not fit to be seen yet."

"What happened?"

"A flux, my Lady." Fenner shook his hands dry and picked up a towel. "Wait, my Lady!" He went into her father's room and Campion heard a moan of terrifying pain before the door blessedly closed.

Caleb Wright came in with fresh sheets. He paused at the door. "My Lady?"

"Caleb?"

"You're to go to Mistress Sarah and say I sent you. She knows what to do."

She frowned. "What is it?"

"You go, my Lady, you go at dawn, and don't you bide questions." Caleb gave the order, nodded at her, and went into the room of pain.

Campion went into her father's sitting room, a room he had not used in years, and leaned her forehead on the window pane. It was cold on her skin. Footsteps hurried in the corridor. She heard the housekeeper shouting for hot water, for towels, and Campion stared into the night over Lazen, the deep night of empty darkness, and knew the death, horror and shadows of which Christopher Skavadale had spoken were pressing close. She shut her eyes on her tears. Her father was dying.

"Caleb sent you?"

"Yes."

Mistress Sarah, who looked older than the rings on the heath, hooked the pot crane toward her. The ceiling of her cottage was low and blackened by smoke. Bundles of dried plants hung on the low beams. "Fool Fenner be up there?"

"Yes."

"Flux?"

"Yes."

The old woman spat at the fire. "Rector?"

"Yes."

"No good mumbling psalms. Good Lord will take him or not." She pushed the scarf back from her thin hair and stared at Campion. "You've grown well, girl." Mistress Sarah reached for a knife. "I delivered you. Easy as pulling giblets, you was. Why your mother had to have a Londoner for her last, I never will know. Killed her sure as Cain. And killed the babe. But I wasn't good enough, oh no. Not Sarah Tyler. Might be that I deliver live babies, but I bain't be from London." She had opened a cupboard and taken down a cloth bag.

Campion smiled. "I hope you'll deliver mine, Sarah."

"Be a fool to have aught else, not unless you wants to die. How old are you girl?"

"Twenty-five this month."

Mistress Sarah laughed. "God! You be late! I had nine by then!" Chickens pecked in the sunlight at her back door. "Pass me a bowl, girl, wooden one. Marrying a lord, are you?"

"Yes."

"Pull the glitter off him, girl, and he'll piss like a peasant. Don't you let him bring no Londoner to your bed. Bed indeed!" She sniffed. "Spit them out on a birth-stool, girl, like the good God meant us to." She took the bowl. Out of the bag she brought a white lump that she sniffed. She made a face, then cut the lump into fragments. A nauseous smell seeped through the rich odors of herbs and flowers. A dog on the settle whined in displeasure. "You be quiet! Bain't for you, be for his lordship."

"What is it?"

"Not your business, girl." She had picked up a pestle and was pounding the nauseous smelling fragments. "Why anyone needs London I don't know. I never went more than a mile from here. My Harry, he once wanted me to go to a fair in Dorchester. We took a ride on old Gattin's wagon and I told them to put me down at Sotter's Farm. The edge of the world, I told them, and I never been so happy as when I walked back that day. Now, you come or stay, girl."

The old woman went out of her back door. Her front door opened onto the Mill Street, but the back led directly to the beech trees which bordered the Shaftesbury road. A goat, tethered to one of the trees, made a run for them. Mistress Sarah hit it as it jerked at the end of its rope, then scurried, bent backed, into the piles of leaf mold between the trees.

Campion followed. The neighbors, seeing her, touched their forelocks.

Mistress Sarah was raking her hands through the old leaves. "My mother taught me this, and her mother before her, but it bain't be good enough for Londoners. Oh no. They knows better. I don't doubt your father paid that London doctor a rare fortune to kill his wife and child! Learning be a great thing, girl, lets you make a fortune for nothing. Still, your father knows better now. There." She had picked some of the brick-red fungus that grows on dead leaves. "Come on, girl. And if I don't live to see your first, then you use my youngest daughter." Mistress Sarah hit the charging goat again. "She knows what to do."

"I will, Sarah."

The old woman cut the red fungus into shreds. "Stops the pain, this, you tell Caleb that. Gives dreams, too."

"What is it?"

"Not your business." She repeated her earlier answer with a frown. "Your business is your business, girl, but this is mine. If the day comes when all the business of Lazen is in the Castle, then that be the day the Castle must go." She mixed the red and white scraps and poured them carefully into a white linen bag. She pulled the drawstring tight. "There. That's for your father with my respect. He's a good man."

Campion took the bag. She hesitated, knowing what answer she would receive, but decided that the question, in politeness, had to be asked. "What do I owe you?"

"Be off with you! You knows better than that, girl! Go on!"

She climbed into the chaise and the coachman shook the reins. She smiled at Mistress Sarah. There would have been a time, Campion knew, when a woman like Sarah Tyler would have been burned as a witch, but Lazen had its reasons for protecting such women. The Castle provided the small cottage and, as rent, Mistress Sarah provided the old medicines. Campion looked at the white linen bag and prayed for a miracle.

She gave the bag to Caleb Wright who pushed it into a pocket. When she asked him what it was, he frowned. "Why do you think he's been sleeping, my Lady?"

"Dr. Fenner's laudanum?"

"Fenner! He couldn't put a tired cat to dreaming! I've been giving him Mistress Sarah's physic these last two weeks. Now you go on in. Your father wants you."

The Earl said nothing as she entered. He just held out his hand for her to hold.

She took the hand and sat on the bed.

He looked worse than she had ever seen him. His skin was white, the lines deep, his mouth pulled down. There was sweat on his forehead where she wiped it with her hand. The room stank.

Father and daughter stayed in silence. Downstairs, on the gravel forecourt, the loud voices of Lord Culloden's officer friends shouted and laughed.

He winced. "Get rid of them."

"I will."

"Tell them to go to hell."

"Father!" She said it soothingly, stroking his forehead. He calmed. His mouth twitched in a brief smile.

"Fenner's an idiot."

"He's tried to help you."

"Doctors can't help. They just lie and take their fee."

She stroked his head. "What did he say?"

The head turned on the pillow with agonizing slowness. "He told me I'm dying."

She smiled, though there was a prickling at her eyes. "You said doctors lie."

"Not this time. Not this time. I told him he wouldn't be paid if he lied to me." He smiled at his small victory. "You know I once rode from here to Werlatton in a straight line and I took every damn fence and every damn stream? Now look at me."

She said nothing. She stroked his forehead and held his hand.

His smile was a death's head face. "I won ten guineas for that. My father said it couldn't be done. No one's done it since."

"No one will ever do it again."

There was silence again. The voices of the cavalry officers were farther away. They were trying to cram themselves into the small boat that was used to clean the lake. From outside her father's rooms came the sound of stiff brushes on the carpet.

He sighed. "I suppose Mounter will want to come and mumble over me."

"Not if you don't want him."

He shrugged. "Must do the decent thing." The thought amused him, or perhaps it was the next thing he said that caused the smile to crease the corners of his eyes. "The Bishop said that heaven is year round grass with stiff fences."

She smiled. "And no plow?"

"No plow." He blinked. "And foxes that run for God-damned ever." His face suddenly tightened as he said the last three words. He clenched his teeth and the breath hissed on his lips. He was pale as the sheets. He closed his eyes, opened them again, and looked into her face. "If I'd kept the dawn start I might not be in this bed."

She smiled sadly. Her father had changed Lazen's hunting tradition. Instead of the dawn meet in the mists he had unleashed the hounds at mid-morning when the foxes had digested their night feeding and would run faster. Her father, in just such a fast chase, had fallen at a hedge and his horse had rolled on him. He had never complained. What was planned for the fox was due to the hunter, he would say, and over the years of his paralysis and pain he would always have the master to his room to tell him news of each hunt.

Her father's hand tightened on hers. "Which King died in Berkeley Castle?"

She smiled at the odd question. "Edward II."

"You're much too clever for a girl. Know how the fellow died?"

She shook her head. Her father grinned his corpse's grin. "They put a horn into his ass and then ran a hot poker up it."

"They didn't!"

"They did. Not a mark on him, they say. Straight up! He preferred tupping men, you see, so it was revenge."

"Oh." She smiled. He liked to shock her, but it seemed this story was not for that purpose.

He closed his eyes to fight the pain. His hand tightened feebly on hers, then relaxed. "That's what the pain's like, my love. Again and again. Like a red hot poker in a royal ass. God knows why I deserve it."

"You don't."

"Mounter says it's God's will. I shall have a word with the Almighty about that."

She smiled. "Perhaps the pain will go away, father."

He looked at her. "You never were a fool, so don't start being one now that I'm dying." He squeezed her hand again. "Did you see Sarah?"

"Yes."

"How is she?"

"She hasn't forgiven you for the London doctor."

He gave a weak smile. "She never will. She called me a damned fool in the market place in front of the whole damned town." He smiled. "She was right."

"What did she give me?"

"Something to make me sleep."

"To make you better?"

"Better." His hand tightened again and she saw the rigidity in his jaw, the flicker in his eyes, and she knew that a spasm was racking him. Tears showed at her eyes, tears she was determined not to shed.

He looked at her. "Can't stand women who cry."

"I know." It came out as a sob.

He pulled her with feeble strength so that her head was on his shoulder. He put his thin, weak arm about her and let her weep.

"Campion," her father said later. "Bloody silly name that. I wanted to call you Agatha, but Campion runs in the bloody family. I suppose you'll have to call one of your daughters Campion, poor little bugger."

She laughed as she was supposed to laugh. She felt exhausted by crying.

She had spent the day with her father, watching him sleep fitfully, talking, sometimes laughing. A succession of visitors had come to the room, some welcome, some not, but all curious. Now, as dusk fell beneath a great bank of black cloud in the west, she was alone with him again. He had told the doctor, the rector, even Caleb, to leave them together.

He turned his head. "Fenner says this could last for days, God help me." It was the nearest he had come to complaining. He looked at the four golden seals at her breast. "You know my father knew the first Countess? He was six when she died."

"I know."

"They say she had a tongue like a whip." He smiled. "She was a great, great lady. That's what you have to be now, my love."

It made her cry again.

He patted her hand. He sighed. He closed his eyes, moaned, and she waited for the spasm to go. He seemed exhausted by it. He rolled his head toward her. "You're not happy about marrying Culloden, are you?"

"No."

He grimaced, but whether in pain or at her answer, she

could not tell. He sighed again. "Do you remember that alder tree at Werlatton?"

"Yes." The tree was in truth two trees. They had begun as saplings side by side and, in a spring storm, the saplings had been wind-lashed so that they twined about each other. Campion saw them much later, before the fire that killed her elder brother had burned the tree down. It began as two trunks and then, four feet above the ground, the trunks joined in a writhing, lumpy mass before, glorious above the knotted wood, a single trunk grew smooth and straight.

Her father smiled. "Think of marriage like that. You start separate, there's a period of joining which has to be difficult, and then it comes right. It just takes time. Two people don't grow together without problems."

"I know."

He tried to smile. "I hope you know. You need a husband."

"I do?" She tried to make the question light.

He nodded. "If Toby dies, my love, then you'll need a man here to keep Julius in order."

"Toby won't die."

"He's riding a high horse, my love. I don't blame him. Young men should do that." He gripped her hand. "Marry soon, marry quietly if I'm dead, but marry."

She nodded.

He smiled. "Light the portrait."

There were silver holders either side of the painting of her mother and Campion pushed candles into the sockets, took a taper, and lit the eight wicks.

He stared at his dead Madeleine. "She was a joy. You're like her."

"You're making me cry again."

"Do you remember your mother teaching you the minuet at Auxigny?"

She nodded. It had been on the lawn by the moat, across from the Mad Duke's magical shrine, on a night that was stupendous with stars, and her mother, when Campion was still a tiny girl, had taught her the intricate steps of the minuet and then, joy on her face, had gone into a peasant dance, romping and free, singing the tune aloud and holding her small, laughing, capering daughter by her hand and waist in the moonlight.

Her father smiled. "The two of you looked more beautiful than the stars."

She looked at him. "I love you."

"I know that, fool."

She cried.

He waited till she was calm. "Tell Caleb to bring me Sarah's mixture."

"Now?"

"Now."

He winced again, and she thought of the red hot poker of pain that slammed up him. She went to the door. A dozen faces looked at her in the ante-chamber. "Caleb?"

The Earl said his goodnights to rector, doctor and servants.

He told her to stay.

He smiled at her. "Leave the rents alone; if the cottage is happy then so is the Castle, and always ride the wettest furrow of a plowed field."

She laughed at the hunting adage at the end.

He held his hand to her, took her within his arm and hugged her close. "I love you, child."

"I know." Beside the bed Sarah's mixture of white and red made a sediment in a glass of brandy. Her father looked at it and grimaced.

"Looks like liver fluke."

"It will make you sleep."

"I know." He hugged her. "Remember what I told you.

Marry. Don't let the crucifying bastards get their hands on Lazen."

"I won't, father."

"I wish I could have seen you marry."

"You will, father."

He grimaced. "Promise me you'll marry?"

She kissed him. "I promise you."

He stared into her eyes. "I love you, Campion Lazender."

"I love you, father."

"Don't cry. Don't cry. For sweet Jesus' sake, don't cry."

There was thunder in the night, a racking, splintering, crashing storm that brought boughs down in the park and flooded the banks of the lake.

In the morning there was a sharp west wind. The sky was ragged with driven clouds.

William Carline, steward of Lazen Castle, climbed to the topmost point of the Great House at dawn. He dropped a rope-tied bundle at his feet.

He rarely came up here. He allowed himself a moment to stare from the high, stone balustraded platform. He looked from the town with its mixture of thatch and red tile to the thick wind-tossed greenness of the eastern woods. To the north was the blackthorn of Sconce Hill and to the west stretched the fertile Lazen valley. The "Little Kingdom" was damp and shadowed by cloud. The wind lifted his sparse hair, the same wind that flattened the smoke from the castle smithy eastward.

He untied the halyard of the flagpole, then stooped, picked up the great, colored bundle, and pushed the toggle of the bundle into the halyard's loop.

There was one more toggle and loop to join, and then he ran the bundle to the very top of the pole, pulled on the slack, the slip knot came apart and, like a damp flower opening, the great standard of Lazen fell, unfolded, caught the air, and snapped noisily in the wind. Scarlet, yellow, blue and green, a banner that had flown over this valley for centuries, a banner that had seen the family ennobled, that had been added to as they married other noble families, but which still bore the proud bloodied lance-head of the Lazenders. The banner stretched out in the storm's wake of wind.

William Carline leaned back, watching the flag for a second, and then, as if the task was a burden, he pulled the halyard once more.

Unusually, on this morning of wind, a knot of people stood at the Castle entrance. They were townspeople and they too watched the flag.

They saw the great emblazoned standard spreading its glorious colors against the low, dark clouds, and then it sank to the half and stopped.

Vavasour George Aretine Lazender, Fifth Earl of Lazen, widower, father and cripple, was dead.

15

They buried the Earl in the vaulted crypt of the old church. He was carried the short distance from the castle in a hearse drawn by black-plumed horses.

The sixth Earl was not present.

Sir Julius Lazender was not present.

When it was done Campion stared down into the vault. On her father's velvet draped coffin, bright in the gloom, was his coronet with its eight silver balls.

Beyond it, shadowed, were the other coffins, their velvet palls faded and matted, their coronets misted by cobwebs. The first Campion was there, the first Countess, the first woman to wear the seals that now hung on Campion's black dress. There, too, was Campion's mother between the new, vivid velvet and the tiny coffin that bore the child whose birth had killed her.

She stared. Beside her, embarrassed, was Lord Culloden. "Should we go, my Lady?"

She ignored him. She stared at the palled coffins. One day, she thought, she would join that company. One day her name would be chiselled stone on this floor, worn over the years to a dull inscription. *Hic jacet* Lady Campion Culloden.

Lord Culloden stirred beside her.

Or perhaps, she thought, she would be buried with the

Cullodens, buried in some strange church with her lozenge shield fading on the nave's wall.

She looked up. The Bishop, the Rural Dean and the Rector watched her across the opened floor. She smiled sadly at the Bishop. "Thank you, my Lord." She pulled the veil over her face and turned away from the crypt.

She walked from the church into the sunlight. She kept her head high. Until her brother returned she was Lazen. She would be a great lady.

The castle seemed silent after the Earl's death. The visitors went, the great rooms and long corridors were quiet. Flax sheets covered the furniture in the earl's room. His bedding and mattress were burned. Campion moved the portrait of her mother to the Long Gallery.

She was busy. A quarter day was due and she had to sign letters and seal them with the castle's great seal. She had done it often enough for her father, now she did it for the sixth Earl. She heard nothing of Toby.

She wrote to Lord Paunceley, prevailing on her father's old friendship, and begging his Lordship that Toby should be brought back from France. There was no reply. The news from the Vendée, where Toby helped the rebels, frightened her. She dreaded the post, the London newspapers, the sound of hooves on the gravel that might be a messenger bringing the tidings of another death.

She heard nothing of Christopher Skavadale. At night, when Lazen seemed empty, she would remember the kiss, but it seemed now to belong to a distant past, a time when her father was alive, when Lazen had a purpose. The search for love's wonder was drowned in grief, in hard work, just as the black drapes of mourning dulled the castle's rooms.

Lord Culloden went to London. He said he would return in a month. Their marriage was postponed.

The wedding gifts were still piled in the Yellow Drawing Room. The townsfolk had given her a splendid, beautiful picture of the Castle. Campion herself was in the foreground of the picture, driving her phaeton behind high stepping bays at the Castle gate. The painting was meant to hang in the large room of Periton House. Campion no longer rode to see if the plaster dried on the walls.

She schooled Hirondelle, riding the mare to the lonely chalk hills north of Lazen, galloping under clouded skies of summer, and slowly, as the crops ripened to harvest, she felt her old obsession return. Skavadale, Skavadale. Hirondelle reminded her of Skavadale. As her grief mellowed so the dark, slim, lively face came back to haunt her waking dreams. "He'll come back to us, Hirondelle." She would say it on the lonely hilltops, her voice snatched by the summer wind into emptiness.

Her evenings she spent in the Long Gallery. She played old, half-forgotten tunes on the harpsichord. She would look sometimes at the portraits of the first Countess in her old age and she would see herself as she would look in age, and she wondered if, when she had that gray hair and that straight back, she would reflect on a barren, wasted life. Mrs. Hutchinson, Carline, the Reverend Mounter, all thought she was obsessed by melancholy. She was thinner, her lovely face shadowed. Letters were sent to Uncle Achilles. Dr. Fenner was called to the castle, but Campion refused to see him.

Yet one morning she suddenly seemed brighter. She took breakfast and ordered Wirrell, the estate steward, to come to the castle. She walked with him to the lake, her voice crisp and her manner energetic, and the castle was glad that she seemed to have recovered some of her old, happy ebullience.

They were less happy with the task she had set them.

She had ordered the sunken barge to be taken from the water.

A footman who was a strong swimmer looped chains over the prow, hooking them beneath the swell of the Lazen escutcheon. The fence of the park had to be taken down to give the horses room to haul westward, yet even with thirty horses being urged on by grooms and farm-workers it seemed the barge could not be shifted.

She insisted they keep trying. She ordered a rope tied to the pavilion and pulled sideways to rock the boat in its mud bed and, as the pavilion pillar splintered, so the great teams jerked forward and Wirrell shouted to keep them moving and the men cheered because at last the hull had freed itself from the clinging slime of the lake's bed.

Campion laughed with the soaking, happy men as the boat came, smeared and stinking, lurching up onto the bank with the water pouring from its sprung planks. She saw the cutlery, broken crystal, and smashed china on its deck. George Hamblegird, who feared he would have to rebuild the craft, scratched his head beside her. "Better let her dry out, my Lady, before we lift her onto a wagon."

She smiled at him. "I don't want it lifted onto a wagon, George. I want it burned."

He looked at her in astonishment. "You want what?"

She was walking away from the barge. "I said burn it!"

Some thought that her father's death had turned her brain, but the order had come in the voice of a great lady and the order was obeyed. It took two days, the wood was so wet, but by cramming the soggy interior with pitch smeared lumber and tinder, the boat was burned. At night Campion could see the dull red of the fire, and by day there was a smear of smoke that drifted over the park. When it was done, and when the barge was just scraps of blackened timber on the scorched grass, Hamblegird brought her a curious, knobbly lump of silver. "Reckon that be a knife we didn't find, my Lady, melted right down!"

She put it on the Long Gallery mantel like a trophy.

Yet if burning the boat in which she had accepted marriage was her private gesture, there could be no such public gesture. In August, in a flurry of dust, outriders, carriages, and servants, Lord Culloden returned. With him, whether by accident or design, came Uncle Achilles and Cartmel Scrimgeour.

She felt as if the tribe of men, the capable, authoritative tribe, had come to end her days of sad freedom. There was a sudden air of decision in the castle, like a cold wind in a warm house.

Lord Culloden, the day of his arrival, begged to walk with her in the Water Garden. Mrs. Hutchinson, bundled with shawls against an unseasonal north wind, sat in an arbor of roses to watch them where they paced the walks.

Campion, a black parasol over her head, kept her elbows tight to her side so that Lord Culloden could not take her arm. She walked slowly, stopping often to stare into the slow moving, shallow canals where the carp swam among the lily pads. Lord Culloden seemed to turn his body toward her as he walked. He gesticulated. Mrs. Hutchinson, half dozing among the roses, thought how solicitous he looked as he spoke so earnestly to Campion.

"I worry for you, dear Campion."

"I would not have you worried, my Lord."

Their shoes seemed loud on the gravel. From the lawns beyond the Garden House came the slithering whisper of scythes.

Lord Culloden took off his black hat, frowned at the red lining, then put it back on. "You would not see Dr. Fenner?"

Campion stared at the gravel ahead of her. "I am not ill, my Lord."

"You're thin, my dear, very thin."

"I've always been thin." She said it defensively and stopped on one of the bridges. She stared into the water.

Lord Culloden leaned his back against the bridge. In London Valentine Larke had given him good news, news that the French government forces were closing on *Le Revenant,* and that soon, very soon, Larke expected to hear of the death of the sixth Earl. Larke also told Culloden that the Fallen Ones were demanding a swift marriage. "I don't care if she's in mourning! She has to be tied up, my Lord. There must be no loose ends that can be dragged out into the open. Marry her!"

Culloden looked sideways at her. Light was reflected from the canal, light that rippled on her face as it had on that day in the pleasure barge. He thought how beautiful she was, like a shy, wild creature that had to be tempted with exquisite cunning into the nets of the hunters. It was a pity she must die, though he was consoled by the knowledge that, before she was sacrificed, he would take her in marriage. And then? He still did not know how she was to die. He pushed the problem away and turned, so that his elbow was beside hers. He touched a finger to the ends of his moustache. "Your uncle and Scrimgeour asked me to talk with you."

She looked at him. So the conjunction of their arrival was no accident. She looked back at the wind-rippled water, bright with lilies. "You needed to be asked, my Lord?" A fish moved in the dark shadows beneath her and she knew she had been churlish. It was not Lord Culloden's fault that the Gypsy haunted her dreams. She looked at him. "I'm sorry, my Lord."

As an act of contrition she let him take her elbow. He talked softly but persuasively. He talked of a danger to Lazen, of the future's uncertainty, of Toby's irresponsibility. She protested at that, but it was true.

Toby should be here, not pursuing his futile vengeance in France.

Culloden spoke of Sir Julius. "Rumor says he's drunk twenty hours of the day. Rumor says worse."

"Do we listen to rumor, my Lord?"

He shrugged. "Can you imagine Julius taking up residence here? How will you spend your days, my Lady? How will you stop him destroying the pictures, the treasures, the books? And how will you spend your nights?"

She said nothing. She stopped at the north west corner of the garden and stared at the white temple across the park. If it was Skavadale's hand, she thought, that held her arm, then she would not want to shrink from the touch. She let the wind catch her parasol and used the sudden motion to disengage her elbow.

Lord Culloden took a deep breath. He folded his hands at his back. He cleared his throat. "I once asked for your hand in marriage, dear lady," he sounded acutely embarrassed, "and now, with great trembling, I do so again."

She stopped. She looked at him quizzically.

He smiled. "I would bring to your life some solace and joy. I fear more unhappiness, I fear your cousin, I wish only to protect you as I once had the honor to do."

The memory of her rescue on the Millett's End road always brought a pang of guilty debt to Campion. She looked down at the gravel. "My Lord?"

His voice was low and urgent. "It is seemly to wait, dear Campion, to wait till the mourning is over, but I fear for you if we wait. You will forgive frankness?"

"I would be grateful for it, my Lord."

"We should marry. We should have a quiet ceremony. Later, when the unhappiness is forgotten, we can celebrate. It is your uncle's belief that your father would have wished it so, and it is Scrimgeour's opinion that we should wed and wed soon for Lazen's sake."

She said nothing. She turned and walked along one of the paths. She had promised her dying father that she would marry, that she would have Lord Culloden to protect Lazen. That promise was heavy in her, as heavy as the promise that Skavadale would return.

She thought how she leaned on the Gypsy's promise, leaned on it as if her life was not her own, but in the hands of some benevolent fate. She waited for the Gypsy to come back as if he could free her from her own promise.

Yet she knew Christopher Skavadale did not have that power. What was between herself and the Gypsy, what had happened on that guilty, star-bright night, was a thing of shadow. The reality was the castle, her brother's absence, the promise she had made to a dying man.

She looked into Lord Culloden's face, seeing the lineaments of middle age, the heavy face of a man who would be master of a great fortune. She could see him big in a saddle, his voice confident, a man of few ideas and those irrefutable. Yet, she supposed, that was what Lazen needed. She did not think him a bad man. The worst that she could say of Lord Culloden was that he had a moustache, that his waist filled perceptibly, and that his touch did not make her veins thrill with excitement. "I will think about it, my Lord."

"I ask nothing more."

She thought that he asked for a great deal more, but she smiled, said that the wind was chilling her, and went indoors.

Dinner that evening was an uncomfortable meal, the conversation more notable for its silences than its words, and Campion was glad to leave the three men to their port, walnuts, cigars, and the chamber-pot that was taken from its place in the sideboard.

She went to the Long Gallery where, an hour later, Uncle Achilles found her.

She smiled as he sat beside her. He put his boots on the window seat, shook his head, and imitated Cartmel Scrimgeour's unctuous voice. " 'What exquisite port, what splendid refreshment!' "

She smiled.

Achilles d'Auxigny laughed. "It was execrable port. I ordered the very worst from your cellarmaster because I knew Scrimgeour wouldn't know the difference. I then kept the brandy for myself!" He waved at the decanter he had brought with him. "You don't mind?"

"Of course not."

"Or if I take a cigar?"

"Please." She watched as he lit the cigar from a candle. "You've come to lecture me, haven't you?"

He nodded. "As an uncle, a bishop, and a sinner it is my solemn duty."

She said nothing. The smoke from his cigar drifted into the night beyond the window.

Achilles poured brandy. "Poor Lord Culloden. Poor puzzled Lord Culloden. The English are so bad at being puzzled, so very bad. It means that God isn't doing what they expect him to do. Poor Lord Culloden."

She had to smile at his extravagant tone of voice. "Poor?"

"The silly man, my dear Campion, has somehow got it into his head that you do not wish to marry him." Achilles smiled at her. "He's quite right too, isn't he?"

He looked at her so impishly that he made her laugh, a rare sound in these weeks since her father had died.

He smiled at her laughter. "And I am here, dear niece, to tell you that you should marry him." He made a rueful face at her. "Your father wanted it, I think you need it, and I'm sure Lazen needs it. Mr. Scrimgeour," and here

Uncle Achilles made his voice pompous, "is most insistent that you marry Culloden. The only sensible thing for the girl to do!" Achilles smiled at her. "Forget love. It's a dream. It might come, it might not, and it doesn't matter. Love is a fancy for the unfledged. Marry him and make Lazen safe, then find yourself a nice, warm lover if you need one." His face was mischievous. "You could even try the Prince of the Gypsies."

She looked at him in alarm.

He laughed. "Don't worry, my dear niece. I did not tell Lewis the truth." He tapped ash into a porcelain bowl. "I saw you leave the ball that night. Did you go to our noble savage?"

"No." She looked defiantly at him. "I was feeling faint."

Solemnly he raised the hand which bore the ring of the Bishop of Bellechasse. "*Te absolvo.* You are the worst liar I know, Campion Lazender."

She felt ashamed. She could not look at him. "Nothing happened, uncle."

"Of course not. You're not that foolish!" Achilles smiled. "Poor Campion. Do you find your Prince very appealing?"

For some reason the line from Pascal came into her head and she quoted it softly. "The heart has reasons that reason doesn't know."

Achilles laughed. "My dear child! Pascal, eh? You do have a bad attack, don't you? Pascal is so eloquent, so charming! Man is the fallen King! How we fear the infinite far spaces! And what does it all boil down to? To nothing. Pascal was a small man who dared not let go of God's apron strings. Dear, dear Campion, what reasons can the heart have that will remove the awkward fact that your Gypsy is just that, a Gypsy! A servant! A peasant!"

"He's more than that!"

"Oh." Achilles mocked her. "Do tell me."

She shrugged. "He works with Toby, not for him. He works for Lord Paunceley, like you do!"

Achilles stared at her, frowning. "He told you that?"

She nodded.

His voice was suddenly chilling. "If he told you that, then he was being very foolish. Does he aspire to you? He told you to impress you, yes?" She said nothing. He looked at her profile, bent toward the table, and his voice was harsh. "You have to give him up, Campion."

"I know." She said it feebly, unhappily. She had hoped against hope that Uncle Achilles would understand, yet she knew that Christopher Skavadale was not of her birth. For all his scorn of convention, Uncle Achilles could not blind himself to that brutal fact.

Achilles stared into the night. "You will forget your Gypsy. You will rule your heart's reasons, Campion, and I will never embarrass you by talking of him again. We shall pretend that this conversation has not taken place." He smiled as she looked at him. "Are we agreed, favorite niece of mine?"

She smiled sadly. "Agreed."

"So!" He blew a smoke ring. "Do I have to inflict the tedious Scrimgeour on you? He will be unctuous, he will be insistent, and he will give you a hundred good reasons why you must marry and marry quickly. Do you want to talk with him?"

She shook her head. "No."

"Then you must talk to me."

She sighed. "I know what you're going to say."

"How boringly predictable you must find me."

She smiled. "I'm sorry, uncle." She stood. She walked slowly to the gallery's western end, turned, and stared at him where he sat so elegant and neat in the candlelight. "You want me to marry Lewis, uncle." She said it flatly.

"I don't care if you marry the King of Prussia, my dear, but I care that you're married and married well. Lewis is convenient, he serves your purpose. Your purpose is not love. Your purpose is property. You don't have to share a pillow with him, just make sure that if you have a child it looks vaguely like him." He laughed.

She ran a finger down the golden seals at her breast. "Do you want an answer now?"

"I couldn't bear an answer now. You're altogether too emotional, you would undoubtedly weep, and I would be forced to go to bed with a guilty conscience." He smiled. "However, the day after tomorrow I shall return to London, doubtless with the egregious Scrimgeour beside me, and I would like to know by then."

"That soon?"

"And if the answer is yes, dear niece, then I shall be back in two weeks to lead you to the altar."

"Two weeks!"

He stood. "I've never thought you foolish, Campion. You're one of the few people I know worthy to be a relative of mine, so think about it, be sensible, and give me your answer tomorrow." He spoke kindly, even lovingly, but with stern purpose.

She stared at him, then nodded. "I will tell you tomorrow." She turned to the window, staring into the shadows of the night for the dark horseman who would come back, but the shadows were empty. She was alone.

In the Vendée the rebellion was being crushed. The government was winning.

They won by ruthlessness, by burning the crops, poisoning the wells, and slaughtering the peasants. If they slaughtered all, they reasoned, then they would be bound to kill the guilty. God, as a Pope had once said, could sort the innocent from the rest.

The guillotine never stopped in Nantes. The blade rose and fell to the sound of the crowd's pleasure.

The machine of death had to be fed. The peasants from the rebellious Vendée were a constant supply, yet some people yearned for the old days when the well-dressed aristos had been dragged up the steps to be laid on the soaked board. And on that same night in September when Campion spoke with her uncle in Lazen's Long Gallery, there was hope, at last, that a real aristo would be brought for the crowd's amusement.

A man had come to claim the reward for *Le Revenant,* for the English Earl who fought in France, for Toby Lazender. The man, on a dank September evening, guided a column of troops through a dripping, silent pine forest toward the village where *Le Revenant* had his hiding place.

The Colonel who had been an army butcher no longer led the troops. His report on the bungling at Saint Gilles had guaranteed his death, a report written by a Captain Tours who was now a full Colonel and took care to write his own reports. Colonel Tours commanded the troops on their slow, dusk approach.

Colonel Tours' troops were ill trained. They feared the rebels who had such fatal expertise in ambushes and sudden death. The soldiers moved slowly. Night threatened to end the operation by imposing chaos on the half-trained men.

Tours had hoped to surround the village and then slowly tighten his cordon of bayonets and bullets. Yet the onset of night forced him to abandon the plan. As the shadows stretched long in the dusk he ordered an immediate and frontal attack.

He had been fortunate so far. Not one sentry had been in the pine trees and his men had reached the lip of the valley unseen. He stressed to the officers that the attack must be fast, that the men must carry their bayonets quickly to the enemy, that speed would win this battle.

He shouted them forward.

A ragged line of uniformed men burst from the tree line and ran across the small, damp fields. Hedges slowed them, as did their lack of shoes and the gnawing hunger in their bellies, yet Tours drove them toward the small village where panic could be seen in the torchlit street.

The first muskets twinkled at the village edge, bright sparks in the twilight that left small clouds of drifting white smoke. The noise of the balls fluttering overhead made some of the troops dive to the ground.

"Get up, you bastards! Up!"

More muskets fired from the village. Tours swore. He could see the villagers escaping, running into the safety of the farther hills. He shouted at his men to hurry.

A musket ball clanged on his scabbard, another tore at the leaves of a hedge behind him. "Fire! Fire!"

The troops fired a massive volley. The noise rolled like crackling thunder, echoing back from the hills, and then the thunder seemed to grow, to fill the air, and, as he burst through the bank of smoke left by the volley, Tours saw that a house had exploded in the village. "Go! Go!"

He guessed that one of his men's musket balls had struck a lantern that had spilled onto a powder barrel. Whatever, the shot had caused the explosion and the explosion had taken the heart from the village's defenders. They were running.

Tours felt an immense anger. *Le Revenant* would escape again, and the last soldier who had let *Le Revenant* escape had climbed the wooden stairs of Nantes' guillotine. "On, you bastards, on!"

The troops, panting from the charge, ran ragged into the village's single street.

They took no prisoners, there were none to take. The rebels had fled.

There was scarcely anything to plunder, only some coarse bread, some cheese, a goat, some wasp-eaten apples, and two dozen chickens.

The house that had exploded burned fiercely, the rafters collapsing in a shower of sparks. The heat was extraordinary, making the men stay a good thirty yards from the roaring flames. At least one man had died in the explosion, for his body lay close to the back door of the house, the man's head almost beneath the fallen, white hot roof beams.

Colonel Tours was not interested in the dead man. He cursed his own men, cursed their failure, tried to think of a glib excuse that would persuade Citizen Marchenoir in Paris why they had failed again.

His men did not care about Citizen Marchenoir. They cared for the good boots they could see on the corpse. Good boots were a rarity in the France of liberty.

They found a hook in one of the village barns, a rope in a stable, and they tossed the roped hook to snag the corpse before the fire destroyed those good boots.

They had to throw the hook a dozen times before it caught in the dead man's clothes. They pulled the corpse back from the scorching, terrible flames and eager hands reached for the fine leather riding boots. They had agreed to cast lots for them.

The top half of the corpse was horribly burned, the head and shoulders almost shriveled to half their size and blackened by the flames.

Tours watched them. He was tempted to order them to give him the fine boots, but what use were boots to a doomed man?

"Colonel! Colonel!" One of his officers was shouting. "Colonel!"

"What is it!"

The Captain brought Tours a sword that had been hidden beneath the half-shriveled body.

The hilt was still hot. The snakeskin grip had been browned by the heat. Tours drew it.

It was a lovely, lethal weapon. The steel shone in the brilliant light of the fire. The officers looked enviously at the Colonel.

The blade was engraved. Tours held it so that the light struck at an angle and peered at the design. He saw a coat of arms, lavishly rich, supported by armored knights and surmounted by a coroneted beast. Beneath it was a motto, two words of English, "Dare All."

The shield bore a smeared lance head, the sign of Lazen, and slowly, unbelievably, it dawned on Colonel Tours who the dead man was.

In a French village, looted and gutted, beside a house that burned itself to fine ash, Colonel Tours was looking at the body of Lazen's sixth Earl.

There would be no coronet in his grave, no dusty plumes on his horses, no velvet for his pall.

Le Revenant was dead.

The next evening, as they waited for dinner, Campion surprised the three men by saying she was not hungry. She took a bottle of wine, a glass, and walked out of the castle. Mrs. Hutchinson tried to follow her, but Campion insisted on being alone.

She went to the temple.

She sat on the wall and stared at the incised zodiac.

She had argued with herself for so long. She believed in the magic of love, that the stars could fall to silver a world, yet duty mocked her belief.

Duty was marriage. There was no need to love, only a need to make the lawyers happy, to preserve the house.

She thought of Skavadale. She thought how her body had shuddered when he touched her. She thought of his arms about her, the kiss, she thought of his words that he had himself mocked, but said all the same. Stars in her eyes, lilies at her feet, and love in her hands.

Yet the arguments spilled like water held in her hands. If Toby died then Sir Julius would crawl out from wherever he hid in his foulness and she knew that she could not spend her life fending him off or protecting the treasures of the house against him and his friends. She would need a man.

And if Toby did not die? Then she could not marry a Gypsy, a man known to the house as a groom. She wondered why not.

She smiled into the sunset and spoke aloud. "I can do whatever I like."

But the words sounded strange to her. She had duties. She had been reared, not to extravagance and careless fancy, but to responsibilities. You live in this house, her father had told her, because you deserve to.

She thought of the Gypsy's promise.

She thought of her own promise.

She stood.

She held the bottle over the steps, paused, and tilted it. She watched the wine fall like a libation to the old gods, the gods who had made a creature fairer than the dawn, and then abandoned it.

Cartmel Scrimgeour, standing with Lord Culloden in the window of the Music Room, frowned. "What is she doing?"

The answer was a discord played on the spinet, a sound that made both men turn round.

"She's growing up," Achilles d'Auxigny said. "She's discovering that the world isn't a warm cradle, but a great cold, horrid, open vastness. She'll cry when she sees it. Any child would cry if they could see the waste spaces of adulthood. Childhood's end, Scrimgeour. Childhood's end."

The lawyer laughed. "I'm sure I don't understand you at all!"

"I'm French," Achilles said in curt explanation. He closed the lid on the keyboard and walked into the evening to meet his niece.

She told him she would marry Lord Culloden in two weeks time.

He put one arm about her shoulders and led her to a back door of the castle. He took her that way so that no one should see her tears.

She would be married.

16

Old men dozed.

Young men yawned and wondered which drawing-room they would conquer the next day.

A knight from the shires snored gently, his ample belly rising and falling. Flies walked among the horse hairs of the Speaker's wig.

It was an autumn evening, yet the heat in Britain's House of Commons was as oppressive as on any mid-summer night. Great mats had been hung at the open windows, mats soaked in aromatic liquids to fight the stench of the River Thames.

"Believe me!" The voice rose in the chamber. "Those who attempt to level, never equalize!" There were a few murmurs of agreement. Some of the opposition slumped lower on their benches. Valentine Larke was one who murmured agreement.

A member entered the far door and walked carefully within one of the two woven lines that ran the length of the carpeted central aisle of parliament. If two opposing members faced each other with their toes on the lines, then neither could reach the other with a drawn sword. Thus, by toeing the line, was the peace of Parliament maintained.

The newcomer was searching the government benches.

He saw Larke, smiled in recognition, and came toward him. "I've become a message boy!" He gave Larke a sealed paper, then glanced toward the orator. "Oh God! Burke on his hobby horse? I suppose one had better listen." He sat wearily.

Larke pulled the gummed red wafer from the paper.

He unfolded it. The message was in French.

Not a muscle moved in his face as he read it. To anyone watching it would have seemed as if the message was of trivial interest. The flat, bland eyes read it twice, then he leaned over to the man who had brought it. "Who gave it to you?"

"Fellow outside, Larke. Handsome beggar!" He saw he had not satisfied Larke. "Tall, blue eyes, black hair, young. Civil sort of fellow. Apologized for troubling me. Not a bit, I said . . ." He spoke to air. Larke had stood and, with a curt bow to the Speaker, left the House.

Valentine Larke crossed Westminster Bridge and turned right toward Vauxhall. He walked fast. It was a warm night, the river's effluent stinking. He shrugged off the whores who accosted him as he came close to the Pleasure Gardens.

He stopped at the entrance and, for two pence, purchased one of the black masks which were popular with the Garden's clients. Yet he did not go inside. He could hear the music and laughter, but his summons did not lead to the shadowed walks and private arbors of the Vauxhall Gardens.

He put the mask on.

He carried a heavy stick which he thumped heavily on the cobbles as he walked into a small, slinking side street that led to the river. The street was dark. It was a likely place for footpads, yet Larke's size and the confident sound of his stick carried him safely to a windowless brick building.

The building had large, double doors like a warehouse. A single torch lit the entrance. Cut into one of the doors was a smaller door on which Larke knocked hard.

A shutter was pulled aside. An eye inspected him. "It's a guinea to come in. Two for the bottom tier, three for company."

"Fetch Harvey."

"Who are you?"

Larke pounded the heavy stick on the door. "Fetch Harvey!"

A minute later, without paying a penny, he was inside the notorious Harvey's Palace. The proprietor bobbed in front of him, telling him what a privilege it was, and would he like an artiste for company? Larke snarled at him to be quiet. "What staircase for room six?"

"The third, sir. Over there, sir."

"Now leave me."

"Some wine, sir?"

"Leave me!'

It was dark inside Harvey's Palace. The building was a huge, echoing, brick-built cavern. In its center, like a grotesque half-built ship supported by timber balks and surrounded by spidery scaffolding, was a great wooden bowl. Chinks of light slashed from between its planks. The room was oddly silent, though Larke guessed that in the high cabins that were built above the bowl were probably a hundred or more people.

Stairs rose between the scaffolding, rickety stairs that creaked as Larke slowly climbed to the first tier of rooms. He had to peer closely to see the number six crudely chalked on one of the doors. He knocked.

"Come!"

Larke entered. He found himself in a square room, its walls, floor and ceiling made of wood. It had a table, three chairs, and a wide bed crammed into its small space. One man waited for him, a man sitting in shadow who growled as Larke closed the door. "Take the mask off, Belial."

Larke felt a shiver of pure fear. When he had heard that the Gypsy had delivered the message he had thought he might find the Gypsy himself here, or even some other emissary from Marchenoir, yet the man who waited for him was no emissary. It was Lucifer himself.

The leader of the Fallen Ones was swathed in a great, black cloak. He had told Larke to remove the mask, yet he wore an identical one himself. The black nosepiece appeared on him like the beak of some dark bird of prey. His eyes glittered behind the holes of the cheap lacquered disguise. "Come and sit, Belial."

On the far wall, beside which Lucifer sat, was a curtain. Bright light showed at its edges. Lucifer, as Larke edged by the bed, gestured at the table on which were plates of cold food. "Eat if you want, it's foul enough."

Larke, before sitting, pulled the curtain back, letting in a flood of light.

He was looking down from a hooded window. The upper half of the bowl was entirely composed of similar windows, tiered above each other, and all hooded so that the patrons of Harvey's Palace could not be seen from any other window. They could see only down to the floor of the bowl where, six feet below Larke, two girls writhed on a carpeted floor. Their naked bodies glistened.

As Larke watched, a hatch opened at the bowl's side. He sensed a sigh from all the hidden, hooded windows.

A man struggled through the hatch. The sigh turned to quiet laughter.

The man's monstrous body defied belief. He was huge.

His naked, grease-smeared flesh wobbled as he heaved and grunted and finally rolled onto the floor of the pit. His fat hung in great dewlaps. He had breasts that fell to his navel while his belly, like a sack of fat, hung like an apron. He grinned from beneath a yellowed wig that made him look uncannily like the King. He turned to lay on his back and the great rolls of greased fat quivered and rippled and settled as the man spread his arms and legs wide. The two girls made small, squeaking noises as they crawled toward him and as, like white worms on a huge yellow slug, they pulled their thin, sinuous bodies onto the quivering slapping mound of his heaped, bunched flesh. Larke let the curtain drop.

Lucifer sneered. "Squeamish? Or are you worried that this place takes profits from your own whorehouses?"

Larke looked into the masked face. "This is my place."

Lucifer laughed. "Then you might serve decent wine. This stuff is piss and vinegar. And for Christ's sake, sit down."

Larke sat. He was nervous. He had never met privately with Lucifer, only Marchenoir did that. Lucifer spoke to Moloch, and Moloch sent the coded messages with the Gypsy to Belial, and Belial spoke with Chemosh. That was how it should be, yet here was Lucifer, his eyes glittering like pale stones, sitting in the dusty darkness of Harvey's Palace.

Lucifer poured some wine for Larke. "Tomorrow, in Paris, there will be an announcement." He spoke in French. He pushed the glass toward Larke. "Moloch will announce that an enemy of France is dead. *Le Revenant.* The Lazender boy. The sixth Earl is dead. Burned to an ember. Dead."

Dead. Valentine Larke stared at Lucifer. Slowly, as the news dawned, he smiled. Toby Lazender dead! The sixth Earl dead! The Fallen Ones victorious!

Lucifer laughed. "Surprised you? Thought it would never happen? Well, he's dead. Burned to death, and just to make sure they're chopping off his charred head today with Dr. Guillotin's machine." He raised his glass. "Dead."

Larke raised his own. He felt the enormity of this news grow in him like a stupendous bubble of joy. They had done it! They had won!

Lucifer sipped his wine. "Moloch has done well, Belial."

Larke nodded eagerly. "He's done well."

From beyond the curtains came grunts and slaps, moans and cries. The two men ignored the sounds. Lucifer scratched beneath the nose-piece of his mask. "Moloch has done well. You have done well." He paused to sip his wine. "Chemosh has yet to do anything!"

Larke frowned. He had sponsored Lord Culloden for the Fallen Ones and if Chemosh failed it reflected upon Larke. His voice was guarded. "He's marrying the girl on Saturday." He looked sharply at the dark-cloaked man. "My God! If she hears about her brother's death . . ."

"She won't! I told you it's not being announced till tomorrow." Lucifer paused to sprinkle pepper and lemon juice on an oyster. "From Paris to Lazen must be at least six days!" He tipped the shell's contents onto his long tongue and his adam's apple slipped up and down his thin throat. One of the girls in the pit screamed. There was laughter from the tiered cabins.

Lucifer leaned back in his chair. "Where is the new Earl of Lazen?"

"In one of my houses." Sir Julius was a virtual prisoner who fed, drank and whored at Larke's expense. He had the pox, he had a skin disease, and he could hold little in his belly.

Lucifer traced a star on the table with spilled wine.

"You go to Lazen in the morning, Belial. I want you to arrive during the wedding service on Saturday. You can do that?" Larke nodded. Lucifer spoke softly. "Take men with you. Take the new Earl. Let the girl get married, then break the news of her brother's death to her."

Larke smiled. It was dawning on him that the plan had worked, had really worked! The fifth and sixth Earls were dead! Julius was the seventh, and he had signed his life away, while the girl, the final obstacle, was to be married. They had won. The Fallen Angels, unseen, unheard, and unsuspected, had taken the greatest fortune in England and made it theirs.

The girl screamed in the pit again. Voices in the cabins shouted for more. Lucifer smiled. "How many girls die here?"

"Two a month? More in winter when it gets busier."

"And the bodies?"

"The river."

Lucifer's black, shining mask looked toward Larke. "What are your plans for the Lady Campion Culloden?"

For a moment Larke wondered if Lucifer was suggesting that she should be brought to this place. The thought amused him, but he hid his smile. "Marriage and death, just as we planned."

"That was not what we planned." Lucifer's voice was gratingly low. "I thought we planned to give her the pox, to disfigure her. It was Chemosh who decided to marry her."

"Which he will do," Larke said defensively.

"Then how will she die?"

Larke shrugged. In truth he did not know what Lord Culloden had decided. "A riding accident? It seems the girl likes horses."

"When?"

"I don't know."

Lucifer did not speak for some seconds. From the pit

came gasping sounds, low moans, and the slap of flesh. The shining black mask was staring at the table. "If her father dies, and her brother dies, and then she dies, will there not be men in this country who will take some small interest?"

Larke nodded. "I made that very point to Chemosh."

"And his solution?" the mask looked at Larke, who could do nothing but spread his hands helplessly.

"I don't know."

"If indeed he has a solution." Lucifer leaned back. "Our friend Chemosh must think himself most fortunate. He'll be plowing a pretty field, yes?"

"Indeed."

"I must thank you, Belial, for sending the portrait to Moloch. He was most pleased." He paused, and his voice was like the whisper that echoed in the Mad Duke's shrine. "Most pleased."

"Good." Larke was nervous.

"Moloch, who has done well," and the voice was lower still, nothing but a sinister sibilance from the hunched, dark figure, "would like to meet the girl." He laughed.

Larke said nothing.

Lucifer seemed to shiver, as if controlling some terrible emotion. "Moloch has a peasant's appetite, a priest's cruelty, and the strength of an ox. Would you like to see the girl with Moloch?"

Larke lipped his lips. It was known among the Fallen Angels that Lucifer favored the grim Frenchman most. "It would be amusing."

"But difficult?"

Larke nodded agreement. "Of course."

"Not difficult at all. And most convenient." Lucifer laughed. "Think about it, Belial. Suppose the world thinks that the girl went to France to fetch back her brother's body. Such devotion! And suppose, in France, she is caught by Citizen Marchenoir and killed. Who will be surprised? Who will be suspicious? It would be her own fault. The world will say, truthfully indeed, that she was foolish to do such a thing. Does the scheme not answer our difficulties?"

The mask was close to Larke's face, close enough so he could feel Lucifer's breath. Larke nodded. "It would answer them."

Lucifer chuckled hoarsely. "So how would you get her to France, Belial?"

Larke shrugged. He was scared of this man, this clever, clever man. "It will need thought."

"It will not," Lucifer laughed, "because I have thought already. I will make her walk to Moloch like a lamb. I will pluck her across the channel and she will walk like a bride into Moloch's arms. She will die, and we will have Lazen."

There was silence, but for the sounds from the pit. Larke looked at the dark, masked face. He hesitated, but sensed Lucifer wanted the question asked. "How?"

The mask turned to him. "By reason. How else? But there will be a sacrifice that I shall ask of you, Belial."

Larke hid his nervousness. He nodded. "Whatever you ask."

"I ask for Chemosh."

Larke tried to divine what was behind the brittle, beaked mask. "Chemosh?"

"Chemosh. I am not pleased with Chemosh. He lacks, Larke, a certain ruthlessness? Besides, I am not sure he is not half in love with the girl. Are you certain he will kill her?"

"He says so."

"He says so, but he does not say when. I think it is time for Chemosh to die and for the Fallen Angels to gather, Belial. So listen to me." Lucifer spoke for ten minutes.

He spoke concisely, his orders clear, and when he had finished his pale eyes, behind the shining mask, were close to Larke. "You do understand me, Belial?"

Larke nodded. "I understand."

"She will die in France, because there will be no suspicion if she dies in France; yet she will go to France willingly, out of her own foolishness." Lucifer chuckled softly. "Now you may leave me." The dismissal was abrupt and callous. "You must prepare yourself to travel tomorrow."

"And you?"

"I am always prepared, Belial. If not, how could we succeed?" He laughed his dry, humorless laugh and then, with his thin hand, plucked back the curtain. He turned and his black, beaked mask quested over the sill to stare into the pit. "The dark haired girl is pretty."

Larke glanced down into the arena. "Yes."

"The river, you say?"

Larke nodded. "The river."

The mask turned to Larke. "How old would you say she is?"

"Thirteen?"

"She has the body of a ten year old. Send her to me, Belial. Just as she is."

Larke picked up his mask. The curtain dropped and Larke, looking from the door, saw Lucifer like a cloaked, dark bird; something evil, hunched and clawed in a foul corner.

"Remember, Belial! Be surprised by nothing you see at Lazen!"

Larke went. He paused on the dusty, dim landing, and, as he tied the strings of his cheap mask, he felt a dread of this man who planned so cleverly, thought so clearly, and whose day of victory was now less than a month away. At Auxigny, where the shrine of the Mad Duke waited, the

Fallen Angels would gather again, and this time the body that would be sacrificed, that would be pawed by Dagon and carried by him to the beasts of the dark woods, would be the body of Lady Campion Lazender.

Uncle Achilles arrived in a whirl of powder and perfume. "I'm late! My God!"

"It's all right, uncle!"

"You think so? My wig isn't dressed! My breeches have to be pressed. That fool of a servant has torn my lace jabot! I've got nothing to wear now, nothing!"

She laughed. "Uncle!"

"I am late because of mother. She has been impossible! Quite impossible! A polyp in the nose. It is painful. I grant her that it is painful, but the operation is so utterly simple! You sit in the chair, put your head back, and the best surgeon in London goes snip! My dear! You would have thought her virginity was being pried from her! Such a fuss! She thinks her beauty is impaired for eternity! I have had enough, dear niece! I can take no more! My God! Are you wearing that?"

"Yes."

Achilles stalked about her bed as though something peculiarly nasty lurked there. "It is white," he said dubiously.

"What's wrong with it?"

He gestured helplessly with his hands. "It lacks a certain frisson of excitement? It does not cry joy to me. It is, in truth, a plain dress."

"It's a plain wedding," she said grimly.

"So you chose that?"

She had not wanted to wear the beautiful wedding dress for this delayed, simple ceremony. Instead she had chosen a dress of white silk, simply cut, with a high neck. "It's got balloon sleeves," she said defensively.

"I hoped you wouldn't mention them, Ah, well!" He

sighed and sat on her chaise longue. "Too late to change it now, I suppose."

"Uncle!"

He smiled at her. "I forgot! You have this strange objection to letting me watch you undress. Very well, niece!" He plucked a gold watch from his fob. "I shall return in a half hour! And then?" He stood, he kissed her on both cheeks. "And then I shall lead the most beautiful girl in the world to the altar."

She laughed at him. She wanted to cry. She would be married.

She carried the last roses of summer.

There was a sigh from the servants in Lazen's Old Church. Never had such beauty walked to its altar to be married.

Her face, thinner since her father's death, had shadowed cheeks that only served to enhance her loveliness. Her eyes were bright, shining like her hair that showed beneath the great, silk hat.

About her neck hung the four seals of Lazen, the golden jewels of the evangelists.

Lord Culloden touched the points of his moustache. She smiled shyly at him and then Uncle Achilles let go of her elbow and she heard Lord Culloden's spurs clink as he turned to face the Reverend Horne Mounter.

This was not how she had imagined marriage. She had thought to be married with her family about her. She had thought she would be married in Lazen and that her children would grow with Toby's children to fill Lazen with laughter, tears, ponies, games, nursemaids, happiness and life. Instead this marriage seemed furtive, secret, shameful.

Lord Culloden made the responses in a bluff, confident voice.

She made them nervously. She felt oddly embarrassed to be saying the words in front of the servants. She found her thoughts drifting down, down beneath the flagstones, down to those velvet-palled coffins with their coronets that lay beneath her feet. She thought this service was not worthy of them. She thought the first Campion would not approve, that perhaps even now she should turn and walk from the church, suffer the embarrassment, but then the Reverend Mounter demanded that she hold out her hand. Duty held her. She would not run.

She held out her left hand and felt the smooth, dry touch of Lord Culloden's gloves as he put the ring onto her finger. It slipped easily over her knuckle. The gold was pale in the light of the church. She curled her fingers tight. The ring felt strange.

No horseman had come. No shadow within a shadow to give her hope. She had watched the driveway each day, but Christopher Skavadale had not come. She had thought of him each hour of each day, but he had not come back.

Then, almost with surprise, she heard the Reverend Mounter pronounce them man and wife. Lord and Lady. Lady Campion Culloden. For better, for worse, and the town choir, that had insisted on coming, opened their mouths as the instrumentalists followed Simon Stepper's beat and played their flutes, cellos and violins. She hardly heard the music. She saw the mouths open and shut, saw the smiles on the faces, the tears on Mrs. Hutchinson's cheeks, and then Lord Culloden took her elbow, she turned, Uncle Achilles stepped aside, and she looked up at the tall, moustached man who smiled beside her. This stranger, her husband.

The sunlight beckoned at her door.

Servants waited there, petals in their hands, and she walked beside her husband to the future she had feared so much and she made herself smile, made herself look happy, and then they were under the archway, the music fading, the cheers rising, and there, facing her, laughing all over his pug-like, ugly, toothless face, was her cousin Sir Julius.

She stared at him. His face was a shock. There were no teeth where he smiled, just a pit of red flesh that mocked her. Why had he chosen to come now?

She looked away from him. She smiled at the servants who applauded her, laughed as the petals tickled her skin, and then William Carline was standing in front of her and his head was shaking, his face white, and alone among the servants he did not smile. He was trying to speak, his mouth opening and closing and she frowned, not understanding, and he pointed with a trembling finger to the castle roof.

Campion, the petals bright on her white silk, looked into the blue sky and the roses in her hand, the last blooms of summer, dropped to the gravel.

Lazen's banner, which she had ordered raised for this one day, was lowered to the half.

Julius's laughter was like a hollow jackal's cry.

Toby was dead.

Uncle Achilles gripped her shoulders. "Perhaps it isn't true, my dear."

"Oh God!" She was shaking. "Oh God!" Petals still clung to her long, white skirts. She brushed at them. "Burned to death?"

"We don't know. Paris lies! You can't trust Paris these days."

They were in the Entrance Hall. Mrs. Hutchinson cried beside her. The Reverend Horne Mounter frowned helplessly.

There was laughter upstairs, the crowing, savage

laughter of her cousin. She could hear him shouting. "Mine! Mine!" A woman laughed with him; a raucous, shrieking harpy's laughter. Campion frowned at Achilles. "Who is that?"

"Some woman with Julius."

"Woman?"

He shrugged. "A woman."

"Mine!" came the voice. "Mine!"

"It's not his. Lazen is not his!"

"No." He tried to comfort her.

She turned, pulling her shoulders from Achilles's grasp. "My Lord?"

Culloden, who stood awkwardly in the sunlight by the front doors, frowned. "My dear?"

She pointed up the stairs. "Tell them to stop! Tell them this house is in mourning and I want silence!" This was why she had married him, to control Julius. "Tell them to stop!"

He looked up the stairs. The laughter was maniac's laughter. There was a cascading crash of china, splintering and loud, a shriek of triumph from the woman, more laughter, and still Culloden did not move.

"My Lord?"

Her anger took away her tears.

Achilles tried to stop her, but she moved too quickly. Mrs. Hutchinson screamed in alarm while the Reverend Mounter, pale-faced, hurried after her.

She lifted her white skirts and took the stairs two at a time. She felt a rage that astonished her, a flat, cold, intense anger at what was happening to her house.

The noise came from the Yellow Drawing Room. She hurled the door open.

Julius seemed to be fighting the girl. They both laughed. He pawed at her, tried to tear her clothes from her, and Campion saw that the Meissen porcelain,

Achilles's gift, had been swept from the table by their lurching, laughing fight. Plates, saucers, cups, dishes and bowls lay in a shattered heap. The girl, Julius tugging at her skirts, trampled more of the precious plate.

Campion strode forward.

Julius turned.

She slapped him hard about the face. "Stop this!"

He roared in anger. He reached for her, his hands clawing at the silk dress, but the Reverend Mounter threw his heavy weight onto the seventh Earl, drove him back against the screaming, laughing girl, and all three fell in a scrambling heap on the broken Meissen.

Campion heard hands clapping behind her, clapping slowly like the beat of a funeral drum.

She turned, her face still stiff with anger, and saw a dark clothed, middle-aged man standing in the doorway. He had eyes as flat and hard as any she had ever seen. His hair was ridged and glossy black. He clapped once more then walked slowly into the room's center.

Other men followed him, strange men, big men, in the center of them was Achilles, his wig awry, his face flushed with indignation. He came to her.

She frowned. She straightened her back. "Who are you?"

The man ignored her. He looked at Julius. "Get up." He spoke to the new Earl brutally.

Lord Culloden came into the room now and Campion saw the men's faces grinning as they appraised her. They had hard, scarred faces. They stood like men confident of their muscular power. She looked at the middle-aged man who seemed to be their leader. Her voice was cold. "Who are you?"

He looked her up and down with disdain on his hard face. "My name is Valentine Larke. Doubtless you have heard of me."

"No."

"Your ignorance does you no credit." He turned to a huge man who stood beside him. "Give the Earl and his whore a bottle, Mr. Girdlestone."

The girl giggled. She was dark-haired, her skin pocked with scars, her bodice unlaced. She walked with Julius toward the huge man who produced, from his coat pocket, a bottle of gin. The Reverend Horne Mounter, his hands cut by the porcelain fragments, stood on Campion's right, Achilles on her left.

Valentine Larke turned to Lord Culloden. "Take your bride to your rooms, my Lord. We do not need to detain you."

"Larke!" Campion's voice was so sharp, so sudden, that everyone in the room seemed to jump. Even Valentine Larke was taken aback by the cold, pure authority that the voice held. She stepped forward. "You give no orders in this house, Larke." She turned to Uncle Achilles. "I would be obliged, uncle, if you would ask Simon Burroughs to bring some of his men. There is rubbish that needs to be cleared out."

Achilles smiled. "I should be delighted."

His movement to the door was halted by a sliding scrape of steel and the appearance, in Larke's hand, of a sword. Larke smiled. "Lady Campion. I think it would be better if you ordered your dancing master to stay in this room."

"Dancing master!" Julius laughed. He capered grotesquely as he pointed with the gin bottle at Achilles. His toothless mouth made his words sibilant and hollow. "Dancing master!"

Larke rounded on him. "Quiet!" He turned to Lord Culloden. "My Lord?"

Culloden smiled. "Larke?"

"Take your bride, my Lord. She is not needed here."

"You paltry little man!" Again she shocked the room.

She took another step forward. "Will you threaten me with your sword, Larke?"

"If you don't shut your face, Campion Culloden, I'll lift your skirts and tan your arse. Now be quiet!"

"You will . . ."

"Quiet!"

Both of them were silenced by a crash, a huge, heart-stopping thumping smash that made Campion spin around to see that Uncle Achilles had pushed the statue of Ceres, that he had not liked anyway, from the table to the floor. He had done it to quiet the room, and his ploy worked. He stepped forward, every eye on him. Campion could sense her uncle's nervousness as he stared at Larke. "Mr. Larke?"

"Yes?" Larke frowned, but Achilles's tone had been conciliatory.

Achilles put a hand on Campion's arm. She could feel her uncle trembling. He smiled again. "I fear there may be a misapprehension, Mr. Larke. The Earl," and here he bowed toward Julius, "is not the inheritor of Lazen. I surmise you have come in his party, yes?" His French accent added an odd authority to his words. He did not wait for an answer. "My dear niece, the Lady Campion, is the legal holder of this castle. If she requests you to leave, then I suggest you do so. Do it quietly, do it now, and no more will be said." He tightened his hand on Campion's arm as she began to protest. He hurried on. "If the Earl has misled you, then doubtless you can take the matter up with him at your convenience?" He smiled. "I think you owe Lady Campion an apology, Larke?"

There was silence. Campion put a hand on top of Achilles's hand in silent thanks.

Valentine Larke slid his sword into its scabbard. His bland, dark eyes looked at Campion then back to Achilles. "You say she is the holder of this castle?"

"Indeed."

"While I am the holder of Sir Julius's inheritance."

Achilles smiled. "I hope you did not pay highly for that dubious privilege."

Larke ignored the comment. He pointed to Lord Culloden. "That is your niece's husband?"

"Indeed."

Larke smiled. "Then what is hers is now his? Yes?"

Campion saw the smile, and saw too the small answering smile on Culloden's face, and she felt as if the floor of the Yellow Drawing Room was opening into a great, dark, vacant space. Larke saw her consternation and laughed. "Lord Culloden and I are partners in this thing." He spoke to Achilles. "I did not come, dancing master, in the Earl's party. He came in mine." He looked at Culloden, and the triumph was an open smirk on his face. "My Lord?"

"Larke?"

"Do you wish me to leave?" He said it with mocking, faked humility.

Culloden's spurs rang as he walked forward. "I wish you to stay, Larke. You're a guest of mine, a most honored guest." His voice seemed utterly strange to Campion. It had a languid, amused, and vicious tone.

Achilles was gripping Campion's forearm so tightly that it hurt.

She glared at Culloden. "You will . . ."

"Quiet!" Larke shouted at her. "You speak once more, girl, and I'll put you over my knee. Lewis!"

"Larke?" Culloden smiled and touched his moustache.

"Take your wife and do what is customary on these occasions. Mr. Girdlestone?"

The huge man stepped forward. "Mr. Larke?"

Larke pointed at Campion. "Make sure she gives no trouble to his Lordship."

Girdlestone smiled. There was something in that smile that reminded Campion of the man who had leered down at her on the Millett's End road, who had dribbled his spittle onto her naked breasts, and the memory panicked her, and the panic made her turn, tearing herself from Achilles's grasp and pushing behind the Reverend Mounter who stood appalled at all he had heard.

"Stop her!" Larke shouted.

They would have done, too, except she was not running for the main doors with their gilded pediments, but for a small door that was covered with the same silken paper as the walls. It was a hidden door for the servants, a door by which they could come quietly and unfussily into the room, and it led to the servant's corridor that wound about the north side of the castle and allowed the maids and footmen to move about Lazen without intruding on the great rooms of state.

Even then, as she swerved and opened the door, they might have caught her, except that Abel Girdlestone collided with Uncle Achilles and Campion heard her uncle's despairing, falling cry as he was hurled to the floor. She heard the Reverend Mounter shout as he, too, tried to block her pursuers.

She ran. Suddenly she was no great lady. Suddenly she was a fugitive. She heard the boots and voices erupt into the corridor, she had turned a corner, had run past a dozen doors, and then she threw herself recklessly down the back stairs which led to a footman's pantry. She shut its door silently and stood, panting, listening to the commotion above her. The pantry opened into the garden and she guessed, as she heard the shouts above her, that she would have to leave that way.

The sound of her pursuers was loud. She heard them throwing doors open, and then the clatter of heavy boots on the stairs. It was time to run. It was time to run for her life, and she felt a sudden, savage impulse that she would make those bastards rue the day they had first heard of the name Lazender. She would fight them into their grave. She touched the golden seals, the jewels of Lazen, then opened the garden door and ran for her life.

17

She ran toward the stable block. Once there she would be surrounded by Lazen's servants and could plan what she must do next. First she must find safety, then she would attack.

She heard a shout behind her, a voice bellowing from a window in the castle. She ignored it. She clutched the bouncing, heavy seals in one hand and gathered her long, white, wedding skirts in the other. She heard feet on the gravel of the driveway, from beneath the bridge which joined the Great House to the Old House, and two strange men were running from its shadow, coming fast toward her, cutting her off from the stables. They were shouted on by other voices behind.

She ran in desperation, unable to find a single friendly face. She swerved away from her pursuers, going to the left of the mound that once was the castle's keep, going toward the beehives that were busy on this warm, autumn day. Beyond the hives stretched the empty lawns. She turned.

She put her hands on one of the beehives, waited, and the two men came grinning about the shoulder of the small hill and Campion pushed the hive over, hearing the first buzzing protests of the bees, and then she was running again.

She went away from the castle. She ran north to the tangled blackthorn of Sconce Hill.

The shouts of success turned into bellows of pain. The men had run into the panicking, angry bees that swarmed on them, stung, were tangled in their hair, their clothes, and the two men stumbled like blind men, arms clutched over their heads, while Campion ran from their screams toward the dark bushes of Sconce Hill.

She was going away from the castle, away from help, but she had no choice. The men who had pursued her from the Yellow Drawing Room were already on the north lawn and running toward the stables. Sconce Hill was her closest refuge.

She heard their shouts as she changed direction. Her breath came in great gasps as she climbed the lower slope, then the first branches of thorn tore at her sleeves, she ducked, and was in the shadows.

She dared not stop. She forced her way up an overgrown path, the thorns clutching and tearing at her wedding silk. She tried to work her way to the right, toward the slope nearest the stable block, but the thorns blocked her, forcing her to the very top of the hill.

She stopped there, where the ground was hummocked by the old fortress built by Parliament's troops in the civil war.

She listened.

She crouched in the remains of an old ditch that had once protected the besieger's guns. She clutched the seals that hung about her neck.

She heard voices shouting. One loud, crisp voice seemed to be giving orders, but she could not hear what those orders were.

The thorns had half torn the wedding bonnet from her head. She pulled the pins out and threw the hat away from her.

She heard the thrashing of thorns being beaten down with heavy sticks. The sound came from the south east slope of the hill. Her pursuers had cut her off from Lazen and now, like beaters, they would drive her off the hill into the waiting ambush.

She ran again.

She ran westward, knowing that once she was across Lazen's northern drive she would be in a larger tract of woodland. Her shoes were tight and awkward, slowing her on the uneven ground, but she forced herself on, ducking beneath branches, running through nettles, startling pigeons up from their roosts, scrambling desperately down the thorn-choked slope to the road. The spines snatched at her great sleeves and tore her skirts.

She stopped at the edge of the thorns. Wild garlic grew thick here, its smell pungent. The air was loud with insects. She crouched. Her face was sticky with sweat. Her hair was coming free. She looked up and down the road, but could see no one. Her pursuers were driving her away from the castle, but they had not yet surrounded her. It would only be moments, she knew, before the first men appeared to her left, running up the road to block her retreat from Sconce Hill.

Her dress was caught in a last spike of thorn and she wrenched it free, hearing the silk tear, and then she could run again, across the ruts of the road, through the sudden, bright, treacherous sunlight, and into the shadows of the trees beyond.

This was a beech wood, the trunks of the trees far apart and the undergrowth sparse. She ran for the bushes at the slope's crest, knowing her white dress was an easy sign for her pursuers. At the crest the beeches gave way to a mixture of oak, hazel and elm where, in the safety of their shadows, she hid herself in tall ferns.

She crouched.

She could feel sweat trickling between her breasts. It was sticky on her flanks, her hands, her neck, her spine.

She wiped her hands on the sleek smoothness of her wedding silk. Her left thigh was bared from hip to knee by great rents in the dress and petticoat. She tried to pluck the silk into place, but the tear was too big.

Her hair fell about her face, the strands sticking to her skin. She pushed them back, then stiffened.

She could hear horses on the northern road, their hooves loud on the gravel by the gatehouse.

A red squirrel scuttled noisily up an oak. She crouched low in the tall ferns. The wood seemed loud with the burbling call of pigeons. She listened for the voices of her pursuers.

Culloden was in league with Larke, and Larke with Julius. She could only think that Julius had conspired to evade the provisions of her father's will. Culloden and Julius! She felt a great angry sorrow at what had befallen this house. Toby killed, and now this foulness that had invaded Lazen.

She would not cry. Her enemies had come, but they had not taken her. She would not cry yet. She would fight.

To her right was a broken bough of oak, its bark damp and thick with fungus scales. She pulled it toward her for a makeshift weapon and the bark scraped against a white mushroom that gave off a foul smell. She wrinkled her nose and then bent closer to the plant. She saw the yellow-green tinge, the collared stalk, and knew it was no mushroom. It was the deathcap toadstool and she had smelled it before this year; it was the same nauseous stench that had made the dog whine in Mistress Sarah's cottage. It was this that she had fetched for her father.

She stared at it, for a moment even forgetting her pursuers. Her father had requested his own death. The pain had conquered him, but he believed he could die in the knowledge that she would marry, that she would be safe. With that confidence he had finally ordered his own death; the dreadful, swift end of the deathcap, and she felt a pitiful anger that his trust had been broken by Lord Culloden, just as her own had been broken. Yet Lord Culloden had not taken her body, only her words, and she would see him in hell yet.

She crouched in the ferns, her crude weapon soiling the hem of her wedding dress. She would go to the Rectory. She must get a message to Cartmel Scrimgeour. If she could just avoid capture then she would win. She knew it.

She heard dogs barking.

She parted the ferns before her face. The open spaces between the beeches were empty. A glint of gold on her left hand looked strange. It was her wedding ring.

In sudden anger she forced the wedding ring from her finger. It had seemed to go on so easily, yet now it would not come off and she twisted it, pulled it till her knuckle hurt, and at last it came free and she threw it away, seeing it bounce once in a bright splinter of gold light before it disappeared into the thick leaf mold beneath the beeches. She flexed the fingers of her left hand. Her right hand took hold of her crude club again.

A horseman appeared on the track beneath her.

She did not recognize the man. She could just see him between the thick leaves, a man dressed in dark clothes who stared at Sconce Hill. He looked once to his left, glancing at the open space between the beeches. His horse staled on the track and the noise carried between the trees to her hiding place.

She was crouched in a tiny ball now, just as she used to crouch as a child when Toby hunted her. She remembered the delicious fear of those games. The wood had seemed much larger then, much more frightening, made even more so by Toby's stories of warlocks and goblins and girl-eating ghouls. Those childish stories were coming true.

She heard the dogs again, baying in the music of the hunt, and she realized that the castle's hounds had been unkennelled. She smiled. Did they think the hounds would hurt her?

She wondered how long they would take to search Sconce Hill. Once they knew she was not there they would come into these larger woodlands and she knew, fearfully, that she must move. Yet every move would take her farther from Lazen, farther from the refuge she needed this night.

Two hounds burst onto the track beneath her, tails wagging, and the man shouted at them to move back into the undergrowth. He carried a whip that he cracked at them, shouted again, and Campion used the noise he made to cover her own as she rose from the ferns and ran farther west.

The woods opened here into a great tract, crossed by rides, a jungle of bushes and trees, dazzling sunlight on the greens, golds, and yellows of autumn. Her feet tore at the grass, the dead leaves, the ferns. She ran down a gentle slope, always keeping close to the bright open space of the park. This night, if she avoided capture, she would go in the darkness across the park and turn east toward the town.

She hid amongst a tangle of laurel and wild privet.

She waited. She could see the roof of the temple beneath her. She was thinking how the dome needed a coat of limewash when there was a loud noise behind her, she turned, stifling a scream, and saw a deer had come into the wood from the park. The deer sensed her presence and it thumped away, scut flashing white, and there was stillness again.

A cloud shadow raced over the park, darkened the wood, and shivered her with fear. It passed and the sun was bright again. There was a cool breeze on her forehead.

She listened to the birdsong, judging that while it was uninterrupted then her pursuers were not close. Once a woodpecker startled her. She was biting her lower lip.

They had not expected this. She felt a surge of defiant pleasure. They thought they had beaten her! She had done what the first Campion had done, she had defied her enemies! She gripped her crude, fungus covered club.

She thought of Toby. For his sake she would defy them, for his sake she would beat them, and for his sake she would take Lazen back. For the sake of her dead brother she would see these men in hell for this day's work.

Then there was the sudden jingle of a curb chain and the solid thump of a hoof. A voice called out, not far off, and she recognized Lord Culloden. "Not here!"

God! But he was close! He must have approached so silently, the sound of his horse's hooves muffled by the grass and leaf mold. She could hear his horse moving, she could hear him patting its neck and murmuring to it, she could hear the creak of his saddle and then there was another sound, even closer, and she watched in horror as one of Lazen's bitches came romping into the privet; nose up, tail wagging, barking in pleasure.

She petted it desperately. It pushed its nose into her face, licked her, turned to rub its stern on her crouching shoulder, rolled over to be scratched and then started all over again. Like most hounds it received no human affection. It seemed to want the lack made up on this warm afternoon.

She willed the hound to go away.

Culloden whistled.

She pushed at the bitch. It licked her face, wriggled in ecstasy, and she pushed again. It barked playfully.

"Come on, damn you!" Culloden's angry voice sounded almost above her. She pushed at the hound, who thought it was a game, and then the leaves above her head shook and she looked up to see her husband's astonished face. He had pulled the privet back to find the hound, instead he stared at Campion.

He sat his saddle in shock as if, though hunting her, he had not expected to find her, and then he bellowed out a great "hollo!" The fox was sighted. He was calling in the other hunters and Campion, knowing it was useless, scrambled out of the bushes on the far side from him and ran.

She heard his laughter. She heard the hooves.

She was running as the deer had run. The hound ran with her.

She twisted, she turned, she doubled back, she ran where elders grew close and a horse could not gallop, but always at the corner of her eye Culloden's bright uniform flickered among the leaves and trunks. His horse crashed through undergrowth while his voice summoned her other enemies to head her off. She went into coppiced timber, twisting between the withies, and saw, waiting on the far side, one of Larke's men who laughed because she was trapped.

She stopped.

She gripped the cudgel, knowing it was useless, but not willing to surrender without a fight. Sweat stung her eyes. Flies buzzed at her forehead.

Two more horsemen rode into the coppice. The hounds, bored with the poor sport, streamed toward the deer in the park.

Lord Culloden dismounted. He told the three horsemen to guard the coppice's edges.

The coppice was uncut, its tight branched trees too close to permit a horse access. Culloden had to edge sideways to force a path between them. He smiled at her. "Good afternoon, wife."

For answer she held the damp oak branch ahead of her.

He laughed. His face was gleaming with sweat. He touched his moustache. "What a pretty leg you do show, my dear."

She dodged between two trees. She was slim and could move faster in the small coppice, but she was surrounded. Culloden laughed. "We have all day, dear wife. And then our wedding night." He lunged suddenly, forcing branches apart, and she twisted away, a twig lashing her cheek, then turned and struck at him. Her club bounced off the withies and Culloden laughed again. "Playing games after your brother's death? It's hardly seemly, my Lady."

A voice shouted from farther up the wood and one of the horsemen twisted in his saddle and shouted back. All her pursuers were coming now, a band of men to watch her humiliated. She plucked uselessly at the white silk of her dress, vainly trying to cover her leg. Culloden smiled. "You'd give us better sport if you took the dress off, dear wife. You want to run naked and take a ten minute start?"

One of the three horsemen laughed. "Do it, my Lord!"

Culloden smiled at Campion. "Why not? I've never hunted a naked female." He lunged at her, snatching the hem of her dress and she screamed, twisted away, and heard the silk tearing as she ducked under a spread of branches. She felt his strength pulling on her skirts and she forced herself away, scrambling on the ground as he tugged at her. The silk tore, she could feel her petticoat tearing, and then she was free and she turned and lashed with her oak club. He laughed triumphantly and brandished a swatch of stained silk. "Now for the rest, my dear."

The front of her skirts had almost gone. She beat at him with the club again, but the springy, slender withies that separated them protected him. He smiled. "I'll give you two minutes, wife. Either you come quietly to me, or we'll hunt you through the wood. First man, first serve, yes? So what will you do?" He laughed.

She hit blindly with the club, shaking the slender branches and making Culloden step back.

A voice shouted again from the wood, this time the shout more urgent, and the sound of it made Culloden turn his head. Campion twisted and wriggled deeper into the coppice. She could hear more hooves, more shouts. Her dress was caught again and she pulled it fiercely, hearing it rip further, then she turned again with her club raised to beat at the man who had stood beside her at Lazen's altar.

But Lord Culloden had not followed her. He was staring up the slope with a puzzled frown.

Campion could see men on foot. They were far off, running slowly in the heat toward the coppice. They shouted a warning and she saw what she had dared not hope for.

She saw a horseman who rode as no other man rode, a horseman of arrogant confidence and dark splendor. Beside him, empty saddled and stirrups flapping, came Hirondelle.

Campion wanted to shout this triumph aloud. She wanted her joy to fill this wood. He had kept his promise.

A black-dressed man on a black horse, a sword in his hand, riding toward the coppice with a smile on his face and, as Campion's heart leapt with sudden joy, he touched the flanks of his horse and came at her enemies in a gallop.

Christopher Skavadale had come back.

The first of the three men spurred to meet the Gypsy.

The man drew his own sword and rode so that his right hand would meet the Gypsy's right hand and Campion held her breath as the two men came close, as Skavadale's horse swerved and she saw the Gypsy toss his sword from his right to his left hand, spear it forward, and the wood was filled with a terrible, rising scream and the man was folded on the steel, falling, blood bright as his body turned, and Skavadale let the weight of the man tear his twisting blade free of the spilling guts.

The other two horsemen were riding to help the first, but the first man was already dead, his blood in the leaf mold, his belly opened, his body dragging from one stirrup so that his guts trailed in the dead leaves.

He had kept his promise. He had come back. She laughed with the joy of it and she saw his face, thin and bright-eyed, lit with the relish of battle.

Lord Culloden was pushing through the coppice, Campion forgotten, as the second man swung his sword in a great blow at the Gypsy, but the black horse turned at the last moment, taking the man's target away, and Skavadale's sword, back in his right hand, butchered down to the man's skull.

A pistol banged, the noise clattering pigeons up from the trees, filling the wood with alarm.

Two men were dead, the third threw away his pistol that had missed and drew his sword. He had never seen a swordsman so fast or a horseman so good. To run was to invite the Gypsy's blade in his back, to go forward was to meet death, and he did neither. He sat still and parried the first lunge so that the swords rang in the wood like a struck anvil and then the man screamed because the blade had twisted beneath his guard and was rising to his throat.

Skavadale did not wait to watch the man die. He turned, letting his horse's motion razor the steel through the man's neck and Campion put a hand to her mouth as she saw the blood fountain up, bright against the turning leaves. She was shaking.

He wore black breeches, black boots and a black shirt. His sleeves were rolled up, his tattooed eagles flecked with blood. He turned from the last death and plucked the reins of Lord Culloden's horse, drawing it away from the coppice and from its owner who stood now at the coppice's edge. Skavadale leaned over, took Culloden's pistol from its saddle-holster, aimed, and fired.

The shot echoed through the wood.

The bullet churned leaves in front of Larke's men who ran toward the coppice. It checked them. They had seen three men die in the time it took to draw a breath, and none wished to join the dead who lay sprawled on the leaves. The first man, his horse panicked, bumped and jolted as his corpse was dragged through the undergrowth.

Skavadale turned back.

She felt her breath catch in her. His face was so strong, so implacable, the eyes harder than stone. His sword point dripped blood as it dipped toward Lord Culloden's face. She thought the Gypsy was going to kill the cavalry officer, but Skavadale smiled. His stained sword point was within an inch of Culloden's eyes. "Remember me, my Lord? The Prince de Gitan?" The sword came forward, forcing Culloden to step back. He made no effort to raise his own sword.

The Gypsy forced him back another step. "Drop your sword, my Lord. Then mount."

Culloden, terrified of this man who had killed with such speed and skill, obeyed. The men on the hill, a hundred yards away, watched, but dared not come forward.

"My Lady?"

"Mr. Skavadale?" Her voice was weak.

He smiled, a smile of joyous welcome, of a secret shared. "I owe you an apology, my Lady."

"An apology?" She had dropped the makeshift club.

Christopher Skavadale glanced at Culloden who was mounting his horse. He looked back to Campion. "I should have been here yesterday, but Rom magic doesn't control the channel's winds. Can I suggest you come with me?"

She scrambled out of the coppice. Hirondelle waited for her and Campion, modesty gone to the wind, climbed astride the saddle. Her legs were bared by the torn dress.

Culloden was shaking with fear.

Skavadale, his bloody sword still drawn, glanced once more at the men on the hill, then backed his horse until it was behind Lord Culloden. "Give me your hands, my Lord."

Culloden frowned. "I've given up my sword!"

Skavadale smiled. "I'll tear out your spine if you don't give me your hands."

There was no fight in Lord Culloden. Meekly he put his hands behind his back and Campion saw him wince as the Gypsy tied them. The men up the hill fired a single pistol shot, the bullet ripping at leaves overhead and frightening the birds once more. Skavadale looked with disdain at the men, then smiled at Campion. "Now we can go."

She glanced down as they rode away. The last man to die lay with his head half severed, just like the man on the Millett's End road. She almost gagged. Flies crawled on the blood and gaping flesh, and then Hirondelle stretched her legs and she rode behind the Gypsy out of the wood. He had come back. Amidst the stench of blood and the ring of steel he had come back. She laughed aloud. He had come back.

* * *

No one pursued them. Skavadale led Culloden's horse by its reins, Campion followed, and they rode westward until Lazen was out of sight and then the Gypsy turned south. He smiled at her and spoke in French. "I didn't expect you to run for the hills!"

"Expect me?"

"I was in the house!" He glanced at Lord Culloden. The Gypsy's drawn, blood-matted sword had mesmerized his Lordship. Skavadale looked at her bared thighs and smiled. "It seems a pity, my Lady, but perhaps you should take this." He pulled a cloak from the straps of his saddle and tossed it to her. "You'll have fresh clothes at Periton House."

"Periton House?" She was spreading the cloak like a blanket over her legs.

He grinned. "I took the liberty of sending some of your servants to Periton House. You don't mind?"

"Mind?" She seemed to be in a daze. One moment she had been hunted through an autumn wood, the next she was riding across a water meadow with the Gypsy. Skavadale smiled.

"I don't think you can go back to the Castle yet."

"No." That much seemed obvious.

"So there's some bedding, food and servants at the other house. You'll be comfortable enough." He laughed and urged his horse into a canter.

Campion followed. He was arranging her life and somehow, though she was more than capable of arranging it herself, it felt good to be looked after. She laughed again. He had come back.

That night the Gypsy sat on the floor of Periton's half finished kitchen and cut a sponge into squares three niches thick. Campion, wearing a dress of blue linen beneath a black cloak, watched him. Edna, her maid, had brought the clothes. She had brought news of the Castle, too. It was, she said, all confusion. The new Earl gave orders, Valentine Larke gave orders, and no one knew what was happening. "They're foul, my Lady. Talk to us like dirt!"

A dozen servants, led by Simon Burroughs, had left Lazen. They guarded Periton House this night, including the empty tack room where Lord Culloden had been locked for the night.

Edna sat in the kitchen with Campion. The smell of damp plaster was made worse by the smell of lard that Skavadale had melted in a huge pot on the fire. He was busy with the sponge, slicing it with his knife, but he obstinately refused to explain why he did it.

He spoke in French with Campion. He said he had come to Lazen because he feared for her, that he had cause to fear for her.

"Cause?"

He cut the last piece of sponge into halves, then took a ball of twine. "You had a portrait painted once. You wore a cream dress and held flowers?"

"Yes." She frowned at the seeming irrelevancy.

"Where is it?" His blue eyes shone in the candlelight.

She shrugged. "I gave it to Lord Culloden."

He had cut a length of twine and was tying it about one of the lumps of sponge, compressing the sponge until it resembled an odd, string tied ball less than an inch in diameter. "I carried that portrait, my Lady, from England to France. I had orders to give it to Bertrand Marchenoir."

She stared at him. She wondered if she had heard correctly. "You did what?"

He started on the second lump of sponge with another length of twine. "I'm Marchenoir's messenger. I can't read his letters because they're in code. But Marchenoir did say one thing to me." He grunted as he tied the lump tight.

"What?"

"How much he'd like to be the one who killed you." He looked up at her with a quick, apologetic grin. "He didn't merely say kill, but I'll spare you the rest."

She was appalled. Edna, who spoke no French, watched her mistress's face. Campion's voice was low. "Kill?"

"So he said." Skavadale was tying the next lump. "It seems, my Lady, that your house has enemies. They killed Toby's bride and they want to kill you." He spoke mildly, as though they chatted about the weather or the prospects of harvest. He began compressing the next scrap of sponge into a tight ball. "Why would your husband be in league with Marchenoir?"

She shook her head. She had thought earlier that Lord Culloden had leagued himself with Julius just to evade her father's will, yet Skavadale's casual sounding words hinted at a stranger, darker, more terrible cause. Nothing made sense. Her thoughts flitted as uselessly as the moths that flirted with the candles in the kitchen.

Christopher Skavadale tossed another finished ball onto his small pile. "Mystery after mystery, my Lady!" He smiled at her. "So tomorrow morning I'll squeeze some answers from Lord Culloden. I think that what he tells us will give Lazen back to Toby."

She was silent for a few seconds. "You don't know?"

The sob in her voice at last made him stop his strange activity. He frowned at her. "Don't know what?"

"About Toby?" He shook his head and she had to swallow to make her voice clear. "They killed him."

"Who did?"

"The French!" She gestured helplessly. "They found his burned body. They cut his head off."

Skavadale laughed.

She stared at him in shock. "Didn't you hear me?"

He started on the next square of sponge. "They cut his head off?" He laughed again.

"Mr. Skavadale?" Her voice was cold.

His oddly light eyes looked at her. He smiled. "Why do you think he's called *Le Revenant?* The creature come back from the dead?"

She said nothing. She sensed what he was saying, but the news was too good to believe, and somehow his studied attitude of carelessness made the news even harder to accept.

He smiled. "You mustn't tell anyone. Don't even thank God in your prayers."

"He's alive?"

He smiled at her. "The French found a body with Toby's clothes and Toby's sword. We burned the head so they wouldn't see that the man didn't have red hair." He grinned. "We had to take a chance with the rest of him, if you understand me. What I'm telling you, my Lady, is that your brother is alive. He's well. But no one must know." He raised his voice as she started to smile. "No one! We don't know who your enemies are. They may have spies in your own household! No one must know! You don't even tell Lord Paunceley! You don't tell anyone! You don't tell her," he nodded at Edna who was bemused by the sudden urgency in his voice, "you don't tell your uncle, you don't tell the lawyers, you tell no one! Everyone must believe Julius is the new Earl, everyone! Only three people know Toby's alive. He knows, I know, and now you know."

"He's alive?"

"He's alive." He took another piece of sponge and twine. "Lazen's been under siege for months. It seemed the only way to get your enemies to show themselves was to give them what they wanted: Toby's death." His eyes met hers again. "Swear to me you tell no one."

She nodded. "I swear." The news was coursing through her in waves of disbelief followed by inane joy. She wanted to laugh, she wanted to cry, she wanted to hug this man who had teased her with the news. "Is it true?"

He smiled at her. "It's true. I promise you."

"He's alive?"

He laughed. He was tying the last ball of sponge. "My Lady. Your enemies are laying a trap for you. Your brother and I are laying a trap for them. They think he is dead. They must go on thinking that he is dead. But *Le Revenant* is alive."

Her incredulity turned to belief and, not caring what Edna thought, Campion put her arms about his neck and kissed his cheek. "Thank you."

Edna stared open eyed. The castle had gone mad. A wedding, a chase, an invasion by brutal, loud men, and now this!

Skavadale laughed. He touched her cheek in a quick, gentle gesture. "It's Rom magic, my Lady. We bring the dead to life."

She laughed. "And that?" She gestured at the tightly bound sponge balls. "More Rom magic?"

"More Rom magic." He tied the balls to a heavy, iron fork and took them to the slow bubbling pot of lard. He put another log on the fire, swung the pot-crane toward him, then dropped the sponges into the boiling fat. He pushed the crane back over the flames.

"That pot, my Lady, will give us all the answers."

She laughed. She had woken this morning dreading the day, and now she sat in an unfurnished house and felt that she had joy enough to fill Lazen's valley. "What is it? Tell me!"

"Just sponge balls." He laughed. "We boil them for twenty minutes, take them out, let them cool, and that's it!"

"That's what?"

"Rom magic." He smiled. He was beautiful, she thought, a man of such sudden, striking handsomeness that she wanted to hold him and never let him go. He laughed at her. "Then we wait for the dawn, my Lady."

He would say no more. He looked at Edna whose face was shadowed with tiredness and he lit a candle for her and told her to take her mistress to the blankets that were laid on a bedroom floor. "Sleep, ladies. You have a busy day tomorrow."

Campion smiled. "I won't sleep tonight."

"You will. You'll be safe." He took her hand, put it to his lips, and his kiss was warm on her skin. He gave her a secret, mischievous smile that seemed to promise wonder. "Goodnight, dear lady."

She went upstairs with Edna and, to her surprise, while the greasy balls of fat-soaked sponge cooled in the night, and while the Little Kingdom waited for the morning and for the magic of the Rom, she slept.

18

The first desperate scream woke Edna. The maid, terrified, clutched Campion beneath the blankets. "My Lady! My Lady!"

Campion held her. Both girls listened, wide-eyed, as the scream came again. "Dear God!" Campion scrambled out of the warm shared bed. "Stay there!"

She pulled a dress over her petticoat, pushed her feet into shoes, and plucked the cloak from their makeshift bed. She ran down the uncarpeted stairs and out into the back court.

Simon Burroughs, Lazen's huge coachman, stood guard at the entrance to the stable yard. He had orders, he said, to let no one inside except for her. "Giving him a rare time, my Lady!" He said it cheerfully as, in the dawn's damp chill, he opened the gate for her.

"Give it to me! Give it to me!" Lord Culloden was screaming. His eyes were wide, bright with tears, and his hair was untied, hanging lank beside his unshaven cheeks. "Give it to me! For the love of Christ! Give it to me!"

She stopped, astonished.

His legs were hobbled with rope, his wrists tied, his breeches stained with vomit. He turned as she came into the yard and, ludicrously, he fell to his knees and raised his hands like a beggar. "Make him give it to me, my Lady! Make him give it to me!"

His gorgeous uniform hung open. He shook.

Behind him, sitting on the mounting block, Skavadale smiled. He had a long coachman's whip in his right hand. "Good morning, my Lady!" His voice was cheerful.

"What have you done to him?"

"Make him give it to me!" Culloden shuffled forward on his knees. "My Lady! Please, my Lady!" The tears dripped from his cheeks to his torn stock. There was vomit on his waistcoat.

Campion stepped around him. Her voice was shocked. "What does he want?"

"This." Skavadale lifted a tin flask.

"What is it?" She was frowning. It was not easy to see a man so humbled and broken, even this man who yesterday had tried to strip her naked and hunt her through Lazen's woods.

Skavadale smiled and offered her the tin flask. She took it and felt a liquid sloshing inside.

"What is it?"

"It's an old Rom trick, my Lady." He glanced at Lord Culloden who stared beseechingly at the flask in Campion's hands. "What does a farmer do with a pig that dies of a mysterious disease?"

She frowned at the seemingly irrelevant question. "Buries it, of course." A pig that died of disease was a mass of poisons. No sensible man ever used such a carcass for food.

Skavadale glanced at the kneeling, crying Lord Culloden, then stooped and picked up the one remaining sponge ball. He smiled at Campion. "Supposing you're a hungry gypsy. You make these balls as I did last night. You soak them in hot lard, then let them cool. And when the fat has hardened, my Lady, you cut the string away."

She saw the marks where the twine had bound the sponge. "The cold fat holds the sponge tight, my Lady, and you feed a half dozen to a pig. They'll eat anything. That one," and he jerked his head scornfully at Culloden, "threw up the first four but I said I'd ram them down his gullet with a sword if he didn't keep them down." He tossed the sponge ball in his hand. "So the pig eats them, my Lady, and the cold fat holds the sponge together, but what happens when it reaches the pig's stomach?" He turned from her to a bucket of water that was on the mounting block. Steam rose from the surface. Skavadale dropped the ball of sponge into the pail.

Campion stared into the water.

White tendrils drifted and faded from the larded sponge. A scum appeared on the water and the sponge began to open as the fat left it. The cold lard held the sponge compressed, but as the lard melted, so the sponge welled back to its full size. Skavadale laughed.

"The stomach's a fine warm place, my Lady, and the sponge expands and blocks the intestines. You can't digest sponge. It just stays there and nothing gets past it. The pig dies. It's not a nice death. And we gypsies say that we'll take the diseased carcass off the farmer's hands. We save him the bother of burying it. He thinks we're fools who'll poison ourselves, but instead we eat well for a fortnight." He laughed and pointed at Lord Culloden. "You've got a week to live, my Lord! You'll die with your belly bloated and your guts in agony!"

Culloden struggled to his feet and hobbled toward them. "Give it to me!" he screamed.

Campion was frowning. She held the flask up. "So what's this?"

"It dissolves sponge, my Lady. It hurts, but he'll live." He looked scornfully at the broken cavalry officer. "All he has to do is tell you what he's just told me. All of it.

Then you can decide whether you want him to live. If you do, give him the flask. If not?" He shrugged.

She stared at Culloden's weeping, beseeching, desperate face. The man was in terror. She wondered if already there was a pain in his belly, a pain that would grow as his intestines were blocked tight and his death came closer. "Give it to me!" He held his bound hands toward the flask.

"Talk to us, my Lord," Skavadale mocked him. "Talk to us."

He talked. Campion, standing by Hirondelle's door, listened.

She kept the flask in her hands, the flask that would give Lord Culloden his life, but after his first answers she forgot the flask and listened in horror to his babbling, pleading voice.

She heard the names Chemosh, Belial, Dagon, Moloch and Lucifer. She heard of the ceremony in the Mad Duke's shrine. She heard her husband say how he had murdered the girl for his initiation. The story had to be teased from him, admission after reluctant admission.

She heard that the Fallen Ones wished to take Lazen, that the marriage was part of the plan. She heard and was horrified.

Once Culloden pushed his fingers down his throat in an attempt to vomit, and Skavadale curled the lash of the whip about his Lordship's boots, pulled, and the tall, golden haired cavalryman slammed to the ground and the lash cracked above his face and he stayed still.

Skavadale's voice was like the whip. "Go on, my Lord."

She heard, with shame and anger, how Lord Culloden had hired the man to attack her. He told the story hesitantly, in terror, and the Gypsy cracked the whip about his head, not touching him, forcing the story out.

Lord Culloden told how he had brought the man from

London and paid him to rape the Lady Campion Lazender, to give her the pox, to scar her, to make her unmarriageable. "But then I saw you! I saw you! I couldn't do it!"

Skavadale laughed. "He decided to marry you himself. How noble!"

She listened and it seemed as if she dreamed, except that the crack of the whip was real and the babbling, pleading, sobbing man was real, and the tin flask of liquid was heavy in her hands, and she heard of the Fallen Ones, of the names of the angels who had fought God, and she listened as Skavadale cross-examined Culloden about the ceremony at Auxigny.

She listened. She could hardly believe what she heard, yet the evidence of the flask was in her hands. He pleaded for it, begged for it, wept for it, and bit by bit Skavadale took more from him.

Lady Campion Culloden must die. Her husband, who knelt like a serf before her, had promised to break her neck and leave her beside a hedge as though she had fallen from her horse.

The Gypsy tossed his whip down and walked behind Culloden. "With your brother dead, you are the only person to stand between them and Lazen. They plan to kill you. This thing," and he nudged Culloden with his boot, "will give Lazen to the Fallen Angels. Ask him why."

She did, and Lord Culloden talked of revolution in England, of using the money of Lazen to rot the government and arm the Corresponding Societies who admired the French revolutionaries. He babbled about Julius's debts, about Larke, about Marchenoir, and he pleaded for his life. He shuffled on his knees, his pink cheeks smeared with tears, his hands held high, and he swore on the Bible and all the saints that he had never meant her harm, never.

She looked scornfully at his plump, tear-stained cheeks. "You were going to hunt me naked yesterday. First man, first served? Or did I hear wrong?"

"I'm sorry! I'm sorry!" He raised supplicant hands to her. "I'm sorry."

The Gypsy stood behind him. He took a pistol from his belt and pulled back the flint. He levelled the gun at her husband's head. "Shall I give him the cure, my Lady, or you?"

She held the flask in her hands. With two steps she could give this man life.

She looked at the broken man. She thought of her face scarred. She thought of the would-be rapist dribbling on her naked breasts. She thought of Lucille dead. She thought of the lies, the deception, the honor cast away by a man of rank, she thought of the death that the Fallen Ones had planned for her. She thought of her father's trust betrayed, and she thought of the slow, careful, long plot that had curled its tendrils about Lazen. For months now, while she had agonized about love and marriage, they had plotted to kill her and take the Little Kingdom. She heard again his mocking laughter as he had tried to strip the skirts from her in the wood.

"Please, my Lady! I beg you, my Lady."

She thought of her father.

She unscrewed the cap of the flask.

"My Lady!" Culloden's face was shaking. "Please, my Lady!"

She stared at him. This was the man who was to save Lazen! This miserable, shaking coward was to be her shield and strong right arm. She looked at Skavadale and nodded. "You."

He fired into the base of Culloden's neck.

The head jerked up, eyes wide, mouth opening, and she saw the horror in his eyes as blood spilled bright from his mouth and then he slumped forward, still on his knees, his head on the cobbles in front of her.

The smoke drifted through the stable yard. A horse whinnied.

She stared at Skavadale. She had ordered a death.

He smiled. He was cleaning the burned powder from the pan of the gun. "There is no liquid that I know of, my Lady, that dissolves sponge."

The body, with an odd, bubbling sigh, slumped onto its side. The early sunlight glinted on the silver wire epaulettes of the gorgeous uniform.

"What?"

"There is no liquid that dissolves sponge." He laughed. "That's just water. He was a dead man, my Lady, from the moment I pushed the sponge down his throat." He looked grimly at the body. "I just wish the bastard could have told us more."

"More? Wasn't that enough?"

"No." He pushed the pistol into his belt. "Who's Lucifer? I've not heard that name before. Larke we know, Marchenoir we know, but Lucifer? I tell you Lazen's not safe till Lucifer is dead."

She stared at him. She felt dazed. She felt sick. The shot still rang in her ears. She looked at the body and saw the gold hair at the base of Lord Culloden's skull stained with blood, and suddenly she threw the flask away and ran to a corner of the yard.

She retched until she was empty. She crouched, half leaning on the wall, and her stomach heaved again and again and her breath came in great gasps. Each time she thought of the bloodstained golden hair she wanted to vomit again. The sun had glinted on the gold. She had seen his skin pink beneath each hair. The blood was bright and red and matted and flecked with bone and burned by flame and she threw up again as the memory persisted.

She had her eyes closed. She remembered the head jerk up as the bullet struck, the eyes astonished on her, and then the welling blood that had gleamed, swelled and run down his chin. She retched again.

She spat. She wiped her mouth. She wanted to cry. The waste of death appalled her, yet she had nodded to Skavadale. She had demanded it. She groaned.

She felt weak as she stood up. The buildings of the stable yard seemed to be turning. Horses stared from half open doors.

She had seen three men die yesterday and felt nothing like this. But this death she had ordered. The body lay curled as if asleep.

Skavadale crossed to her. His strong hands took her shoulders. "It's all right, my Lady."

She looked up into his slim, dark, vivid face. "I'm not used to this."

He smiled. "I am. It's my life."

"That?" She frowned toward the body.

"Lord Paunceley pays me to kill Britain's enemies."

Her mouth tasted foul. "Do you enjoy it?"

His eyes flicked between hers. He smiled. "What I will enjoy, my Lady, is breeding the fastest horse in the world. But before that can happen, we have things to do." His hands still gripped her shoulders as if he tried to pour his strength into her. "The first thing we do, my Lady, is take Lazen back from the bastards."

She smiled at that, a small nervous smile. "Yes."

"And then we go to France."

She stared at him in shock. "France?"

"Because only if you go to France will the Fallen Ones gather. If you want peace, my Lady, you must help me kill Lucifer."

She shook her head. "I can't go to France."

He smiled. "I want you to come to France, to Auxigny."

"No." The word came out almost as a sob. She had seen death, had seen its waste, had seen blood dark in bright hair. She would not go to the land that had embraced death like a lover. She shook her head. "No."

He wiped her chin with his strong, warm fingers. "Yes, my Lady. Yes."

She stared into his eyes. She saw the strength of him. "I can't go to France."

He smiled. "You are the last creature God made. You may do what you like. You can walk through blood and you will be safe."

She shuddered. The first flies were dark on Lord Culloden's neck. "I need some tea, Mr. Skavadale. I need a dish of tea."

She came to Lazen at midday.

She came in fury.

She carried a riding crop. To her right was Christopher Skavadale, a sword at his side and a pistol in his belt. To her left was Simon Burroughs, a horse gun huge in his hands.

She ordered the body of Lord Culloden, like a challenge, to be thrown on the forecourt. He lay there, a gaudy corpse that denied Valentine Larke his mastery of the castle. The flies crawled on the plump face.

Men watched her from the windows. She ignored them.

She climbed the steps, walked into the pediment's shadow, and went into the castle. She had come home. Her head was held high and her face was set like stone.

She looked at the footman who had opened the door. "Where's Larke?"

"The Big Library, my Lady." The man grinned with delight.

Her shoes were loud on the marble floor. She led her men to the door and flung it open.

The library table was covered with books and papers, the tally of the rents and harvest, the lists of Lazen's property, the documents of the richest earldom in England; the records of the Little Kingdom.

Valentine Larke was standing. He had been given a few seconds warning of her coming. Six men were in the room with him, but not, she noticed, Sir Julius.

She walked toward Larke, skirting the table, ignoring his men, ignoring the huge Abel Girdlestone, ignoring the men whose faces were swollen from bee stings.

She stopped in front of Larke. He looked from her to the Gypsy, recognizing the man who carried his messages to France, and he tried to work out why this man should be here, with this woman, and then he saw Campion's arm move, he flinched, but the crop sliced into his face, came back and struck him again.

Skavadale's voice was casual. "Another step and you're pig food." He hefted the pistol in his left hand.

Abel Girdlestone, who had been moving toward Campion, froze. Simon Burroughs laughed.

Campion looked into Larke's face. "Yesterday, Larke, you threatened to put me over your knee. Was it my ass you were going to tan?"

Larke said nothing.

Campion's voice was cold. "Simon?"

"My Lady?"

"Bend him over!"

The huge coachman came forward. He grinned. He took Larke by his crinkly, glossy black hair and bent him over his knee. He plucked up the tails of the politician's coat. "Like that, your Ladyship?"

"Like that. You are about to discover, Larke, that you have made a mistake."

She thrashed him. She lashed him with the crop and her fury was in her arm and there was a joy in the punishment. Larke twisted, but he was helpless in the coachman's grasp. He yelped with pain.

She tossed the crop onto the table. "Let him up."

She waited until Larke was standing then pointed at the window. "My husband, Larke, is dead. What rights he had over this property died with him. You are not welcome, Larke. You have made an enemy. You have made an enemy of the house of Lazen. I would advise you to hide somewhere and pray we never find you. Out!"

There were tears in his eyes and a twist of fury on his face. He, who hated the aristocracy, had been humiliated by a mere girl and there was nothing he could do. Nothing! And then he remembered Lucifer's words, that he should not be surprised at anything which happened at Lazen, and he gaped at the Gypsy and he thought that there was a chance of revenge after all! Revenge at Auxigny! He pointed a finger at Campion. "I will pay you for that!"

"Out!"

The door to the library opened and Skavadale turned, pistol rising, to see Uncle Achilles gaping at the scene. He blinked at the Gypsy, then saw the anger and pride on Campion's face. "Campion?" His voice was incredulous.

"You're blocking the door, uncle. These men are leaving."

They went. They were cowed by her, terrified of her, and they huddled through the door and down the steps and stood uncertain, their belongings stranded within the house, and then the first men from the stables appeared, alerted by the grooms come back from Periton House. Larke saw them stoop to pick up stones, and suddenly he and Abel Girdlestone were leading a running retreat, past Culloden's body, pelted by dung and stones and pursued down the drive by jeering servants.

Three more men were found in the house and sent running by the footmen. Campion strode the corridors, throwing open doors, leading a triumphant, joyful band of footmen and maids. Mrs. Hutchinson joined Uncle Achilles, hurrying behind the noisy throng. William Carline, hearing the news that spread like wildfire through the huge castle, found Campion in the Yellow Drawing Room.

He bowed to her, his face quivering with happiness. "My Lady."

"The flag will be lowered to the half for my brother, Mr. Carline."

"Of course, my Lady."

"And where is my cousin?"

He gestured toward the rooms that her father had occupied. She turned. "Simon? Mr. Skavadale? Come with me."

She walked beneath the pictures of horses. She walked to her father's rooms and pushed the doors open.

She saw the girl first. The London whore stood in the bedroom door frowning at the noise in the Castle.

The girl wore a dress that had belonged to Campion's mother, an old fashioned, gorgeous dress of flounced scarlet taffeta and lace, one of the many dresses that her father could not bring himself to throw from her old dressing room. It was the dress she wore in his favorite portrait, and now the dress was tight on the painted whore.

About her neck were Campion's mother's jewels; the rubies that her father had given his bride on her wedding day, the diamonds that he had given her each year.

"Take that dress off!" Campion's voice was cold and bitter. The girl backed away.

"Who in Christ's name?" Julius, a robe hastily wrapped about him, came to the door, and Skavadale stepped past Campion, took him by the throat and pushed him backward. Julius fell on the bed, bounced back with his fist ready to punch, but Skavadale hit him first, hit him hard, and growled at him to stay still.

The girl looked to Julius, back to Campion.

"I said get that dress off!"

"But . . . ."

"Off!"

The girl fumbled at the hooks, the laces. Campion's anger was awesome. "And the jewels!"

The girl unclipped the necklace, took the bracelets from her wrists, the rings from her fingers and the diamonds from her ears.

"Get the dress off!"

Burroughs laughed. The girl wore nothing underneath, not even a petticoat. She stood naked.

Campion walked to the girl's own clothes. She kicked them toward the naked whore and, as she did, a golden watch fell from the skirt pocket.

"Wait!"

There was silence. Campion felt in all the pockets. Slowly, on the table by the window, she made a small pile of treasures that the girl had stolen and hid in her clothes.

"Simon?"

"My Lady?"

"Open a window."

He hurried to obey. Campion scooped all the clothes up, bundled them, and hurled them out onto the gravel of the forecourt. She turned to the white faced girl. "You leave this house as you are. That way I know you can steal nothing as you leave! Go!"

The girl shook her head, terrified.

"Go!"

She ran. Campion ignored the laughter outside. She turned and looked at her cousin who lay on the bed, his toothless mouth open. "Simon?"

"My Lady?"

"What premises are empty in Lazen?"

Burroughs frowned. "There's the old stable house, my Lady. It's not clean."

"You will put the Earl of Lazen into the old stable house. He is not allowed into the Castle. He will not come into my presence."

"Very good, my Lady." Burroughs was grinning.

"With those exceptions," she turned to the coachman, "he will be treated with the respect that his rank and his behavior merit."

She looked out of the window to see the naked girl, pursued by mocking servants, snatching her clothes from the gravel and running ungainly past the dead body. "And Simon?"

"My Lady?"

She pointed to Culloden's body. "Ask someone to bury that filth."

She stalked from the room. She strode through the castle, throwing its windows open as if to scour it clean, and her anger was mixed with laughter as she remembered the joy of beating Valentine Larke with the crop. All London would know of that!

She ordered a bath drawn, ordered an astonished William Carline to prepare a bedroom for Mr. Skavadale in the Garden House, and watched as the belongings left by Larke's men were taken to the smithy fire.

She laughed. She was a great lady and she had taken Lazen back.

She sat in the Long Gallery after dinner. It was a sweet, autumn evening, the shadows long in the valley, the swallows quick above the misting, silver lake. There was the smell of ripeness in the valley, of apples lined on racks, of leaves burning.

Uncle Achilles, a bruise on his forehead where he had

been trampled by Girdlestone the day before, was alone with her. He had arranged it so, asking Skavadale to give him this time with her. The servants had brought Campion tea. Achilles had brandy and a cigar that he cut and lit.

He put his boots on the window seat and stared at the clouds which were delicate against the sky. "I owe you an apology. It seems I was wrong about Lord Culloden."

"It seems everyone was wrong. My father, you, Scrimgeour, me." She shrugged. She remembered Culloden pleading in the stable yard. "He was a weak man, uncle."

"And now you've found yourself a strong one?" He smiled at her.

She did not want to talk about the Gypsy. She half suspected that Achilles had arranged to be alone with her, but she was in no mood to be lectured about her birth and responsibilities. She changed the subject. "I'm sorry about your Meissen. It was the best present and they broke it."

He waved a hand in dismissal. "There's always more Meissen, dear Campion. I shall flood you with it. I'm sorry about the statue."

She laughed. "You're forgiven for that."

Two swans flew over the castle, turned, their great wings touched pink by the setting sun and then, riding the air on spread feathers, they glided down to seethe onto the still water of the lake. Achilles watched them. "I think God made swans in one of his better moments." He smiled at her. "Why were you never presented at court?"

The sudden question surprised her. "I never wanted to be."

"Every other girl was!"

She laughed. She hated London, hated the court, and had never wished to line up with the other nubile daughters of the aristocracy to shuffle across the floor and curtsey to the King, all the while being ogled by the courtiers. "Father called it the Royal Fatstock Auction. He gave me a choice and I chose not to go. And I've not regretted it, uncle."

"When were you last in London?"

She frowned. "Three years? Maybe four."

He tutted. "You really should go into society, dear niece."

She laughed. "I am a widow since this morning, uncle, and already you are trying to marry me to some lord."

He blew a smoke ring and watched it drift toward the window. "How about the Prince of Wales?" She laughed and he frowned. "I'm serious!"

"Uncle!"

"I think I could bear having a niece as the Queen of England."

"I'm sure the Queen of England could bear having you as an uncle, but it will not be me, I promise you that."

"He'll fall at your feet. Rumors of your beauty have reached London, you know."

"You're embarrassing me." She sipped her tea. "I really can't believe that you want to marry me off so quickly. You'll forgive me if I say that your last suggestion did not turn out entirely happily?"

He shrugged. "I beat about the bushes, isn't that what the English say?" He laughed at himself. "I merely suggest to you, dear niece, that you can marry the very highest in the land."

She made a wry face at him. "As against the lowest?"

He shrugged. "Your words, my dear, not mine."

"I am not thinking of marriage, uncle." She said it tartly.

"No." The smoke from his cigar wafted through the window. He sighed. "You're in love, though. I can see it. I warned you against it, but you wouldn't listen. You think that nothing matters in all creation but one other person, as if all this," he waved his hand to encompass the whole planet, "was made as a shrine simply for two people."

He had spoken with unnatural vehemence. She looked at him. "Is there anything wrong with being in love?"

He nodded. "I have known some of the great men of this world, my dear Campion. I have watched them plot and plan and calculate their every move, I have seen them tread the dangers of power with exquisite skill, I have admired them! And then I have seen them in love! No calculation, no plotting, no care, no plan, no wisdom, just a lust that tugs them like blind fools into misery. Why?" He frowned at her. "Why, when we are so clever, do we allow this one decision, this one most important decision, be governed by the same emotion that drives a boar onto a sow?"

She smiled, but her voice was cold. "Uncle, I don't think I want to talk of love this night."

"No." He tapped ash into a bowl. "I didn't think you would. So talk of something else. Talk of the Fallen Angels." He said their name with pure scorn.

At dinner she and Skavadale had told Achilles of all that had happened, all that Culloden had said. Only one thing had she held back, and that with difficulty; the news that Toby still lived. She had wanted to shout that news from the rooftop, but Skavadale had been adamant. No one must know.

Achilles smiled. "The Fallen Angels! What a piquant name! It amuses me how grown men like such stupidities. The *Illuminati*! The Fallen Ones! Lucifer! Moloch! Belial!" He laughed. "How apt that they chose my father's shrine! A place built by a madman for their lunacy. But have you thought that there might be a method in their madness?"

"Method?"

"They want you dead. What better place to kill you than in France?"

She stared at him. "I don't know what you're saying."

"Oh, but you do. No one, dear Campion, has ever said you were a fool, but are you as clever as you think? They trapped you before, didn't they?" He blew another smoke ring and watched it drift away. "They trapped you. They arranged for a man to attack you and they sent you a Lord on horseback, a sword in his hand. What chance did you have? Every kitchenmaid dreams of such things! He rode straight into your life, all the doors magically opened by his seeming bravery!" He looked at her almost mockingly. "Have they done it again?"

"No, uncle."

"Have they sent you a man more handsome than the devil? Sent you a man who could break any woman's heart. Let her fall in love, let her have the sun and the moon! Let the stars be jewels in her eyes! Send her the Gypsy!"

"No!"

"It was all so convenient, dear Campion! He just happened to be in the right place at the right time. Not a moment too late! At the last second, when Lewis is tearing the clothes from you, a tall, handsome Gypsy rides to your rescue." Achilles made a gesture of wonder. "Does it not sound familiar? Twice? The kitchenmaids would envy you! But are you so blind that you can't see that these things do not happen by chance! Once, maybe, but twice?"

She stared at him, shook her head. "He killed Lewis. He killed three other men!"

"And when Lewis rescued you, dear Campion, he killed his own man too. The parallels, my lovely niece, are horribly precise."

"No!"

Achilles let her protest echo and fade. He sighed. "Tomorrow, he says, he goes to see Lord Paunceley?"

"Yes." She was miserable.

"We don't even know that he knows Lord Paunceley!" He looked at her. "I think I shall go with him."

"Go with him?"

"He claims he works for Paunceley. His Monstrous Lordship has never mentioned him to me." Achilles shrugged, as though that might not be entirely surprising. "But this is a plot against us! Against our family. It's our relatives who die, Campion, not Paunceley's. So I shall go with your Gypsy and I will find out if he does know Paunceley, and I shall find out if that depraved monster supports your Gypsy in wanting you to go to France."

"But I won't go anyway!"

"Not even for love? Not for a love put there by the Illuminated Ones? The Fallen Angels?"

"I won't go!"

"You'd be a fool to go." He said it tartly. "Remember I have my own shadowy friends in Lord Paunceley's world. Do nothing, dear Campion, till I find out who this Gypsy is."

She nodded. "I will do nothing, uncle."

He reached a hand to her and patted her arm. "I am sorry if I have made you sad, dear niece."

She shook her head. "You haven't."

"Oh but I have!" He gestured and the candlelight caught the dark red stone of his episcopal ring. "Lovers have such a propensity for sadness, it is as essential to them as happiness. Only intensity of emotion convinces them that love is real. They cannot settle for contentment, oh no! It has to be the peaks of ecstasy or the chasms of melancholy, and they never understand that to throw up everything for one moment's joy is to risk an eternity of boredom." He smiled. "I feel a preaching mood coming upon me; I shall be quiet."

She said nothing. The darkness spread from the east, a velvet, soft darkness on Lazen. Lucifer still lived and she knew, staring into the enfolding night, that while he lived there would be no peace in this valley.

"A game of chess, dear niece?"

She played, but her mind was elsewhere. She had thought that the Gypsy's swift sword had cut the tendrils that wrapped about Lazen, that he had defeated her enemies, but now it seemed that the man she would love could be the man who had been sent just to make her love. Love tore her, love tormented her, love drove her.

She advanced her black knight. Achilles sighed and took it with his bishop. The small horseman, sword raised, went from the board and her queen was threatened. She could not win. She was in love, and love's misery, on this night of victory, engulfed her.

19

Lady Campion Lazender, she refused to allow anyone to address her as Lady Culloden, had an overwhelming desire to tell Simon Stepper, bookseller of Lazen, to have a bath. It would be too hurtful, she decided, so instead she opened the upwind library windows and sat on the low, cushioned sill. "Did you discover anything, Mr. Stepper?"

"I'm rather proud to say I did, yes!" He laughed to himself, a habit he had caught over the lonely years of sitting in his dusty shop waiting for customers. He pulled his bag of books onto the table and settled himself happily in a chair. He wore a scarf summer and winter which he twitched now to dust the cover of a large leather volume. "Do you have the *Tractatus* by the Abbé Ferreau?"

"No," Campion said.

"A mere four guineas, your Ladyship, and I could leave it now?" He peered hopefully over his spectacles.

"Of course." She smiled.

"Splendid, indeed!" He laughed. "Well, now, I've marked the places. His Latin is execrable, not what one would expect of the Roman Church, dear me, no! Would you care to look?" He pushed the open book toward her.

Campion kept her judicial distance. "Please, Mr. Stepper, I had rather you told me."

"Of course. Well then, let me see, let me see!" He pulled the book toward him. He wore gloves that had the tops of the fingers cut off. The pages of the book crackled as they turned. "*Illuminati.* Founded by a man called Weishaupt, Adam Weishaupt of Ingolstadt. I was there once, my Lady, many years back. I seem to remember a very fine Polyglot Bible, the Plantin, of course. Very fine. Beyond my humble means, of course, but . . ."

"Mr. Stepper?"

"What? Oh, of course!" He laughed. "How very wayward of me, indeed yes. We spoke of the *Illuminati?*"

"We did." She had asked Simon Stepper, the man whose mind ranged extraordinary distances in the confines of his book stacks, to discover what he could about the *Illuminati.*

He turned a page. "Of course the Abbé Ferreau is not, I think, the most reliable of authorities? A mere gossiper, my Lady, and his Latin is bad, most bad, doggish indeed." He laughed. "One might expect such Latin at Cambridge, but not in the Roman Church, indeed, no. Ah! He says, my Lady, and you will forgive a free translation?"

"Of course."

He peered at her over his smeared spectacles. "Although I daresay that even my humble translation will be an improvement on the original!" He laughed. "Doggish indeed. Woof, woof. Dear me! Where were we?"

"The *Illuminati?*" She hid a smile.

"So we were. So we were." He put a filthy fingernail on a line, frowned, and adopted the solemn, portentous voice he thought appropriate to the written word. "They aim to establish and, let me think, propagate? Yes, propagate a new religion, my Lady, which is based on enlightened reason! Ah! They think they know what that is, do they? Dear me! Where was I? Yes. They wish to establish a universal and democratic republic, dear me!

They aim to overthrow the existing church and governments of the world!" He leaned back, shaking his gray head. "Ferreau may be wrong, of course."

"I think not," Campion said quietly.

Stepper had not heard her. "On the other hand you must remember that Weishaupt started the movement in 1776!"

She frowned. "1776?"

"The Americans, my Lady? The rebel Washington?"

"Of course."

"A bad year! Indeed so. Nothing will come of it, of course. The red men will drive them into the sea and that will be that!" He shook his head and tutted. "I believe there's a fine press in Philadelphia, I saw a very satisfying Ovid. Very sad, very sad." He reflected on the coming cataclysm in America until Campion, helping the breeze with one of the fans left over from the wedding, gently took him back to the *Illuminati.*

"Yes! Of course! Dear me!" He fished in his bag and produced another book. "You have Balthazar Bleibacht's *Discourses,* my Lady?"

"Not to my knowledge."

"Three guineas?"

She smiled. "Of course."

"Splendid, splendid! Not that I know much of Bleibacht. Execrable printing, of course, I never did like black letter. Still, he has something to say, let me see, let me see. Here it is!" He took a feather from the page. "The *Illuminati,* he says, are believers in Illuminism. I always wonder why Germans have to state the obvious. Let me see now. The possession of an inner light! That makes sense, what else does he think Illuminism is if it isn't that, eh? He says they're very secret. Ferreau concurs in that. Highly organized! They need to be! Overthrow the world's governments indeed!" He laughed. "What else now, let me see, let me see. Ah yes! Bleibacht says they believe that the ends justify any means! Any!" He tutted.

It all made sense to Campion. A secret movement devoted to republicanism and the overthrow of established monarchies. A movement of ruthless purpose. Behind her she heard wheels on the gravel of the driveway. The harvest was coming in, the wains loaded with grain. "Do the books say if the movement has spread to England?"

"No." Stepper was polishing his spectacles on the end of his scarf. "They merely say, my Lady, that it started in Germany, was driven south by the German Princes, and found a home in France. That's hardly astonishing, I suppose. Any lunatic can find a home there these days. Thomas Paine, indeed!" He chuckled at another private jest as he turned back to the *Tractatus*. "Ah! Ferreau says that they're very strong in Italy."

"Italy?"

"Indeed, yes. Ah! Here we are! A statement of purpose, no less." He laughed to himself, twitched the scarf closer about his neck, and frowned as he translated for her. "To deliver the peoples of the world from the tyranny of priests and kings!" He tutted. "Whatever next! Extraordinary people!"

A new voice startled both of them, a voice of harsh ugliness and loud confidence. The voice was rude, sudden, and mysterious. "Extraordinary indeed!"

The shouted words made Campion lean forward and she saw, at the library door, a man more ugly than she could imagine. An old man with a malevolent, leathery face beneath an ancient, filthy wig. A man with a small head that seemed to quest about the room on an unnaturally long neck. A man whose mouth seemed lipless and eyes lidless, a man of reptilian menace. He was wrapped in a great cloak. He pushed the helpless, protesting footman aside and walked farther into the library.

"Cagliostro. Mesmer. Laclos. The Anarchasis Clootz, Restif de la Bretonne, and let us not forget the Count Donatien Alphonse Francois de Sade, now secretary of a Revolutionary Committee in Paris. All extraordinary!" He stopped. He glared at her. "I presume you are the Lady Campion Lazender?"

She stood. Her voice was icy. "I am. And you, sir?"

"Paunceley, of course." He nodded to her in what she supposed was meant to be a bow. "And who in Christ's name are you?" He pointed a finger at Stepper.

The bookseller smiled. "Stepper, Simon, sir. Bookseller."

"You stink, but you're right. They are extraordinary people. The *Illuminati* indeed! Cagliostro's a crook, Mesmer's a fraud, Laclos is a fool, Clootz is a clown, de la Bretonne a pornographer, and de Sade!" He pulled a chair from beneath the table and sat. His ugly face looked at Campion and his mouth twitched with amusement. "De Sade, my Lady, requires his valet to sodomize him while he tups whores. I tell you not to cause offense, but to satisfy your evident curiosity. You have finished with this man Stepper Simon?"

She was offended, not by his words, but by his manner. She felt more than offense, she felt awed by him. He had come into the room as if he had a perfect right to dictate to her, and he took for granted that she would know his power and influence. Yet she would not be cowed by him. "My business with Mr. Stepper is not concluded, my Lord."

"Then I shall wait for your attention." He took a book from his pocket and Stepper, his professional interest aroused, leaned over the table.

Lord Paunceley gave the bookseller a ghastly smile. "The *Riche Heures de Madame la Dauphine*. Illustrated. Twenty-five guineas."

Simon Stepper blushed.

Campion tried to ignore Lord Paunceley, smiling at the bookseller instead. "You found out more, Mr. Stepper?"

But Simon Stepper had been flustered by Lord Paunceley's sudden appearance. He shook his head nervously. "Indeed not, my Lady."

Lord Paunceley laughed harshly. "Then go, bookseller! I need her Ladyship's attention!"

She turned on him. "My Lord! You have refused to answer any of my letters. You come here unannounced, and you presume to give orders where you have no authority. I would be obliged if you would desist!"

He looked at her with feigned astonishment. Slowly, his cloaked shoulders heaving, he began to chuckle. He pointed at her. "That's it! Attack an old man! Would you like to hit me? Shall I get you a pistol to shoot me with? You!" He twisted around to the footman who still stood in the doorway. "You!"

"Sir?" The footman was as terrified as the bookseller.

"Before her Ladyship slaughters me I would like some tea and a fire lit. Quick, man! I may not have long to live." He looked back to Campion. "I have taken the unpardonable liberty of ordering a fire in my bedroom. Christ in his insane heaven, but it's cold!"

"It's the warmest autumn for years!"

"That's it! Bully me! I'm just an old man so you can bully me! I prayed, I hoped, I begged for the winter of my years to be peaceful, but I must be insulted by mere children. You!" He pointed at Stepper. "You're still here! Your stink offends me! Go!"

"Mr. Stepper!" Campion checked the bookseller's headlight flight. She was tempted to order him to stay, but something warned her that she should not oppose Lord Paunceley yet. Besides, it would be a relief to get the odorous bookseller safely into Lazen's open air. "I shall see you from the Castle."

She escorted him into the Entrance Hall where strange servants were piling Lord Paunceley's luggage. She smiled at Stepper. "I do apologize, Mr. Stepper. He is an old friend of my father, so perhaps he can take these liberties."

"Not at all, my Lady, not at all." He was wrapping the scarf about his neck. "Sticks and stones may break my bones, my Lady, but not mere words. Oh no!" He laughed to himself. "And to say that I smell! Most amusing." Now that he was out of Lord Paunceley's presence, the bookseller was regaining his usual optimism and jauntiness. "I have some volumes that perhaps ought to be in the Castle's library, my Lady?"

She made a polite response. She was trying to edge him toward the door when, with a clatter of boots and laughter, it was thrown open and she was staring into Christopher Skavadale's smiling face.

The doubts evaporated. Every doubt that Achilles had put into her head, and which had festered during these last ten days, disappeared. She had remembered his face, but not the life of it, not the bright, vivid life that stabbed at her and made her smile to see him. She had missed him.

Another man came to the door and Campion used the stranger's presence to shake the bookseller loose. Skavadale bowed to her and gestured to the newcomer. "May I present Mr. Geraint Owen, His Lordship's secretary? This is the Lady Campion Lazender."

Owen bowed. "I trust you will forgive this intrusion, your Ladyship."

"Owen!" Lord Paunceley's voice was plaintive from the library. "I'm cold, Owen! I'm being insulted! I'm thirsty! Owen!"

The Welshman smiled at her. "You will forgive me, my Lady?"

Campion nodded. She saw the bookseller to the door, telling him to bring whatever books he thought necessary for the library, and then she turned to the Gypsy. She could not hide her happiness. Achilles, she thought, could not be right. This man, this splendid, smiling, handsome man could not be her enemy. "You came with Lord Paunceley?"

"Yes."

She laughed. "He's a monster!"

Skavadale nodded. "True. And how's your own monster?"

She shrugged. Julius still lived in the Old Stable House, drunk for much of the time, guarded day and night by servants. Dr. Fenner was treating his pox with mercury. "He's alive." She said it dubiously and looked up into the Gypsy's face, feeling the familiar pang that he gave her. "Why has Lord Paunceley come?"

"Let him tell you."

"He wants me to go to France, doesn't he?" Skavadale nodded, and she shook her head. "I'm not going!"

"I've already told him that."

A servant went past with a tray of tea, another carried a basket of logs. Campion turned to the library.

It took ten minutes for Lord Paunceley to make himself comfortable. The tea was too weak, the fire too slow to start, and he querulously demanded that the windows be shut. Like a shaggy, bad tempered beast he arranged the library for his comfort as if, on this fine autumn day, he was settling for the winter. Only when the last footman had left, and when he was satisfied with the tea and oatcakes, did he turn his ugly face on Campion. "You are privileged, my Lady!"

She thought he meant that she was fortunate to live in Lazen. She nodded. "I know, my Lord."

"I have not left London these three years, apart from visits to Tyburn! Yet here I am! I have come, at considerable inconvenience, to your very door! You are privileged indeed! Do you know why I have come?"

She said nothing. Paunceley sucked noisily at his dish of tea. He plucked the cloak over his knees. He looked slyly at her. "Your uncle came to see me!"

"I know."

"He thought the Bastard didn't work for me! Ha!"

She frowned. "You mean Mr. Skavadale?"

"Mister!" The word delighted Lord Paunceley. "You hear that, Bastard! She calls you 'mister'! Ah! You cheer an old man up, dear Lady Campion, you lighten my old age. Mister indeed!"

Skavadale smiled at her. "His Lordship does not believe that the Rom marry, my Lady."

"Marry!" Lord Paunceley cackled. "What do they do? Dance naked around a cauldron at a coven?"

The Gypsy smiled. "We're not like your family, my Lord, we marry in church."

Paunceley smiled. "I suppose I shall have to call you 'mister,' then. Or would you prefer a knighthood, Bastard? Sir Christopher Skavadale? My God! They gave that dauber Reynolds a knighthood! Sir Joshua! I suppose anything can happen if you have a mad, fat, German King." He looked at Campion. "Which language do you prefer to use?"

"Whatever your Lordship prefers."

"I prefer Russian. Speak Russian, do you?"

"No, my Lord."

"God knows why Vavasour didn't educate you. Because you're a girl, I suppose. Waste of time educating girls. They only grow into mothers and think they're clever because they do what any cow can do. All right! French!" He sipped noisily at his tea. "I was sorry about Vavasour. I liked him." He grimaced at her. "Pity about your brother, too."

"Thank you, my Lord."

"Can't say I was sorry about Culloden. A shooting accident?"

"So the Coroner said, my Lord."

He laughed. He dipped an oatcake into his tea and then sucked at it. "So your stinking bookseller, my Lady, has told you all about the *Illuminati?*"

"He has told me what he could, my Lord."

Paunceley looked at the Welshman. "Tell her more, Owen. Illuminate thou her!"

She decided she liked Geraint Owen. He had a quick, nervous smile, expressive hands, and an easy manner. He confirmed all that Stepper had told her, and then added more. "They have secrets within secrets, my Lady, small septs to perform specific tasks." He pushed his long dark hair back from his pale face. "We think one such sept was behind the massacres in Paris a year ago, almost certainly another is the guiding group for the politics of France." He shrugged as though he hardly expected to be believed. "And Mr. Skavadale seems to have discovered another group, my Lady. The Fallen Angels." He smiled.

She was sitting in the window seat. It seemed strange, with the Lazen valley golden behind her, to be hearing of these plots and secrets.

Paunceley scowled at her. "So that's it! A group of toads who call themselves the Fallen Angels! They want Lazen, it seems." He peered at her with his small, fierce eyes. "And your uncle tells me that you won't go to France to destroy them!" He said it with evident astonishment.

"No, my Lord."

"Why ever not? I thought you girls enjoyed jaunts to France! My sister always enjoyed jaunts to France. Why won't you go?"

"I have learned to value my life, my Lord."

"Christ and His angels!" Paunceley guffawed. "Value

your life! You sound like a threadbare Wesleyan! Have you been born again, my Lady?" She said nothing and he plucked the fur-edged cloak tighter to his thin body. "Do I have to explain it all to you as if to a child?"

"If you wish, my Lord."

He scowled. "Your uncle claims you are not a fool. So be intelligent now. The *Illuminati,* my Lady, seek to take over the fortune of Lazen. To do that they need to kill your brother and yourself. They have been successful with your brother. That leaves you. You have avoided one clumsy attempt, does that make you feel there will be no more? You are suddenly immune to attack?" She said nothing. He scratched beneath his wig. "From this day on, my Lady, you are in danger. Every servant, every guest, every traveller on your roads may carry your death. Suppose that you marry? Suppose that, God help you, you spawn a child? Then that child is in danger, too!" He twisted his hands together as if wringing the neck of a baby, then waved dismissively at her. "So you'll die! Your suckling infant will be dead, and Lazen will be lost! And all because you wouldn't go to France! Well! I couldn't care! I'm an old man! Soon they'll be burying me!" He twisted to look at the Welshman. "Make sure it's in the Abbey, Owen! In the choir! I won't have a drafty grave!" He turned back to her. "So? You'll go?"

"Go?" She frowned. "My Lord, if I am in danger then I am perfectly capable of guarding myself."

He groaned. "Listen to her! You're saying what half the dead nobles of France said! Don't you understand, my Lady? They wish you dead! You will live in fear so long as Lucifer lives. Kill Lucifer, and you may rock your whining brat into slumber. But so long as Lucifer lives, you fear."

"I do not understand, my Lord . . ."

"You're a girl, that's quite reasonable."

"I do not understand, my Lord," and she did not hide the anger in her voice, "what purpose my going to France serves."

"You don't understand?"

"No, my Lord."

Paunceley stared at her. There was something malevolent about his reptilian face as he slowly smiled. "Two weeks from now, Lady Campion, the Fallen Angels are going to gather at Auxigny. All of them. They will gather for one purpose." Slowly his hand came from his fur robe and a thin finger jabbed at her. "You are that purpose. But if you are not there, girl, then they will not gather, and if they do not gather then they will not be in one convenient place where my Bastard can kill them. Do you understand now?"

She looked at the Gypsy whose face showed nothing, then back to Lord Paunceley. "No, I don't understand."

Paunceley scowled. "Tell her, Bastard."

Skavadale smiled at her. His voice was soft. "Bertrand Marchenoir has offered me a place among the Fallen Angels. The price is that I deliver you to Auxigny. They will think I have come to join them, but I will have come to kill them."

"There!" Lord Paunceley leaned back in his chair. "What could be simpler? A jaunt to France? A little betrayal, a little death, and you'll be back before the wheat's milled. In my youth I would have asked for nothing more!" He looked at Owen. "You've got the Harvest Whore at Weymouth, yes?"

"The *Lily of Rye,* my Lord. Yes. She's waiting."

The vile, dirty-wigged, ugly face came back to her. "So what in Christ's name is so worrying? We provide the boat! The Bastard looks after you! He kills your enemies, and he's very skilled at that, and then you come home!"

She said nothing. They all seemed to be waiting for her reply, but she gave none. She looked at Skavadale. In a sense, she thought, her uncle had been right. The Gypsy was working for the Fallen Ones as well as for Lord Paunceley, but which had his loyalty? She remembered Lord Culloden telling of the girl he had killed at Auxigny, of the death that was required as a sacrifice for every new Fallen Angel, and she shuddered to think that she was to be the next victim. She searched the Gypsy's dark, strong face and she could not believe that this man was an enemy. The silence stretched.

The Gypsy sighed. He was sitting on the library steps. He looked at Campion with a flicker of sadness, then shrugged to Lord Paunceley. "I have another girl who can go, my Lord."

Paunceley looked at him. "You do? So what does she look like?"

"Blonde hair, same height." He shrugged. "Of course, we'll have to pay her."

"She's used to taking money, is she?" Paunceley laughed. "Is she beautiful, this whore of yours?"

The Gypsy nodded. "She's thought beautiful, my Lord."

"What girl?" Campion asked.

Paunceley scowled at her. "If you will not help us, my Lady, then pray do me the courtesy of not interrupting us!"

She stood, inflamed by his rudeness. "What girl?"

The Gypsy shrugged. "She's an actress."

"So was Nell Gwynn," Paunceley laughed. "Every whore calls herself an actress! There aren't enough theaters in Europe for all the actresses!" He looked at Skavadale. "You'd better take her. Bastard."

"She'll go in my place?"

Paunceley's voice was suddenly savage. "Lady Campion, I would not sacrifice a shilling to save this house, I couldn't care if the *Illuminati* turn it into a whorehouse. But I do care about Britain. It may have a fat King and it may be filled with more fools than a carnival, but I would not like to see it seething with gibbering revolutionaries who will disturb my declining years. I am paid to keep the lunatics in Parliament, not to have them rampaging in our streets! Lucifer, my Lady, will turn this country into another France, a blood-filled charnel house! So I must kill him. That's why fat George employs me! And if you will not help me, then, by God, I'll pay every trollop in town to go in your place!" He looked back to Skavadale. "Pray excuse my intemperate interruption, Bastard, and tell me about this lubricious maiden you will escort through France?"

Campion was staring in astonishment at the Gypsy. "You mean this girl will call herself Campion Lazender?"

He nodded. "Of course!"

"She will not!"

Her words were almost shouted. Paunceley smiled. It had been his idea to invent a fictitious girl who would go in Campion's place. He looked at her. "You can't forbid it."

She was astonished at the jealousy that had stabbed at her, the jealousy of some unknown girl having this man's company in France. She looked at him. "How are you going to travel in France?"

"With the Rom as far as Paris, after that the public stage."

There was silence.

Paunceley chuckled. "Perhaps the actress would be better, Bastard? I doubt whether the Lady Campion could endure the discomfort."

She ignored him. She stared at Skavadale. She thought of Achilles' warning, yet was not this assemblage in

Lazen's Library proof that the Gypsy's loyalty was to Paunceley? Every scrap of sense warned her not to go, but at the same time she was being offered a chance to be alone with this man, away from servants and chaperones and gossip. She swallowed nervously. "And what happens at Auxigny?"

Skavadale smiled. "The girl is my bait. She draws the Fallen Ones and I kill them." Everyone in the room was staring at her and Skavadale took the opportunity to silently mouth another message. "Toby."

So Toby would be at Auxigny.

Geraint Owen cleared his throat. "We'll provide you with passports, travel permits, all the papers. It really will be safe, my Lady. We send men into France all the time!"

"How many come back?"

He smiled. "Most."

She touched the seals of Lazen at her breast. "If we went, when would we go?"

Paunceley smiled. "Tomorrow?"

"Tomorrow!"

"Unless you have other things planned?" he said sarcastically. "A small tea party, perhaps? Some friends to giggle with you!" He held up a hand to ward off her angry protest. "Do not tell me I am rude, Lady Campion! Remember I am made in God's image!" He turned to Skavadale. "Take your whore, Bastard. This one can't endure a small insult, and France is one great insult these days."

Skavadale said nothing. He watched Campion. He waited.

She knew she would go. Achilles' advice notwithstanding, she would go. She would go because Toby was there, but above all she would go because, if she did not go, then another girl would take her place.

She would go to the land of death and madness. She

would go to France and she knew, as the three men watched her, that she did it in the name of love.

She took a breath. She thought this was the most fateful decision she had ever made, but if that kiss in the Temple, the touch of his hand, if that magic that had seared through her meant anything, then she must trust him. She looked at the tall, light eyed man who could set her soul aflame. "I will go to Auxigny."

That night, as Campion slept, Lord Paunceley waited alone in the library.

A decanter of port was at his elbow, a book on his lap, candles beside him. The fire glowed red.

He heard the door open, there was a second's silence, then it closed with a soft click. The reptilian face lifted from the book. "Gitan?"

"Oui."

"Come where I can see you."

Christopher Skavadale sat on the hearth fender. The fire lit one side of his face.

Lord Paunceley stared into the dark, thin face as though he would read it like the book on his lap. Then he gave his thin, mischievous smile. "She's more beautiful than sin, Gitan."

"Yes."

"I haven't seen a girl so lovely in fifty years!" Paunceley sighed. "And so innocent! Do you like them innocent, Gitan? Do you have a taste for purity?" Lord Paunceley sipped his port. "She's in love with you. That's why she's going, isn't it?"

Skavadale shrugged. "How would I know?"

"You would know, Gitan, you would know." Paunceley stared at him. "How sad, Gitan, that you were born in a ditch, eh? You'd make such a couple!" He laughed softly.

"But it can't be, can it? You can't marry her, so you'll take her to Auxigny instead, yes?"

"Yes."

Paunceley stared at him. In the Hall outside a clock struck one. Paunceley smiled a subtle smile. His voice was suspicious. "Did you tell her that her brother was still alive?"

Skavadale paused, then nodded. "Yes."

"How clever of you. Does she believe you?"

"She believes me."

Lord Paunceley closed his eyes. His harsh, grating voice was hardly louder than the sound of the log fire. " 'Now the serpent was more subtle than any beast of the field which the Lord God had made. And he said unto the woman, "Yea," ' " and he drew out the last word to a long, lascivious syllable and opened his eyes to stare at the Gypsy. The fire flickered and the candles shivered. "And what name, serpent, have you chosen from the angels?"

Skavadale smiled. "Thammuz."

Paunceley quoted the Bible again. "The 'women weeping for Thammuz,' yes?" He laughed softly into the bright, light eyes of the Gypsy. "You'd like to be called Lucifer, wouldn't you? It would suit you!" He waited, but the Gypsy did not respond. Paunceley smiled. "So what can I do?"

Skavadale took a sealed letter from a pocket. "This has to be delivered to Larke."

Paunceley grunted as he leaned forward to take the letter. "You're telling him to go to Auxigny?"

"Yes."

Paunceley put the letter inside his book. "So innocent, so pure, so ready to be ravished. Do you ravish her, Gitan? Do you go to her in the night and make her moan?"

"No." Skavadale smiled.

"More subtle than any beast of the field." Paunceley laughed. "But you will, Thammuz! Before you deliver her to Auxigny, you will!" He waved his hand in dismissal. "Goodnight, Gitan! Oh, thou most excellent servant, goodnight!"

The Gypsy went on silent feet to his room in the Garden House, and Lazen, beneath the infinite spaces of the dark sky, slept.

20

They lay in the sandhills that stretched inland, the dawn limning the spiky grass, and the sea crashing dully behind them. The gulls cried in the wind over the foam.

Christopher Skavadale was beside her. He watched the road below them. "I always knew you'd come."

"Why?"

He smiled. "It's in the blood. Your father did it, your brother did it, perhaps your children will do it."

"I hope not." She shivered.

She was dressed as a gypsy with dark heavy skirts, a blouse, a vest, two aprons, and a headscarf that was bright with small gold disks. She felt conspicuous and foolish, yet Geraint Owen, the nervous, quick Welshman had explained why they used the gypsies to travel the dangerous, well guarded coast roads in France. Strangers, he had said, were always suspect in France, yet gypsies were the one kind of stranger that no one was surprised to see.

She travelled with false papers, though her true protection lay with Skavadale. He had a paper signed by the Committee for Public Safety itself, a paper that would command instant obedience from any French soldier. They could, Skavadale said, have used the paper to commandeer a carriage, yet he preferred the hidden, secret travel of the Rom. It was best, he explained to her, that they did not attract attention. She believed that he preferred, for at least a few days, to show her his own people.

They waited for *vardoes,* the gypsy wagons with their bright-painted roofs. When a *vardo* was built, he explained, the seller would stand inside the wagon at night with a lit candle in his hand. The buyer would prowl about the outside, and if so much as a single chink of light escaped through the narrow, jointed planks, then the *vardo* was reckoned to be unsound. If light could get through, then so could rain.

She would travel the autumn roads in a *vardo,* sharing it with an ancient gypsy woman. Just to be in this country, Campion knew, condemned her to death, but as she waited for the travelling people to come to this rendezvous, she felt oddly happy. This was an adventure and perhaps he was right, perhaps it was in her blood. Beneath her clothes she carried the seals of Lazen; she had debated whether to bring them, but she had thought they might give her strength. She was in France for Lazen, but so much more besides. The heart has reasons that reason does not know, and she travelled with the Gypsy.

Ababina seemed older than Mistress Sarah. She was a tiny, white haired lady with skin wrinkled a thousand, thousand times. She still kept her own horse, fetched her own water, lit her own fires and cooked her own food.

There were five *vardoes* in the group, the other four all driven by Ababina's grandsons. On the second day, as Campion sat beside the old woman on the driving board, and they followed the wagon in front that clanged with buckets and chains and had four dogs tied to its back axle, the old woman tapped her pipe on the footboard and said she had once seen the old King of France.

"You did?" Campion asked.

"Yes, *rawnie.* He was an angel. He rode in a chariot of fire and gold."

Later, much later, Campion realized she meant Louis XIV who had died seventy-eight years before.

"Of course I was only a child," Ababina explained. "I'd only had one baby then."

Each hour was full of strange stories, yet not all were believable. One of the grandsons, a surly, dark bearded man who earned a living as a blade-sharpener, had a scar on his face that ran from his temple to his chin. Ababina said that he had fetched the scar as a tiny child when the cow that he had been put to suckle trampled on him. She laughed at Campion's disbelief. "You'll learn, *rawnie,* you'll learn."

Rawnie meant "great lady." Christopher Skavadale, whose single earring marked him as a leader of the Rom, insisted that she was treated with respect.

Her travelling papers, forged in London, gave her name as Shukar. Skavadale had chosen it.

She tried to learn some Romani from Ababina, yet there was not time to learn more than a few nouns. *Grai* was horse, *jakel* was dog, *pal* was a friend, and a man who had the *tacho rat* was a man of true Rom blood. It was not thought fit for such a man to marry a *gaje,* a non-gypsy.

At night Christopher Skavadale pointedly slept far from her wagon. It was not the Rom way, Ababina said, for a man and a woman to share a bed before marriage.

She asked Ababina where the gypsies came from.

The old woman shrugged. "Who knows? Our enemies say that Eve lay with Adam when he was dead, and we are the result."

There were stories that the gypsies could curse people,

could master fire, and that they stole fair-haired children. Ababina laughed at Campion's gold hair. "They'll think that we stole you."

Campion asked the old woman whether Ababina meant anything or was it just a name?

"It means Sorceress."

Campion smiled. "And Shukar? Does that mean anything?"

The old woman laughed. "It's what your man calls you!" Except that Christopher Skavadale was not her man. He was *tacho rat,* and she was *gaje.* But at least, as *gaje,* she was better than the tinkers. Tinkers, to Ababina, were the lowest of the low.

The Rom, Campion found, were scrupulously clean. She helped Ababina scrub out the *vardo,* she helped wash clothes in a stream and was surprised to find that the womens' clothes were never washed with the mens'. To do so was to be unclean. She learned never to put shoes on a table, and never to wear white. White was the color of death.

To be unfaithful was to court the punishment of losing an ear or a hand. To be a whore was filthy, unfitting for Rom, to be as bad as the *gaje.*

"Why do the *gaje* hate you?" Campion asked.

"They say we stole the swaddling clothes from the baby Jesus. They say we made the nails for his cross."

Campion laughed.

Ababina smiled. "Because we're free, so they envy us. Because we see the future, so they fear us."

"And can you see the future?"

The old woman clicked her tongue at her dogs. "Anyone who lives can see the future. You just have to trust what you see." She looked ahead to where a small village straddled the road and she spat at the verge. "Soldiers."

* * *

Christopher Skavadale rode a horse borrowed from one of Ababina's grandsons. He dismounted and went into the guard house.

The *vardoes* stopped in the village street. The villagers surreptitiously crossed themselves, preferring to risk the wrath of a regime that did not like religion than to run the dangers of the gypsies' evil eye.

The soldiers, less fearful, walked slowly down the line of wagons. They asked for papers. They stole the dead chickens that hung at the wagons' sides, not knowing that the gypsies had stolen the fowls earlier in the day for just that purpose.

The soldiers carried muskets. They had bayonets sheathed at their belts. Their feet were bare or stuffed into straw filled sabots.

A soldier stopped beside Ababina's wagon and reached for their papers. He took them, glanced at them, and handed them back. He could not read.

He looked at Campion. "You're not a gypsy."

"I am."

He laughed. Two of his companions joined him, and they called to the other soldiers so that the troops crowded about the *vardo* and stared at the gypsy who had golden hair showing at her scarf's edge.

"You want money, gypsy?"

She said nothing.

The man reached out with his musket and hooked the muzzle beneath her skirts. He lifted them and the soldiers cheered as they saw her calf. "Come on, girl! A livre from each of us?"

She said nothing.

He pushed the musket higher, jerking her skirts back down over her knee and she twisted away, pushing the skirts down, and the man reached out and caught her wrist. He pulled her down so that her face was close to his and she could smell the onions on his breath. "I'm offering you money. If you don't say yes, little one, I'll take you for nothing. Now what's it to be?"

She was terrified. She felt inadequate. She sensed that another girl, more used to the world, would have known how to deflect them with laughter and boldness. She knew they sensed her fear, they had found themselves a victim.

He pulled her farther toward him and more hands reached up to take her shoulders to haul her clear of the wagon. She screamed, and they laughed.

"Come on, beautiful! We'll steal you back from the bastards!"

She half fell from the wagon seat, both arms held by soldiers, and they began to drag her toward one of the houses. A hand snatched the scarf from her head and a whistle of appreciation sounded as her gold hair spilled in the sunlight.

The pistol shot froze them.

She pulled one arm free.

An officer ran toward the men, his face appalled, while behind him, on the steps of the guardhouse, Skavadale reloaded his pistol.

"Leave her," the officer shouted, "for God's sake! Leave her!"

The soldiers frowned. She was just a gypsy, a nobody, a girl to rape with the freedom conferred on them by liberty's uniform.

The man who held her left arm, the man who had lifted her skirts, pulled her toward him. "We offered the bitch money!"

"Let her go!"

The officer's command over his men was tenuous, but behind him Skavadale walked slowly toward the soldiers and they fell back before his air of comfortable confidence. The man let go her right arm.

Skavadale walked past her. He took the man by the throat and hit him twice over the face. "Well?"

"Captain?" The man appealed to his officer.

Skavadale hit him again, harder. "Well?"

The officer's face warned his men to make no trouble.

Skavadale lifted the soldier by the throat. He did it without apparent effort, his eyes on the man's eyes, and, when he held him six inches above the ground he suddenly dropped him and brought up his right knee.

The man screamed, fell, and curled on the ground with his hands clutching his loins.

Skavadale turned. "My papers, Captain."

The officer handed over not a passport or a travel permit, but a folded sheet of paper that bore a red seal.

The soldiers watched in silence as Skavadale helped her back onto the wagon. They sensed that they had been fortunate. The guillotine, these days, was utterly without discrimination. Skavadale rode beside her. "Are you all right?"

She nodded. She had been appalled. She was ashamed that she had not behaved better.

He smiled. "Next time tell them they're not men enough for you, that you don't ride donkeys, only stallions."

Ababina laughed. "You'll learn, Shukar, you'll learn."

They parted from the gypsies to the west of Paris. The sky was smeared with the city's smoke. There was a chill in the air, the hint of autumn's ending. The birds had been flocking south for three days now, flying over the *vardoes* and gathering in great swarms in the golden trees.

Ababina was the last to say farewell. She kissed Campion on both cheeks. "*Ja develesa,* Shukar."

Campion smiled. "Which means?"

"Go with God."

"And Shukar? What does that mean?"

The old woman laughed. "It means beautiful. Remember one thing."

"What?"

The old woman looked at Skavadale who had relinquished the horse and now waited for her. "He's frightened of you."

"He's not frightened of anything!"

The old woman laughed. "He chose the *gaje* world, Shukar. Do you think it doesn't frighten him? He won't show it, but in your world he feels as strange as you in ours." She shrugged. "It's his choice."

She kissed the old woman. "Thank you for everything."

"*Ja develesa, rawnie,* and I think you do."

The greatest change Campion could see in Paris was in the clothes of the people. It was dangerous, Skavadale said, to be seen flaunting wealth, and so the inhabitants, even those who had money, adopted a protective costume of dirty rags. Most wore rosettes of red, white and blue, similar to the one that Skavadale pinned on Campion's shawl.

The houses were festooned with patriotic banners, the colors bright, the slogans preferring death to loss of liberty. Yet the houses also had the names of their inhabitants painted on the doors so that the soldiers could search to find those who slept without permission in Paris.

Skavadale took her to the Section *Bonnet Rouge* and sent her upstairs to the Revolutionary Committee. "Ask for a permit to sleep in the Section."

"You're not coming?"

"I'll be a moment." He smiled. "You'll be safe."

Eight men sat at the table. They seemed to spend all

day in the room that was smothered with posters exhorting the world to revolution. The table was littered with half-eaten food, wine bottles, dice, and playing cards. Women cooked in a kitchen next door, their laughter loud, their heads bright with red caps of liberty.

The men stared at her.

One man took her papers. He glanced at her passport, but frowned for a long time at her forged *Certificat de civisme* that guaranteed, in this age of liberty, that her political views were acceptable to the revolutionaries. He sniffed. The room buzzed with flies.

One man looked her up and down. "Why are you in Paris?"

"To seek work."

That made them laugh. "You could earn a fortune without leaving your bed, *ma poule*!"

She smiled.

Skavadale had paused to buy a bottle of apple brandy. Now he stood in the deep shadow outside the Committee room. His voice startled her. "She's not a gypsy."

She felt panic sear through her.

The men, who ruled this section of Paris, stared at her.

Skavadale spoke again. "She's an English aristocrat."

They looked at the shadows by the door. She felt her stomach turn into churning, liquid fear.

One of the men suddenly roared a great welcome. "Gitan!" There was an explosion of laughter.

Skavadale shook their hands one by one. "You're getting fat, Michel." He punched a friendly fist into the man's stomach. He had a word for everyone in the room, knew their nicknames, and happily sat with them and offered them his gift of brandy. He jerked his head at Campion. "My woman. We need an inn."

"Just one room, eh?" One of the men laughed. "You're a lucky bastard, Gitan!"

Skavadale grinned. He patted the chair beside him and Campion sat. They scribbled the permit she needed and pushed it to her.

The man called Michel grinned at her. "You'll prefer me, gypsy girl! I'm a man of substance!"

She took the brandy that Skavadale gave her. She was still liquid with terror inside, but she forced a smile onto her face. "I never ride donkeys, only stallions."

They laughed. She was in Paris.

That night she lay beneath an open window and watched the clouds and smoke skein before a crescent moon.

She had never travelled without a horde of servants. She had never been in an inn where the innkeeper was not solicitous for her comfort. She had never been in such danger.

There had been times since she had landed in France when she had felt lost, lonely and frightened, yet those times were few. She had hated it when the soldiers grabbed her, but even then she had known that Skavadale was near, that he would come for her, that she was safe. Just as now, lying alone in her narrow bed, she felt safe because he was downstairs.

Tomorrow they would take a coach for Bellechasse, and from Bellechasse they would cross the mountains to Auxigny. And at Auxigny, she knew, all the answers would be found. Not just to Lucifer and the Fallen Ones, but to the questions that had mocked her these twelve months. Love, her uncle had said, was an illusion. Nothing more.

Then this, too, was an illusion. This journey, this madness, this adventure.

He had told her once that the roads never end, yet it seemed to her that they would end, not in sadness, but in the mysteries at Auxigny. After that, she told herself, the old roads would be gone. She smiled. She was in France and she was happy.

She knew that the machine stood in the Place de la Revolution, yet somehow it was a surprise to see the twin shafts rising above the crowd's heads. She stopped, frowning.

"What's the matter?" Skavadale was carrying their bags toward the stage terminal. "Oh, that!"

"Dear God!"

"Don't use English."

"Did I?"

He smiled. "Yes."

But it was a shock, like finding that the Green Man really did live in the woods or that witches circled the moon on broomsticks. It was there, sticking into the sky like nothing she had ever seen, but was oddly familiar all the same. It was close by the great plaster statue of Justice that loomed over its own victims' deaths.

She suddenly gasped. "They're using it!"

"Of course! They do every day!"

She took his arm. "Come on!"

She had seen the crowd there, but had somehow not thought that they watched an execution. The sight of people walking through the huge square had convinced her that nothing was happening, and it was only the flicker of the blade climbing the twin shafts that had told her that Paris had become so used to this sight that most passers-by did not even stop to watch. Death was a commonplace now. She wrinkled her face. "It smells!"

"They want to build a 'sangueduct.' "

"A what?"

"A gutter to carry the blood to the Seine." He smiled down at her. "So much blood has soaked into the square that it stinks."

She heard a thump and a cheer. She tried to ignore it, but Skavadale stopped and she had to stop with him. She looked up at him. "Can't we go on?"

"Look at it."

She looked. A woman was climbing the steps. Even at this distance Campion could see how her hair had been chopped short. Paris, with rough humor, called the haircut that was given to every prisoner *"La Toilette."*

One man took her right elbow, the red-aproned executioner her left, and the third man her legs. The third man held a rose between his teeth. The woman was thrown forward, face to the plank, and, while the man with the rose in his teeth pulled a strap over her back, so the executioner brought the neck brace down.

He stepped to one side, jerked the rope, and she heard the scraping rattle, the thump, and the cheer of the crowd.

"You can open your eyes now."

"Oh God!" She could see the headless body being heaved off the platform. I'm going to be sick."

"You are not." He walked her up and down the cobbles.

She heard the scraping, grating fall of the blade, the thump, and the cheer. "How many more?"

"Till there's no one left to kill."

Edmund Burke had prophesied this. He had said that the revolution would try to purify itself by blood and fire. She was here, where the cleaning was being done, where peasants were being executed for saying they thought the revolution a mistake.

She heard the machine. The thump seemed to go through her soul.

Blood smelled thick.

It was all so casual. People passed through the square about their business and did not even look at the guillotine. Death was so common that it was not worth a glance.

It was casual, but horribly efficient. No one escaped because there was not time to organize an escape. If she was arrested this day then she would be tried the next morning, found guilty, and be at the guillotine within three hours. No one escaped.

The cheer sounded again.

A prisoner was allowed no defense and the prosecution needed to bring no evidence. To be accused was enough. The lawyers who dominated this revolution insisted that a defense merely confused the issue. Revolutionary virtue, they said, would guarantee justice.

She looked at the crowd, at their happy faces, and she wondered if she could see the townspeople of Lazen standing like this beneath twin uprights that held a slanting blade, and she thought that truly the faces were no different. Small children, bored by the machine, chased pigeons on the cobbles. Lovers held hands. People laughed.

A man climbed the steps. He turned and called cheerful words to the prisoners behind him, and then his elbows were taken, he was swung forward, and she clung to Skavadale, gritted her teeth, and watched as the red aproned man pushed the neck clamp down, stepped back, and released the rope.

She made herself watch.

The blade was stained.

It fell slowly for the first two feet, then she heard it, she was holding her breath, and it crashed down and she saw the fountain of red that provoked the cheer, and the executioner was hauling the blade up while his assistants, one still with the rose in his mouth, released and lifted the body. Blood ran down the slant of the blade, collected, dripped.

"Oh God." She let her breath out.

They called it sneezing into the basket. She supposed

that the man who now climbed the steps, hard on the heels of the one who had just died, would lie on the plank and see, just inches beneath his gaze, the severed heads of the men and women who had been his companions a moment before, their dead eyes staring at the blood-soaked weave of the basket like fish in a creel.

The thought made her put her face into Skavadale's black coat. She heard the blade fall again.

He patted her shoulder. "Don't show it! It's dangerous! You can die on the machine for disliking what it does."

She forced herself to look.

The executioner had tied the blade so it was suspended two feet above the brace. He straddled the plank on which the victims were tied, wiped the blood from the blade's edge, then felt in his back trouser pocket for a stone. She heard the commonplace sound of steel being sharpened, a ringing, scraping, homely sound. Christopher Skavadale still held her shoulders. "He takes the blade home with him."

She frowned, uncertain what the significance of the remark was.

He smiled at her. "Otherwise people would come here to kill themselves at night."

"No!"

He nodded. "Yes. Have you seen enough?"

"Too much!"

He led her away. Behind her she heard the scraping rattle, the thump, and she thought how she, too, had become used to death in just these few moments. She looked at Skavadale. "Why did you make me watch?"

For a few steps he said nothing, then he shrugged. "It exists. It's there. You can't ignore it."

She wasn't sure that the answer was satisfactory. "But you made me watch!"

He stopped. He looked into her eyes and Parisians,

passing by, were struck by the man and girl and thought it a miracle that such love and beauty still lived in a city crouching beneath the stench of blood. He smiled at her. "Does your uncle ever go into the kitchens at Lazen?"

She was used to his apparently irrelevant questions by now. She shook her head. "No."

"Does he ever visit the smithy?"

"No."

"The cottages?"

"No. Why?"

"You do."

She shrugged. "So?"

"So who knows more about Lazen? You, who see it all? Or your Uncle Achilles, who never leaves the gilt and plasterwork."

She smiled. "I live there."

"And you see it all. You can't go through life and pretend that it doesn't have bits that reek of foulness. It must be wonderful to sit at a great dinner, but is your enjoyment spoiled because you know of grease in the kitchen or blood in the slaughterhouse?"

She frowned. "I'm not sure I understand."

He gestured at the machine. "It exists! It's as real as Lazen!"

She shivered despite the sunshine that warmed Paris. "Are you telling me that's the alternative to Lazen?"

He smiled. "No, my Lady. Auxigny is the alternative to Lazen. Shall we go?"

She walked through Paris with him and it seemed like a dream, an adventure, love's madness that was leading her to the heart of evil, to the Mad Duke's shrine, and to whatever lay beyond the road's ending at Auxigny.

21

"You know where you are?"

She nodded. Dusk was touching the trees of the valley dark, filling the spaces between the trunks with mysterious shadow. Beyond the hill was Auxigny, her mother's childhood home, the lair of the Fallen Ones.

Skavadale led her between small ricks of drying hay. She could smell the pines ahead. A colony of rooks were noisy to her left, screeching like harpies as they fought and tumbled in the air above their black nests.

They crossed a plank bridge over a small stream, and went into the woods.

They climbed toward the high crest that would reveal Auxigny. Once or twice, where rocks cropped up on the hillside to bar their way, he would give her his hand and the touch of his warm skin was comforting.

The slope became steeper and he stopped more frequently to help her. They were climbing in dark pine woods. She passed the fragile, white lattice of a dead raven, the fox-scattered black feathers still lying on the pine needles.

Skavadale was weighed down with two big leather bags, both of them roped to his left shoulder. He wore a sword. He carried two pistols and an ammunition pouch, yet he moved as easily as if he carried nothing.

It had been a sharp, bright autumn day, but the effort of climbing the hill made her as hot and sticky as if it was summer.

The sky, glimpsed between the tall pines, was darkening to the east, while above her, spreading westward beyond the ridgeline, the sun reddened the thin, high clouds. Skavadale led her quickly, wanting to reach the crest before the sun disappeared.

His hand pulled her up one last barrier of tumbled stone, the sun shone huge and red into her eyes, and below her was Auxigny.

Like a secret jewel cradled by dark hills, the chateau of Auxigny stood in the center of its deep valley.

The light touched red on the two moats and slashed crimson on the windows of the south front. The white walls rose to the blue-black slates of the pointed turrets. She had half expected to see the chateau burned, to see the windows as black, empty holes, but it looked as it had always looked, beautiful and serene, the proud home of the Lords of Auxigny out of which armed men had ridden, laws had been issued, and justice had come like vengeance on the lesser mortals below.

It was beautiful and intricate, but seeing it now from this high crest above the tops of the pines beneath her, it seemed so very different to Lazen. Lazen sprawled, it was part of the town, it opened on to every part of the estate, while Auxigny, proud Auxigny, was secretive and aloof. There were two entrances only; the southern bridge that crossed the moat and led to the great facade, and, at the north, the bridge which led to the shrine.

The shrine, to the north of the chateau, was surrounded by its own, smaller moat.

The Mad Duke had come close to bankrupting the family to build his shrine. It reared like a grotesque fantasy on its artificial island, with walls of green marble and turrets of polished black stone that jutted about the copper-lined dome. There were no windows.

The bridge which crossed the smaller moat, the bridge leading directly to the windowless shrine, was not built of stone. It was a wooden drawbridge.

The Mad Duke had ordered the drawbridge built. The first miracle of his shrine was the order for his servants and tenants to go to worship while he ostentatiously stayed on the chateau side of the moats. The drawbridge would be drawn up and, minutes later, he would appear in the shrine. The peasants and servants would dutifully applaud his walking on the water despite their memory of digging the tunnel that led beneath both moats. The village *curé*, knowing the Duke's madness, had indulged the harmless lunacy.

Campion stared from the high crest. The chateau, this night of autumn clarity, looked splendid and unchanged, as though the machine which beat in the heart of Paris had not stained this beauty with its splashing blood.

She looked beyond the chateau, following the line of the stream to where the valley opened to the west. The small town of Auxigny guarded the valley's head. Its roofs were touched red by the setting sun so that it seemed, from their place on the mountain, as though the town glowed like great embers where the river ran past the hills.

Skavadale watched her, a half smile on his sun darkened face. "How long since you've seen it?"

She smiled. "Five years?"

"It hasn't changed."

Except that it was owned by the government now, confiscated from the d'Auxignys. Uncle Achilles, she realized with surprise, was now the Lord of Auxigny, except there were no more Lords in France. She thought sadly how much he would have loved to live here. He would have filled its elegant, high rooms and wide, moat-edged lawns with music. He would have liked to be the precious jewel within the jewel of Auxigny.

Skavadale picked up the two leather bags. "We must go on, my Lady."

He led her left, striking obliquely down the steep slope which faced Auxigny and the setting sun. They had come from Paris by the public stage, leaving the vehicle at Bellechasse and taking this long, hidden approach across the hills. To her left reared the high peaks, rocks touched crimson above the pines, while to her right was the valley where the chateau, glimpsed between the tips of the trees, seemed like a precious doll's house far beneath her.

She could hear water ahead and knew they came close to the waterfall that glinted high over the chateau. She had never been this high in these hills. She had sometimes stared from the windows of the chateau at the high, bright fall of water and wondered where the stream came from. Her mother had told her that there was always a rainbow at Auxigny's waterfall, that whenever the sun shone the colors would dance above the spray. In her child's mind she would think of the waterfall as a far-off, magic place, like a glimpse of heaven above her head.

She came to the waterfall now, to where the water seethed into a pool carved from the stone by the force of its fall, then split into a rock-strewn course that foamed down the hillside to feed the moats of Auxigny.

Beside the pool was a grassy clearing. There was a long, low hut built against the rock face, an affair of pine branches roofed with turf. It was a summer shelter for shepherds, a refuge from the wolves and the weather. Skavadale smiled. "Your home tonight." She noticed the care with which he chose his words. Her home, not his. He would sleep outside, as he had guarded her door each night since they had left the Rom.

He had brought food, water and wine. Within the hut was old bracken for a mattress. Outside, where the grass gave way to a rock ledge that overlooked the valley, Skavadale lit a fire, working as ever with economy and skill, teasing the flames, feeding them, so that as the sun spilled its last glorious light on the far rim of the world they sat by the burning pine-cones and watched the darkness cover the land beneath.

She smiled at his profile. "Should we have a fire?"

"They'll think we're shepherds bringing a herd from the summer pastures."

There was a rabbit to eat, with bread, cheese and wine. They sat at the edge of the clearing, where the slab of rock still held the heat of the sun. Behind them the water roared in its endless, seething fall.

Auxigny had disappeared. No lights came from the building that had once blazed with light, no fires warmed the magnificent rooms of gold and white.

The town was lit. Campion could see the small, wavering points of flame that showed where torches burned. One small light crept achingly slow along the hidden fine of a road, a coach coming late into Auxigny.

They had been oddly silent as they ate.

She knew why. They had travelled across France and, in all that time, it had been as if their meeting in Lazen's Temple had never happened. Yet this silence proclaimed that it was not forgotten. As slowly, as inexorably as that light crawled along the dark road toward the town below, she knew that they had waited for this moment.

She knew it, and because she knew it, she made her voice casual. "Tell me what happens tomorrow."

"Again?" He smiled.

She gestured toward the hidden chateau. "It seems more real now."

"You're frightened?"

She smiled. "No, Mr. Skavadale. I come to France so often these days. I quite frequently act as a lure for a mad pack of killers."

He laughed softly. He lit one of his small cigars and the light touched red on his strong face. Tomorrow, he said, they would go down from the mountain and she would wait in the woods while he found Toby. Toby was hiding in Auxigny, waiting for their arrival.

She thought how polite they had been for these days. It was as if they had silently agreed not to talk of that night in Lazen's park. Only once, as the guillotine rose and fell behind her, had he obliquely made any mention of it. They had been polite, treating each other with a delicate formality.

And by now, he said, Toby should have unblocked the old tunnel by which the Mad Duke walked on water. And tomorrow night, while the Fallen Ones watched Campion in the lit shrine, Toby would come from the gloom of the crypt to kill from behind while Skavadale killed from in front.

"Will there be soldiers?"

He shook his head. "No." He drew on his cigar and she watched the smoke fade in the air over the valley. He shrugged. "A few, maybe."

"A few?"

"Marchenoir's an important man. He'll want to impress his home town with an escort, but they won't trouble us. They won't know about the Fallen Ones, and they won't be allowed into the shrine."

"And how do we leave?"

He laughed. "We walk out, of course. We show our papers and we simply walk out."

She stared at him. He was so confident, so utterly confident. She remembered the guillotine, the commonplace machine of death that soaked blood onto the cobbles, and she knew that he had made her watch so that she would see the horror and not be afraid. He walked through terror and he was confident.

Yet Ababina had talked of his fear. Like the men and women who climbed the steps of the machine he had learned to hide his fear. That, she thought, was the secret of fear.

She looked back to the lights of the town. The carriage lamps had crept closer now.

She was frightened of the next day. She knew she must hide that fear.

She drank wine. She sat with her knees drawn up and she looked into the darkness beneath her. "Mr. Skavadale?"

"My Lady?"

She paused before asking her question. They had waited so long and now she would start to lead them toward that private, secret place. But first he must tell her a truth. She looked at him. "Did I really need to come?"

The wind stirred the pines. He did not look at her. "You had to come for Lucifer to come."

She frowned. He was evading her. "We'd beaten them already, hadn't we? Toby's alive, I'm alive, Lazen is safe!" She stared at him. "Lucifer's beaten, Mr. Skavadale!"

"He still lives." He looked at her, seeing the taut expression on her face, and he knew that she was demanding the truth from him and that without the truth there could be nothing between them. He had told her half truths and now he must go further. He spoke gently. "You need not have come, my Lady. We could have protected you. We could have killed Larke, and that would have been sufficient."

She said nothing. She had known all along, she supposed, that she had come, not for Lord Paunceley, and not to defeat the Fallen Angels, but to be with this man.

He smiled. "But we do want Lucifer."

"Of course."

They had said the words as if to reassure each other that their purpose was not to go to that mysterious place of love where only the truth would do. They were being polite still, fearful of the trembling moment.

The carriage lights crept into Auxigny. She heard, above the water's sound, the hiss of air on an owl's wings. She thought she saw the bird slide menacingly across the dark sky, a night-hunter seeking blood in the valley.

The silence stretched. She was staring at one small, yellowish light in the town that twinkled faintly like a star, sometimes seeming to disappear, then becoming bright again.

She turned to him in the silence and saw that he was looking at her. Neither spoke.

She had known this moment would come, and, now that it was upon them, there was an embarrassment in her. For one year she had dreamed of this man, dreams as forbidden as lust, and now she was with him, high over the world, in a private place to which, she knew, he had purposefully brought her.

She turned away from him. She stared at the tiny, flickering light in the town and she thought how she had been used by men in this affair. By Lucifer, by Culloden, by Paunceley, even by this man who sat beside her. The thought made her frown. She had come into a world of deceit and shadow, a world where the Gypsy hunted just as the owl did that swooped into the great chasm of darkness. He had brought her to this place of rock and water and solitude for a hunter's purpose.

She touched the rock with her fingers. "Did you ever hunt foxes?"

"Yes."

"I remember my first hunt. I was frightened." She stopped, and the Gypsy, knowing better than to say anything, said nothing. She stared, huge eyed, over the valley. "I was only a child and they took me to where the fox had been killed. They blooded me." She turned and looked at him almost defiantly. "My father cut off the fox's brush," she said, "dipped it in blood, and smeared it on my cheeks. I should have been excited. Every child wants to be blooded, but I hated it. I felt sorry for the fox." His hand made a gesture in the darkness, but what the gesture meant she could not tell. "Do you know what I'm saying?" she asked.

He smiled at her, his teeth white against his dark skin. "I know that you still hunt."

"Yes." She paused. "I like it. I don't know why. It's the horses, I suppose. Foxes have to be killed," she shrugged, "but it's the horses. It's the excitement. You can gallop a horse in exercise, but it's to no purpose, is it? Not really. But in a hunt!" She shook her head. "In a hunt it's different. You don't care about the obstacles, you ride for the life of it, for the sheer life of it! But then comes the end, and I never go close."

"Never?"

She shook her head. "Never."

The water fell and seethed in the pool. A sickle moon of brilliant clarity was rising in the north, its light silvering the pines beneath them. Campion was looking at the stars, tracing the sword of Orion's belt. "I think you told me a lie once."

"I did?"

She looked at him. "So I'll ask you again." She could feel the heavy, golden seals of Lazen trembling against her skin. She paused, because she knew she was going into a place of dreadful mystery. "What happens at the end of your story? When man finds his creature?"

"The last creature that God made?" His voice was as soft as the small wind in the pines, as soft as the air on an owl's wing.

"Yes." She was remembering him standing on the steps of Lazen's small temple. "You said you didn't know the end."

He smiled. He was staring into the great empty night above Auxigny. "She will be fairer than the dawn, and in her eyes, stars. At her feet grow lilies, and in her hands, love." He stopped, and though it was not a cold night, it seemed to Campion that her skin crawled with chilliness. He looked at her. "We make our own endings, my Lady."

She shook her head. "You know better, don't you?"

"I do?"

"Because there isn't an ending, is there?" She was staring at him with a frown. "The hunt is everything, isn't it? There's no joy in an ending. Do you find your creature, discard it, and hunt another? Is that the story's ending, Mr. Skavadale? That there is no ending, just another hunt, another chase?"

He shook his head. "No."

"You enjoy this, don't you? You're a clever man among clever men and you're playing a game. Lucifer hunts Paunceley and Paunceley hunts Lucifer, and if either did not exist then they would find another enemy. And Toby!" She looked down into the dark valley. "He likes the hunt, doesn't he? Do you all hope that it will never end?"

"You need not have come," he said simply.

"I know." She would not look at him.

"And you need not go to Auxigny tomorrow."

"I know that."

She had been used by these men and brought down paths reeking of blood, and she had come willingly because, when she had first seen this man, she had thought him more splendid than any man she had ever seen. She understood, well enough, that Lucifer's death was desirable, that the Fallen Angels should be broken, but she understood, too, that her part in their downfall was foolish. She had come, like a besotted child, come for the moment itself, and suddenly the years beyond this moment seemed dark as night.

She had wanted love, but now she was scared of it, as if the glory of the moment might fade and she saw what Uncle Achilles had tried to tell her, that love's instant could be as bright and brief as the fall of a shooting star. She was frightened.

The Gypsy stood. She heard him walk to the fire, heard him add wood to the blaze, then heard his steps as he came and crouched behind her. She could smell the good smell of horses and tobacco on him. His voice, as it had been at the temple, was like the darkness itself, soft and beguiling, gentle in her hearing. "So ever since the world began, my Lady, the Rom have hunted for the creature that is fairer than the dawn. We have ridden the mountains, we have crossed the dead lands, and always we have been hated and scorned because men fear us. We have been cold, we have been hungry, we have seen our children die, and we have listened to men ask us why we do not build houses and grow crops to be like them." He paused. Her hand was pressed to the golden seals at her breasts.

His voice was gentle. "The story does end, my Lady."

"How?"

"The Gypsy finds the creature, and he knows she cannot be beaten or whipped or broken, so he gives her the one thing that he wants from her. He gives her love."

She thought that the beating of her heart would fill the whole chasm of the dark and come echoing back from the high rocks until the whole night was filled with her trembling. "You know what love is?"

"Love is wanting for the other person what they want for themselves. It is never seeking to change them. It is seeing them in the morning and in the evening and being glad that they live." And as he spoke he reached forward and stroked her hair, as gently as the touch of silk, stroking the shape of her head to the skin of her neck. "And you will forgive me, my Lady."

"Forgive you?" She did not move from his touch.

"When I say that I love you." He leaned forward and kissed her neck and still she did not move. "And forgive me when I say that I wanted you to come here, and that I have not used you, but that I have wanted you, and for that temerity, I am sorry."

He leaned away from her, and her neck was cold where his warm touch had been.

There was silence between them. The moon was as bright and sharp as metal, its light cold and silver.

His voice was still soft. "And you must know that no harm will come to you. You only risk love."

She stared into the night. "Tell me how the story ends."

She thought he would never reply. The moment seemed to stretch, and the sound of the water was like a torment to her and she felt her heart throbbing the gold against her skin and she knew that she trembled, and when he did speak she almost jumped because his voice was so near. "I want to be with you always, my Lady, to be astonished."

She was shivering. "Astonished?"

"At God's last creature."

His hands touched her shoulders and, obedient to their pressure, she turned. The moon touched her blue eyes silver, shadowing the places beneath her cheekbones and mouth. Very slowly he leaned forward. He kissed her. His lips brushed her cheek and his hands held her shoulders and he whispered softly in her ear. "And I would marry you."

She held him, her arms about his body, and she pushed her head against the leather of his coat. "I thought when I first saw you that you didn't notice me."

She sensed that he smiled. "I thought you would never notice me, my Lady."

"I used to look for you in the Castle. I'd go to the stables just to see you."

"I used to hope that you'd come." He kissed her cheek, her forehead, her eyes, and she kissed him back and still she trembled. She had her eyes closed, not daring to look at his face. When he kissed her she shuddered. She moved her cheek against his cheek as if she could melt into him, as if she could hide in him.

He drew his face from hers and raised his hands to her hair. He pulled the combs and pins loose, releasing the pale gold to flood onto her shoulders. He gently stroked her hair. "Why did you come, my Lady?"

She thought he was more beautiful than any creature she had ever seen. "I wanted to know how your story ended."

He gave her a quick smile. "The ending is what you make it."

"I know."

His hands were suddenly still on her hair. "So what is your ending, my Lady?"

She saw the worry in his eyes, the flicker of fear, and she understood that he had risked foolishness in asking her, that his confidence was a mask, and his gentleness a sign of what was masked, and she wanted to hug him because of it. Instead she touched his face, his thin, savage, hawk's face. "I will marry you."

He smiled a smile of such happiness and such relief that she wanted to laugh. His eyes were searching her face as though he would draw into his memory a picture of this moment that would last forever and he shook his head in wonderment, took her shoulders in his arms, and held her as if he would never let go of her, never again spend a moment without her.

She wanted to say something, she wanted to laugh with happiness, but there was nothing to say, not even when he leaned away from her, took her hand, and drew her to her feet. He smiled, he stepped toward the fire, and she went with him onto the grass. His dark, splendid face was lit by the flames. "I love you."

She looked at him, knowing the bravery it must take for a Gypsy to ask a Lady to marry him. She knew what he asked now. "I know." She could hardly speak.

He let got of her hand and, without letting his eyes move from her eyes, he put his fingers to the laces at her throat.

The fear, delicious and tremulous, beat like wings at her. She stared into his oddly light eyes. He watched her, and because she made no move, he pulled the laces free, put his hands on the collar and pushed the coat from her shoulders.

The coat fell.

She swallowed. Her heart was beating like a young colt's when it fought against the bridle. Still she stared at him, and he leaned forward and she shut her eyes and his mouth was warm on her mouth and his tongue flickered on her eyelids and his lips brushed her cheeks and she pressed her face into his face as his hands, strong and firm, stroked her from the nape of her neck to the small of her back. She shivered, and she felt the small juddering as his fingers pulled at the knot of her skirts.

He took his face from hers. She kept her eyes shut. She felt the strings at her waist come loose and she held the skirts with her fingers. Her heart was pounding the seals at her breast.

His fingers touched her face. "You have only to say no."

She could hardly make her voice sound. "Tell me you love me."

"I know no better way, my love."

She felt his breath on her face, then his lips touched hers, warm and hard, and she kissed him back, her eyes closed, and his hands were at her throat, his strong, quick hands, and the night air was cool on her skin as he undid the buttons one by one.

She could not have believed, not in all her waking dreams, that she could feel such fear and such delight and such apprehension and she hid her face on his face, fearing so much, fearing that he would despise her, that he would laugh at her, and then his strong hands were at her shoulders, his palms warm on her bare shoulders as he pushed the blouse back.

His hands pushed the cotton blouse down her arms. Her breasts were touched by the night air, by the swinging laces of his coat, and when his hands reached her hands she had to let go of the skirts.

She trembled. Her clothes lay at her feet. She stood naked, but for the pagan gold that hung between her breasts and caught the light of the thin, hard moon.

He put his arms about her, as if to hide her nakedness from herself, and she shook because all the magic that men had denied was sweeping about her, his arms were around her, his hands on her skin, and she let him lift her and lay her down, and the fear was filling the darkness and the grass was cold. Her eyes were closed. She did not want him to take his arms from her. If he held her he could not see her, and she shook her head with a kind of despair as he lifted himself from her and then, gently, he laid her coat over her body, covering her from her neck to her feet.

She opened her eyes. She lay nervous and still, childlike, not daring to speak, fearful that one sound or movement would break the spell which held her.

Neither did he speak. Slowly, watching her eyes, he took his coat and dropped it on the grass. He unlaced his shirt and pulled it over his head. His chest was dark in the moonlight, sleekly muscled. He pulled his boots off, his eyes still on her, and then, unbuckling his belt, he stepped from his breeches and she lay, silent and still, and thought that his beauty was like the slender, shining, long muscled beauty of a thoroughbred.

He came toward her, knelt, and put his hand on the coat.

She shook her head.

He bent toward her, his dark hair brushing her face, and he kissed her cheeks, her lips, her hair. "I love you."

She felt the coat lifted away and she made no move.

She closed her eyes. She wanted to hold her breath. He looked at her a moment, seeing how lovely she was, and then he put his mouth on her mouth.

His hands stroked her long flanks, her waist, her thighs. He kissed her. His fingers writhed in her hair, then spread it like a golden fan upon the grass. His hands moved down her face, her throat, her breasts, and his touch was gentle and she moved to it, wanting it, feeling the glory that she knew love could have, though still her eyes were closed as his hands stroked down to her legs and his lips were soft on her mouth. His knee pressed on her knees. She put her arms around him, her fingers digging into his back, and slid her cheek against his cheek so that her closed eyes were buried in his hair. His knee pressed on hers and she yielded. She kept her eyes tight shut, and the small, small wind was on her skin like a caress and he was in her and he moved his mouth to hers and she cried out once, held him tight, kissed him, and she held him so tight and wanted to cry out with the pleasure of it. Her mouth was open, she was kissing his face, and she pressed up from the grass and pressed again, and then she felt the great shudder and he cried out in a noise that was more flattering to her than any words he could have spoken. They still moved, she still held him as if she wanted to hold him against all the people who would deny them this.

And slowly they became still.

The wind was cold on her. She kissed his face. Her eyes were still shut. "Is it always like that?"

His voice was soft. "They say the first time is the worst."

"Who's they?"

"The people who do it a second time."

She laughed. She opened her eyes. She was happy.

He slid from her and stroked her body from her face to her knees. The seals of Lazen were like barbaric gold between her breasts. He kissed her, following his hand down her body, and she stared at the stars and soared among them.

He kissed her breasts, her belly, her thighs, and he drew himself back to her face and smiled at her. "I love you."

She looked into his eyes. "I love you." She said it as a test and found it true. She pulled him and he lay on her again, their bellies slippery with sweat. "I love you," she paused shyly, "Christopher?"

"I love you," he paused, "Campion?"

They laughed at their embarrassment.

She touched his face. "I can't cook."

"I'm marrying you for your servants." He kissed her nose. She kissed him back and rolled him over so she lay on top of him. She propped herself on her hands and smiled at him. "You brought me here to do this, didn't you?"

He smiled. "Yes."

"We could have gone into the town and met Toby, yes?"

"Yes."

She made a face at him and he laughed.

She felt his hands laying plucked grass on the small of her back. It tickled. She felt him stirring beneath her and she lowered her head to kiss him and she marvelled at the passion, at the dawn in her life of this magic. She was in love and she made love with him again and the glory of love was in her and about her and she held him, skin against skin, against all the nightmares of a dark world that would deny this glory. She had found love.

Later, in the small hut, she woke to find that she had rolled away from him in her sleep. She crawled out of the cloaks and blankets and went to the doorway. She crouched there, naked in the cool of the night, the wind cold on her thighs and shoulders.

There was a gray light, a wolf-light, to the east.

The embers shivered the air above the gray ash.

She felt like an animal, like a wild beast for which anything was possible. She had lain with her man on a mountain top and she smiled into the darkness. She was happy.

She stood and walked to the ledge of the rock where her clothes and his still lay, heavy now with a dew. She stood naked on the ledge, staring down at the misted valley where her ancestors had reigned, where they had danced to the music and built their great house. Auxigny. Had even one of them, she wondered, ever stood naked above the whole valley? Perhaps only the first people who ever came to this place and found the valley with its water and rich soil had stood like this on its crests.

She raised her arms to the wind, letting the cool air wash about her, she closed her eyes, lifted her head, and heard his footsteps.

She turned.

Skavadale smiled at her. "Do you know what you look like?"

She laughed. It was odd, she thought, how quite suddenly there was no embarrassment in standing naked before him. He had made her feel beautiful. "Tell me what I look like."

He looked at her, the gold bright on her skin. She was pale and slim and naked in the wolf-light. "You look just like the Nymph in the picture."

"Like the Countess?"

"The swimming Countess."

"You saw it?"

He laughed at her shocked surprise. "I saw it."

She went to him, her arms wide, and she thought that his dark, bare, muscled body was more beautiful than anything she had seen, and she hugged him. She raised her face and kissed him. "You need a shave."

He tugged his forelock. "Yes, my Lady." He smiled at her. "You don't have regrets?"

"What is there to regret?"

He smiled. His hands explored the curve of her back. "Will you really marry me?"

She smiled, but her voice was stern. "Do you think I'd be here like this if I wasn't going to marry you?"

He kissed her, then turned to stare at the dawn mist which shrouded the lower valley. "The world will say you married badly."

"Then the world is wrong." She touched his cheek. "I'm marrying a man, the world will be jealous." She thought of Achilles. She thought of the shiver of scandal that would run through England's society. She laughed. If they could see her now! She was naked in a cold dawn and a man was stroking her breasts and kissing her face and she put her arms about his neck. "We have only one duty to the world."

"Which is?"

"To show them a good marriage." She stroked his face, exploring it with her fingers. "Will you be happy?"

"Yes."

"You won't miss the adventures?"

He was teasing her hair with his fingers. He kissed her. "I don't think I'll be bored ever again."

She had never guessed that she could feel this way. His hands flickered on her and she laughed.

"What?" he asked.

"I was going to ask you if people only did this at night. It seems a rather unnecessary question." She laughed again. She had always been quick to laughter before her father died and now, as she pulled him onto the dew wet grass, she knew the laughter had come back.

And afterward he remade the fire and she put their wet clothes to dry beside the flames. They sat cloaked on the hill's rim and watched the dawn, like bars of silver, shine through the pines beneath them. The chateau was hidden by mists.

She smiled at her man. "What do you do today, Prince of Gypsies?"

He smiled. "I shall kill your enemies."

She touched his face. "I love you."

He held her hand. "God knows what the world will say of it, my Lady."

She was not the daughter of Vavasour Lazender for nothing. She looked at the mist-shrouded valley and her voice was scornful. "The world can roger itself, my Lord."

And above them, unseen by them, the planet Venus faded as the sun rose. Some men called it the day-star, it shone above them where they kissed, and others called it Lucifer.

22

Bertrand Marchenoir was the first of the Fallen Ones to reach Auxigny. A full regiment of infantry came with him, the men straggling into the town behind Marchenoir's coach. The first company was hurried ahead to form a guard of honor in the courtyard of the inn. Their Colonel hastened to open the carriage door himself.

Marchenoir stepped down into the dusk light. He wore a dark green cloak on which was sewn a tricolor rosette. He looked about the yard. "When I grew up here, Colonel, I wasn't allowed in this inn yard. I was too dirty, too poor, too hungry." He turned to his servant who was climbing from the rear of the coach. "Make sure it's the best room!"

"Of course, citizen."

"And order a *cassoulet* for me! You know how I like it cooked."

"Indeed, citizen."

Marchenoir walked slowly down the line of the troops, fixing each man with his eyes as though he could personally read the soldier's mind. At the end of the rank, instead of turning back into the yard's center, he walked beneath the stone archway into the main street of Auxigny. The Colonel walked beside him.

Marchenoir looked right and left. The street was hard rutted and dusty. Dogs scavenged its gutter. One lifted a leg against the Tree of Liberty, a pole with a red hat perched on top that was an essential now in every French town. Those of the townsfolk who saw him kept their faces turned away. Marchenoir seemed not to notice.

He walked toward the bridge and, reaching it, leaned on the stone parapet to stare into the shallow river. The Colonel was nervous. The revolution was undoubtedly splendid, and had undoubtedly brought liberty, equality, and fraternity, but that did not mean that members of the Committee for Public Safety were safe when they walked among their subjects.

Marchenoir pointed downstream to where some low hovels appeared to grow out of the mud banks of the river. "My home, Colonel."

"Indeed, citizen."

Marchenoir nodded. "One day that hovel will be a shrine. Frenchmen will travel miles to see it. They'll forget Versailles, Colonel, but they'll remember that hovel! Proof that strength belongs to the people, not the bloody aristos." He pointed farther away, to where a gap in the range of hills showed a deep shadowed valley where stood, far in the dusk's gloom, a great, white building. "The Chateau of Auxigny, Colonel." He shook his head. "When they rode from the chateau they sounded a trumpet to tell us that our betters were coming, that it was time for us to grovel in the mud like beasts, to bow our heads lest we looked upon the daughters of Auxigny!" He took the hat from his head and made a mock bow toward the chateau. "The daughters of Auxigny! Do you know, Colonel, that the old Duchess used to let manservants come into her room when she bathed? She'd be naked and they'd bring firewood. Do you know why?"

The Colonel shook his head. "No, citizen."

"Because a servant was not a human being! She didn't mind a lap dog seeing her in the bath, so why not a servant? They were the same in her eyes." He smiled a bitter smile. "They say she was ugly as sin, which is why her mad husband took his God-damned pleasures elsewhere." He stared at the far valley, then waved his hat toward the shambling hovel where he had grown up. "You see that house, Colonel?"

"Yes, citizen."

"That house was assessed for tax. We paid tax! We had nothing, but we paid tax! And you see that house?"

The Colonel stared at the chateau. "I see it, citizen."

"They paid no taxes! They were the nobility!" He spat over the parapet. "But I sent the last Duc d'Auxigny to sneeze in the basket. I did that." He laughed to himself. "My mother died in what passed for a bed, but I put him beneath the blade!"

The Colonel had heard that it was the d'Auxigny family who had plucked Marchenoir from his muddy obscurity, recognized his talent, and paid for his training as a priest. This did not seem the moment to ask for confirmation of the story, nor to mention the other gossip that tied Citizen Bertrand Marchenoir, tribune of the people, even closer to the great chateau that stood in its lone valley. No one now would dare to voice the rumor that the town whore had given birth to the Mad Duke's bastard.

Marchenoir put on his cocked hat. A green feather rose from the inevitable tricolor rosette. "What's your name, Colonel?"

"Tours, citizen."

"Ah! You're the man who caught *Le Revenant!*"

"Indeed, citizen."

Marchenoir led the Colonel toward the inn. "You did a great service, Colonel, and tomorrow you will do another!"

Tours had been ordered here, but he did not know why, nor what was expected of his regiment. To ask was to court disfavor, to earn disfavor was to court death, and no man was so liberal with death as Citizen Marchenoir.

Marchenoir stared at the town with dislike. "Tomorrow, Colonel, you obey my orders. Tomorrow night, at dusk, you surround the chateau. What happens inside is none of your business, and once the night is over, Colonel, you will forget that it ever happened."

"Forget, citizen?"

"You will forget, Colonel, because some knowledge can be dangerous knowledge. You will have to trust me."

Tours nodded. "Yes, citizen."

Marchenoir looked up at the inn. His heavy face, that struck fear into his enemies, suddenly broke into a smile. "Things change, Colonel! There was a time when they threw stones to keep me out of this place."

The innkeeper brought the *cassoulet* to Citizen Marchenoir's room. He brought the best wine and, once he had set the table with the inn's finest chinaware and lit the tall candles, he nervously waited on the great man himself. To the innkeeper's relief the food gave satisfaction. It was bolted down hungrily and even earned a nod of approval from Citizen Marchenoir who pushed the empty plate away. "Take it away." The innkeeper came obsequiously forward and Marchenoir looked at the man. "You remember me, Jules?"

"Of course, citizen." The innkeeper was nervous. "With pride, of course, citizen."

"Ah! Pride! A dangerous emotion, citizen."

The innkeeper went white. "Pride in you, citizen."

"Of course, of course." Marchenoir leaned forward and lit a cigar from one of the tall candles. "You remember that your father wouldn't let me in here, eh?"

"My father was his own worst enemy, citizen."

"How true, Jules, how very true. He was glad enough for my mother to be here, though, wasn't he? He took his slice, yes?" Marchenoir laughed. "But not me. Not me." He looked about the comfortable room with its tall, curtained bed, its two windows that looked eastward toward the mountains, and its big fire. "Did my mother work in this room, Jules?"

"I wouldn't know, citizen." The innkeeper edged toward the door, but Marchenoir waved at him to stay.

"You think she earned her livres here, eh? Until your father threw her out because he found a prettier whore, yes?" He stared at the frightened innkeeper. "Do you have a whore in the inn these days, Jules?"

"No, citizen." The innkeeper smiled nervously. "We have some apple pie, citizen? Or damsons? The damsons were specially good this year!"

Marchenoir's eyes were like death. "Damsons, Jules? Damsons?" He blew smoke toward the innkeeper and leaned back. "I looked into your main room as I came in, Jules. You're very busy!"

"Indeed, citizen."

"And there was a young whore serving your tables, Jules. Green skirt and a white blouse. Very fetching, I thought. Had you forgotten she existed in your happiness at seeing me again?"

The innkeeper almost hesitated, hearing his own daughter described, but he managed to hide his consternation and smile ingratiatingly. "White blouse? Green skirt? Yes, citizen, I know her."

"She can fetch me two more bottles of wine." He waved the innkeeper away.

When the man had gone Marchenoir stood, loosened his corset, and went to stand by the window. It was a clear night, the stars bright above Auxigny, the sickle moon rising over the hills to touch silver on the river.

His servant had put the small, gilt-framed portrait of Lady Campion Lazender on the table by the window and Marchenoir picked it up and stared obsessively at the girl's extraordinary beauty. It was hard to believe that this portrait was not just a painter's fantasy, yet Gitan had sworn that it scarce did her justice. Tomorrow, Marchenoir reflected, he would find out. Tomorrow he would have Lady Campion Lazender's tall, slim body for his reward. She was the last daughter of Auxigny, the last and the most beautiful, and tomorrow she would die. He felt the anger in him, the terrible, unassuagable anger. He would kill them all for mocking him when he was a child.

He stared into the night again. The eastern hills were dark except for one tiny spark of a fire high on the slopes above the chateau. He guessed that shepherds were coming from the high summer pastures, bringing their goats and sheep down to the valleys. When he was a child he would sometimes carry big cans of ale to the high pastures and he would skirt the great chateau and wonder what splendors lay behind the red-curtained windows. Now he knew what lay behind the red velvet. Girls like this one in the portrait that he held, like jewels in a locked box, but he had forced the lock and he would take this one tomorrow.

The door behind him opened.

He turned. He frowned.

A woman stood in the doorway with two bottles of wine. She wore a white blouse and a green skirt, but she was not the girl he had seen in the main room carrying the tray of tankards high over her head. This woman was older, much older, with a face that had once been pretty and now seemed filled with terror. He scowled. "Well?"

"The citizen wished for wine?"

"Who sent you?" He knew, but he wanted to hear from

this woman's lips that the innkeeper had tried to cheat Bertrand Marchenoir.

She trembled. "My husband."

Marchenoir walked toward her. She had been beautiful once, and there were vestiges of that beauty left on her face that was so terrified. "Your husband?"

"Yes, citizen."

"And the girl?"

"Is my daughter, citizen."

He understood. So the mother had come instead! He watched as she put the bottles on the table. "Your daughter is too proud to bring me wine, citizeness?"

He could see how hurriedly this woman had pulled on the blouse and skirt. The husband had undoubtedly sent her thinking that she would not attract Marchenoir. Undoubtedly, too, the daughter would have been sent on some errand by now, sent safely to another house in the town. The innkeeper, Marchenoir thought with anger, was playing a most dangerous game.

The woman seemed to shiver. "My daughter's not well, citizen."

"Oh? Not well?" He pushed the door closed and latched it. She looked at the latch, then back to him. He smiled and pretended concern. "She's not well! A sudden illness, yes? She was well enough an hour ago!"

She touched her stomach. "A sudden pain, citizen?"

"Oh!" Marchenoir laughed. "So what do you propose for my happiness, citizeness?"

She tried to smile, a feeble effort, and Marchenoir found her terror suddenly annoying. He frowned at her. "Do you remember me?"

"Yes, citizen."

"I don't remember you. You grew up in Auxigny?" He walked close to her.

"Yes, citizen."

He pulled the bonnet from her head and the pins from her brown hair. It fell to her shoulders. "Where in Auxigny did you grow up, citizeness?"

"Behind the town hall, citizen."

"Ah! The Draper's Row?"

"Yes, citizen."

"No wonder we didn't meet. You wouldn't talk to dirty little boys who lived beyond the river, would you?"

"Citizen?" Her eyes were wide.

He looked at her with loathing. "Get ready, woman."

She took off the blouse, the skirt, and kicked off the shoes. She stood, naked and weeping, the brown hair tousled on her thin shoulders.

Marchenoir walked slowly forward. "You're a fool."

"Citizen?"

"Get out! Get out! Get out!" The rage came from nowhere, thrusting up like a red surge. "Get out!"

She fled, scooping her daughter's clothes, unlatching the door, and running in terror past the astonished sentries in the passage.

Marchenoir kicked the door closed. There was no joy in power so easy, there was no pleasure in the tears of a woman from Draper's Row.

He looked at the portrait on the table. There was joy, and there was pleasure, for that was a bitch who he would haul from her pinnacle and in doing it he would make a new world.

He took one of the bottles that the innkeeper's wife had brought and brooded at the window, staring at Auxigny. Tomorrow was the day of Lucifer. Tomorrow.

When the day-star had faded and the sun was dancing a rainbow in the spray of the waterfall, Skavadale led Campion from the high place where they had loved in the face of the world's scorn.

They crossed the stream and went down steep paths through dark woods toward the valley. Journey's end, the Chateau of Auxigny, was still shrouded by a white mist that flowed softly toward the town.

The mist cleared slowly. First Campion saw the blue-black slates of the turrets, rising out of the vapor like some fairy-story castle instead of a place that had been given to evil. She stopped in a clearing to watch the last shreds of mist unveil the placid, steel-smooth waters of the moats. Auxigny.

She thought how her journey had begun when this man, now her lover, had come to Lazen a year before. She wondered when it had begun for him.

He smiled when she asked. "Four years."

"That long?"

"Paunceley's been hunting the *Illuminati* for longer, but that's when he started me on the hunt." He led her from the clearing. "It's one of Paunceley's private obsessions. He hates secret societies, he says they're sewers, and I'm the rat that he sends in to explore them." He laughed.

She could smell the fresh dampness of the pines. The ash trees that clung to the rocks were bare, the twigs beaded with dew. "Why," she asked, "if Lord Paunceley's behind all this, couldn't I tell him that Toby is alive?"

Skavadale did not answer at once. He had stopped at a bend in the path and was slowly examining the way ahead as if looking for enemies. She saw his tense stillness and guessed that it was not just his eyes and ears that he used, but a kind of animal instinct that would warn him of danger. She saw him relax. He gave her his quick smile. "Because in the sewers, my Lady, you trust no one."

She remembered him saying that nothing would be what it appeared to be. Nothing. "You don't trust him?"

"When Toby was to come to your wedding it was Lord Paunceley who told the French where the boat would collect him."

"Lord Paunceley?"

"He said he wanted to know if the French really were interested in Lazen."

"How do you know?"

He smiled. "Because I was his messenger, of course."

"You told the French?"

"Yes."

"But Toby could have died!"

"I told him, too." He said it as if such duplicity was the most natural thing in the world. "It wasn't really until I saw your portrait that we were completely sure that they were interested in Lazen. We go this way." He led her away from the open pasture of the valley, deeper into the trees.

"But Lord Paunceley was my father's friend! He wouldn't attack Lazen."

He laughed. They had reached the floor of the valley and he led her toward a forester's hut that was roofed with pine branches. "I don't think Lord Paunceley has a friend. He just has lesser enemies. If it's not offensive to you, I'd imagine that he liked your father because a cripple was no threat to him." She said nothing. He gestured at the hut. "Welcome to your home for today."

The hut was damp, small, and lonely. "Can't I come with you?"

He shook his head. "I can move faster on my own. Besides, you've got a long night in front of you. You need rest."

"You'll bring Toby back?"

"Yes." He smiled at the anticipation on her face. "This afternoon."

She put her arms about his neck and held his face

close. She liked the smell of him, the strength of him, the shiver of desire that he gave her. She had thought, as she followed him down the mountainside, that he was a man who had always walked alone, had stalked the treacherous roads with only his own wits and strength to keep him alive. Perhaps it was that, she thought, that was so desirable; the desire to tame this tall, lean, self-sufficient man. She looked up at him. "You don't really need anyone, do you?"

He smiled at her. "To love someone isn't to need them."

"It isn't?"

"No." He kissed her with the tenderness that she liked so much. "If you need someone then you lack something."

"You make it sound very simple."

"It is." He stroked her hair. "What's the matter?"

She was shivering, but not from the cold, nor desire. She shivered because they were in this dark valley, this place of the Fallen Ones, and her happiness, that seemed to be so close, still had to survive the ordeal of this night. He stroked her hair, he kissed her, and then he left her. He went, he said, to find her brother, and then, united again, they would go to the shrine of madness and to Lucifer.

By the time the Gypsy reached the inn, Valentine Larke had arrived and was sitting in Marchenoir's room. Both men welcomed Gitan, though the Englishman showed reserve. The memory of their last meeting still rankled.

Bertrand Marchenoir offered him wine, but the Gypsy said he preferred water.

"You're certain?" Marchenoir asked.

"I have to give answers tonight."

Marchenoir shrugged. "The questions are easy, Gitan. You've been in the *Illuminati* long enough to know the answers. Still, water it will be. You've got the girl?"

"I've got her." The Gypsy turned to Larke as Marchenoir went to the water jug beside the bed. "I owe you an apology, sir."

Larke's hard, bland eyes looked up. "An apology?"

"For the deception at Lazen. I didn't know what she planned to do."

Larke shrugged. "Give me revenge tonight." His words were edged with bitterness. He would beat the girl tonight for what she had done in Lazen. He would beat her until she screamed. "Just give me revenge tonight."

Gitan nodded. "It will be given." He turned to take the water.

Marchenoir stared at the Gypsy intently. "She's here?" He asked it as if he could scarcely believe it to be true.

Gitan smiled. "She's here."

"You enjoyed travelling with her, eh?"

"Enjoyed?"

"Come!" Marchenoir leaned back in his chair. "You tell me you cross half of France with a girl and don't bed her? Did you find her to your satisfaction, horse-master?"

Gitan kissed his fingernails and nicked them outward.

Marchenoir laughed grimly. "Lucifer was right about you. They can't say no to you, can they?" He waved dismissively at the Gypsy's shrug. "Lucifer said you would get her here. For that, Gitan, well done."

Larke sneered. "She thinks she's in love?"

Gitan laughed. "Love is a dream. She's come for reality. She thinks her brother lives. She thinks I'm meeting him now and that we're planning your deaths."

Marchenoir frowned. "Innocence! What it is to be innocent! When I was a priest, I would look at all the little girls come for their first communion and I would think how innocent they looked! So virginal! But what were they, eh? Tubes of flesh and slopping liquid just waiting for a lout to make them pregnant! Pretty at seven, but at twelve they turned into wet-lipped, udder heavy brutes. Animals!" His face twisted with sudden distaste, then, just as suddenly, he smiled. "So let us discuss tonight's arrangements, shall we?"

Marchenoir took charge of the discussion. He wanted, he said, this night of triumph to have a solemnity to it. Dagon, the mute giant, had prepared the chateau. All that Gitan now had to do was to deliver the girl at dusk. "There'll be no one there, Gitan. She'll think it's empty."

Gitan nodded. Larke smiled. Slowly, upon the Fallen Angels, was dawning the realization that success was at hand. The fortune of Lazen would drop into their hands, its slender thread finally sliced through by Lucifer's subtle cleverness. All that was now needed was the girl's death. "And that," Marchenoir said, "is mine to give." Beside him, beside the portrait of Campion, was a leather covered box. He undid the catch, opened the lid and there, gleaming in their velvet racks, were surgeons' knives. Their previous owner had died under a different blade. The steel shone like silver. Marchenoir touched one of the scalpels with a blunt finger. "For all that is past," Marchenoir said softly, "her death is mine."

The day of Lucifer was half done. Moloch, Belial, and the man who would be Thammuz were gathered. It waited only for the night and for the coming of Lucifer.

"Where's Toby?" She ran through the trees to meet the Gypsy.

Skavadale kissed her, but his face was clouded. "There are problems."

"Problems?" Alarm made her voice loud.

"You remember Dagon?" She nodded. Lord Culloden, when he babbled in the stable-yard, had spoken of Dagon.

"Dagon's looking after the chateau." Skavadale took her arm and walked with her. "Toby hasn't managed to unblock the tunnel yet. He's gone there now. We're hoping that Dagon has to get the shrine ready." He hugged her as if to reassure her. "It will be all right, I promise you." He sat by the hut and pulled both pistols from his belt. "Toby's going to wait for you in the Music Room. As soon as the tunnel's free and Dagon's gone, he'll be there."

She nodded. She feared parting from her man this evening, yet she knew that the ceremony of the Fallen Ones demanded that he went to the shrine first. It was a relief to know that Toby would be there for her. "Is he well?"

Skavadale smiled. "Disgustingly."

"Did you ask him about us marrying?"

He laughed. "We had other things to talk about, my love, like tunnels and enemies and killing people." He was tugging at the flint of one of his pistols, making sure that it would not slew in its jaws when the trigger was pulled. He smiled at her. "Are you worried he'll disapprove?"

"I'd like him to approve."

The Gypsy smiled. "He likes me, if that's any help."

"It helps." She felt one of the shivers of fear. This whole night's success depended on Toby breaking unseen into the shrine and attacking the Fallen Ones from the rear while Skavadale fought them from in front. She looked at her man. "Is it going to be all right?"

He smiled at her. "It's going to be all right."

Her face was frowning. "But what if he can't unblock the tunnel?"

"Then I have to kill all of them myself." He said it calmly, as though the odds were in his favor. "But Toby will manage it." He snapped the trigger, sending a bright shower of sparks from the steel. He obsessively tested the flint's seating again.

An hour later they stood among the long shadows at the edge of the trees and stared at the chateau across its meadow. Nothing moved, except the birds that nested on its abandoned ledges and the uncut grass that stirred like a crop of hay in the wind. Impulsively she put an arm about her man's waist and felt his own arm come about her shoulder.

She stared at the chateau. She had never liked coming here as a child, despite its elegant splendors, and now she wondered if that had been a feeling caught from her mother. Her mother had hated this place, had hated her father who had believed he was God and who had dressed his servants in white robes and golden wigs. It was not surprising, Campion thought, that her mother had turned from Catholicism with such ease, or had taken to Lazen's less formal ways with such alacrity. It was no surprise, she thought, that Uncle Achilles had been so cynical a priest.

She laughed nervously and Skavadale looked at her. "What?"

"I was wondering what my uncle would think if he could see me now."

"He'd think you were mad."

"Perhaps I am." She smiled. She thought that love was a kind of madness, a fine madness.

The western sky was golden. A few clouds stretched like skeins of smoke on the horizon, skeins that were colored crimson and seemed to glow with an internal fire. Soon they must leave. They must walk out of the trees and cross to the bridge that led to Auxigny.

Skavadale touched her arm. "Shall we go?"

She looked up at him and thought, suddenly, that his face looked grimmer than she had ever seen it before, as if the difficulties he faced were greater than he had told her.

She nodded. “Yes.”

They walked onto the meadow and it seemed like walking onto a stage.

The light was fading. The valley was dark shadowed. The walls of the chateau reared high above them.

Her feet grated on the gravel drive. It was overgrown with weeds. The white bridge over the moat still had its statues of the Roman Emperors. As a child she had thought they were the wreathed deities of the dark forests about Auxigny.

She stopped on the bridge. The waterweeds were dark in the moat, the lily pads thick and touched scarlet by the low, slanting sunlight. She suddenly wished she was not in the homespun gypsy clothes. Coming back to Auxigny, if only for Achilles’ sake, she wished she was in some light, white, soft gown that would bring to the fading chateau a memory of its lost elegance.

Skavadale led her over the bridge, under the gatehouse from which no banner flew, and up the great drive.

Weeds grew on the gravel and between the flagstones of the broad steps on which the servants used to parade to greet Auxigny’s guests.

There was a ragged piece of paper nailed to the door, its ink faded and smeared by the weather. It proclaimed that the Committee for Public Safety had confiscated the house. It threatened penalties if anyone dared enter this property of the people.

Christopher Skavadale ignored it. He stooped and picked up three white stones that made a small triangle in the shadow of the doorpost. “Dagon’s at the shrine.”

“How do you know?”

“Patrin.”

She smiled. “Which is what?”

"The way the Rom leave messages. Crossed twigs by horse-dung means there are enemies in the next village, things like that. I told Toby to leave the stones here if it was safe."

"So we can go in?" Her voice was suddenly happy at the thought of seeing Toby.

He smiled. "You can go in. I shall watch for Dagon. You know where the Music Room is?"

"Better than you." She laughed, then felt another shiver of fear. "What if Toby's not there?"

He put his hands on her shoulders, bent to her face, and kissed her lips. "Then he's still working at the tunnel. Be brave."

She rested her cheek on his for a few seconds. "I love you."

"I love you."

She clung to him. "How many women are going to be jealous of me?"

He laughed. "Not as many as the men who will envy me."

Night was coming to the day of Lucifer. She had been drawn to the dark valley where the Fallen Ones would gather, and where, as Lucifer had prophesied, she now walked of her own free will into the chateau of Auxigny.

23

It had been glorious once, it was glorious still. The great entrance hall rose with massive columns of marble to a painted ceiling where, wreathed by clouds and leaning on balustrades of gold, robed gods stared disdainfully at the humans beneath. The two staircases of white stone curved in vast, triumphant ramps on either side of the ballroom entrance.

She stood for a moment. It was so familiar and so changed. The tapestries, that had hung huge on the side walls, were gone. The furniture was lost, all but for a few sad pieces. The carpets that had marked paths on the floor had disappeared. The floor itself, which on her last visit had been polished to a mirror brightness, was now dull and scratched.

The chandeliers still hung, too big to be easily taken down, though now the crystal chains and drops were draped and wrapped and thick with spiders' webs.

The silence in the great house was like a tomb.

The gilding of the pillars and high ledges seemed flat, as if the brightness had gone from the gold leaf. She could smell the sharp, sour stink of cats.

The windows were boarded up. She wanted to take a great hammer and smash the boards down, to let in the glory of the last sun to lighten and emblazon the hallway.

Instead she walked on the dusty, dull floor toward the great double doors that opened onto the ballroom. Leading from the far side of the huge room, its windows opening toward the shrine, was the Music Room.

She felt herself smiling. It had been so many months since she had seen Toby, months of worry, pain, and death, and now he was here and she wanted to see his face.

One leaf of the doors was ajar. She edged through it. "Toby! Toby!" But the ballroom was in darkness. No windows opened into this, Auxigny's largest room.

She stood for a few seconds in the doorway. Slowly her eyes became accustomed to the gloom and, in the small gray light that seeped from the open front door, she saw the pillared arcade that ran around the ballroom like a cloister about the vast, sunken floor. She walked into the arcade where, not so many years before, the names of the mighty were announced as they came into the candlelight. The far end of the huge room was entirely lost in shadow, the doors to the Music Room shut.

It was odd to think that once this place glittered as bravely as any palace. The cloistered edges of the dance floor had been rich with the jewels and scandals of France. Now it was dark, empty as a great tomb buried in the desert's silence for centuries. Her shoes scuffed the debris left by the looters who had swarmed like rats into Auxigny.

"Toby!"

All the doors were shut, doors that led to reception rooms and antechambers, to the card room where her grandmother would dictate the play of her opponents' hands. Straight ahead of her were the Music Room doors, dimly visible now in the dusty gloom.

She heard footsteps behind her, footsteps in the Entrance Hall and she turned, expecting Skavadale. She felt relief that he was coming to share the ordeal of this massive, dark room. "Christopher?" It still seemed odd to use his name.

A man appeared in the doorway. He was a dim silhouette, watching her, and she frowned. "Christopher?"

Then the fear started because she saw that the man was huge, a great shambling dark creature who stared in silence at her, and she knew this was Dagon.

She shouted Skavadale's name, the shout given desperation by the sudden fear that surged in her.

The hinges of the door moaned. It shut, leaving her alone in the absolute darkness. "Christopher! Christopher!"

There was no answer.

She went to the Music Room doors, feeling her way up the steps, and found the handles would not move. She beat with her fists on the bronze panels and she called her brother's name and her voice echoed futilely in the great, dark ballroom. She was alone. She was in Auxigny, drawn there by Lucifer, locked there by his servant. She was alone.

Valentine Larke and Bertrand Marchenoir shared a carriage. It slewed onto the bridge, its wheels noisy on the weed-grown gravel, and stopped at the foot of Auxigny's main steps.

Gitan waited for them. He sat on the steps smoking one of his small cigars.

Marchenoir alighted and spread his arms in an expansive gesture of welcome. "She's here?"

"Inside." Gitan sounded laconic.

Marchenoir began to laugh. He pulled the Gypsy to his feet and lumbered him about the gravel in an ebullient, clumsy dance. "You clever bastard, Gitan! You clever bastard!" Even Valentine Larke smiled to see Marchenoir's delighted antics.

The soldiers were astonished by Marchenoir's capering, yet another madness to add to a day of lunacy. They had brought two wagons from the town, wagons that contained flambeaus, thick torches of twisted straw that had been soaked in pitch. There were also a score of small barrels which, with the torches, had to be carried to the rear of the chateau.

The soldiers had no idea why they had been brought here, or why, as the sun sank over the far town, they were ordered to make a cordon about the chateau and the moated shrine. One company had to prop the unlit flambeaus in the barrels which flanked the path leading from the chateau's north door to the Mad Duke's marble fantasy. Other men tested the drawbridge, pushing on the levers until the counterweights raised the wooden slab. They let it sink again.

Valentine Larke, strolling with Marchenoir toward the shrine, looked at the ring of soldiers. "We're well guarded."

Marchenoir laughed. "Against nothing, my friend, but they add a kind of solemnity to our victory, yes?"

Larke smiled. There was solemnity this night, he thought, the solemnity of a great occasion, of a secret victory, of a rite that would be performed and a pact sealed and a new world forged from the debris of ancient kingdoms and superstitions.

They turned when they reached the high bronze doors of the shrine. They could see Gitan pulling away the planks that barred the Music Room doors. Marchenoir smiled. "He'll be a worthy member."

Larke, whose spirits were not so high as the Frenchman's, shrugged. "This time last year I hoped the same of Chemosh."

Marchenoir patted Larke's shoulder sympathetically. "He served Lucifer's purpose, my friend. Perhaps that is all any of us can hope to do." He gestured for the Gypsy to join them.

A wind stirred the littered water of the moats, it bent the grass of the meadow in slow, rippling waves. The west was a furnace of gold and crimson, touching the heads of the northern clouds scarlet and slashing light on the high waterfall. It was night already in the shadow of the trees, where, at the meadow's edge, a vixen made her first kill, snarling over the dead rabbit and the blood-smeared grass. Night was coming and victory close.

Dagon, the huge mute who looked after Auxigny, lit the candles in the shrine. He was not a man who was swift of understanding. He knew he had to guard this place and he did it ferociously. The youngsters of the town were told that he liked to eat small children who dared cross the moat. They believed the story.

He liked the loneliness of his job, though he was pleased that his master came back this night. Dagon enjoyed the ceremonies. He wondered if he would have to kill the girl who waited in the ballroom, or whether that pleasure would belong to another.

It took more than half an hour for all the candles in the recessed shelf to be lit. When it was done, Dagon went down the stairs, through the corridor that led from the shrine's inner room, and down to the crypt. There was a handle in the crypt wall, like a well handle, and he grasped it, turned, and the chains clanked in their metal pipes to lift the iron shutter up from the ring of light.

The Gypsy was standing in the entrance of the shrine. He watched in amazement as, slowly, like an artificial dawn, the chamber was flooded with brilliant light.

Marchenoir chuckled. "Impressive, eh?"

Gitan smiled. He had never seen Bertrand Marchenoir in such high spirits, so playful. "Extraordinary."

"Let there be light!" Marchenoir declaimed. "Though in truth it's nothing more than a giant hooded lantern." He slapped Gitan's shoulder. "Come on, my friend, time for you to get ready."

He took him to a small room that opened from the entrance hall. The room had a table, but no other furniture. A small window opened into the shrine and Marchenoir said it was here that the trumpeters used to hide so that, when the doors opened to reveal the Duc d'Auxigny in his finery, the men could play a hidden fanfare to their unlikely deity. Marchenoir laughed in derision, then said he would come back in five minutes.

Gitan shrugged. "What do I do?"

"Undress!" Marchenoir smiled. "I'll collect your clothes. The girl will have to wait in here. We don't want her ruining your coat or coming out swinging your sword!" He laughed at the thought, then smiled at the Gypsy. "We've come a long way, Gitan."

The Gypsy remembered this time a year ago when Marchenoir had come to the stinking prison cell in Paris and offered him the traitor's path. He nodded. "A long way."

"Yet the best is to come." Marchenoir smiled. "Forward, ever forward."

In the crypt beneath the room where the Gypsy took off his clothes Dagon was cradling his brass-mounted blunderbuss. He breathed heavily. In his head he was singing, crooning to himself, for he knew that his master was coming this night. He rocked the great gun and wondered what would happen to the golden-haired girl. She must die, of course, for they always died when they came here, and her body would be clawed by the beasts and torn by the ravens. He laughed to himself and he waited for Lucifer.

* * *

A coach came from the town. The windows of the coach were curtained. The glass flashed red as the coach turned over the stone bridge. The soldiers watched as a cloaked man, a hat pulled low over his face, stepped slowly from its interior.

The man stared up at the facade of the chateau, turned, then walked through the overgrown gardens. He walked slowly. He ignored the soldiers and, perhaps because of his slow, purposeful walk, or perhaps because of the extraordinary aura of authority that he radiated, the troops no longer thought this night a mere piece of useless lunacy. There was menace in Auxigny.

Bertrand Marchenoir stood at the shrine's entrance, the Gypsy's clothes and sword still in his hands. The cloaked man looked at him. "All is prepared, Moloch?"

"Yes, Lucifer."

Lucifer turned to look at the sunset then, abruptly, led Moloch into the shrine.

The Fallen Ones had gathered.

The sun sank in molten glory. The blue-black tiles of the chateau's turrets were the last part of the buildings to be touched by the gilding sun. A hawk, that nested on the roof, slid black against the darkening sky.

One by one the torches were lit. They flamed smokily, red and black, a line of fire from the castle to the shrine. The wind snatched at the flames and drove the smoke toward the dark mountains.

The soldiers prepared. The drummers rammed the leather loops down the side ropes to tighten the skins of their instruments.

Colonel Tours, who did not understand any of it, knew only that to disobey was to die. He waited till the sky was dark, till the day of Lucifer was night, then nodded. "Begin."

The end had come.

* * *

She was shivering with fear. She had tugged at the handles of the doors to the Music Room till her hands were sore, but they were firmly locked. She did not know how long she had waited. She had groped her way around the walls and tried each door, then sat on the steps of the cloistered arcade and the fear seeped into her soul as the chill of the huge, empty chateau crept into her bones. She had known she would be frightened, but not with this slow, dark terror. She feared her brother dead, and she feared betrayal.

She fought the fear by imagining what happened in Lazen this night. The harvest should be in, the rickyard full and the long storerooms ripe with the smell of racked apples. She thought of the dairy with its light walls, clanging pails, and the white painted steps where the girls liked to sit in the evening to watch the men come back from the fields. The thoughts of home made her want to cry.

The drumming began.

She was thinking of the Long Gallery, imagining being back there with Christopher Skavadale beside her, when suddenly the noise came muffled from the Entrance Hall. She backed away from the war sound, the insistent, unending rattle of the sticks on tight skins.

Then light came. She heard the noise first, the crashing of the great doors at the other end of the ballroom and she turned, crying out in panic, to see the locked doors of the Music Room had been thrown back to show the red brightness of the torches that led from the north front of the castle to the shrine.

The drumming was closer.

The rhythm was insistent and dreadful and then it seemed to swell, to grow like thunder, as if clubs beat on the doors to the entrance hall. She backed away. She touched, through her blouse, the seals at her breasts. The world was flame and noise, horror and menace, and the panic was beating like black wings in her.

She touched the seals again, the jewels of Lazen. She would not show her fear, she would not give them that pleasure. They might kill her, but they would not see her defeated.

The resolve almost went as the doors to the entrance hall were hurled back, forced by heaving soldiers to crash with a deafening echo against the walls.

She had to stop herself from screaming.

This was the enemy and they had come for her. She could see, silhouetted by the flames of torches behind, the drummers who kept up their insistent rhythm of death. Behind them were men with muskets who flooded into the ballroom, made a line, and came toward her. Each man was a black shape. Before them, on the tittered floor, their shadows stretched monstrously. Their boots crashed on the floor in the rhythm of the drums.

They came slowly, like soldiers of a burial party, drummed on by the unrelenting noise, the slow beat of death that forced her toward the passage of flame.

She was being driven like a deer. She remembered, from when she was a small child, the terrible hunts of this chateau, hunts that would make her hide in her room, refusing to watch the wasteful cruelty. The peasants would go into the hills with their drums and horns, their clubs and bells, and drive the deer down to the valley's head. There more peasants waited, forming a great corridor that forced the deer to run past the chateau. They galloped in panic on the meadow that faced the moat, where, on the bridge, the Duke and his party waited with loaded guns. The slaughter would soak the meadow red while panicked deer, terrified by the noise and smell, stampeded into the moat to be shot as they swam.

She stumbled on the far steps, caught her balance, and went through the opened doors into the Music Room.

The doors in the side walls were barred shut. She could only go toward the corridor of light that led to the shrine.

The drums slammed behind her. The feet of the soldiers, in ragged, slow tread, pressed close on her.

She went where they wanted her to go, into the garden. There was nowhere else to go, she was being driven like the deer into the corridor of death.

Now there were more soldiers. Soldiers who stood with the flamelight on their fixed bayonets. They stood behind the twin lines of torches, stopping her from running into the darkness of the gardens. Their faces seemed blank.

She had no choice. She must go on, down the passage of fire to the great shrine built by the Mad Duke who had thought he was God.

She walked.

She thought of the men and women who had climbed the wooden steps in Paris. They had gone with dignity. She would do the same. She would not run like a frightened beast. She would walk.

Love had filled her and love had changed her and love had led her here and she had to fight the insidious certainty that she was in a trap, that she was betrayed. Death felt close, as if it brooded for her in the windowless shrine, and she was glad that, before she had walked into this web of steel and fire, she had been loved. The wind drove the heat of the torches into her face, drew the acrid smell of tar smoke into her nostrils.

She climbed the first bridge. The torches flickered on the dark water. Soldiers lined the narrow neck of land between the chateau's moat and the moat of the shrine.

She crossed the second bridge. The firelight glinted on the wooden uprights. The tread of the soldiers was close behind her. She stared at the shrine and remembered Lord Culloden babbling of the girl's death. This was the place of death, and there was nowhere to go, but inside.

The drumming behind her stopped.

She turned to her pursuers. The cordon of soldiers had contracted, leaving the chateau behind, surrounding only the shrine and its moat. They watched her in silence, the flames reflecting on their bayonets. Three men stood on the drawbridge to close the doors of the shrine behind her. Other men stood by its chains to maroon her within the building when the doors were shut.

She would not show them fear.

She turned, climbed the steps, and went where her enemies had wanted her to be. She went into the shrine of the Fallen Ones.

She was alone.

The doors crashed shut behind her, the echo deafening.

It was almost pitch dark in the lobby, the only light came faint through an open door to her left.

When the echo of the great crash of the closing doors had faded she heard, as if from far away, the sound of voices. They seemed to come from the dimly lit room and she climbed two steps to look inside.

The room was empty except for a heavy table. There was a small aperture on the opposite wall. The light came from that unglazed window.

The voices rose and fell.

She went into the room. She went cautiously, as if expecting to be hurt, but the room had no surprises. She looked through the window into the marble shrine.

Skavadale stood with his back to her. He was naked. His black hair was tied back and the earring glinted in the brilliant light which cast an intricate coronet of shadows about his tall, muscular body. He stood in the center of the marble floor.

"What is your name?" The voice, a hoarse whisper seemed to come from nowhere and everywhere.

"Gitan."

"And what is your desire?"

"To join you."

Silence.

She watched. The light was brilliant on marble and mosaics, on gold and whiteness, on the superb, tall, naked man who had loved her.

"What is your name?"

"Gitan."

"What gives light?"

"Reason."

"What gives darkness?"

"God."

"How do you know this?"

"Reason."

She told herself that this was what she had expected, but she knew she deceived herself. She had not expected so many soldiers, she had not expected the drums, the torches, the flames on bayonets, and nor had she expected to feel these terrible uncertainties about the man who stood so splendid before her. Toby had not been in the chateau. Toby had not come to her. Nothing that Skavadale had said about Toby had come true.

Another voice, also a whisper, echoed mysteriously about the great chamber. "What protects the weak?"

"The law."

"What is above the law?"

"Reason."

A third voice whispered. "What is death?"

"Nothing."

"Why did you come here?"

"To serve you." He spoke boldly.

"Whom do we serve?"

"Reason."

"What bounds does reason have?"

"It can have none!" He said it triumphantly, and his voice echoed in the marble chamber and lingered like the voice of a conqueror.

She felt cold tendrils of horror. She had the sudden agony of betrayal, not the betrayal of an ally who is revealed as an enemy, but the infinitely worse betrayal of love. She had loved this man, but the sudden triumph in his voice put terror into her soul.

"What is your name?"

There was something familiar about the whisper, something in the grating, hoarse voice that echoed in her mind, echoes of a voice heard in Lazen, a mocking voice.

"Gitan."

"Henceforth, Gitan, you will be Thammuz."

There was silence.

He stood naked and tall in the candlelight. Never, she thought, could such a man have existed before; so strong, so vividly beautiful. In action, she thought, how like an angel, a Fallen Angel.

She thought of his touch on her body, his gentleness, his legs by hers, his smile, and she bent her head and rested her forehead on the sill of the aperture and thought she would cry. Toby was not here, she was alone with her enemies, and she no longer knew who was her friend. Yet, when he had loved her in the mountains, when he had stroked her and soothed her and filled her with a shudder of love, had he been lying? If that was a pretense, she told herself, then nothing was real.

"Come forward, Thammuz."

She looked again. She was in the utter despair of love betrayed. He was joining her enemies, he was picking up from the white marble steps a folded garment of black and gold silk.

"You may wear the robe of a Fallen One, Thammuz."

She felt a sudden angry scorn of the mummery. She wanted to laugh at them, to mock them, to scream derision at these fools who cloaked their evil in such tawdry trumpery.

Thammuz unfolded the robe, opened it, and pulled it over his head. The sleeves hung loose. He pulled the cowl over his head. The robe, that she wanted to find so derisory, looked magnificent on him.

The voice, that nagged her with its echoes, whispered again. "You are one of us, Thammuz, but you must prove your worth." The Gypsy stood unmoving. The voice spoke again, so low that Campion could scarce catch the words. "You brought us the girl, Thammuz?"

"Yes, master."

"Call me Lucifer." The sibilance seemed to hang in the chamber that was like a tomb.

"Yes, Lucifer."

Another voice spoke, a louder voice; a voice that had a note of mocking triumph in it. "Why did you bring her, Thammuz?"

He replied with a similar triumph, with a laugh of confidence in his voice, and Campion almost cried out in fear as she heard him. "I have brought her for you!"

"Fetch her!" The words echoed in the chamber.

Thammuz turned. Campion saw the glitter of his eyes deep under the black and gold cowl, and she went back in the room, back to the heavy table, knowing that she could not fight, could not resist, could only wait for the victory of reason and the end of Lazen. Panic beat inside her and she waited for the man who had loved and brought her here.

Until this moment she had thought that her life was so

blessed, so charmed by love, that she could not be hurt. She had come to France for love, but she had come to Auxigny because she believed in that love. Now, suddenly, as she heard the inner doors of the shrine open, that belief seemed childish. She was in terror.

She gripped the seals of Lazen as if they could give her strength. She saw light flood the lobby, and then the robed man with the blue, glittering eyes came into the room.

Thammuz had come for her.

24

A scream sounded in the shrine,

The silver cowl of Lucifer tilted up. His voice was mild. "He's a fine looking man."

The scream came again and faded into sobbing. Valentine Larke smiled. "She's putting up a fight!"

"Poor thing." Marchenoir opened the box of scalpels and stroked one of the handles. His voice was mocking. "Waiting for her dear brother!"

Lucifer's silver cowl turned toward the knives. "How you do enjoy death, Moloch."

"I got used to it quickly enough, didn't I?" Marchenoir said. "It was common enough in this valley, except in the chateau, of course. We could die of hunger and there were fat dogs up here."

Lucifer laughed his dry laugh. "Your father, Moloch, was a Duke. Belial's father was an Earl. You both hate what gave you life."

There was silence. The candles were bright on the polished black table.

The girl screamed again and Lucifer's cowl moved impatiently. "What's keeping him?"

"A farewell rogering?" Marchenoir made his voice light. Somehow the mention of his and Larke's aristocratic fathers had been chilling. He lifted one of the knives. "Skins like white silk, they have. They must bathe once a bloody month."

"Once a day," Lucifer said dryly.

"In milk," Larke added.

"Christ in his heaven!" Marchenoir laughed. "That would stop you pissing in the bath."

Their laughter was cut off by a new scream, by the sound of feet dragging on the great chamber's floor. Lucifer spoke softly. "Progress, I do believe."

They stood. They moved in a susurration of silk robes, each man going back to his small observation hole in the wooden doors. They waited for Thammuz to bring his sacrifice for their victory. Behind them, on the stone table, the candles shone on the gleaming steel of Marchenoir's blades. They waited.

Skavadale dragged her through the inner doors, into the splendor of the candle-lit chamber that seemed so oddly empty as though the marble and porphyry and mosaics waited for a great tomb in the circular floor.

She fought him. She beat at him with fists, but his strength was huge and he half carried, half dragged her down the steps to the center of the room.

He wrenched her about, facing her toward the far wall, and forced her hands up behind her back so she could not move.

She waited. She could hear her own breath as the loudest thing in the room. She sensed she was being watched.

"Thammuz?" The voice was a sinister whisper.

"Lucifer?" Skavadale's voice was strong in her ear. Her hair had half fallen about her face. The gypsy clothes had been tugged ragged on her. The ring of candles made their shadows spread and mingle about their feet.

The whisper sounded again. "Tell her what you are, Thammuz."

His voice was strong. "I am *Illuminati!*"

"Tell her where her brother is, Thammuz."

"In a common grave."

"Tell her who betrayed him, Thammuz."

"I did!"

She sobbed. His hand wrenched her arm higher.

The whispers seemed to mock her, to laugh at her, to echo about the cold marble of the big chamber.

"Who deceived her, Thammuz?"

"I did!" He shouted it, startling her, shouting it in a yell of victory, and the yell seemed to provoke a great crash that was like the world's ending, a ringing, clanging, grating, hammering clash that echoed in the marble walls like all the thunder of a season's storms poured into one room and one moment.

The candlelight went out with a crash, plunging the room into blackness, leaving only the tiny spots of light where the holes were drilled in the false marble.

She screamed.

The scream echoed and she fed it with another, filling the room with her fear, rivaling the noise of the great iron shutter that had fallen over the candles.

Instinctively, though they could see nothing from within their small chamber, the three robed men looked up. Marchenoir frowned. "The chain must have broken."

"Open the doors." Lucifer's voice was crisp.

The scream still echoed as Marchenoir and Larke pulled back the doors, spilling a softer candlelight onto the sunken marble floor where the girl, who looked so pitifully pale and frail, stood in her captor's grip.

Campion gasped. She looked at the Fallen Ones; three robed men, two in black and gold, and one resplendent in silver. She could not see their faces that were hidden by the deep cowls. This was trumpery, she knew it, yet they were oddly impressive as, on silent feet, they came to the top of the marble steps.

The silver cowl tipped as Lucifer stared up at the shutter. She saw the glitter of his eyes, then he raised his right arm and gestured one of his companions forward.

The man seemed hugely bulky beneath his gaudy robe. He pulled back his cowl and Campion saw the face that gave Europe its bad dreams, the enemy of kings and courtiers, the heavy, savage, triumphant face of Bertrand Marchenoir. He walked down the white marble steps and his eyes, that had looked on so much death, were bright with the anticipation of this moment.

He stopped four paces from her. "I am Moloch!"

She said nothing.

"I am your death." He stared and felt his anger stir. The girl, even dishevelled and frightened, was more beautiful than he had dared hope. "Daughter of Auxigny! You thought me an animal. You made me bow to you. You thought me dirt." His face twisted in a spasm of hatred as he spat at her. The spittle flew past her head.

"I never knew you!"

"Knew me! I was the peasant! But you will know me, by Christ's blood you will know me!" His voice was rising in a passion of hate to fill the echoing chamber with his threat. "Let us see you, girl! Let us see what you are!" He raised his arms and stepped toward her and he reached with his huge, strong hands for the neck of her clothes to rip them in rage from her body that he knew would be like white silk and on which he would spill his awful revenge until he panted and was slaked.

"Now," whispered Christopher Skavadale.

"Scream!" He had said as soon as he appeared in the small room. "For Christ's sake, scream!"

She stared at him in horror.

He seemed to ignore her. Instead he went to the table, stooped, and felt beneath it. "Scream!"

"Scream?"

"Scream!"

She screamed.

"Louder, for Christ's sake!"

She screamed as though she wanted to wake the dead.

He groped under the table and brought from the hooks that were screwed there his two pistols. He had hung them by their trigger guards when he had undressed, praying that Toby had remembered to put the hooks in their place. "Turn around."

She frowned.

He hissed at her. "Hurry, woman! Turn! Scream!"

She turned and she felt his hands tugging her blouse from her skirts and then the cold barrels of the pistols were next to her skin, were being rammed inside her waistband, and he was pulling the blouse down to hide them. Her throat hurt from the screaming. "Where's Toby?"

"If he killed Dagon, he's downstairs. Scream!"

She screamed. He turned her round, looked at her with a look of pure joy on his face, that same look that she had seen in the autumn woods behind Lazen when he had killed for her, and he smiled. "Listen!"

He had told her exactly what they would do. As the light went out in the great crash he had tugged the pistols from her belt. He pushed one pistol into her right hand and she felt his fingers warm on her skin as he pulled back the flint.

His voice whispered in her ear as the doors were pulled back. "Courage. Keep your eyes open as I taught you."

He had taught her by taking her to the guillotine. There were times when horror had to be faced.

The three men faced her.

Skavadale's voice was softer than wind on fur. "I love you."

She almost smiled. This was why she loved him, not because he was a difficult man to be tamed, but because he thought her worthy to walk the lonely paths with him. She saw it at that moment, as clear as the sun reflected from Lazen's lake, that love had bound them, that it was not she who gave a gift by stooping from her rank to marry him, but that he, from his competence, loved her. She was filled with love for him, she sensed the happiness that waited for them, because she too thought him worthy. All that she wanted, all that she dreamed of in her life, this man would help make possible. He trusted her. Love, as nothing else can, filled her and made the difficult possible.

Then the silver-gloved hand gestured the big man forward, and she saw the face revealed, knew it was Marchenoir, and the brutish, smiling, gloating man came toward her and she listened to his ravings and her fingers gripped the pistol which felt slippery in her palm. He stepped forward, his hands rising to tear the clothes from her.

"Now," whispered Christopher Skavadale.

Skavadale moved away from her, moving to the left, and she brought the pistol around in her right hand and she saw the eyes of the big man glance down and she hurried, stepping back, pushing the pistol forward and his hand seemed to strike down as his mouth opened in a snarl.

She pulled the trigger.

It was harder than she could have believed.

She had fired many guns, but the pistol trigger seemed to resist like a stuck key, his hand was coming down to knock the gun away and she jerked her finger, trying to remember what Christopher Skavadale had told her, and then it seemed as if a mule had kicked her.

The noise exploded in the room.

The gun jerked back, her wrist flaming with pain. She was half dazzled by the fire, stunned by the noise and the kick of the gun, and she kept her eyes open as he had told her, stepped back, and she saw the Frenchman stumble. He pawed at her with his right hand, bellowed like a clumsily gelded calf and fell onto his left knee. His hands clasped his hip as blood welled between his fingers.

She stepped farther back. Her ears rang with the echo of the shot, Christopher Skavadale was walking forward, his pistol pointing at Belial and Lucifer who stared at the sudden blood and hazing smoke.

Marchenoir was on his knees, shouting in pain, his blood staining the floor. Skavadale had told her to bring the pistol up beneath his chin and blow his head off, but he had been too quick for her, the trigger too stiff. He was helpless, though, his hip shattered. He looked up at her, anger and astonishment mingled on his face, then Lucifer moved.

He took one step, just one, and he had placed himself behind Valentine Larke.

There was one bullet in Skavadale's pistol, a bullet that, if he fired, must hit Larke. Lucifer smiled. "Who are you, Gitan?"

"Your enemy."

"Then you are a fool. You will die a fool's death."

There was a sound in the passage behind the shrine, a scraping sound like a beast dragging itself on stone. Campion saw a shadow there, a shadow within a shadow that seemed monstrous in the darkness, and in the shadow's hand was a great, brass mouthed gun and Lucifer, turning to the shadow, laughed. "Had you forgotten Dagon, fool?"

Skavadale fired.

The bullet entered the shadowed cowl, struck it back, spraying blood high in the air to spatter the marble wall of the chamber, and Valentine Larke, his forehead holed by the ball, fell back into the silver robes of Lucifer.

"Dagon!" The silver-robed man screamed at the deaf mute and raised his arm to point at Skavadale and Campion. "Dagon!"

But Dagon was dead, his throat sliced so that his great head hung bloody in the crypt, and the man who held the gun turned it on Lucifer and Campion laughed aloud.

He had red curls, unruly and uncut, and he grinned at her with the same old mischief and delight. "Hello, sister."

Le Revenant had come back from the dead, and Campion, the sudden blood and horror wiped out by his presence, ran to him, eyes bright, laughing, and put her arms about his neck. "Toby! Toby!"

Skavadale took the big, brass-mouthed gun from Toby's hand. Campion hugged her brother. "Toby!"

He had tears in his eyes, tears of joy, and he laughed because he seemed unable to say anything. With rough affection he stroked her head with hands scraped coarse by tearing down the stubborn stones of the blocked passage.

Behind them, like a broken animal trailing a red slime, Marchenoir pulled himself over the floor. He looked up at Toby Lazender and knew that this was his enemy come back from the grave. Marchenoir, forgetting that he had preached a dead God, crossed himself.

Christopher Skavadale, the gun held easy in one hand, walked to Lucifer.

The silver-clad arms tried to fend him off, but he was helpless against the Gypsy's strength. Skavadale pushed the cowl back and Campion, at last, saw her enemy.

This was the man who, with a subtle thread, had drawn her over the sea.

Toby let go of Campion. He turned on Lucifer who, without his hood, looked ludicrous, like an awesome judge who, stripped of his wig, is seen to be a frightened, weak man. Toby frowned. "Why?"

Lucifer said nothing. He looked from Toby to Campion, back to Toby. He had thought Toby dead, and now, seeing him alive, he knew that he had been outplayed by a cleverer hand. He shook his head, as if the gesture of denial would make Toby go away. "No! No!" There was horror on Lucifer's face, the face of a man outwitted who prided himself on his wits. "No!"

Toby pushed the silver-robed man, making him stumble against Larke's body. "Why?" His voice was louder. "Why?"

The man in silver went back from the anger, back into the main chamber, down the marble steps to his bleeding half-brother, the son of the town whore, the half brother with whom, in Auxigny's shadow, he had found a childhood companion in resentment and with whom he had learned mischief and learned mischief's pleasure that became evil. He looked at Toby. "You would not understand!"

Beneath his silver glove Campion could see the lump made by the ring that had belonged to the Bishop of Bellechasse.

"Why?" Toby shouted again.

Uncle Achilles ignored him. He pointed at Campion. "You! I warned you! I told you not to come, but you had to come!" He laughed suddenly, the sound like a flare of madness in a marble chamber built for madness. "I knew you would disobey. I told you, but you wouldn't listen! Society? You wouldn't enter it. You're a woman, but you work like a housekeeper! You're not worthy! I warned you but you preferred him!" He pointed at the Gypsy, and his head shook in a spasm of disgust. "I tried to save you! I tried! But you wanted your own way!" He screamed this last at her.

Toby, Campion, and the Gypsy stood silent, transfixed by the sudden frenzy. Achilles, with a curious gesture of pride, twitched his silver robe into place and looked at Toby. "Do you know what your precious sister is doing? She's rogering a gypsy! Did you know that, Earl of Lazen? That your sister is being tupped by the servant's hall? By a peasant! She forfeited her nobility with her virginity!" He pointed at Skavadale. "To that!"

Toby said nothing. He stared at the raving man who had always seemed so gentle and cynical, but who now spat his words in a shrieking, shrill voice. "I told her not to come, but she would have her own way, wouldn't you?" He looked at Campion. "I always knew how to manipulate you. I would tell you one thing to make you do the other. You could have been a queen, but no! You had to bed yourself with that!"

"Uncle!" Campion's cry was not in protest. It was a cry of pain and affection as if she saw a sick man, but he shook his head at her and raised a silver-gloved hand against her tentative step forward.

"Don't call me uncle! You're not noble! You don't have nobility in England! It's bastard blood, tainted! You don't know what civilization is." The hand pointed at Toby. "Earl of Lazen! Look at you! In Auxigny you wouldn't be fit to scrub stone!" He suddenly shouted as if in great pain. "I wanted Lazen! I would have made it beautiful! I would have made it a refuge in this world, the one place where music and poetry and refinement could live! I would have given England an aristocracy! I would have dazzled your peasant country, your crude King, your beer-sodden people, your sottish women, your sluts, your whores, your fox hunting fools!" The last was spat out. He looked with disgust at Campion. "Look at her! The English got to her, didn't they? In love with a Gypsy! She's not fit to open her legs to an ape. I would have made Lazen great!"

Marchenoir looked up at the man who was his half-brother, who had been his companion in boyhood bitterness, who had been his Bishop. "It was all for you? Just for you?"

"Don't be a fool, Bertrand." Achilles' voice was suddenly and curiously affectionate. "I gave you what you wanted, I gave you Auxigny!" He laughed suddenly, his eyes bright. "Auxigny should have been mine. I was fit for it! I could have made Auxigny into the brightest jewel of the finest aristocracy in the world, but no! I was the youngest son! I was the monkey who should have been drowned at birth! I was fobbed off on the church!" He was shouting again. He pointed at Toby. "You don't deserve Lazen! She doesn't! She's a whore! Making the two-backed beast with a gypsy! Where's the grace? The exquisite detail? Tell me?" He asked the questions with a terrible intensity.

Toby looked horrified. "You're mad!"

"Mad? I fooled all of you!" He stopped, his eyes going from one to the other, his head suddenly jerking in denial because he had been fooled too. "Mad? Look at her! She's mad! In love with a peasant! Love?" Achilles laughed. "Messy love? Sweat on the sheets? Spilling, sticky, messy, slippery, filthy, sweaty love?" The anger came again. "Your place was to be beautiful! To be a woman, a mystery, a gesture with a jewelled hand, a smile! Not heaving on a peasant's body, sliding in his slime!"

Toby went down the steps. He shook his head. "You could have lived at Lazen, uncle."

"Lived! And listened to your endless talk of horses! Horses! What does the English aristocracy think it is? Do you think of nothing but horses and farming?" He backed away from Toby. "There's no manners in England, no elegance, no fineness. I could have given it to you! I could have brought it to you like a gift, you could have shone in the world like a great crown, the inheritor of all that those bastards took away from us here. And you spoiled it!" He cried it in mad agony in this marble hall built for madness.

Campion stared at him in horror. "You ordered me raped!"

"Jesus Christ!" He looked at her with pure scorn. "You were throwing Lazen away! Your footmen slouch! It had to be saved!" His voice was rising again. "There has to be one place where the best of our world can live and grow and dazzle. Don't you understand? If you had gone into society, girl, if you had tried to be worthy of it, I would have let you live! How many chances did I give you? How many? Go to London, I said, but no!" He wailed the last word, his head shaking, and then he stared at the horror in her eyes and gave a casual laugh of pure insanity. "Rape? Yes. Yes. You should have been raped. Your brother should be dead. But I would have looked after you!" He nodded eagerly at Campion. "It was a small price for the glory of Lazen, don't you see that? But with a gypsy? A peasant?"

Bertrand Marchenoir, his robe stiff with blood, stared up at Lucifer. "My mother was a peasant!"

"Don't be a fool, Bertrand!" Achilles laughed. "It's not the same for men! Men can spawn what they like, but women are different!"

Marchenoir shook his head. "You betrayed us!"

"Betrayed you! Betrayed? I gave you France, Bertrand. All I wanted was Lazen!"

Toby stepped closer. "You're mad, uncle, you're like your father."

Achilles stared at Toby with disdain, looking from Toby's unruly hair down to his shabby boots. "I am a Duke." He said it with great dignity, then raised his hand to point at Campion. "And she is a whore."

"You're just a mad bastard." They were the first words Christopher Skavadale had spoken in minutes, and the sound of his strong, careless voice seemed to jar Uncle Achilles. He looked at the huge gun in the Gypsy's hand and suddenly, with a swirl of his silver robes, he turned and ran to the doors of the shrine. "Colonel! Colonel!" His voice echoed from the lobby where he struggled with the huge metal ring-latch. "Colonel!"

Skavadale moved with his cat-like speed. He crossed the sunken floor, past the blood trail, and he stopped at the inner doors and raised the gun. "Lucifer!"

Lucifer turned his head. He stared into the oddly light eyes of the man he had thought he was using for his ambition. He shook his head and the Gypsy fired.

The scraps of iron lifted Achilles up and slammed him against the huge bronze doors that his mad father had put there.

The silver robe was twitched flat on his body. It was spotted with scarlet.

His head, silver hair flecked with his blood, was thrown back.

He sighed, he slid, and his twitching, gloved hands smeared trails through the blood on the bronze doors.

He fell, he rolled on his back, and his belly, where the iron scraps had torn free, looked as if dogs had torn at him. He had been opened from the crotch to his neck, he was ragged tatters of silk and blood and bone and flesh. He was the last Duc d'Auxigny, who had thought himself Lucifer, and he was dead.

* * *

Colonel Tours, standing beyond the drawbridge, heard the shot and heard the rattle of metal on the bronze doors. One of his Captains frowned. "Should we go and look?"

"Christ, no!" Tours shivered. He had been ordered to be curious about nothing, to do nothing, to wait. His men were tight about the small moat. Above him the clouds were silvered by the thin moon.

"We wait, Captain." He wondered who the girl was. If he rose high enough in the hierarchy of power, he thought, then perhaps he too could afford a girl like that.

They waited.

Christopher Skavadale threw the gun down. "I'm putting my own clothes on."

Toby nodded. He was staring at his uncle. He did not look around as Skavadale left the great chamber.

He turned only when Skavadale had gone. He walked past the wounded, bleeding Marchenoir and climbed the steps to his sister. "Is it true?"

"Is what true?"

"You and Gitan?"

She looked into his eyes. She did not know what he was thinking. She nodded. "Yes."

Toby frowned. He was suddenly the sixth Earl of Lazen, the head of the family, and in his voice was astonishment. "You're his lover?"

She put defiance into her voice. "I'm going to marry him."

Toby said nothing for a few seconds. His face was grim. "Marry Gitan?"

"I'm going to marry him." She said it stubbornly. "I don't care what the world thinks. I'm going to marry him."

"Do you know what you're doing?"

"Yes."

"You do? You've thought about it?"

"Damn thought!" She was angry suddenly. "I love him!"

He seemed to sigh. He shook his head. "You don't know what you're doing, sister, truly you don't."

"Tell me." She said it sharply.

"You're marrying a man of no birth." He saw her stiffen and ignored it. "Of no name, apart from a name given him by an eccentric Lord. A man of no fortune and no standing." He paused. "Isn't that so?"

She shrugged. "I don't care."

He put his hands on her shoulders and she shook them off. He went on in the same tone of voice. "You're marrying the strongest man I know, who doesn't stoop to malice or cheapness. Other men judge themselves by him and find themselves wanting." He smiled into her upturned face which slowly dawned with the realization that he had teased her. "You're also marrying the best damned horseman in the world so I won't have to pay for his advice. And you're marrying the luckiest bastard that ever lived." He kissed her on the nose. "That's what you're doing. And why are you crying? You know I can't stand women who cry."

"I'm not crying." She hugged him.

He laughed at her. "He even asked my permission. I thought it was most polite."

"When?"

"After he first saw you."

"He did?" She smiled. "What did you say?"

"That if he was mad enough to want you, he was welcome to you."

She laughed. Happiness seethed in her like the mountain pool beneath the waterfall, then she thought of the happiness that had been denied to her brother. "And what will you do, Toby?"

He shrugged. "I think I want Paunceley's job."

"You do?"

"I shall come and visit the two of you and you can envy me." He smiled at her. "Or I you, whatever." He let go of her, walked to the table, and picked from the wooden box the largest of Marchenoir's knives. He stared at it, then gave her a smile. "But before all that, I have one more thing to do, just one." He turned the blade so that it flashed in the candlelight. "Perhaps you'd better join Gitan?"

She nodded. She looked at Marchenoir. He was her half uncle, his bitterness sprung from the same mad root as Achilles' envy. She was suddenly glad that Gitan was so sensible, so strong. If the world would not accept him as her husband, then that was the world's loss.

She walked down the passage. She heard her brother say the name Lucille and she flinched as a scream echoed in the marble hall and was abruptly cut short. It was done.

They left through the tunnel when midnight was past. The soldiers who guarded the gatehouse recognized Skavadale as one of the privileged friends of Bertrand Marchenoir. They knew better than to ask who his companions were.

Toby led them westward, away from the hills, going to where he had horses hidden for their escape. They rode toward the sea and the ship that would take them home. They stopped as the dawn blazed from the mountains and they turned to look behind them. The seals of Lazen hung in the sunlight, glorious and safe, and Campion, thinking of the tall, golden woman of the Nymph portrait, thought how the fortune of Lazen had been founded by love and now preserved by it.

The bright sun was shadowing the cleft in the mountain where the soldiers still guarded the shrine of the dead, the shrine of the last Duc d'Auxigny. Campion frowned. "Why did he do it?"

"Mad," Toby said.

"It was his duty," Skavadale said.

"His duty?" she asked.

"He believed."

"He was mad!" Toby said.

"So he was a mad believer. A fanatic."

Campion stared into the dawn. Like a glint of gold she could see the streak of the waterfall high in the mountains. "Poor Uncle Achilles." She looked at the tall, light-eyed man who was her lover. "He must have been so disappointed in me."

"Your footmen do slouch. It's quite true."

She laughed. She would go with Christopher Skavadale to Lazen, she would marry, and they would breed a horse that was faster than the north wind. She held out her hand, Skavadale took it, and she leaned over to kiss him and to feel his arm about her.

She felt his skin on her skin. She was an aristocrat with the blood of kings, and he was a man. He loved her, and she knew it, and she remembered how she had felt when the Fallen Ones came forward in the shrine, and she knew that her life's dreams were safe in this man's hands as his were in hers. "I love you."

He laughed softly. "You see? It does exist, it really does."

The Earl of Lazen coughed. "Are you two finished?"

She made a face at her brother, then turned her horse. She went to that place where all the roads begin. She rode, hand in her lover's hand, for love.